Red flags.

Not blush red, orange red, wine, or ruby red. No, bloody red flags. Did you see them, Claudia? Did you?

Did you see any red flags?

That's the question they asked me over and over again, hoping to find answers. Hoping to understand what no one could. Signs. Were there any signs Monday was in trouble? Did you see anything out of the ordinary, anything unusual?

No. Nothing.

In so many words, they called me a liar. That hurt more than losing my best friend.

If Monday were a color, she'd be red. Crisp, striking, vivid, you couldn't miss her—a bull's-eye in the room, a crackling flame.

I saw so much red that it blinded me to any flags.

MONDAY'S NOT COMING

MONDAY'S NOT COMING

A NOVEL BY
TIFFANY D. JACKSON

 KATHERINE TEGEN BOOKS
An Imprint of HarperCollins Publishers

Katherine Tegen Books is an imprint of HarperCollins Publishers.

Library of Congress Control Number: 2018933268
ISBN 978-0-06-242268-2

Typography by Erin Fitzsimmons
19 20 21 22 23 PC/LSCC 10 9 8 7
❖
First paperback edition, 2019

For my daddy and my Pop-Pop
who let me fly but were always there to catch me.

SEPTEMBER

This is the story of how my best friend disappeared. How nobody noticed she was gone except me. And how nobody cared until they found her . . . one year later.

I know what you're thinking. How can a whole person, a kid, disappear and no one say a word? Like, if the sun just up and left one day, you'd think someone would sound an alarm, right? But Ma used to say, not everyone circles the same sun. I never knew what she meant by that until Monday went missing.

You wouldn't think something like this could happen in Washington, DC, a city full of the most powerful people in the world. No one could imagine this happening in the president's backyard. That's the way us folks in Southeast felt too. If they say we live in the shadow of the nation's capital, then how could one missing girl flip it inside out?

My doctor says I shouldn't talk about this anymore. But then that podcast came around, re-examining all that happened, poking holes in a burnt cake to make sure it's done. Like the color pink, somebody always sees the story different. Some see rose and magenta, and others see coral and salmon. When at the end of the day, it's just regular old pink.

For me, the story started the day before the beginning of eighth grade. Our last year of middle school, what I thought would be the best year of our lives.

THE BEFORE

"Ma, have you seen Monday?" I asked the moment I walked out the gate at Reagan Washington National Airport, my hair still in fuzzy summer braids, skin browned by the southern sun.

"Sheesh! Can I get a hello first? I ain't seen you all summer either," Ma chuckled, her skinny arms stretched wide as I dove into a joy-filled hug.

Every summer, Ma sent me down to Georgia to stay with my grandmamma for two months. Monday and I would write letters to each other with funny drawings and ripped-out magazine articles, keeping up with the latest neighborhood gossip and music. But that summer was different. Monday never responded to any of my letters. Without them, the summer had crept by like a runaway turtle. I loved Grandmamma, but I missed my room, missed my TV, and most of all, I missed Monday.

Lights twinkled off the Anacostia River as we crossed the bridge onto Martin Luther King Jr. Avenue, the Nationals baseball stadium in the distance. The moment we turned off on Good Hope Road, I noticed old posters still pasted to an abandoned building at the crossroads: "SAVE ED BOROUGH! It's community! It's home!"

Ma relocked the car doors, her back tensing. A true southerner, she never felt safe in the city, despite living here since I was born. As a distraction, I told her about my unanswered letters. She shrugged, more focused on the evening traffic, mumbling a "Maybe she couldn't make it to the post office." But that didn't make much sense to me. We'd saved our money and bought enough stamps to make it through the eight weeks without each other, since Grandmamma don't like the kids playing on her phone and my cousin already hogged up the line talking to her man. Monday knew I hated writing, but we promised to keep in touch, and you don't just back out of promises. Not with your best friend since the first grade.

"I don't know, Sweet Pea," Ma said, stopped at a light by the liquor store and gave a nervous wave to someone she recognized outside. "She probably got caught up with something. But once she knows you're back, I'm sure she'll be by."

The light turned green, and Ma slammed on the gas

for two blocks before making a sharp left at the Anacostia Library, then a right onto U Place. Home. She parked on the street in front and I jumped out of the car with my book bag and sprinted for the door. I ain't gonna lie—every summer I kind of hoped to come back to some miraculous transformation. Not that I don't like our house, I just love surprises. Like, running down the stairs Christmas morning, I always expect to find a fresh coat of terra-cotta paint on the walls, a new couch to replace our beige sofa set, stainless steel appliances to replace our rusting white ones, and a new staircase banister, one that wouldn't cry when you leaned on it.

As soon as I walked in and found nothing had changed, I dropped my bag and used the phone by the stairs to call Monday. Maybe she was too wrapped up in taking care of her little brother and sister this summer to write. Whatever the reason, I'd let it slide since I was about ready to bust I had so much to tell her. One ring in and some automatic lady told me I have the wrong number. I only knew two numbers by heart: Monday's and my own.

"Girl, you on that phone already?" Ma huffed, dragging my suitcase in the house. "Why, you don't let no grass grow under your feet!"

"Monday's phone not working."

"Probably off the hook or something," she said, locking up the front door. "Now hurry up and get the comb. We need to start on this hair. Sheesh! I should have told

Momma to take out these braids before you came."

I took the stairs two at a time and opened the first door on the right. My room was exactly as I left it, a mess. I mean, my twin bed with its deep eggplant bedspread had been made, and the lavender walls where I hung all my artwork between music and movie posters were all still in place. But I hadn't had time to clean up the tent Monday and I made with a bunch of old sheets and throw pillows during our last sleepover before I left. It still sat under the shelf near the window, facing the back of the library across the street.

"Claudia! Hurry up!" Ma shouted from downstairs.

"Coming, Ma!"

I grabbed the comb off my white vanity, noticing a fresh coloring book and pencils sitting on my chair. Daddy must have left it before heading out on another delivery.

"Claudia, let's go! We'll be up all night!"

Ma and I spent the rest of the evening tackling my braids, then washing and straightening out my hair. Exhausted, I finally climbed into bed close to midnight, ignoring the gnawing in my stomach. Something wasn't right, but I couldn't put a finger on it.

"Claudia!" Ma yelled the next morning from the kitchen. "You're gonna be late for your first day!"

Every year Ma would holler, wanting me to run down the stairs all crazy and be surprised by the big breakfast she always made for the first day of school: pancakes with a syrupy smiley face, scrambled eggs with cheese, grits, and beef sausage links.

So I played along, jumping off the last two steps and running into the kitchen dressed in my school uniform and new sneakers, greeted by the table laid out with my feast.

"Surprise!" Ma said, springing from her hiding spot, her short auburn hair still in pin curls. Sometimes in the light, little specks of gray peeked out behind her rose-gold highlights.

"Thanks, Ma," I laughed, hopping into my seat.

"Lawd, I cannot believe you're going to high school next year. I'm such an old woman now."

"Ma, you don't act no older than me."

She grinned, cupping my face. "That's no way to speak to your mother. Okay, Sweet Pea, hurry up and eat your breakfast. You don't want to be late for school and keep Monday waiting."

Ma knew the right words to light a match under my butt. What was I going to say when I finally saw Monday? I mean, how could she just leave me hanging all summer?

"Ma, can Monday come over after school today?" I asked between pancake bites.

She laughed. "Y'all waste no time. Okay, she can come. Just . . . check in with Ms. Paul first, okay?"

I dropped my fork onto my plate. "I thought you said

I didn't have to go to the library after school anymore. I don't need no babysitter!"

"Not a babysitter," Ma said, feigning innocence. "Just . . . want you to go say hi. Ain't nothing wrong with you checking in so someone knows where you are. Breadcrumbs, Claudia. Always good to leave breadcrumbs."

"I wouldn't need to leave breadcrumbs if I had a cell phone," I muttered into my lap.

Ma huffed. "Listen, I ain't going down this road with you again. We agreed, once you start high school, then you can have one. Now, come on, let's go."

I strapped on my new book bag—navy with violet swirl designs. Monday had the same one except in pink, her favorite color. We picked them out right before I left for Georgia. I called her two more times before leaving, just to check. No answer.

Ma always drove me to school on the first day, taking off a few hours from the veterans' canteen. They'd miss her for sure, leaving their kitchen a mess without her running it. But she always says, "You only get one shot at your kids, so you need to hit the bull's-eye."

We pulled up to Warren Kent Charter School, behind a line of other cars waiting to drop off at the big fenced-in yard where all the kids gathered by grade before the first bell. Pressing my greasy face against the glass, I scanned the sea of red-and-navy-plaid uniforms for my matching book bag.

"Ma, I don't see Monday," I said, trying to hide my panic. Monday always arrived first to school, sometimes two hours before anyone else even thought of showing up.

"I'm sure she'll be here soon," Ma said over the steering wheel, inching to the drop-off point. "Now, have a good day at school, Sweet Pea. Remember to call me as soon as you get home."

An avalanche of uncertainty tumbled down, pinning me to my seat. I couldn't step one foot out of the car without seeing Monday first. School didn't seem real or possible without her. And the idea of walking out there *alone*, with all those kids . . . *BEEP! BEEP!* A horn blew behind us.

"Oh, shut up!" Ma yelled out the window before turning to the back seat. "Sweet Pea, what's wrong? You're not nervous, are you?"

When she used that squeaky, nasally voice, felt as if I was strapped in a car seat with a bottle rather than being a year away from high school. If I didn't start acting like it, I thought, she'd never stop treating me like a baby.

I shook my head. "Naw, Ma. I'm good."

Another horn blew, more aggravated than before. *BEEEEEP!* Ma rolled her eyes and smiled, looking straight through my act.

"Claudia, she'll be here. She's probably just running late or something. Now, look over there." She pointed into the schoolyard at one of the lunch monitors holding up a sign that read "Eighth Graders." "See, your class is right there.

Why don't you wait in line, and save her a spot? I'm sure you got a lot of catching up to do with your other friends too. Okay?"

The line of my classmates—my archenemies—stretched long. Without Monday by my side, I was jumping alone into shark-infested waters . . . dripping in blood. But Ma didn't know Monday was my only friend.

"Um . . . Okay."

She grinned. "Now, come give me a kiss."

Clicking off my seat belt, I leaned forward, kissed her cheek, and she wrapped an arm around me in another tight squeeze. "I love you so much. Have a great first day!"

Squeezing back and not wanting to let go, I whispered, "Love you too," and climbed out of the car with a brave face, but my lungs pinched shut.

Warren Kent ain't a big school, around a thousand students, but when you put us all together, we sounded like a million. Shrieks of kindergartners blew out eardrums. The third and fourth graders ran circles. The sixth and seventh graders hugged and giggled, reunited after months apart. This will be Monday and me when she shows up, I reminded myself over and over again to keep from running back to the car. I peeked over my shoulder at Ma, who was still watching from her spot, cars beeping behind her.

She's right, I thought, I'm tripping. Of course Monday would come. She never ever missed a day of school.

But I still gulped as I approached my class. Everyone looked older, more menacing, the boys taller and the girls had filled out. I wondered if I looked different too. Maybe Monday did and I didn't recognize her. Shayla Green stood at the top of the line, an evil smirk growing across her pretty brown face. She whispered into Ashley Hilton's ear, with her new mini gold hoops. They stared, giggling. I whipped around, ready to run back to the car, but Ma drove off, and all my bravery evaporated.

"Oh snap, dyke bitch is back," Trevor Abernathy cackled, his white button-down shirt making his rich black skin glow. The others snickered—monsters in uniforms. I kept my head down and stood at the end of the line. Trevor skipped around and yanked at Shayla's ponytail.

"Boy, I ain't playing with you," Shayla snapped.

He danced around, trying to escape her swinging arms as the others egged him on.

So immature, I thought. Look at them, a bunch of dummies. How they expect to get into any good high school acting like that? At least I know they won't be following me nowhere. One more year, then it'll just be me and Monday. But until then, Monday needed to hurry up and get here before the wolves closed in.

Seconds ticked by, the yard buzzing as everyone checked out each other's hairstyles, cuts, fresh sneakers, jewelry, and book bags—accessories were the only way to set yourself apart. I flipped open my compact, smoothing down my edges and slicking on another layer of clear cherry lip gloss. I mean, I looked cute, but it was hard to relish in it when the one person I wanted to see me more than anyone wasn't there.

Monday usually wore her hair in braids, but we'd decided that for the first week of school we'd try new styles—more grown-up looks. You know, to practice for high school. But without our regular catch-up, I worried she might have forgotten our plan. I stared at the gate, checking my watch.

The bell shrieked, and the lines of students began falling into the building, starting with the kindergartners, then the first graders. Monday's brother, August, should have been with the fifth graders, but he was nowhere in sight. And her sister Tuesday—wasn't she supposed to start kindergarten?

"Where are they?" I mumbled to myself.

My bony knees clapped together as they called our line and we trickled in slowly. I never took my eyes off the gate, hoping at any moment she'd come running through it, panicked and out of breath, her hair glistening with that coconut oil she loved. We would hug in relief and she'd be by my side again—the world back to normal. But the gates swept out of sight and were replaced by the beige brick walls of our school. The heavy dookie-brown doors slammed shut behind me like a period marking the end to that dream.

• • •

"Hello, class. My name is Ms. O'Donnell, and I will be your homeroom and first-period teacher for the school year," she said as she wrote her name on the board. "First rule: attendance is taken only when you are in your seats before the second bell rings."

Ms. O'Donnell, a name I would grow to hate over the year, taught eighth-grade English. She had short, curly graying-blond hair and a white face full of deep lines behind huge glasses. She was dressed in high-waist pants, a canary-yellow T-shirt, and ugly brown loafers. We'd met her last year on Move Up Day, and one of the older kids had said she was the meanest teacher in the school—maybe the whole planet.

"Now, when I call your name, raise your hand. Trevor Abernathy?"

Trevor finished snickering with his boys just in time. "Here."

"Arlene Brown?"

"Here."

As she went through roll call, I noticed how packed the room was. Every seat taken—not a single empty desk left for Monday. Where would she sit when she showed up?

"Claudia Coleman?"

"Here," I announced, raising my hand and wiggling my fingers so the light would catch off my new manicure, lilac with pink metallic stripes. I added the pink for Monday.

"Carl Daniels?"

"Here."

Wait, she didn't call Monday Charles? Monday's name always came before mine. Does she have the wrong list? Did they move Monday to another homeroom? Maybe, but, I mean, Monday would have told me. Wouldn't she?

"Hey, Sweet Pea. How was your first day?" Ma said as soon as she walked in from her shift, carrying a few bags of groceries.

"Monday didn't show up!"

After school, I called Monday's number five times and the automatic lady told me once again that I was wrong. On a day we should have been comparing class schedules and locker assignments, I spent the afternoon watching reruns of *Dance Machine*, coloring in my new books, and trying to relax on a bed of sharp needles.

"Really?" Ma frowned. "Well, maybe she'll be there tomorrow. Just be patient!"

I tried to be patient. After all, if I asked too many questions, I could draw attention to the fact that I had no friends, and it'd be open season for nonstop teasing. But Monday didn't show up on Tuesday, Wednesday, or Thursday. By Friday, with my stomach clenched tight from all the knots it tied itself into, I mustered up enough courage to ask one of the kids that lived in her complex if he had seen her.

"Naw," Darrell Singleton said, standing by his locker, packing his school lunch leftovers in his bag. "Haven't seen her all summer." Darrell was the biggest kid in the whole school, towering over everyone with a greasy, meaty face full of hills, valleys, and potholes. His uniform barely fit, and his locker forever smelled like the rotting food he squandered.

"All summer? You sure?"

"Yeah. Why, wasn't she with you?"

Darrell has had a crush on Monday since the fourth grade, but she never paid him the time of day. Of all people, I was sure he would have been checking for her. I clutched my math textbook to my chest.

"I was away all summer."

"Oh," he mumbled, squirming more than usual. "Well, I saw her mom a couple days ago. She stopped by next door. . . ." His voice drifted, eyes darting away. Everyone knew the house next to Darrell's was what Monday called the pit stop. Folks from New York to Florida stopped by, dropping off or picking up packages. Any drug you could ever think of, the pit stop had your twenty-one flavors.

"What about her brother or sisters?"

He scratched his head, thinking. "I don't know. Maybe."

Even though I wasn't allowed to go over to Monday's without an adult, I pedaled my purple bike down the sidewalk—not brave enough to ride in the busy street.

With Ma wrapping up her double shift and Daddy on the way home from his last delivery, I had a short window of opportunity to disappear. A whole week and no word from Monday? Something was up, and I had to find out what, with or without them.

Maybe Monday had the flu again. She'd had it before, out of school a month. But why hadn't she responded to any of my letters? And if she was sick, why hadn't her brother shown up for school either? Could they all be sick? And what's up with her phone?

Monday lived in Ed Borough Complex, one of DC's biggest public housing areas—a village of identical cream row houses, stacked together like Monopoly houses, shaded by giant trees along the river, sectioned off by highways, about fifteen minutes away from my house. As Ma and Daddy would say, Ed Borough was the hood! I mean, no part of Southeast is a cakewalk, but Ed Borough . . . you don't want to be caught there late at night.

In all the time I'd known Monday, I'd never been inside her house, not even once. Ma wouldn't allow it, and neither would Monday, for reasons I wouldn't know until much later. Whenever we dropped Monday at home, Ma would wait for her to walk inside, jittery, looking over her shoulder every second, triple-locking the car doors.

So I pedaled fast, past the Ed Borough apartment complex sign, up two blocks, past the famous basketball court that hosted the summer league tournament, and stopped at the path leading to Monday's house. I leaned my bike against the tall tree shading over the building and walked up the cracked cement sidewalk. The dingy brown door of house number 804 had no doorbell. I knocked twice, my blood pumping. I had never been this close to her house before.

A television hammered through the door. Someone watching *The Simpsons*, so loud they could probably hear it in the White House. I knocked again, picking at my chipped nail polish as a thought leaped through my head: Monday hates *The Simpsons*.

"Who is it?" a woman barked, her voice punching through the door.

"Hi, Mrs. Charles? It's Claudia."

There was a pause, some shuffling and grumbling before the locks clicked and the door cracked open to a slit. A yellowish eye peered out.

"Who?"

"Um . . . C-Claudia," I stammered.

She stared as if she didn't recognize me—as if she hadn't known me almost my entire life. My skin went cold, hands drenched in sweat. Mrs. Charles opened the door halfway, positioning herself in its frame so I couldn't see inside. She was a tall woman, one of her boobs the size of my head. She stood in a man's tank top, black sports bra, and red basketball shorts, her hair wrapped with bobby pins. I never noticed it, but she had the same paper-bag complexion as Monday.

"Claudia?" Her face scrunched up as if I stank. "What you doing here?"

I couldn't think with the television blaring behind her. What *am* I doing here?

"Um . . . is Monday home?"

She blinked twice and shifted her stance, her hands on her hips. "She ain't here."

"Oh, um. Is she coming to school on Monday?"

Her blackened lips cocked to the side as she snarled. "Why you asking so many questions? I said she ain't here. Now, go on! You know your bougie-ass mother don't want you around here."

The whole neighborhood could hear her yelling, but they couldn't smell the liquor on her breath like I could. Every hair on my body stood up, calling to my bike. She had never talked to me like this before. Maybe I crossed a line by coming to look for Monday, asking her questions and talking fresh to grown-ups, as Ma would say. But I couldn't just *go*. Not when the other half of me was missing.

"But . . . where's Monday? Is something wrong?"

She lunged toward me. I stumbled back, tripping over a crack and landing hard on the concrete, scratching my thighs on some scattered pebbles without a moment to scream.

"I said, she ain't here! NOW GO HOME!"

My throat closed as she stood over me, leaning so far down we could have bumped foreheads. Her hands balled into fists as her leg cocked back, ready to kick through my side. A siren went off in my head, but I couldn't feel my feet or move. Frozen to the ground, I braced for the pain. But she stopped short, glancing past me. A curtain pulled back in the window of the house next door.

She sniffed and glared at me, as if still deciding what she wanted to do.

"Get your ass out of here," she mumbled, slamming the door shut.

My elbows collapsed and I fell flat on my back, coughing out air, the TV sounding as if it was right beside me. On the ground, trembling, I stared up at the passing clouds, wondering how Monday could live with such a monster.

On Saturday, Daddy came home from what he called a short trip, down to Texas and back. A truck driver for a car factory, he drove brand-new shiny cars to dealerships around the country and could be gone weeks at a time, depending on the schedule.

"Hey, Sweet Pea!" he said, lifting me up as soon as he walked through the door, giving me a raspberry on my cheek.

"Daddy! Stop that! I'm not a baby anymore," I said, trying to sound serious but giggling regardless.

He laughed. "You're always gonna be my baby girl!

You had dance class today?"

"Dance don't start till next week."

"Well, let me know what size leotard I need to join you."

"Cut it out, Daddy!"

"I'm serious. I can at least fit in an extra large. Just got to lay off the chicken wings."

"Daddy!" I laughed as we headed into the kitchen.

"Well, I hope you've been at least getting out the house some. Maybe take that bike around for a spin."

I winced a smile, thinking of my long ride back from Monday's house.

Ma stood at the stove, frying up some catfish. Hot corn bread and lima beans sat on the table. Daddy kissed her neck and she squirmed, shooing him away with a dish towel and a grin. Those two lovesick teenagers can make a whole room gag.

Ma and Daddy met at a truck stop outside Atlanta where Ma was flipping pancakes. Daddy says it was love at first sight, happily volunteering to take the long route down south just to see her. After six months, he asked her to marry him, bringing her home to DC. He was twenty-nine. Ma had just turned nineteen.

Daddy is a big, burly man with a shiny bald head and arms the size of toddlers. He played football in college, defense, before hurting his knee junior year. With no scholarship, he had to drop out. But Ma says college isn't for everyone. Degrees don't mean you're smart, and Daddy's the smartest man I know. He saved every dime he made as a truck driver before meeting Ma. Enough to buy our first home.

Ma pulled the mac and cheese out of the oven, and we sat at the table for dinner—our Saturday-night ritual.

"So," Daddy said, his mouth full. "How was your first week of school?"

"Monday wasn't there."

"Really? Where she at?"

I shrugged. "I don't know."

"You try calling her?"

"Her phone don't work."

"Her phone *does not* work," Ma corrected me, passing Daddy the hot sauce. "You've got to speak proper English, baby. I don't want you going places and people thinking you don't got no home training or nothing."

Daddy smirked at her. "Listen to your mother, Sweet Pea. No matter how crazy she sounds."

Ma gave him a look but blushed at his smile.

I gently wiggled in my seat, my butt still bruised from the fall outside Monday's house. I didn't tell Ma what had happened. She wouldn't care how crazy Mrs. Charles acted—she'd be more upset that I was over there in the first place. But I couldn't shake the look Mrs. Charles had given me or the sharp edge in her husky voice. Monday's mom wasn't the sweetest pie, but she wasn't bitter greens either. And Monday never mentioned anything about her hot temper. Maybe she was just in a bad mood.

"Daddy, can you drive me to Monday's tomorrow?" I figured if I brought some muscle as backup, Mrs. Charles would act right the next time I saw her.

Daddy sighed. "Aww, man, Sweet Pea, can't I sleep in tomorrow? I'm tired as I don't know what. Plus, I got practice with the fellas."

Daddy played the congas in a go-go band called the Shaw Boyz with my uncle Robby. Go-go is music homegrown in Washington, DC. Bands like Junk Yard, Rare Essence, E.U., and the Godfather of Go-Go, Chuck Brown, helped put DC on the map for more than just politics. Daddy and Uncle Robby started their band in high school, back when chop-shop spots were packed for hours. They're not super famous, but to people in Southeast, that didn't matter if you're cranking and shouting out their hood or block. Kids my age don't listen to it like they used to. Monday used to say I was born in the wrong decade.

"And we have church tomorrow," Ma jumped in. "Lest you forget."

I sighed. "No, I didn't forget."

Ma chuckled. "Maybe she's just sick. She probably will be there first thing Monday morning! You know how she do."

The thought made me grin. "Right. Monday!"

Mondays were Monday's favorite day of the week, and not just 'cause she was named after it. She loved the day itself. She'd be at school, early as ever, brighter than sunshine, even in the dead of winter with wind that could freeze our eyelids shut. She'd stand outside the gate, bundled in her thin coat and mismatched scarf, waiting for the doors to open.

"Why you so happy to go to school?" I would grumble, missing the warmth of my bed. "No one is happy to go to school. Especially on Mondays."

She would shrug. "I love school."

I'd roll my eyes. "School don't love us."

She'd laughed. "Mondays are the best days! Like, aren't you excited about the start of a new week? It's like a new chapter in a book. And the best part, even though we at school, we get to be together again—all day, all week."

So on Monday morning, I hopped off the bus and waited by the gate with a slice of Ma's pineapple upside-down cake snuck in my bag. Monday loved Ma's cooking, and being sick for so long, I was sure she could use something sweet. I waited and waited until the bell rang. Monday never showed.

Back at home, I tried Monday's number again, and the same automatic lady told me I was wrong. I slammed the phone down with a scream. I wasn't wrong! We've been friends forever. I knew her more than I knew myself: her favorite color was pink, she loved crab legs and corn on the cob, hated running late, and was allergic to peanuts. Knowing all this, I couldn't ignore that voice shouting in my ear.

Something was wrong.

THE AFTER

I love the dusty particles a fresh colored pencil leaves behind with the first stroke, the sound it makes kissing the page when I'm done filling in voids. That first spot of rich color on a crisp white page, the start of something new. Feels like all I do is color since Daddy read in some article that it's therapeutic for me. Glad he stopped buying those kiddie books and started buying ones with more intricate complex designs. Geometric and psychedelic shapes, mosaics, and mandalas . . . There is a calm in the chaos that most folks don't see.

I take my time picking the right shade. There's a distinct difference between periwinkle and cobalt blue. Has to be right or the whole picture will be ruined.

Without Monday, I felt ruined too.

"Don't you have work to do?" Ma asked, holding a fresh load of laundry.

"It's Saturday," I said with a grin as I lay spread out on the sofa, coloring book in my lap, blasting music. I would watch TV, but Daddy ain't fixed it yet. It sat on two old speaker boxes, untouched for who knows how long.

"That don't mean you can't do your work and get it out the way so you're not rushing to do it after church tomorrow."

"Ma, it's just some . . ." The phone rang and I leaped off the sofa. "I've got it!"

Ma jumped out the way as I scrambled for the cordless. "Hello! Hello?"

"Hello? Claudia. Hi, there, it's Sister Burke from church. How you doing? Is your mother around?"

My heart deflated faster than a pin in a balloon. "Hi, Ms. Burke. Hold on, she's right here."

My arm went limp as I passed the phone to Ma, and she gave me a sympathetic smile.

"Expecting somebody, Sweet Pea?"

I winced, shaking my head, and stomped back to the sofa.

"Hey, Sister Burke," Ma said, balancing the basket on her hip. "Oh, she's doing good. Real good. Being a lazy bum on my sofa but keep her in your prayers, okay? How you doing? And Mikey? Good, good. So you calling about that order, right? Yeah, I'll have them pies for you tomorrow."

Ma had a growing side catering business she'd started a few summers back. People loved her potato salad, chicken potpies, and most of all her BBQ spareribs.

"Dang it," I grumbled. I'd chipped my pinkie nail running to catch the phone. I ran upstairs to grab polish remover out my kit. My kit was on point. Ask me for a color and I got you! Raspberry mocha, thin mint, stone gray . . . I'm so good at painting nails, I could open up my own shop. I told Ma this once and the next day she came home with college brochures.

The color was called devil's plum, a deep matte purple that I accented with tiny lavender rhinestones—just like the color of the journal Monday gave me for Christmas last year. It had been sitting on the bookshelf next to the TV—untouched. Such a weird gift. I mean, Monday knew how much I hated English. And writing outside of school was straight-up torture. But I had so much to tell her. So much I needed her to know that without thinking twice I cracked it open. Gripping my pen with sweaty fingers, I attempted writing a few words, just to make sure I didn't forget anything.

Dear Monday,
Were are you? I got a new bra wit Grandmmma.
Are we the same sise now?

ONE YEAR BEFORE THE BEFORE

"OMG, I can't believe how cold it got. Like, overnight. And look how dark it is already. What's that thing that happens—daylight saving time? When is that again?"

Monday wrapped a pilly red scarf around her neck, shivering in her jean jacket. Actually, it was my jacket that I let her borrow months ago. She didn't have one, and it looked better on her anyways. The wind wrapped around our exposed thighs as cars drove by on our walk home from school. Time to change into winter tights.

"Girl, are you even listening to me? You heard what I said? Pastor wants me, ME, to read the scripture this Sunday. In front of ALL those people! I can't! I'mma mess up and then . . ."

Monday's eyes softened, scratching at her pretty fishtail

braids, secured with a red headband. Monday could braid just about anyone's hair and make it look hot. When she slept over on the weekends, she would braid my hair the same pattern so we'd look like twins at school.

"So, just fake sick," she said with a shrug, sucking on a cherry Blow Pop while I unwrapped my green apple.

"I can't. I'm also in dance ministry, and we have a performance. We've been practicing for weeks. Ma already hemmed my costume and everything."

Monday smirked, her lips sticky red. "Dang, that church got you working hard for Jesus. They paying you or something? Maybe I should join."

"Shut up," I laughed, playfully pushing her.

"I can be in the dance ministry. Watch!"

She skipped ahead of me, exaggerating her steps with her long limbs and swaying hips. During the summer before seventh grade, Monday somehow started to grow a body without me. Her breasts pushed against her button-down and a little booty had popped under her plaid skirt. Twice that week the hall monitors made her do the fingertip test, checking the length of her skirt. I was a stick standing next to her.

She spun around, faking a stoic face, lifting her arms in staggered motions to the sky, then bowing into a prayer pose.

I laughed. "You better quit playing before Jesus strikes you dead!"

Monday jumped up, grinning. "Yo, that was kinda tuff, though. We should add that to the routine when we get home."

"Bet," I said as a low-rider Cadillac creeped by, engine purring.

"Hey, Claudia, what color is that?" Monday chuckled.

"Hmmm . . . it's like a mix of rust and apricot with a yellow undertone."

She laughed. "You so weird. Oooh! Let's stop by the carryout. I'm starving."

Monday dragged me into Mr. Chang's Carryout—the Chinese food spot a few blocks away from home, our favorite Friday after-school snack.

"So, you really think I should just . . . play sick?" I asked as we waited in line.

"You can't just play sick. You gonna have to drop out. That's the only way to keep them from asking you again."

"Drop out? Of church? You crazy! Ma would kill me!"

"Well, what other choice you got? You gonna get up and read in front of all them people? Read *all* them words?"

I gulped, gripping the straps on my book bag with sweaty hands. Monday was right. They would ask me again and I couldn't risk being embarrassed in front of the entire congregation.

"How am I gonna drop out?" I mumbled to the floor.

She shrugged. "Tell your mom you don't want to do it anymore. Say it's corny."

Monday lied with matter-of-fact precision, in a self-preservation type of way. I could never manage it, even to save my own ass.

"Dang, Ma's gonna be so mad." I hated the idea of disappointing her.

Monday grunted, staring off. "She never gets that mad."

When we reached the counter, Monday stepped up to order for us. Being the voice of our duo, she always spoke up first while I hung back. I mean, I'm not really shy or nothing, but Monday was just better at talking to strangers. Folks were just drawn to her, and I hated the idea of sharing her.

"Let me get two chicken and mambo sauce, with extra salt on the fries."

"All that salt ain't good for you, you know," I chided.

She rolled her eyes. "Yeah, Granny, I know. Oh dang, think I forgot my wallet at home. You got any money?"

I give her a look, pulling out the ten dollars Daddy had given me.

She grinned. "Thanks. I'll get you back next time. And we have enough for some iced tea!"

The door swung open behind us and in piled a group of boys, thick 'fros, long black T-shirts and hoodies, one carrying a basketball. I huddled closer to Monday, as her eyes roamed over their gear quick, seeming unimpressed.

"Big news?" she whispered to me in the secret language we made up in the fifth grade. *Are you okay?*

"Noodles." *I'm cool.*

She nodded, taking another look at the boys.

"If ten on the left not safe." *The one on the right is cute.*

"Me right sane?" *Are you crazy?*

She smirked and turned back to the man behind the bulletproof glass. "Dang, what's taking so long? We ain't got all day, you know!"

One of the boys stared at the back of her exposed legs, muttering something to the others before chuckling. I moved closer to her, confused by the jealousy bubbling in my chest.

"Y'all twins or something?" one of the boys asked as the others laughed.

We loved questions like that, since we already walked around pretending to be twins. But we weren't taking their weak bait. Monday cut her eyes as the man behind the glass handed her our food. She grabbed my hand and headed for the door right as one of the boys stepped in our path. She ran into him, chest first, bouncing back.

He smirked, looking her up and down. "My bad, shorty. *Excuse* me!"

A deer caught in headlights, she reeled with a gasp, backing into me. His bulky frame blocked the door while the rest of his friends trickled out of their seats and surrounded us. That trapped and cornered feeling slipped into my skin, and I quickly looped her arm. With a two–step dodge, I rushed his left side, and made an offensive play out the door.

We walked two blocks in silence before she exhaled. "He was cute, though."

"Girl, he was like seventeen! They in high school! Ain't got no business with us."

She shrugged with a smirk. "So. He was still cute. And it's not like we babies!"

That year, the conversation about boys had turned from hypothetical dreams of rappers and movie stars to realities of neighbors and classmates.

"You was feeling one of them, weren't you?" she teased.

I sucked my teeth. "Ain't nobody worried about them bammas. Smelling like they Momma's kitchen grease. Don't look like they had a proper shower in days."

Monday laughed. "Whatever!"

We skipped through the doors of the Anacostia Library, where Ms. Paul sat at the information desk.

"Hi, Ms. Paul," we said in unison.

"Hello, girls! Happy Friday!"

"We're just checking in," I said.

"Just like books," Ms. Paul giggled. "Okay, I'll let your mother know you stopped by."

"Thanks, Ms. Paul!"

Every day after school I'd go to the library, where Ms. Paul would watch me until Ma came home. Ma slipped her a few dollars a week and plates of food at church on Sundays. It was kind of cool. I spent hours in the media center watching movies or flipping through magazines. At least three days a week, Monday would hang with me, and we would use the computers to watch music videos on YouTube. Ma would let us hang out at home, but only if we stopped by first. *Breadcrumbs.*

We took our to-go plates back to my house, washing down our sauce-soaked fried chicken with super-sweet iced tea in my room. Monday had the stomach of a grown man—she could eat enough for three people some days. As I cleaned up our mess, since Ma hated when we ate in my room, Monday grabbed two of my Barbie dolls off the shelf.

"You think them boys would've tried to get with us? Like, for real?" She plopped down on my bed, Ken and Barbie dancing in front of her.

"Yeah. Seems like it."

Monday grinned, her face lighting up as she kicked her legs.

"Hey, girl!" she said, her voice deep like Ken's. *"What yo' name is?"* She switched voices for Barbie. "My name is Claudia. *Hm. Claudia? Nice! How old are you?* Ha, old enough. *Alright, well, let's get it!"*

She shoved the dolls together, making kissing noises and moans.

"Cut it out!" I giggled, swatting her away. "And stop being fresh with Barbie."

"Yes, Grandma," she laughed. "Aight. It's time for rehearsal!" She hopped up to turn on my iPod hooked up to a speaker.

I took my position next to her. "Ready."

"Okay, first, when the music drops, we'll do this!" Monday popped out of a crouching pose, throwing her hands in the air. "Then we'll spin, and break into this." She posed and vogued, her arms motioning like an air traffic controller. *Boom. Beat, beat, step, step.* I recognized the move from a YouTube video of a Texas dance team.

Most afternoons were spent making up routines to songs we'd listen to over and over until I could hear every beat in my head like a pulse. Monday could dance her ass off. Ain't no other way to describe it. I mean, she only had to watch Beyoncé's "Single Ladies" three times before knowing the whole routine. Mrs. Charles couldn't afford dance school. My parents could barely afford it, so I would teach her turns and leaps, and she'd end up doing them better than me.

I followed her lead, adding my own spin to it. We liked talking out our choreography, counting out the steps, and naming our crazy dances—the hot oil and flour, the butt pinch, and the pumpkin patch.

"Girl, loosen up! Why you so stiff?" Monday laughed.

"I *am* loose!"

This was us, in our own world, with our own language and customs. We lived inside a thick, shiny bubble that no needle was sharp enough to pop.

"Hey! You know what?" Monday said, out of breath as she turned down the music. "Maybe we should go to them cheerleading tryouts!"

I stopped dead in my tracks. "What?"

"I heard Ms. Valente talking to Shayla and Ashley about it. Ms. Valente used to be a cheerleader and said it was fun. We should do it too!"

I nibbled at my bottom lip. When did she talk to Ms. Valente without me?

"I thought we were going to wait until high school and try out for the dance team."

"We can do both!"

"But . . . why?"

She shrugged, not meeting my eye. "I don't know. It'd be cool, though. And we better dancers than them anyways."

We had enough problems with Shayla and Ashley that we really didn't need to go crouching on their territory to add to them. "Naw, I don't want to."

"What? You scared or something? Come on, they'd love us! Especially you, you know all them flips and stuff."

She was right about one thing: they would love Monday. Love her enough to steal her away from me.

"Naw, it's just . . . well, we should be working on our routines. Not wasting our time cheering for some stupid boys who always losing games. And I heard *America's Dance Challenge* is probably going to have auditions in DC soon."

Monday straightened, her eyes sparkling. "For real? They coming to DC? When?"

I shrugged, innocently playing it off. "I don't know. Probably soon, though, so we should be ready."

She grinned, nodding her head. "Yeah. I guess you're right. Anyways, let's start with homework before your mom gets home. I have to read that packet to you."

I blew out a sigh of relief. "Probably be easier if I just copied yours."

Folks in Southeast talk about crack often.

How crystallized powder turned DC into a city of zombies during the '80s and '90s, hitting Southeast the hardest. Crack led to desperation, desperation led to crime, and crime led to murders and destruction. Everybody knew somebody affected by it: Daddy's family, Monday's family, church congregations, the Mayor, even teachers at school. Over time, folks rebuilt, families healed, but the evidence remained like a funny-shaped cloud that hung above our heads, occasionally blocking the sun with its memories.

"Hey, Dre! Turn that up!"

DJ Dre from WKYS volunteered to DJ at the Ed Borough Recreation Center annual block party every year. He grew up in Ed Borough and was proud of it. The block party was held by the courts and the whole community comes out to have fun. Balloons, face paint, clowns, barbecue, games, and music. Daddy's band was booked for the closing entertainment. Ma sold her pies, Mrs. Charles played cards with neighbors, while Monday and I ran around, eating hot dogs, dancing by the DJ booth, and playing in the bouncy house with August.

That's the thing, people remember the past and hold on to the rumors. Folks think all of Southeast is so dangerous and ghetto. But we just like everybody else. We love a good cookout, some crankin' go-go, family and friends. You can pick up this block party and put it anywhere in the world.

The Capitol Housing Authority built the Edward Borough housing projects during World War II on land originally given to freed slaves during the 1800s. It was meant to be a place of community, a place to start again, a place for the American dream.

Later on, developers realized how valuable the land was, sitting right on the river, with easy access to the city. Too valuable for black folks to have.

How convenient that crack would ravish the area developers wanted most.

Everyone's afraid of Ed Borough, while Ed Borough should have been afraid of everyone else.

Dancing by the DJ booth, a stray bee made its way from the trash can to the back of my ear.

"Ah," I screamed, running in circles trying to escape it.

"Girl, what kind of dance is that? Relax! It's just a bug."

"Naw, those things kill folk!"

Items Out Receipt

Davenport Eastern Avenue Branch
Wednesday, March 9, 2022 12:09:16 PM

Title: Diary of a wimpy kid : the long haul
Material: Book
Due: 3/30/2022

Title: Monday's not coming
Material: Book
Due: 3/30/2022

"Buzzzzzzzzz." Monday circled me with that mischievous grin that always cut through my butter-leather skin.

"Quit playing," I laughed, swatting her away.

We buzzed around each other, trying to out-buzz each other with fits of laughter in between until we grabbed hands and started spinning, spinning until the world blurred and we fell into the grass, staring up at the passing clouds.

"Girls," Ma called from a table near the grill. "Y'all want some pie?"

"Yes!" we said in unison, and scrambled to our feet.

"Wait now," Mrs. Charles said, lightly jogging over from a card game with a grin. "Let me bring a couple of slices over to the fellas first. Kids don't need all this sugar."

Monday giggled, reaching for a slice Ma had already cut before Mrs. Charles slapped her hand away.

"I said wait!" Mrs. Charles growled. "Damn! Little fast ass won't listen! Fast since the day she was born, I swear."

Monday backed away from her in a frantic panic, crashing into the table behind us. Ma blinked, her brows pinching together. Monday's teary eyes glanced between Ma and me a thousand times before she gulped. No longer buzzing, she rushed to my side and we linked pinkie fingers, her chin trembling.

"Big news?" I whispered. *You okay?*

Monday only nodded.

OCTOBER

Red flags.

Not blush red, orange red, wine, or ruby red. No, bloody red flags. Did you see them, Claudia? Did you?

Did you see any red flags?

That's the question they asked me over and over again, hoping to find answers. Hoping to understand what no one could. Signs. Were there any signs Monday was in trouble? Did you see anything out of the ordinary, anything unusual?

No. Nothing.

In so many words, they called me a liar. That hurt more than losing my best friend.

If Monday were a color, she'd be red. Crisp, striking, vivid, you couldn't miss her—a bull's-eye in the room, a crackling flame.

I saw so much red that it blinded me to any flags.

THE BEFORE

September came and left, and Monday never showed. I called every day, but the same lady would tell me I'm stupid for trying. Last time we'd gone this long without seeing each other, well, at least during the school year, Monday had that crazy flu and ended up passing it to the rest of her family. With a fever of 104, she couldn't even talk. Ma wouldn't let me near her.

I tried to keep myself busy. Coloring, keeping my nails tight, watching Redskins games with Daddy. We even went tailgating at FedEx stadium and Ma barbecued ribs on Uncle Robby's truck bed. Daddy's been teaching me football since I could crawl. Sometimes I think he wishes I were a boy, though he swears he likes being in a house full of women.

But school was . . . lonely. Every day without Monday

made her absence grow bigger and bigger in my head, like the tumor my great-aunt Jackie died from.

"So your *girlfriend* ain't here," Shayla said, standing over my desk as I tried to finish my English packet. "Awwww, you miss your boo? Can't feel each other up in the bathroom no more?"

I rolled my eyes and attempted to refocus, flexing to feel my bubble surround me. Shayla reached down and swatted the paper off my desk. The other girls snickered.

"You dummy, everyone's been finished. Why you so slow?"

The girls cackled behind her. My hand twitched and I reached down for my packet. Shayla stomped on it with her burgundy sneakers, leaving footprints like tire tracks. I jumped up, forgetting she had a good five inches on me.

Ms. O'Donnell tapped a ruler on her desk.

"Hey! Young ladies," she scolded. "What's going on back there?"

The girls scattered back to their seats.

"Claudia, you should be focused on your packet, not chatting with your friends. You're the only one still working on it."

"But she started it!" I said, voice cracking.

"Snitch," someone muttered under her breath.

My stomach dropped as I slipped back in my seat, lips trembling.

"She ain't my friend," Shayla heckled. "She ain't got no friends."

The class laughed as Shayla high-fived Ashley like she'd just scored a touchdown.

"Enough! Everyone take out your books and read chapter three," Ms. O'Donnell ordered. "I want that done *today*, Claudia."

The entire class had finished their packet, and I was only on page three.

The school lunch line ran the entire cafeteria wall. It took twenty minutes just to get a tray, which only left about ten minutes to eat. Monday and I used to entertain ourselves, playing hand games, plotting our dance routines, and picking our favorite go-go remixes. Up until the second grade, Ma packed my lunch every day. Monday's Ma couldn't afford to do that, so I asked Ma if I could get school lunch too. So we could be together—inseparable twins.

Without her, the line went on for eternity. Without her, I ate alone. Being alone made you a target, though, and ain't nobody got time for stupid boys throwing food at your head. That day, I skipped out on spaghetti and meatballs and went looking for the only other person in school that knew her best.

"Claudia? What are you doing in here?"

Ms. Valente, my seventh-grade English teacher,

my favorite teacher of all time, stood cleaning off the whiteboard in her classroom. She was that young, cool, down-to-earth teacher that dressed fly every day and knew all the music us kids listened to. Ma said she reminded her of Halle Berry, and Daddy happily agreed.

"Hi, Ms. Valente."

"Don't 'hi' me. Why aren't you in the cafeteria with Monday?"

I almost tripped over my own feet. "You saw her! Where?"

She crossed her arms with a hint of a smile. "Well, no, not today. But I know she's here—Lord knows she doesn't miss a day of school."

The disappointment felt like a bucket of ice water to the face as all my hopes crashed to the floor.

"She's not here," I mumbled.

Ms. Valente blinked. "What do you mean?"

I shook my head. "She hasn't been coming to school."

"So . . . where is she?"

I shrugged. "I don't know. I was hoping maybe you knew. Or heard anything?"

Ms. Valente frowned and placed her eraser on the table. "Come on. Let's drop by the office and see what we can find out."

Together, we walked down the hall to the main office. She told me about her summer wedding and honeymoon trip she took with her wife to Europe, and I told her about spending the summer with my grandmamma. I always felt I could relate to Ms. Valente, so I had no problem admitting that I hadn't seen Monday since June and I was real worried about her.

"I'm sure there's a reasonable explanation," she said, softly bumping me with her shoulder. "Girls like Monday are hard to lose."

I nodded, praying that was true.

"So, why is this the first time I'm seeing you?" I asked. "Where you been hiding?"

"Ha! Why you miss me or something?"

I giggled. "Sort of. All the other teachers are so . . . boring."

"Well, the school was a bit short on staff and they asked me to teach fifth grade and be a team leader, so I'm in the East Wing this year. But, you know . . . if you miss me, you can always visit the dark side and I can give you some extra homework. I know how you *love* that."

"Anything is better than Ms. O'Donnell."

Ms. Valente raised both of her eyebrows and chuckled. "Ah. She's a tough one. But she's fair. She'll get you ready for high school. I've seen students come back and visit just to admit they were wrong about her."

"We'll see," I sighed. "Just wish Monday was in class with me."

"Well, maybe you'll be in class together next year—in high school. Speaking of, any thoughts about where you want to go yet?"

"Banneker," I said, blurting out my practiced answer. A decision Monday made for the both of us.

"Hey! Now, that's a good school. I know a few students who went there."

"Yeah, but ain't it, like, really hard to get into?"

"I wouldn't worry about all that. You're pretty dang smart, so you'll do just fine. Got any other schools you're thinking about?"

I held my breath, scratching at my sleeve. "I, um, don't know. I guess it depends on where Monday wants to go."

"I know. But where do *you* want to go?"

I shrugged. I hadn't put much thought into it.

She laughed as we approached the office door. "Y'all a two-headed horse, that's for sure."

Ms. Clark sat behind the front desk computer, her lunch spread out, tuna on white bread with a bag of Utz crab chips. Monday's favorite.

"Hey, Susan. Can you do me a quick favor? I'm looking for a student I had last year. Monday Charles?"

Ms. Clark nodded, stuffing one last bite into her mouth before clicking a few keys. I bounced on the balls of my feet, holding back an exploding grin. Ms. Valente put a hand on my shoulder with a smile, but I couldn't calm down. We were about to find Monday!

Ms. Clark stopped typing and peered over her big glasses. "Hm. Not registered."

"Um, okay. How about her little brother? August Charles?"

Ms. Clark smirked. "Wait, the girl's name is Monday and she has a brother named August?"

Ms. Valente raised an eyebrow, her lips tightening. "Yes, like the famous playwright August Wilson."

"And Tuesday Charles," I added. "She should be starting kindergarten."

Ms. Clark shrugged and clicked her computer some more, seeming bored. She shook her head. "Not registered either. Could they have moved?"

Ms. Valente glanced down at me, eyebrow raised.

"Her mother still lives at the same house. I . . . uh, saw her."

"But you didn't see Monday?"

Ms. Valente glanced back at Ms. Clark with a fake smile. "I know I've only been in this school for a couple of years, but back in New York, when a student doesn't show up for class nor register for school, the school follows up. Is that not the case here?"

"A lot of students didn't return this year. Most had to move due to rent going up and stuff. But I'll pass a note along."

THE AFTER

Dear Monday,
Ms. Manis moov me up to Group Five in jazz!
Wit the highschol girls! I was the only 1 she did tht
for. In this Girls are class on dance teams—those
travling ones. Me and Ma and Daddy went to Chili's
to celabreat. Wish you where here to.

"How'd she get in this class?" A girl with thick, short hair
stretched up to the ceiling, then bowed down to her feet,
holding her position and letting her arms dangle toward
the hardwood studio floor. She glanced up, eyeing me in
the wall mirrors of the Manis Dance School for Girls.

"And ain't she, like, twelve?"

Another girl sat in a comfortable split on the floor next

to her, with her hair wrapped in a high bun. Both had the same creamy brown complexion and wore black leotards, pink leggings, and dance shorts.

"Naw, she ain't that young. And you saw her in that last recital? She killed it."

There were ten in the class: a bunch of juniors and seniors, one sophomore, and three freshmen, with me being a strange new addition. A brown horse in a field of unicorns.

"Yeah, but was it enough to jump out of group four, though?"

Keeping my distance, I stretched in the corner by the windows, listening to Daddy's last album on my iPod. Go-go isn't classical music, but I needed the adrenaline boost.

I pointed the new black ballet flats Daddy had bought me toward the windows, holding the arches of my feet, feeling the stretch in my sleepy hamstrings. Warm muscles help you jump higher so you land like a feather rather than a brick. That's what Ms. Manis would say. It's what I loved most about her. The tricks she drilled into our heads with sweet words, how she allowed us to incorporate hip-hop, jazz, and ballet moves into our pieces, how the music she selected didn't make me feel like I was counting sheep.

Another girl, much thicker than the other two, stretched her leg up on the barre next to the mirror with a deep breath. "But shouldn't she be with the little kids 'cause—"

The high-bun girl's smile dropped. "Shannon, quit playin'. Ms. Manis said to leave her alone. So leave her alone."

Short-Hair Girl exhaled as she backed up. "Well, as long as she don't fuck up at recital and make us all look stupid."

I gulped up a few short nervous breaths, pretending to focus, my confidence slipping through soft fingers. What if I didn't belong in Group Five? What if I wasn't good enough? And even if I was, was it worth being hated by another class of girls? I had enough trouble at real school; I didn't need to add dance school to it.

"I wonder what song Ms. Manis is gonna give her for her solo," High Bun said, rotating her head counterclockwise.

I could go a whole dance season without saying a word to the girls in my class. I wasn't good at making new friends. Never needed to. I had Monday, and that's all that mattered. But without her, the void she left stretched far, unexpectedly looping around every part of my life. I found myself wondering . . . what would Monday do?

Ms. Manis arrived, clapping us to attention, and we sprang into formation, the music starting. After warm-up, we moved into more intense steps. In the back of the room, I counted the beats, focused on Ms. Manis's footwork, avoiding eye contact with the others. They might as well have broken out a measuring tape the way they sized me up. But I pushed through. I imagined being in our invisible bubble where their slick talk couldn't hurt me, my force field impenetrable.

For the last twenty minutes of class we began learning the first steps of a routine that would eventually be a part of our big recital in June. An all-black dance school located smack in the middle of DC, our recitals could have up to five hundred spectators—including the mayor and senators working on Capitol Hill. Group Five dancers participated in their category dance, and then each girl had their own separate solo performance before the company-wide finale. It would be my first solo ever. I had ideas for my piece, but I needed Monday around to help me perfect them.

Ms. Manis counted out the steps, and we each took turns with the routine. Short Hair went first, sweeping across the floor, flashing a cocky smirk at me. High Bun was second to last, gracefully stepping, staying on count and leaping into a perfect landing. I bounced on the balls of my feet, waiting my turn. With a nod from Ms. Manis, I sprung, kicked out into a layout, then added one last twirl to a stop. Ms. Manis smiled in approval.

"Excellent, Claudia."

Eyes scorched the back of my head red and I cowered inside my bubble for the remainder of class. Maybe showing off wasn't the best way to make friends.

"Told you she's good," High Bun mumbled with a grin to Short Hair as they passed in the locker room.

"Yeah, whatever."

THE BEFORE

We should be practicing.

That's all I kept thinking as Daddy's album kicked through my mini speaker in the living room. Once Monday got back from wherever she was hiding, we'd have a lot of work to do. We couldn't mess around. We needed to be super tight, so that when we got to high school, making it on the dance squad would be nothing. We'd even be cocaptains. Everyone would want to be us—the best dancers, the most popular girls in school.

Lost in that go-go beat, I caught a glimpse of myself in the hallway mirror, noticing the way my swiveling hips made my ass shake. Slowly, my hands found my knees and I squatted, poking my ass out—a muscle I'm not used to dancing with—and forced it to move the way I wanted.

Monday used to do this, twerk in the mirror like girls in the music videos we'd studied, face stoic and focused as if was she solving a complicated word problem. I'd laugh until tears streamed down my face, but now I see it. The draw. How I went from a little kid to a hot girl in a matter of a few moves. *Sexy.* A word I would never use to describe myself, but at that moment, I saw a glimpse of it. And I liked it.

Ma came halfway down the stairs before busting out laughing.

"Girl, don't hurt yourself!"

"Ma!" I screamed, running away.

"And don't let your daddy catch you dancing like that either. Come on. Let's get you out the house for a bit."

We parked at the Giant supermarket, thick with Saturday traffic. I pushed the cart, while Ma checked off her long list. She planned meals out in advance since Daddy could eat a whole chicken on his own, leaving nothing but dry bones for us to pick from. Ma fussed, calling him a Hoover vacuum but only teasing. She loved how he loved her food.

"Not too fatty there, Chris," Ma said to the butcher behind the counter. "My husband's old and he don't need the cholesterol."

The butcher laughed. "Yes, boss lady. Anything else?"

Ma knew how to flirt with the butcher to pick the best

cuts, and they appreciated her love of roast beefs and lamb chops.

"Beef stir-fry," she said, reading from her list. "Need them strips a little thick, though."

"I got you."

I leaned against the cart full of canned goods and fresh vegetables, burying my face in a *Seventeen* magazine, avoiding Ma's smirk every time she glanced in my direction.

"Oooh, Ma! Look at this red!" I said, pointing to a nail polish ad.

"Sweet Pea, don't you have enough reds?"

"It's not just any red. It's a *blue* red! And it's a gel color! It even comes with a kit."

Ma shook her head, turning her attention to a stack of turkey butts. "Lawd, only you would see the difference."

That's when a sparkle caught my eye. I glanced up and there she was. *Monday.* Standing near the bread aisle. Even with her back to me, you couldn't miss her unmistakable denim jacket—the one with the red striped collar and rhinestones. The one I gave her. My knees gave in and I collapsed against the cart.

"Monday?" I breathed.

She didn't hear me as she made a left down the next aisle. I dropped the magazine in the cart, my sneakers squeaking against the floor as I took off after her.

"Monday!" I called, noticing the relief in my voice, joy bouncing in my chest.

I never ran so fast in my life, chasing a dream after living through a nightmare. I made the corner before my heart crashed into a wall. Up close, the girl in my jacket gliding up the aisle was much taller, but I still gurgled her name.

"Monday?"

The girl flinched as if shot, slowly turning to me.

I gasped, her face almost unrecognizable. "April?"

April's shoulders sagged, as if the very thought of responding to her own name exhausted her.

"Hey," I said, my voice falling flat. The hope that had ballooned inside burst, blood rushing to my head.

"What's up?" she sighed, her voice low and solemn. Monday's older sister looked . . . older. Her pale skin, big black bags under her eyes, had her looking like somebody's mother rather than a sixteen-year-old.

"Um, where's Monday?" I said, staring at my jacket.

April pressed her lips together, staring right into my eyes. "She . . . is visiting my aunt."

"Your aunt?" Monday had an aunt in Laurel, Maryland. But it had been years since she mentioned her. I peeked inside April's cart. Three boxes of mac and cheese, a bag of cheese puffs, white bread, fruit punch mix, and a jar of peanut butter. Monday can't have peanut butter.

"Uh . . . yeah."

"She's staying with her or something? She's already missed a month of school."

April sucked her teeth. "I don't know."

I swallowed, my thoughts not pulling together fast enough.

"Well, you got her number so I can call?"

"My aunt doesn't have a phone right now," she said, gripping the cart. "Anyways, I've got to go."

I scrambled, trying to come up with more questions, just so she'd stay with me longer. Even though she acted like a block of ice, she was the closest thing I had to Monday.

"But . . . when do you think Monday will be back home?"

She gave me a dark look, gripping the handle tighter, her knuckles turning white.

"Claudia. Just . . . stay away, okay?" I took a step back as she moved closer to my face. "Just stay away. Don't do this."

With that, she sped off, abandoning me in the aisle.

Stay away? She knows I came by the house. If she knew, maybe Monday knew. And if so, why hadn't she called me?

ONE YEAR BEFORE THE BEFORE

"No way! There ain't nobody?"

Monday's mouth fell as she sat on the floor across from me in the library after school. We hung out in the back, among the magazine aisles, waiting for the church car pool to pick me up for dance class. August, still too little to walk home alone, flipped through books in the kiddie corner, chewing on Fruit Roll-Ups.

"Naw," I said with a shrug.

"You *fake lying*. You telling me there ain't nobody you like? Nobody you find even cute. Not even Tyrell or Demetrius?"

Tapping my pencil on my notebook, I struggled to finish my essay. "I mean, they cute, but I'm not feeling them like that."

"Then who?" she badgered. "Come on! Tell me!"

I sighed, tired of all our conversation turning to Monday's new obsession: boys.

"There got to be at least one guy." She raised an eyebrow with a smirk. "Unless . . . there's a girl . . . that you, you know, may be feeling."

I looked up from my notebook sharply. "Don't."

She laughed. "Sike, you know I'm just playing with you."

My face grew hot under her fiery questions. I mean, there wasn't a boy I liked or even found cute. They all still seemed so nasty and stupid to me.

"Well . . . there is one guy," I said hesitantly, trying to make my lie believable. "He's cute but he's . . . older."

She laughed. "Of course you'd like them old, old lady!"

"Whatever. Not everyone's got love at first sight like you."

She closed her eyes, her smile glowing. "Did I tell you we sit next to each other in history?"

"Yes. For the thousandth time! Dang."

Grinning, she leaned over and drew on my notebook:
Jacob + Monday.

Jacob Miller: hands down the finest boy in our school. Been fine forever. Every girl liked him and he knew it, which made his cockiness ugly to me. His head was so gassed up he could float over the river, walking around like the king of Southeast. But who could deny his almond-shaped eyes, his crooked smiles, his dimples, his big bush of soft, curly brown hair he pushed back with a headband.

Monday had loved him for so long that I couldn't remember another boy but him. Her eyes would flicker when she talked about him like sparks were caught between her eyelashes.

"I heard him talking with Mr. Ode about applying to Banneker next year." She pretended to hold back a scream as she lay on the floor. "Wouldn't that be cool? We end up at the same high school together? Him on the basketball team, us on the dance team? OMG, OMG, OMG! Like, we could be THE couple. That's why we got to find you a boo, so we can go on double dates and stuff."

"Ain't you putting the cart before the horse? Y'all don't even talk!"

"Only old ladies say stuff like that. I'm working on it, but you're supposed to be helping me."

I laughed, opening my binder. "Whatever. Here, read my essay."

She snatched the loose-leaf paper out of my hand with a mischievous grin. "Only if you help me bag Jacob."

"Yeah, yeah, yeah. Just read it."

She scanned the paper and my back stiffened at her quickly fading smile. She looked up at me, harshness in her eyes.

"Claudia! What'd I tell you about this?" she snapped,

stabbing the sheet with her finger. There could be a number of things wrong with it, so I didn't bother guessing.

"You've got to be careful! We ain't gonna get into Banneker if they put you in the stupid people class. We'll have to go to some other high school!"

I reeled back, her anger unhinging.

"Sorry," I mumbled, holding back tears, playing with a piece of lint on my stockings.

She sighed, her eyes softening. "It's okay. Here, let me just . . . rewrite it for you."

Without hesitation, I handed over my notebook. I had secretly hoped she would offer. She wrote my essays better than I could anyways, but it was the first time she ever snapped at me about schoolwork. She normally had a gentle touch. The idea of going to high school with Jacob Miller was driving her to madness.

"You know, if that happens . . . you can go to Banneker without me."

Her head popped up. "Huh?"

"I mean, you can go there . . . with Jacob."

"What you saying? I'm not going to school without you!"

"Okay," I conceded, taking out my coloring book, needing something to accomplish to soothe my ego.

"We got a plan! Everything's gonna be okay."

"Day Day!" a little voice called out. "Day Day, where are you?"

"Shhhh! August, we over here! Keep your voice down!"

Little feet pattered in our direction before August burst around the corner. He grinned, running full speed through the stacks—his Transformers book bag half open, drinking a juice box with cookie crumbs on his little face, and braids undone.

"Why you such a mess? Tuck in your shirt."

"Look! Ms. Paul gave me some juice," he said, tumbling onto the floor.

"Still don't explain why you such a mess. And what happened to your hair?"

"It itches," he whined, scratching at his scalp.

"That don't mean you take them out in the public," she groaned. "Come here, boy! We can't go home with you looking like this. Mom will kill me!"

August grinned and somersaulted over to Monday. She pulled a long-tooth comb out her book bag and sliced into his 'fro.

"Ow," August cried. "Owwww!"

Monday sucked her teeth. "Oh shut up! Ain't nobody hurting you!"

August whimpered, fidgeting with the buttons on his shirt. Born with ants in his pants and rocks in his shoes, he couldn't keep still for more than a minute.

"Day Day, can we go swimming?"

She swatted at the side of his head again. "Boy, quit playing. You don't swim!"

"But—"

"Shut. Up," she snapped. "Shut it!"

Their brother-sister relationship felt more like a mother-son dictatorship with her harsh disciplines. Spending afternoons corralling him exhausted her.

By the time I finished coloring in the red tail of a baby dragon, Monday was nearly done.

"Dang, you did that quick."

She shrugged. "I'm just used to it."

"I know, but I mean, you can probably do other people's hair that quick too. Maybe even open yourself up a braid shop and make some money." I laughed. "You see all them bammas in school with their hair looking crazy. You can hook them up. Boys got money to get their hair did."

Monday didn't respond, just worked intensely, weaving through to the ends of August hair. Suddenly, the comb fell out of her hand. August scooped it up, quickly turning it into a toy.

"Girl," Monday gasped with a huge grin. "Yo! You're a genius!"

The next day at school, Monday had more sass in her step.

"I can't believe you're about to do this," I whispered, watching her gaze at Jacob, Trevor, Carl, and a bunch of other boys from class huddled in the yard.

"You came up with the idea," she teased, touching up her freshly done hair. An intricate pattern of tiny braids weaved like a basket into two pigtails. She must have spent half the night on them.

"Yeah, but not like this."

She grinned, shoving her bag into my hands filled with her supplies: a comb, a spray bottle filled with water, hair grease, and tiny black rubber bands.

Monday had a reckless fearlessness that made me want to grab her by the neck and stuff some sense in her ears like wet clothes in a dryer.

"Naw, mix up top? Meet press stop!" *Are you nuts? Don't do this!*

With a deep breath, she headed toward the boys. Drawn to the wreckage I was sure would come, I followed.

"Hey, y'all," Monday started. She held her chin up and kept her voice light and easy. "I got a question!"

The boys, stunned by her voice, did a double take and fell silent. Shayla and Ashley, chilling near the entrance, moved in closer while the entire yard watched on. I clutched her bag tighter, ready to run.

"Uh, yeah?" Trevor chuckled, looking at the other boys, appearing as confused as ever.

Monday smirked. "Any of y'all need your hair done?"

The boys glanced at one another, baffled. "What?"

"I can braid y'all hair. Seven dollars a head. Anyone interested?" She asked, her eyes falling squarely on Jacob, his hair pulled back into a messy ponytail.

"Seven bucks, that's all?" Carl asked—his thick hair

looked like it hadn't been combed in a minute.

"Yeah."

He grinned. "Aight. Bet."

"Carl! How you know she knows how to do hair?" Trevor challenged. "Your dumb ass gonna come out looking crazy."

"'Cause, she's a girl! And look at her hair! She hooks her little brother's up too, and he be looking on point. My cousin charges me fifteen, and I be broke as a mug."

The guys shrugged, still looking unsure before Carl waved them off. "Man, y'all lunchin'," he said and turned back to Monday. "Where we doing this?"

"Over here." Monday grinned, directing him to a bench behind us.

The boys formed a semicircle around them as if Monday was about to perform a magic trick, Jacob hanging to the far back. She inhaled deeply before prepping Carl's hair, spraying it with water to soften, deftly detangling and combing out the knots. Carl winced at her heavy hands, and the boys snickered. She carved out several sections, clipping back the parts she wasn't ready to work with, fingers working fast over his strands. Shayla and Ashley stood by, pretending to be deep in conversation, glancing over their shoulders every thirty seconds. Thirty minutes later, the guys stood in awe. Monday nodded at me, and I held up my small compact mirror.

"Yo! Shorty hooked me up," Carl exclaimed. "I told y'all!"

Trevor nodded in agreement. "So, can I go next?"

Later that evening, Monday and I giggled over chicken and mambo sauce in our makeshift tent, reliving the afternoon in detail.

"OMG, I was so shook," Monday squealed, braiding one of my doll baby's hair. "And Shayla's face . . . OMG, she was so heated!"

"Girl, I couldn't breathe watching you! I could've never done that!"

"Yes you could've. Just got to pretend to own that shit until you do," she said, stuffing her mouth with a dizzy smile. "Okay, so! If I charge seven dollars a head and do, like, four boys a week, that twenty-eight dollars a week."

"What about girls? You can probably do their hair, too!"

"Hell, yeah. And YOU!" She sits up on her knees to face me. "You could start charging people to do their nails. We can open up a whole beauty shop at school."

"We can be like, um, what's the word?"

"Entrepreneurs?"

"Yeah! That!"

She dug in our carryout bag, grabbing two cans of Coke. "To making money . . . partner."

I smiled, cracking my Coke open. "Right, partner!"

We crashed our cans together and chugged. Monday giggled, trying to drink the fastest.

"Ha! Beat you!" she cheered, wiping her mouth with the back of her hand.

"Aight! You win," I gasped, coming up for air. "You want to watch a movie downstairs before bed or whatever?"

"Yeah. But let's change into our sweats first and bring our blankets," she said, crawling out of the tent, turning to shimmy out of her sweater. "You know we just going to fall asleep down there."

Climbing out the tent, I froze midway, my mouth dropping at the sight of her purpling skin.

"Dang, what happened to your back?"

Monday yanked down her shirt and spun around, stunned. Her eyes widened with terror, as if she forgot who I was.

"I . . . I . . . uh . . ." Her face went blank for a solid thirty seconds until she coughed out a throaty laugh.

"I fell out of bed," she said with a shrug, clutching the bottom of her shirt. "You know how I be sleeping all crazy."

She didn't sleep crazy. She slept with an invisible boulder on her back. Rarely moving, barely breathing, dead to the world.

"Again?" I said, shaking my head. "Maybe you should be on the bottom bunk."

"Ha! April's not having that. She's already taking half the joint up with all her stuff."

Monday's room was such a mystery to me. I always asked her to describe it since I could never go to her house. She would give a vague description, ending with a shrug and an "It's not big enough." But I had my own predictions: a large cream room, pristine ivory carpet, golden bunk beds with fluffy pale pink comforters, crystal lamps, and a speaker box for an iPod. I don't know why I envisioned it this way, maybe because I wanted the best for her.

"So, what movie do you want to watch?" she asked. "I'm thinking something funny!"

And just like that, she was back to normal. Even though it looked like an army of trolls had beaten her with baseball bats, how could I *not* believe? She was my best friend. If she was lying, it had to be for a good reason.

Right?

THE BEFORE

The essay prompt made my stomach clench up in a way no body part should be able to.

Prompt: Discuss why you wish to attend Benjamin Banneker Academic High School.

I had absolutely no idea.

Monday and I would have worked on this essay together. Alone, the only answer I could muster sounded straight foolish: my best friend wants to go, and we are a package deal.

"Claudia? Did you hear me?"

I focused back on Mr. Hill, my guidance counselor, sitting behind his neatly organized desk in his narrow monotone office.

"Um, sorry what?"

"I said, Banneker is a tough choice," he sighed, cleaning his glasses. "Besides needing a 3.0 GPA and scoring proficient on the DC CAS, you'll need a dynamic essay and recommendation letters from the principal, your math and English teachers, *and* myself. There's also an interview, which usually happens in the spring. Are you sure you're up for all of this?"

Benjamin Banneker High School is one of the top ten selective schools in the city. Selective meaning tough, and I had enough trouble with school. Why Monday wanted to go there so bad, I didn't know. But knowing how obsessed she was, I assumed she must have been preparing to apply, and I should do the same.

"Yes, I'm sure."

He pressed his lips together, readjusting his tie. "Claudia, they are also very strict about your final performance and GPA. From what I've seen . . . your grades . . . are taking a beating this semester. Is everything alright?"

Science labs, history projects, and Monday were the only reason my GPA hadn't sucked—until now. In the few short weeks Monday had been gone, books had gone unread, homework forgotten, tests and papers too exhausting to complete. Why did the hours feel so long, yet the day sped by?

"Yeah, stuff is just harder this year. I ain't the only one, though! Other kids been complaining, too!"

Mr. Hill nodded and smiled. "So I've heard. But they're

offering peer tutors in the Learning Center after school. Maybe you should stop by."

Like a hot coal was down my tights, I shot up, the words *Learning Center* a trigger.

"No! I mean, naw, I'm good," I said, slipping the Banneker application between my textbooks and backing toward the door. "I'll do better. I swear."

"Well, okay."

The class photo hung on his wall by the door sparked an idea.

"Mr. Hill, do you know why Monday Charles doesn't go to school anymore?"

"Monday Charles?" he mused. "Oh. Oh right! Monday. Um, I'm not sure. Believe she moved, correct?"

I frowned. "Naw, she didn't move."

"Oh. Well . . ."

"I tried to call but her phone is disconnected."

"Hm. I think I have two numbers for her. I'll dig it up and give her a call."

"Really?" I grinned. "Thanks, Mr. Hill!"

Mr. Hill stood up. "Anytime. And you're sure about the student tutors at TLC?" he insisted. "Because I can—"

"Thanks for the talk, Mr. Hill. See you later!"

I spun, almost knocking myself out on the closed door, leaving the flaming words behind me and running down the hall before they could catch me.

"It's okay. It's okay. It's okay," I mumbled to myself in the lunch line, my legs bouncing as I stared at the prompt in the application peeking out of my textbook. The walls of my bubble were caving in fast around me. If Monday didn't come back soon and help me push them back, I'd suffocate in a world of my own making.

"You think Monday's mom sent her away because they were lesbians?" a voice whispered behind me.

"Probably," another said. "You heard how they got caught in the bathroom last year, right? Doing nasty shit."

I refused to turn around, no matter how much their words burned holes through my bubble.

"Those were just rumors."

"Hmph. Can't be rumors when you seen it with your own eyes."

"Guess Monday got down with both guys and girls. Living that 'ho life . . . just like her sister."

"You heard about them closing Ed Borough, right?"

"Yeah . . . but the city said they gonna let people move back. Once they build new houses or whatever."

"Ha! I got a cousin who used to live at Cappers. City did the same thing to them. Bulldozed them down, and ain't none of those families got to move back. Think they turned Temple Courts into a parking lot. She and her sister probably living in West Bubblefuck right now."

• • •

The library held millions of stories in a glass house. One good stone throw and the stories could leak out. That's how my bubble felt. One sharp stone and all my secrets would come flooding out. But Mr. Hill will find her, she'll be back soon, I thought.

"Hi, Ms. Paul!"

Ms. Paul looked up from her desk over a stack of books.

"Hi, sweetie. How's it going?"

With Monday not around and Ma and Daddy busy with work, the house felt like an echoing shell. The library at least provided some relief.

"I'm okay. Gonna hang out in the media center."

"Alright, I'll let your mother know you're here."

"Cool," I said, heading toward the back.

"Oh, Claudia! You know, I haven't seen Monday in a while. How's she doing?"

"She's . . . fine," I lied. "Just busy."

"Oh, okay. I was so used to seeing her bouncing around here all summer, I thought she moved or something."

"You used to see her . . . during the summers?"

She chuckled. "Almost every day. Her sister signed her up for the literacy camp every year."

Monday never mentioned going to camp. In fact, she swore she did nothing but hang out at home with her brother and sisters or chill on the basketball court, watching the games.

"Well, anyways, I saw her on the late-return list and thought maybe she moved and forgot to drop her book off."

No way. Monday was relentless about returning her books. She would walk through the pouring rain before incurring a late fee.

I winced a smile. "Well, I can let her know you're looking for it. Which, uh, book was it again?"

Ms. Paul pulled out a paper from the drawer and slid her finger down the sheet.

"Eh . . . it was *Flowers in the Attic*."

My stomach hardened and I backed away from the counter. "Okay. Thanks, Ms. Paul. I'll remind her to bring it back."

Rushing over to the media room, I stopped to collect my frantic thoughts. Monday took that book out a week before I left for Georgia. She took that book out a bunch of times. I remembered the cover, the funny title, the dents she made in the pages as she read it in our tent. Why does she still have it?

Since the third grade, Monday and I went as a trick-or-treat duo. Fairies, clowns, witches . . . eggs and bacon. But we were about to enter high school and needed a more grown-up, sophisticated look. I toyed with the idea of angels or French maids until I flipped through a magazine and landed on the perfect costume: sexy cops—complete with fuzzy handcuffs.

Of course that *was* the plan.

Saturday night, a week before Halloween, I sat at the kitchen table, ready to pull my hair out over a huge history project due the following week. Monday and I always worked on projects together. I handled creativity: posters trimmed with perfect designs, titles made out of cut-up construction paper, replicating old cities with paper-towel rolls and newspapers. Monday handled the content. We landed As every time. We. Always *we*. I didn't know how to work alone. I stopped by Mr. Hill's office almost every day to follow up on Monday. Every time, he said he'd get back to me, and it started to feel like that day would never come.

"Weeks been going by so fast that I didn't even notice Halloween coming around the corner," Ma said, peeling apples in the sink, prepping candy apples for a kid's costume birthday party. Her catering orders picked up around the holidays.

"If it wasn't for this party I would've plum forgot!"

I sighed, digging through my textbook, pulling out phrases and quotes. Cheating, I know, but I didn't know what else to do. My project stank of failure. And the words . . . they didn't look right. Something about them felt off, no matter how many times I scribbled them down. I crumbled up another piece of paper, throwing it on the ground with the rest of the snowballs that surrounded me.

"Heck, I'm surprised you haven't brought up costume

shopping yet. You too big for costumes now?"

I shook my head, aimlessly coloring in the margins of my notebook. Steam swirled inside my bubble, a closed lid on a pot about to boil.

Ma glanced over her shoulder at my half-eaten dinner.

"Sweet Pea, what's wrong? You not hungry?"

Biting my lip, I turned away from the questions that rubbed salt in the wounds Monday's absence created. *"What's wrong? Are you okay? Everything okay?"* Over and over again.

"Aren't you excited about Halloween?"

"No," I muttered, digging my nails into my thigh.

"Really? Why not? You and Monday sure drove us crazy every year when it came to trick-or-treating."

Just the mention of her name sent me into a tailspin. My whole body shook before the tears that had built up over the last few weeks finally exploded.

"'Cause me and Monday were supposed to go as sexy cops and now she ain't here and I got no one to go trick-or-treating with 'cause I got no friends!"

Ma dropped the apples in the sink and ran to my side as I slammed my head into my textbook.

"Hey, hey, hey," she cooed, rubbing gentle circles on my back. "Why you talking crazy? Of course you have friends!"

"No I don't," I sobbed. "Nobody likes me! Nobody wants to be my friend!"

Ma shook her head, as if to say "silly girl" and wiped my tears away with a dish towel. She didn't believe that her only child could be so corny. With a sigh, she cleaned up my dishes, taking a carton of ice cream out of the fridge. I sniffled, ruining the pages of my textbook.

"How about this . . . why don't we go by Monday's house one day after church?" Ma said, her back to me. Her voice sounded unsure as she scooped spoonfuls of chocolate-chip ice cream into two bowls. "I'll have a chat with her momma and see. How's that sound?"

She sat next to me, offering a spoon and a closed-mouth smile. She didn't like the idea, I could tell, but she would do anything to make me happy. I nodded with a sniff and reached for the spoon before she pulled it out of reach.

"But under one condition. I want you to join the teen ministry at church."

"Ugh . . . Ma, no," I groaned, slamming my head back down.

Ma tried to make me join the teen ministry—a group full of nerdy Bible geeks—every year. If kids at school found out, they'd add on another label to a long list I couldn't shake.

"It'll be good for you to make some friends. More friends, I mean. They're even having a little Halloween party. Well, Harvest Party, but they'll have candy, and games. I'm sure you'll have a good time."

It sounded like hell. Especially when I hadn't been to a

party, Bible study, or Sunday school since I quit the dance ministry. Would they even accept me back?

"So, what d'you think? You join the group and I'll talk to Monday's mother. Deal?"

I didn't have many options.

"Okay. Deal."

THE AFTER

Dear Monday,
Happy halloowen! Guess no sexy cop costumes
this year. Can't were that to church. Got two look
decent, so I'm wearing all black. Do you halve my
orang cardigan? I can't find it. Gonna be the dryest
halloowen party in the world. No scary movies. No
costumes. Probably won't even half kandy.

The church basement is a large open space with yellow
linoleum tiles, cream walls, and scriptures written in navy
cursive next to paintings of black Jesus. On the left is a
big industrial-sized kitchen that Ma volunteered in during
the holidays and for our annual soup kitchen day; on the
right are three small classrooms for Sunday school. During

events like Halloween (or Harvest Night, since no good Christian would ever celebrate some devil holiday) they set up chairs and tables against the walls with Christian activities while gospel music hums out of the speakers set up by the media ministry. I stood at the refreshments table, draped in an orange plastic cloth and fall leaves, clutching a cup of lemonade and the last bites of Ma's apple pie she donated. In my red sweater, I was the most festive girl in the room. The party needed some good music to get folks dancing, but I couldn't imagine this crowd twerking.

"Are you going to stand there all night?" a voice said behind me.

Who the hell is clocking my moves like a hall monitor? I thought, searching for the culprit. A boy—tall, muscular, dark skin like Daddy, dressed in black slacks and a lemon shirt that matched the floor—leaned up against the wall behind the snack table.

"You haven't moved from that spot in an hour," he chuckled.

Stunned, my mouth dropped.

"Are you . . . new here or something?"

He laughed. "You kidding? We've been going to Sunday school together since the first grade. Claudia, it's me. Michael."

Moving closer, I stared hard before finally recognizing his eyes. They used to squint when he smiled, his thick cheeks mashing them shut.

"Oh. Hi, Mikey."

His smile dropped. "Not Mikey. Michael. I hate Mikey."

"My bad, *Michael*," I said, rolling my eyes with a grin. Sure, I'd known him my entire life but (and there's no other way to say this) Mikey was always the chubby kid at church. I hadn't seen him since June, when the church surprised him with a gift card for graduating middle school with honors. He'd grown into a giant overnight, the weight melting off him like butter.

"Aren't you too cool to be with us church kids? With your new name and all."

"I'm slumming it," he said, grabbing a handful of cheese puffs, popping one in his mouth. "And Mrs. Duncan asked if I could help set up the DJ equipment."

"What DJ? All I've heard is gospel music on repeat."

"Man, don't act like you can't party to Kirk Franklin," he said, bopping his shoulders.

I didn't remember him being so funny. He'd barely spoken more than three words at a time to me, always so busy helping the media ministry during services and gospel celebrations.

"You right, you right."

"Ohhhh, wait, I forgot. You love you some go-go. Got any go-go gospel tracks you want to request?"

I laughed and it felt good. "Well . . . yeah. You got the Agape band, Radical Praise, New Found Love . . . they some of them got hits you can really dance to."

His face lit up. "Oh, so you *want* to dance? Does that mean you're back and gonna join the dance ministry again?"

My smile dropped a tad. "Nah. I'm just . . . really busy with . . . stuff."

"Aw man. I thought you . . . it's just, you're a really good dancer. But, anyways, I saw you come in, so I figured I'd stay and enjoy the party. It's good to see you."

"Um, yeah," I muttered, confused. We weren't close. Half the time I didn't pay him any attention. Why was he acting so friendly? And when did he get so cute?

"Why you seem so surprised?" he laughed.

"I'm not," I said, feeling my face flush and changed the subject. "So how's high school?"

He cocked his head to the side with a curious stare before grinning. "Man, it's crazy cool. You get to pick your own schedule. You don't have to wear a uniform. There's way more kids. *And* I'm on the football team!"

"Is that how you lost all that weight?" The question slipped out my mouth before I could stop it.

He shrugged. "I guess. But I wasn't that big, was I?"

"Um, naw. Not really."

A group of girls, huddled in a circle, smirked, eyeing us with hushed whispers. Sidestepping away from him, I fixed my hair, wishing I had on a cuter outfit.

"You've never been to the Harvest Party before," Michael said, offering me a cheese puff. "Why not?"

I didn't know what to say without sounding crazy. I

mean, how could I explain what I didn't understand myself? My best friend dropped off the face of the earth and I had no other friends to skip around to collect candy with.

"It's just that I used to go trick-or-treating . . . with my friend."

"Oh," he gasped, like someone socked him in the stomach, his eyes widening.

"But . . . that's kid stuff!" I quickly added, trying to downplay it.

He motioned to the room with a small grin. "And this is better?"

"Dang, you ask a lot of questions!"

Wounded, he stepped back. "Listen, I'm just making conversation. You ain't making it easy. Sheesh!"

My back tightened as I thought of Monday and what she would do. She made friends so easily, even when I didn't want her to.

"Sorry," I mumbled. "Just, this is not what I expected to be doing tonight. But plans changed."

He brightened. "Like my dad always says, shit happens."

"Michael! Cursing in the house of the Lawd!"

"Man, we in his basement. He understands," he laughed. "Hey, you know, we should hang out sometime."

I glanced over at the girls in the corner again, hoping they didn't hear him or see me turn into a cherry.

"Um. Why would you want to hang out with me? We barely know each other."

He shrugged. "I don't know. Just saying, we go to the same church and stuff."

"Yeah, I guess so," I agreed, still uneasy.

"And it seems like you could use a friend."

"How would you know . . . wait, did my ma put you up to this?"

His smile fell into a straight line. "Well, I saw her leaving . . . and I know . . ."

I threw my cup in the trash can and stormed off.

TWO YEARS BEFORE THE BEFORE

"Come on, girls! Dump them bags right over here," Mrs. Charles said, grinning, making room on our kitchen table to spread out. August clung to her leg in his red-and-blue Transformer costume. "I want to check y'all candy before you start eating it. Folks put all kinda pills and razor blades in stuff."

Monday and I fluttered into the house, two bumblebees in yellow-and-black-striped dresses, antennas, and honey pots. Ma came in right behind us, snickering as she closed the door.

"Buzzzzzzzzzz," Monday giggled, circling me.

"Hey, April," Ma said, shaking her head. "What's it doing?"

A glowing April looked up from her seat on our sofa,

with little Tuesday asleep in her arms. She'd offered to stay home with the baby and watch horror movies while we went out trick-or-treating.

"Hey," she whispered with a warm smile across her lips. "She's knocked out cold."

Ma crept over to the sofa, gazing down at Tuesday dressed as a baby pumpkin.

"Awww . . . so precious," she whispered, softly brushing Tuesday's cheek with the back of her finger.

April beamed proudly. "Yeah. Think she can be a little model or baby actress. Need to take some good pictures of her and send 'em to those Hollywood agents."

Ma nodded in agreement—a longing in her eyes. "Yes. She's . . . perfect."

I swallowed, rushing over to her. "Um, Ma? Ma!"

Ma shook out of a trance, blinking as if all the lights had turned on at once.

"Yes, Sweet Pea. Sorry. Say what now?"

"Um, can Monday sleep over tonight?"

"Yes, of course," she muttered.

We walked into the kitchen to find August rolling around under the table and Monday carefully monitoring her mom. Didn't want her stealing any of our hard-earned candy.

"Claudia!" Ma said, glancing at the table. "Did you leave any candy for the rest of the children in DC?"

"Yes! I left them plenty of that mushy stuff Grandmamma likes," I laughed, hopping over to the fridge.

Monday grabbed the cranberry juice with Mrs. Charles watching her every move.

"Janet," Mrs. Charles said in a low voice. "Did you see Dedria's face when she opened that door?"

My ears perked up at the mention of Shayla's mother. Monday and I caught eyes.

Ma pursed her lips. "Yes, I did."

Mrs. Charles shook her head. "Look like that man took a foot to her face this time."

Ma sighed, her eyes flickering in my direction as Monday and I pretended not to listen, pouring our juice slowly.

"Well. I'm praying for her."

"We got to do more than pray," Mrs. Charles said. "That man could kill her."

"That's private married folks' business."

Mrs. Charles's face turned up. "They private business ain't so private when it's written all over her face."

"You can't tell a woman to leave her husband."

"So what you want them to do? Go to therapy or something?"

"Of course not. Don't need some doctor telling them how to handle family business!"

"Well, at least we agree on that. But no man should put his hands on no female. Not ever! I teach my girls that every day. I lived through that long enough to know."

"I know . . . but you can't tell a woman to do something she don't want to do!"

"You can tell her mother, though. She'll listen. She go to church with you, don't she? Think of her daughter. Would you want Claudia seeing you that way?"

Ma blinked hard, her eyes narrowed and the room tensed. Monday and I shared a nervous glance. Our mothers weren't the best of friends. They only tolerated each other for our sake. So we frequently tried to extinguish fires before they spread.

"Excuse me, Ma," I said timidly. "Can we use the computer, please?"

Ma sniffed before taking her glare off Mrs. Charles. "Still doesn't work, Sweet Pea. Your father thinks it got some type of virus."

Mrs. Charles huffed. "You don't wanna be messing with them computers anyways. The government, they watching you on those things. Tracking your every move. They looking at the food you buy, what music you listen to. Hell, they even watching the books you taking out that library."

"Why would they track us at the library?" I asked before I could stop myself.

"'Cause they want to know what you reading." She stabbed a finger in her temple. "Get inside your head and know what you think so they can—"

"Girls!" Ma barked, catching wind of her own tone and cleared her throat. "It's getting late. Why don't y'all head upstairs and get ready for bed."

Monday grabbed her cup, making a run for it.

"Hey, fast ass," Mrs. Charles sneered. "Where's my kiss?"

Monday froze, her face tight. She tiptoed back and slowly pecked her mom on the cheek.

Mrs. Charles smirked. "Alright, you behave!"

Monday nodded quickly before sprinting out of the kitchen. I followed, climbing the stairs slow, worried about leaving them alone.

"Anyway, are you going to talk to Dedria's mother tomorrow or what?"

I stopped, peering over the banister.

Ma shook her head. "Patti, she got to leave on her own terms. It ain't my place!"

Mrs. Charles glared at her. "Janet, that man is going to *kill* her one of these days! Are you going to be able to look yourself in the mirror when he does?"

Ma's face dropped as she wrung her hands together, torn. Her eyes shot up, looking directly at me on the stairs. I bolted to my room and dove into the tent with Monday.

We slurped our juice, listening to Mrs. Charles, April, August, and Tuesday pile into a friend's car and head home.

"You did see Shayla's mom's face, though, right?" Monday mumbled without looking at me. "All them bruises?"

"Yeah," I admitted. "Shayla said she had an accident."

Monday chuckled. "Yeah, the type of accident where her dad's fist had a run-in with her mom's jaw."

"You don't know if that's what happened."

She pursed her lips. "You don't know if that *didn't* happen."

She climbed out the tent, stood at the window, and stared at the library, expressionless.

"What? You see someone in there?" I asked, only half joking as I joined her, admiring our reflection—us as twins.

Monday crossed her arms. "You really think they tracking us? The government?"

I shrugged. "If they are, all they're going to see is a bunch of kiddie books. Books that don't mean we're trying to take over the world."

"Right," she laughed. "Hey! I heard they had a Halloween party at the rec center."

"*You* wanted to go to the rec center?" Monday swore she hated the Ed Borough Recreational Center. Too many kids from her neighborhood went there and she tried to stay as far away from them as possible.

She shrugged. "Maybe . . ."

The next day at church, Ma talked to Shayla's grandma. Mrs. Charles talked to the school. And Shayla's father went into hiding.

NOVEMBER

If Mrs. Charles were a color, she'd be yellow—bright, cheerful, golden rays of sunshine. A ripe banana, a fresh highlighter, sweet like pineapples, tart like lemons, you could lose her in a field of dandelions. One drop of her coloring could turn plain buttercream frosting into the sweetest Easter cake.

But one drop of another color could spoil her brightness. Leave her out in the heat too long and her banana peel would start to rot. The tip of her highlighter blackens with wear. The prickling of her pineapple skin sometimes leaves her impossible to open.

And dandelions are nothing but pretty weeds.

THE BEFORE

If God could hear my prayers, he'd help the mailman lose my mid-quarter grades. He'd make it so that my parents would never see how I was failing almost every class except biology. The pressure pushed down against the top of my bubble like a spatula trying to flatten a pancake. School should have been my biggest priority, but finding Monday topped everything. Once she's back, things will be normal again.

I just need an assist from another player on my team.

"Hi, Ms. Valente," I blurted outside her classroom, paying her another visit in desperation.

"Claudia!" she yelped, confused but pleased. "Uh . . . how's it going?"

"It's . . . going."

She arched an eyebrow. "Hm. You want to share a turkey sandwich?"

"Yeah!"

I sat down, appreciating the decor: grammar posters, Shakespeare quotes, black history trivia. Unlike Ms. O'Donnell, she had a well-cared-for classroom. Ms. Valente was the only English teacher I'd ever liked. She was patient, kind, gentle as a feather but tough as metal. She even worked with me after class. Monday worried she'd know about my problem if I got too close to her. But when you're always cold, it's easy to be drawn to the sun.

"So, how's classes going this year?" she asked, splitting her sandwich onto two pieces of paper towel.

"Hard. Really hard."

"Ha! Then the real work begins in high school. You settled on your choices yet?"

"Um, sort of," I said, trying to pace myself. I didn't want to be too pushy and only use her for information. "I got to write an essay and stuff."

I bit into my half of a sandwich. Ma told me to never take food from strangers, even folks from school, but Ms. Valente was good peoples. I trusted her.

Ms. Valente grinned and took a sip of water. "Well, I can tell something's on your mind. You want to spit it out or do I have to offer you my whole sandwich?"

She always had a way of cutting to the chase. "Naw, you can eat."

"Good! 'Cause I'm hungry," she said, biting into her half with a sly grin.

"I'm . . . just wondering if you ever found out anything about Monday?"

Ms. Valente stopped chewing and swallowed hard. "Wait. Wait. Wait! Monday's still not in school? And you haven't heard from her?"

"Naw. Did you?"

She dropped her sandwich, shoving back her chair. "We're going to the office."

Ms. Clark, also in the middle of lunch, tried her best not to roll her eyes as we entered.

"Yes, Ms. Valente, how can I help?"

"Remember a few weeks ago, I followed up on a student?" Ms. Valente said, tapping on the desk. "Monday Charles? Have you heard anything about her?"

Ms. Clark lazily pushed a few buttons on her keyboard. "No student by that name enrolled this year."

"Yes, we established that the last time," she said.

"Ah, right! Tried to call a few times. Phone is out of service. Social worker filed it with CFSA to follow up."

Ms. Valente blinked, leaning in as if she didn't hear her right. "But . . . that was weeks ago," she challenged. "Anybody stop by yet?"

"What's CFSA?" I asked.

Ms. Clark raised an eyebrow at Ms. Valente, tipping her head in my direction. Ms. Valente winced. "Um, it stands for Child and Family Services Agency."

My tongue went dry and I backed away to keep from asking the million questions roaming around my head without a place to land.

"I know they were going through some reorg after the mayor took office," Ms. Clark added.

"Social worker?" Ms. Valente asked, flustered.

"She had a family emergency but will be back next week."

"Anyone else to take her place while she's gone?"

"Not at the moment." Ms. Clark sighed. "But you know she's on it!"

Ms. Valente rubbed her temple. "Thanks. I'll shoot her a note to follow up."

Ms. Valente gave me an uneasy smile as she led me out into the hallway. "Let's go finish our lunch."

"Why does Monday need a social worker?" I asked after a few quiet steps.

"Some families . . . just need a little help." Ms. Valente forced another smile. "I'm sure everything is fine. Sometimes, it boils down to miscommunication. Wires crossed, missed emails, stuff like that. Adults don't always know how to play nice in the sandbox together. When the social worker comes back next week, she'll stop by and talk to

Mrs. Charles. They'll take it from there. I know you're worried about your friend, but let's not fret about it for now. Okay?"

I tried not to let my imagination run wild, but a picture started to emerge. All it would have needed was a little color to fill it in and make it clear. When I think of social workers, I think of kids being abused. And Monday wasn't abused. She would have told me.

Right?

THE AFTER

When you think of dance, I bet you think of colors like cotton-candy pink and glittery snow white. Not me. I think of gray, silver, smoky charcoal, the shadowing of a number-two pencil. The simplicity can be so beautiful.

I try to look like shadows on a page when I dance. Imagining myself the color of rocks at the bottom of the river, every movement casting a ripple behind the next. The few seconds before I leap off the floor and arch my head back, I'm a perfect summer rain cloud.

"Nice soft arms, Claudia," Ms. Manis said from the corner. The studio felt massive with just the two of us. So much room to twirl and fly without worrying about bumping into the girl next to me. I could close my eyes and just exist.

"Come, let's chat," she said, and I skipped across the floor to join her by the sound system. "Now, my dear, it's time to talk about the piece for your solo performance. I don't know what the other girls have told you, but the reason why I personally select the song for your pieces, rather than letting the students decide, is because I believe in challenging my students. Pushing them out of the box they choose to stay in. Students nowadays will pick songs you hear over and over again on the radio. Songs you know inside out. But the songs I pick for you have an edge that only you can dance to. Now, close your eyes and listen to chords, the words, the melody."

A piano started, strong, steady, beautiful keys. Adele's unmistakable voice cooed out the speakers. "All I Ask."

"It's a slow song," I said, my eyes fluttering open after the second verse. Most of last year's jazz solo performances were fast-paced. Only the ballet dancers kept to the slow stuff.

"Yes. This, being your first solo, I picked a piece that has a mix of grace and fire. Trust me, it's perfect for you. Perfect for healing. Listen to it a few times and become familiar. You'll soon see yourself in the song."

I swallowed back my disappointment. No way I could do the moves Monday and I created to a slow song. Unless she came back and we came up with some new moves.

We wrapped up the lesson and I headed for the locker room, slamming right into High Bun.

"Oh shit," she said, slipping off her jacket. "You scared me. I didn't think anyone else was here today."

She yanked open a free locker, stuffing her book bag and boots inside.

"Uh, hey," I mumbled.

"Megan," she said slowly, as if reminding me. "Claudia, right?"

"Um, yeah."

"You have solo lessons today?" she asked, stretching into a long-sleeve off-the-shoulder top. "Me too. Did she give you your song yet?"

I nodded, forcing myself to speak. "Yeah. It's an Adele song."

"Oh! That should be pretty," she said, grabbing her shoes and leg warmers out her bag. "Well, later."

"Yeah, later," I croaked out, watching her switch away.

THE BEFORE

Two Sundays went by before Ma made good on her promise. After church, we drove straight to Monday's complex and parked in front of her house. The big tree stood almost naked, seeming bigger and scarier than before. Or maybe it was the house. Though no different from the identical ones beside it, something about Monday's house made you want to put on an extra sweater just looking at it.

Ma must have felt the chill too as she peered out the window from the driver's seat, her foot hovering over the gas. She sighed and pulled out her cell phone.

"Hey, baby. Yup, we're outside Monday's house. . . . Just letting you know . . . Okay . . . Yup, yup. Yup, I know. . . . Okay, love you too. Bye."

"Why'd you call Daddy? He already knew we were coming here today."

Ma's face tightened with a closed-lip smile. "It's just good for people to know where you are. You know, just in case. Breadcrumbs, Claudia."

She never felt safe by Monday's. Even when Daddy drove with his glock under the seat, she felt uneasy. Daddy was away that weekend and she had to keep her word, especially after I lived through that party. She flung the car door open, locking it twice behind us. Our heels clicked up the sidewalk as the wind rained dead leaves down on us.

We paused for a moment when we reached the door, and Ma scanned the block once more before knocking. A curtain flapped in the upstairs window.

"Monday?" I mumbled, and Ma looked back at me.

"What did you say?"

"Who is it?" Mrs. Charles barked, and the hairs on my neck stood up.

"Patti? It's Janet," she said, as if already tired from the conversation.

The heel of my flats rubbed against the crack in the concrete that I'd tripped over the last time I had come. Blinds shifted in the upstairs window. Someone was watching us. Maybe it was Monday, locked up in her room. I tapped Ma's arm, afraid to look away in case I missed her face appearing.

"What? What is it, Claudia?" Ma asked, before we

jumped at the clicking locks.

Mrs. Charles yanked the door open halfway and stood in the frame, her face stuck in a scowl, eyes squinting from the sunlight. My stomach clenched.

"Yeah," Mrs. Charles snapped.

Ma nodded, taking in her sweatpants and baggy yellow shirt.

"Hey, Patti," she sighed. "How you doing?"

Mrs. Charles's eyes narrowed. She glared at me, eyebrow rising, then glanced back at Ma. Her face brightened but somehow still seemed malicious, like a blackened sun.

"Well, look at y'all in your Sunday best," she said with a raspy laugh. "I didn't know Christians did door-to-doors. I thought that was just Jehovah's Witnesses. How you doing, Janet?"

Ma painted on a fake smile. "Blessed. And you?"

Mrs. Charles shrugged, her lips turning up. "Oh, you know. Keep on keeping on, I guess. You heard about them trying to kick everybody out around here? They want to bulldoze the whole neighborhood and build condos for white folks. People already started getting them eviction notices."

"I heard," Ma said. "Pastor is talking about forming a coalition. Get folks involved."

"Hmph. He ain't my pastor. Probably get involved so he can put money in his pocket."

"Patti, you know he ain't like that. He'd give his last

dime to help the community. Even to you."

She cut her eyes. "Well, if your savior pastor don't get involved, I don't know how they expect me to raise my beautiful, smart children living on the streets. And you know they about to close down Jak and Co."

"Really?"

"The landlord gone and doubled the rent. Been working there almost fifteen years. Trying to find another job but these white folks just don't want to hire a *black* woman. They don't want me to keep a roof over my children's heads. They just want my home."

Ma nodded as if she understood. With a sigh, she wrapped her arm around my shoulders, pulling me closer. I snuggled next to her coat, inhaling her perfume, feeling safer.

"Well. We just stopped by 'cause baby girl here been missing her friend."

"Really?" Mrs. Charles chuckled. "Well, I told Claudia last time she stopped by that Monday is by her daddy's."

I flinched. Ma gave me a look that could've burned all the hair off my head. I should have known Mrs. Charles would rat me out.

"Oh. She didn't tell me that," Ma said between her teeth.

"You know how kids are," Mrs. Charles said with a husky laugh. "Or *kid*. Since you only could have one."

A hard sucker punch right to the gut. Ma held her breath, her hand gripping my shoulder.

"Well, we better be going, have to start dinner soon. Give our best to Monday, will you? Maybe she can give us a ring sometime."

"Of course. I'll tell her you dropped by."

My flats scraped against the concrete as Ma dragged me back to the car. Once inside, I was met with the death stare.

"So you think you're grown now and can go wherever you please," she snapped. "Just wait until I tell your father about this!"

"But Ma—"

"DON'T say another word until we get home! Can't believe you got me out here looking foolish in front of that woman."

I slumped in my seat, kissing my TV time good-bye, and peered out the window. Mrs. Charles watched us from the doorway, a smile spread across her face, nasty like mustard.

Ma didn't tell Daddy about me sneaking over to Monday's house. She liked using him as a threat. Instead, she made up her own punishments—like helping her prep for Thanksgiving dinner. Family always came to our house for Thanksgiving, since Ma really knew how to throw down. Fights have popped off over her stuffing. Between Daddy's five brothers and sisters, we can have close to forty people in the house at once.

Anyway, my punishment: clean the house from top to bottom, then assist her in the kitchen as her sous chef. Doesn't sound that bad, but if you saw the amount of sweet potatoes I had to peel, green beans I had to snap, celery I had to chop, and greens I had to wash (TWICE!) in a burning-hot kitchen, you'd know why it was torture.

When Daddy came home from his last delivery before the holiday, we were on day three of punishment, and I was up to my braids in shredded cheese. Daddy kissed Ma as she stood at the stove boiling cranberries for the chutney.

"Ladies! You've been busy I see. The place looks good," he said with a grin, stealing a carrot stick from the strainer. He knew if I was in the kitchen helping Ma, I must have done something wrong.

"Yes, your daughter has been an *excellent* help," Ma said, glancing over her shoulder at me.

They continued talking about Thanksgiving plans, the uncles and aunties coming over with my cousins. Most of my cousins were in college, married and/or pregnant with second cousins. I never had a bunch of kids my age to play with, but Monday had always filled the void. I was the last baby in Daddy's family. They thought he would never get married. He says he was just waiting for Ma.

I could barely lift a hand to wipe the beads of sweat off

my forehead, my arms weak from grating while another three giant blocks of sharp cheddar waited for me. Monday would've been drooling over the mountain of gold. Felt strange, her being with her daddy, and not here in the kitchen, helping us. She never really talked about her dad. In fact, I couldn't remember the last time Monday mentioned him. He'd left for good right before little Tuesday was born. So I couldn't understand why Monday would live with him now. And why wasn't April with him too? And why did they have a social worker?

"Baby, you know Tip Charles, right?" Ma asked, not looking up from the pot she stirred. My hand slipped and brushed against the metal.

Daddy grunted. "Tip? Tip from high school, Tip? Yeah."

"You still keep in touch with him?"

He frowned. "That fool? Janet, why you asking about him? Of all people."

Ma shrugged. "Patti said Monday was with him."

My back straightened. Daddy noticed and arched an eyebrow at Ma.

"And?"

"And," Ma said, facing him before glancing at me, "we wanted to check."

"Check on what?"

"On Monday. To see if she's . . . alright. That's all. Since we've known her, that girl ain't never spent no time with her daddy. And we haven't heard from her in weeks."

Right then, I knew Ma didn't believe Mrs. Charles's story about Monday. Even though she was still mad at me, it felt good to have her back on my team.

Daddy sighed. "Janet, it's their family business. It ain't none of ours."

"But we—"

"Just stay out their drama, will you?" he sighed. "I don't wanna get mixed up in their mess."

Ma smiled, doing her best to play it cool, but I knew her temper was growing steadily. The tapping of her foot, her tight smile . . . I wanted to warn Daddy, but I knew it was the only way to Monday.

"Baby, Sweet Pea is just missing her friend. Ain't nothing wrong with calling the man so she can talk to her friend."

"I ain't got the man's number. I haven't seen him in years."

"But maybe you can get it."

"Well, why didn't you get the number from Patti?"

Ma slammed down her dish towel on the counter. "Because I'm asking you to get it, Gerald! You think I didn't think of that before? Do you think I ain't got no sense myself? I'm asking you, my *man*, to talk man to man to that little girl's daddy, and you sitting up in my kitchen questioning me about it. And what I look like going around here looking for some other man's number? You trying to make me look crazy or something?"

A whole frozen minute passed before Daddy cleared his throat and shifted in his seat. Ma didn't get upset too often, so when she did, you knew she meant business. With her hand on her hip and her neck rolling, it always surprised me how such a loud voice could come out of such a little woman.

Daddy sighed, rubbing his head. "Aight. I'll ask around. See if I can get his number."

Ma exhaled and returned to her pot, smiling over her victory.

ONE YEAR BEFORE THE BEFORE

The early-morning sun gleamed off the snow-covered streets as I heard something tap against my window. Melting ice, I thought, and didn't pay it no mind, until it hit harder, trying to break in. I climbed out of bed, wondering why the squirrels wouldn't let me have my rest, reaching the window just in time for another pebble to bounce off the glass right in front of my face and glared down at the sidewalk below.

"What in the hell?"

I tiptoed past Ma's room, ran down the stairs, and snatched the door open. Monday stood shivering with a dizzy smile.

"What you doing here?" I shouted under my breath.

She slipped inside, closed the door behind her, and yanked off her wet sneakers. I spotted my denim jacket under her thin black peacoat.

"I knew you'd be up and I couldn't wait. I have to tell you something!"

She grabbed my hand and dragged me into the kitchen.

"Girl! You're freezing," I said, wiggling out of her icy grip and shaking free of the chill.

"Shhhh! Keep your voice down."

"Well, why you so cold?"

The corner of her mouth pulled up. "'Cause I've been out all night."

"What you mean? Where were you?"

She bit her lip with a dramatic pause. "With Jacob Miller."

"What!" I screamed.

She jumped, covering my mouth with her icy hand.

"Shhhh . . . you got anything to eat? I'm starving."

We grabbed two bowls, a box of Cheerios, sugar, and some milk before running to my room and curling up in our tent.

"Okay, tell me everything," I said, my skin buzzing with excitement, holding my doll baby Pinky in my lap.

A face-splitting smile grew over Monday's spoon as she slurped.

"I snuck out the house last night."

I gasped. "Are you for real? How you do that?"

"I climbed out my bathroom window and jumped down."

"What? How you not dead?"

She chuckled. "'Cause I jumped onto the trash cans right below."

"You stone cold crazy! Why?"

She shrugged. "He asked me to. He wanted to see me."

"You gonna do everything that bamma tell you. You could've broke your leg or something. You can't dance on no broken leg."

She rolled her eyes and giggled. "I was fine. I've done it before . . . when I had to."

That's weird, I thought. Why the hell would she have to climb out a window? Maybe they practice for fire drills or something.

Monday dug around her Cheerios. Her thoughts seemed to drift away—somewhere far, without me. I snuggled closer.

"Well? What happened?"

She bit her lower lip, her eyes glowing. "He asked me to do his hair, said he wanted it to be special and didn't want everyone around. His mom went to the casinos for the night, so we had the whole place to ourselves. I sat on the sofa and he sat right between my legs on the floor. Girl, I was so nervous! My hands were shaking. But I hooked him up. His hair looks crazy good, you'll see. After I was done, he turned on a movie."

I leaned forward, clutching Pinky, hanging on to every word. "And then what happened?"

She gushed, hugging her knees. "And then . . . he kissed me."

"OMG! He, like, kissed you kissed you?"

"Yes, girl! We were lying on the sofa—kissing and stuff."

"OMG," I shrieked, burying my face in Pinky's hair. I popped my head back up. "And then what happened?"

She smirked. "What you mean?"

"Did you . . . you know, do it?"

She chuckled bashfully over her spoon. "No. But he wanted to. But I told him I couldn't until he told everyone we go together at school on Monday."

"So, he's, like, your boo now?"

She nodded, smiling huge. "Yeah, I guess so."

I buried my face in Pinky again and let out an "Eek!" I'd never been so excited!

"Wait a minute. What about your mom? How you gonna explain where you were?"

"I'mma tell her I was at your house," she said, shrugging it off like it was no big deal. "She won't know the difference."

I hugged Pinky tighter. So many questions running

through my head. I didn't even know where to start.

"What was it like? Kissing him? How'd you know what to do?"

"It's just like the movies. When the guy puts his tongue in your mouth."

"Ew. That sounds . . . nasty."

She laughed. "It's not. It felt good. Just got to make your lips soft and open your mouth a little."

I picked up Pinky by the yarns of her hair, flopping her from side to side, mulling it over as a twinge of jealousy surfaced. Monday snuck out the house. She kissed a boy. She was doing all these major things—without me.

Monday's eyes ran over my face. "What?"

"I didn't say nothing."

"Yeah, but you're thinking something."

I shrugged. "Just thinking."

She rolled her eyes. "Come on, Claudia. You my best friend. Ain't no boy gonna come between us."

I didn't know that was even a possibility.

"I know. I ain't worried about that."

She shrugged. "We just got to get you a boo now."

"You know I don't like anybody," I sighed, focusing on Pinky's hair.

"So. You'll learn to like them. I'll ask Jacob. Maybe one of the boys got a crush on you."

"You think so?"

"Yeah. You real pretty. One of them feeling you and

116

ain't saying. But now that me and Jacob go together, I bet they'll holla."

I tensed, clutching Pinky. "But what if they find out that . . . you know?"

Monday turned serious. "Trust me, they won't. Plus, they so dumb they probably won't know the difference. They'll be dying to get with you!"

I bit my lip, holding in another scream. She patted my leg and scooted out of the tent.

"Where you going?"

"Come on, leave Pinky there. We got work to do. We got to do our nails *and* our hair for tomorrow. It's gonna be a big day!"

The next morning for lineup, I arrived early. I didn't want to miss Monday's big moment, anxious to see how Jacob would let everyone know that him and Monday were together. Would he just start holding her hand in the hallway, sit next to her at lunch, or would he make some big announcement like he was running for president? Would he kiss her—in front of everybody? I didn't know if I was ready to see Monday do something so . . . intimate.

Monday flat-twisted the front of her hair, leaving the back out semi-straight. I painted her nails apple red with rhinestone studs on the tips, and she borrowed some of April's makeup. Standing next to me, her skin glowing, she almost looked like a different person.

Jacob stood in his normal circle, cackling with the other boys. His hair did look fly. Monday wove his braids in zigzags, leaving the ends out slightly unraveled. We stood in silence for thirty minutes and he never said a word to her. Didn't even look in her direction. Not even when the bell rang.

"Aye, who hooked you up?" Carl asked Jacob on the way to history. "Braids look on point, cuz."

Jacob shrugged. "Some girl around my way."

"Dang, can she hook up mine like that too? I'll pay her whatever."

Monday fidgeted with her book bag, glancing at me, worry in her eyes.

Scrambling to find comforting words, I whispered, "He's just nervous. Maybe he doesn't want everybody knowing just yet. Boys are stupid."

"Yeah, stupid," she agreed, her voice timid.

I linked our pinkies. "Be cool. He'll come around."

But as the day went on, nothing happened. Not that day, the next day, or the next. He blew by her like she was a ghost. While everyone complimented him on his braids, he remained mute on Monday. And there were only so many reassurances I could give her before they started to sound like lies.

THE BEFORE

The week after Thanksgiving, with everyone's bellies full of Ma's sweet potato pie and peach cobbler, Mr. Hill called Ma to request a special meeting after school. My mid-quarter grades never showed up. Either God answered my prayers or they held them back for other reasons. Reasons I was deathly afraid of.

I waited in the main office, my legs bouncing, praying for another miracle. Mr. Hill strolled in, head down in his files, chewing on a toothpick.

"Mr. Hill!" I jumped up from the bench.

"Oh. Hey, Claudia," he said, eyes shifting behind me. "Are, uh, your parents here yet?"

I noticed my name printed on top of the thick folder and gulped. Whatever was about to happen wasn't going to be good. But if I had Monday, she could help set every-thing right.

"They're . . . on their way. So, um, did you talk to Monday yet?"

"Monday? Oh, oh right. Yes, I called, but the phone was disconnected."

"Yeah. I told you that. You said you had another num-ber?"

"Oh. Thought I did. But I sent a letter to the last address on file to have her call the school."

"A letter? But—"

"Ah, Mrs. Coleman! Nice to see you again."

Ma arrived first, dressed in a sandy-colored long-sleeve dress with her black church blazer. Then Daddy, still in his army-green uniform.

We entered the big conference room with light seafoam walls and long brown cafeteria tables. Ms. O'Donnell sat on one side of the table along with Mr. Hill. Her presence alone made me want to vomit.

"It's no secret that Claudia has been having a rough time this quarter," Mr. Hill began.

Ma frowned, her voice laced with a warning. "Clearly, it's been a secret to us since this is the first I'm hearing about it."

"We thought it might be best to assess the situation first," Mr. Hill said with a half smile. "Didn't want to raise any unnecessary alarms."

"How is our daughter a 'situation'?" Daddy asked, his voice low, bellowing in the half-empty room.

Mr. Hill nodded at Ms. O'Donnell, who refused to acknowledge my glare. She sniffed and opened up a teal folder in front of her. "Take a look at some of her work over the past few weeks. Notice anything?"

Daddy lifted up my book report and I forced myself not to snatch it out of his hands. He read it over, his eyes going wide before passing it to Ma with a blank expression.

"Her letters . . . they're all backward and stuff," Ma muttered reading through it.

"Correct," Mr. Hill said. "Most of her in-class assignments are like this. Clearly she's having difficulty with spelling and basic reading comprehension. I checked with the rest of her teachers, and they have all made similar observations. One even mentioned she seemed terrified of reading aloud and assumed she was just being shy."

Pressure pushed against the thinning walls of my bubble and squeezed. I shuffled and reshuffled a card deck full of excuses and kept coming up blank.

"Her homework from previous years, however, seemed to be impeccable," Ms. O'Donnell said. "I'm curious, Mr. and Mrs. Coleman, do you help Claudia with her assignments?"

Ma raised an eyebrow. "You mean do we *do* her home-work for her? No!"

"Baby, please. Relax," Daddy whispered, rubbing her back.

"She's always done it on her own," Ma said, her voice drifting before glancing at me. "Or with . . . a friend."

I gulped, her gaze burning a hole in the side of my neck, trying to smoke the words out of me.

"Well," Mr. Hill sighed. "We'd like to have her tested and continue evaluations, but our best guesstimate is she could have dyslexia."

The word burned through the air—a word that lived on the back of my tongue, gagging me every time I pretended to read a book. A word I had tried to shield and protect myself from for years. But once spoken, it shot out like a hot needle and popped the bubble I lived in. Exposed to the new crisp air, I shivered, like I never knew cold existed.

Ma and Daddy stiffened, sharing an awkward exchange of glances.

"That doesn't . . . make any sense," Ma stammered. "Her work has been just fine! I mean, the other day she came home with ninety-two on her last math test. We hung it up on the fridge! How can she score damn near a hundred on a test and write like this?"

"I spoke to Ms. Montgomery about that," Ms. O'Donnell explained. "She prints her test and quizzes on blue paper. Commonly, students with dyslexia process information differently. When presented in such a way, color reduces confusion. It's one of the key identifying traits I picked up on."

Ma shook her head, struggling to find the words.

"But she's never had problems before, and she's been in this school since the first grade," Daddy said. "Isn't this something you should have caught a while ago?"

"Yeah," Ma huffed. "How come they didn't check for that on them standardized tests y'all be stressing over every year?"

"It's possible she's flown under the radar," Ms. O'Donnell said, glaring at Mr. Hill.

"With all these teachers up in her face every day, I don't understand how my *child* could fly that plane alone and no one notice until the year before she's supposed to go to high school," Ma snapped.

"Sometimes these issues materialize in other ways, as a form of distraction," Mr. Hill started carefully. "Could explain some . . . behavioral issues Claudia's had over the last year."

Daddy holds Ma back from lunging at them.

"Issues? You mean when you let crazy people take pictures of my child and spread them all over the internet? You mean like when that boy touched her butt? Issues like that? She had every right to box that boy's ears in."

"Yes, but that hasn't been the only fight she's been in," Mr. Hill said.

Ma's eyes dropped to her hands, her expression softening.

Daddy glanced between us and I stopped breathing. "Wait a minute! What other fights?" Daddy asked.

"We'll talk about that later," Ma whispered, not looking up at him.

Daddy shook his head, his lips pressed together. "So what are the next steps for something like this?"

"Well, like I said, there are a few official steps and procedures," Mr. Hill said. "But once it's all worked out, Claudia will be identified as a student with learning disabilities, which qualifies her for certain supplemental tools to help her manage and succeed."

Tears prickled against my eyelids. Without my bubble protecting me, every bone in my body ached to run and dive into my tent. With Monday. The world felt raw without her.

"I know it may not seem like it right now but this is actually a good thing," Ms. O'Donnell offered with a painful smile.

"I don't see how my child suffering with this for so long—undetected—could be a good thing," Ma said, though not as fierce as before. "Clearly this has affected her studies and could affect her choice of high school."

"You are right. It's unfortunate we are just learning this now, and it's too late to right all the wrongs," Ms. O'Donnell said. "But knowing is half the battle. Claudia is an extremely bright student. Every teacher has said such. With the proper tools, she'll accelerate without question!"

"And we will, of course, do our best to push her through to graduation," Mr. Hill added.

Ms. O'Donnell rolled her eyes at him. "But our main objective will be to provide resources. Immediately."

Mr. Hill seemed to hold back a comment, giving Ma a pained smile.

"I think it'd be best if we discuss this in private," Daddy sighed before standing. The teachers leaned back, thrown off by his height and build. "Thanks for your time. Come on, Claudia."

The three of us walked in silence to the car before Ma finally broke.

"Well, they got some nerve! First, they start accusing us of doing her work for her, then they admit they messed up, then they talking about this is a 'good thing.' A good thing? How they in her face all day and not see something right in front of them?"

"Not now, Janet," Daddy said.

"And that Mr. Hill, talking about how they gonna 'push her to graduation.' Sound like they just wanna get rid of her—make her someone else's problem instead of trying to help her. Sounds like they worried more about their ranking than our daughter!"

Daddy spun around to face her. "Janet! I said. Not. Now."

Ma's mouth hung open. Daddy huffed and continued toward the car.

We sat parked in silence for almost ten minutes, Daddy deep in thought, gripping the steering wheel.

Ma sighed loudly and clicked on her seat belt. "Well, I don't understand what you mad at me for."

Daddy turned to her, his eyes narrowing. "Fighting in school? You never said nothing about that. What else has been going on while I'm on the road? What else you not telling me? What else have you been *lying* about?"

Ma glared at him as she coldly crossed her arms. "Take me home."

Daddy's eyes softened. He knew he'd gone too far. He cleared his throat and started up the car. As we drove by Ed Borough, Monday swallowed up my thoughts. None of this would have happened if she were here to help me. They would have never found out. I can't believe she would leave me high and dry like this. She knew I needed her. She knew!

"Daddy, did you ever talk to Monday's daddy?" I blurted out.

Daddy grunted. "You need to stop worrying about your friend and start worrying about them grades. I don't want to hear another word about that girl. Not one more word about Monday until your grades are up! You understand?"

DECEMBER

I saw Jacob Miller not too long ago, coming out of the movies with some girl at Gallery Place Chinatown. We hadn't seen each other since "it" happened—when the police were questioning everybody about Monday.

He'd fallen hard from grace after they found her. Bouncing from school to school, kicked off basketball teams, smoking, drinking until he couldn't stand up straight. As Ma would say, he don't know his ass from his elbow anymore. They say what happened changed him. I don't believe that. I think he still using Monday. But if *it* did change him, then good. I hope *it* fucked with his head the way he fucked with Monday's. I don't feel a bit sorry for him.

But Ma says everyone deserves forgiveness.

That's why if Ma was a color, she'd be pink with her sweetness. A tender flower, a bubbly pop of chewing gum, two scoops of strawberry ice cream. Silly in her girly ways, her color deepens with love, until she glows fuchsia— bright and bold, unstoppable.

But when she is not fed the riches that life promises, Ma pales, remaining but a tint above white, a color aching in want.

ONE YEAR BEFORE THE BEFORE

"I can't believe he's gonna carry me like this. He SWORE he would say something." Monday wrung her hands around an empty water bottle, staring at the tiles on the floor in the school bathroom. Three weeks since their first kiss, and even though they linked up over the weekends, he still ignored her at school.

"He told me this weekend. He said he would finally tell people now. Shit, I'm so stupid."

"It's not your fault," I said. Even though I wanted to say that this is what happens when you step out of the bubble. No good could come of it. But the told-you-so speech didn't seem right with tears in her eyes. How was I gonna get her to look over my English paper before class?

"What am I going to do?" She sniffed, her face wet.

I pulled her into a hug, and she buried her face in my shoulder, holding on tight. I squeezed her back, and she yelped.

"What? What's wrong?"

She stood there for a moment, staring at me—deciding. Even after years of friendship, she measured my worthiness. Finally, with a sigh, she pulled back the collar of her shirt, exposing her chewed-up shoulder, throbbing red under her bra strap.

"Oh shit," I whispered, inching closer to see the teeth marks. "What the hell happened to you?"

"August. He keeps having these . . . tantrums. Been attacking us out of the goddamn blue."

"Why?"

"I don't know," she said, slipping her shirt back up. "Just, don't tell anybody, okay? I'll worry about him later. But what am I going to do about Jacob?"

"Girl, just forget about him. He's an asshole!"

"I can't, Claudia." Her face went hard. Her voice grew deep and the air changed around her. "I can't. Not after . . . naw. I want to know why he's trying to carry me like this. I need to know."

The bell rang, and she collected her books off the floor and stormed out into the hall. Afraid of what she might do, I raced out after her.

Jacob stood in the hallway outside of English class, his braids in a fresh style, whispering in the ear of some girl leaning against the lockers. The sight of him was the match that lit Monday on fire.

I didn't want her hurt more than she already had been, so I grabbed hold of her arm and pleaded. "Non-slipping plus. Him non-paying." *Don't do it. He's not worth it.*

She gave me a dark look and knocked my hand off before charging toward him.

"Hey! We need to talk," she snapped, bringing the entire school hallway to a stop.

Jacob grinned. "What we got to talk about?"

"You know exactly what. So you just gonna pretend we didn't do anything this weekend?"

The girl standing next to Jacob glanced between them, backing out of the line of fire.

"Man, whatever," he said, waving her off as he turned away.

"No," Monday said, grabbing his arm. "You're gonna fucking talk to me."

He snatched his arm back. "Aye, get off me! I don't know where you been."

A circle formed around us, and my heart shifted up to my throat.

"Tell everyone who really did your hair, Jacob! Tell them how you called me up to come over your house this weekend. Tell them!"

"You lunchin'. That ain't happened!"

"Ohhhh . . . you went over Jacob's house?" Trevor

asked, appearing out of the growing crowd, fake punching Jacob. "So, you hit that?"

Jacob grinned at him with a sly shrug. "Well, I don't kiss and tell, but if she wants to put it out there that she came by my spot, I ain't gonna lie."

Monday gasped, her eyes growing huge. "How you gonna lie like that in front of my face?"

"So did you or didn't you?" Trevor challenged.

"Of course she did," Shayla said, busting through the crowd. "She a 'ho, just like her sister, fucking every dude on the courts."

Monday jerked back, clutching her books to her chest while trying to mask her shock. No one had ever brought up April in school before. Even I felt the sting of her words.

"I didn't," Monday yelled, shaking her head.

I tugged on her arm, trying to pull her away. No one was going to believe her. Life outside our bubble was blunt and cruel, and I had had enough of it to know when it was time to retreat. Monday fought me off.

"Tell 'em, Jacob!"

Jacob huffed and rolled his eyes.

"Aight, she right. I didn't bang her," he relented with a slick grin. "She said she only like doing it with Claudia, 'cause they lesbians!"

The hallway erupted with laughter. Monday and I looked at each other, bewildered, the joke lost on us while

Jacob high-fived his friends.

Lesbians? Because we were best friends? Boys can be so childish, coming up with the dumbest excuses for the foolishness that they do.

But for some reason, and I'll never know why, something snapped in Monday. Maybe because he dragged me into his chain of lies and she wasn't about to let him hurt me too. She charged at him, fist in the air, and conked the top of his skull and then slapped the hell out of him with her books. He went face-first into a locker and fell to the floor. An "Oooooo!" hissed from the other students.

Jacob jumped up, enraged. He shoved Monday into a locker, pinning her. Monday dropped to the floor with a scream as he pulled her hair. The wind went out of me. At that moment, seeing my best friend dragged and thrown around like a doll, something turned inside me, bursting through my skin, and I saw nothing but red.

"Get off her," I screamed, tackling his back like a monkey, hitting his head with my balled-up fists. But none of my blows felt strong enough to crack through his thick skull. I dug my freshly painted nails deep in his neck and scratched.

"Ahhh, stop," he hollered, releasing Monday to swat me off. His hand caught my cheek, and I fell to the floor with a pathetic thud. Monday sprung up at the sight of me on my knees.

"Don't you touch her!" she screamed, and kicked him

in the nuts. He cried out, falling to the floor before she swung her leg back and kicked him again. She kicked and kicked—each kick to the gut more powerful than the last. Everyone's laughter turned into hushed whispers and then silence.

"Aren't you gonna help him?" someone said to Carl, frantic.

"Naw! My momma would kill me for touching a girl."

Light bounced off the sweat on her brows as she straddled him. She slammed against his head and I caught the unfamiliar glimpse of rage in her eyes. Stunned, I couldn't make myself move. I'd never seen her so . . . violent.

"Well, someone has to help him," Shayla hollered behind me. "She's gonna kill him!"

But no one moved, all too mesmerized by the scene of the most popular boy in school being overpowered by a girl—a girl who up until that moment had never made much of a fuss, who some barely noticed. That is, until she stepped out of our bubble.

Jacob's grunts turned into whimpers, then full-out cries as he spat blood. A teacher finally broke through the crowd, and just as we were a package deal in the ass whupping, we were a package deal being dragged to the principal's office kicking and screaming.

"It's okay. She'll understand," I whispered on the bench.

"No. She won't," Monday said, wiping a tear from the

corner of her eye, her clothes askew, buttons lost, tights ripped, with hair pointing in every direction. "She's going to kill me."

I had only been to the principal's office once before, when a boy touched my butt in front of Ms. Valente. She'd dragged him by the ear to the office and Ma almost lit the school on fire.

This time, though, we'd ganged up and attacked a boy in the hallway. We sent him to the hospital bleeding. I expected Ma to be the first one flying in screaming. Instead, Mrs. Charles entered the office like a prowling lioness, glancing at us on the bench by the door. If looks could kill, we'd be a hearty dinner for maggots. Monday shifted closer to me, her color draining. I mean, what kid isn't scared of their mom? Hell, Ma still jumps when Grandmamma calls after her. But the look on Monday's face, you'd swear Lucifer had walked in the way her eyelids pulled back. Quickly, we linked pinkies.

"Oh boy," Ms. Clark muttered behind her desk, and called the principal.

The principal stepped out of his office with a heavy sigh.

"Hello, Mrs. Charles," he greeted coldly. Mrs. Charles held a blank face.

He gave her a recap with stoic calm. All the while Monday trembled next to me.

"We will see if the Millers plan to press any assault charges, but for now . . . there is a mandatory suspension for fighting."

Mrs. Charles didn't flinch at the statement like we did. She turned to us and asked, "So what happened?"

Monday could barely breathe, so I jumped in first.

"Jacob Miller was spreading lies about Monday, and she told him to stop, but he wouldn't listen."

"Lies? What kind of lies?"

"Saying that . . . they were . . . doing it," I said.

Mrs. Charles frowned. She glanced at Monday, whose eyes were locked on the floor. For a moment, I thought I had said too much, that I had only made the situation worse, but Mrs. Charles turned back to the principal. "Listen, I don't know what you heard, but I know my child. She would never lay hands on some boy unless she had reason. She knows better."

The principal crossed his arms. "We were told she assaulted him first. That she approached him in the hall."

"I SAID I don't care what the fuck you *heard* happened. Did you ask her WHY?"

"It makes no difference," he stated. "We have strict rules about fighting on school property."

She pointed to Monday. "You let that little nigga spread lies about my daughter . . . have her looking like some 'ho and you gonna tell me . . . wait. What the hell is that?"

Mrs. Charles marched over to us and I held my breath, my soul fleeing. Monday flinched and leaned away with a whimper before Mrs. Charles snatched and yanked at her collar. My heart slapped against the floor like a heavy sponge. I hadn't noticed the speckles of blood on her shoulder, leaking through her shirt.

"The fuck is this?" she asked Monday before turning to the principal. "Why she got bite marks on her shoulder?"

Monday's whole body shook as she whimpered. She tried to cough out words but couldn't even spit out air. The look on her face . . . all I could think about was saving her.

"It was Jacob," I cried. "He was biting her!"

Monday's mouth dropped as she turned to me.

Mrs. Charles released Monday, storming toward the principal.

"You talking about that boy going to the hospital—why hasn't MY daughter been looked at?"

The principal stammered. "We didn't . . . I mean, she didn't say . . ."

"That little nigga gonna spread lies about my daughter, chew up her shoulder, and you busy talking about what SHE did? She's a female! He shouldn't be touching no damn female! PERIOD!"

Mrs. Charles's screams brought the entire office—maybe

137

the whole school—to a standstill.

"She ain't never acted up in this school before. EVER! She was defending herself! I should be pressing charges too."

The principal glanced at me. "Claudia, you can go back to class now."

"No! She's staying right here since she's the only one here decent enough to defend my child. A school full of fucking adults and you letting some boy, some MAN, touch my child!"

Mrs. Charles went on like this for another twenty minutes, and by the time she was done, Ma had arrived, and we were excused for the day—with no more talk of suspension.

"So explain to me what happened again, 'cause I'm still not understanding," Ma said once we were outside. Even though Mrs. Charles had saved us from suspension, there was no stopping Ma from tearing into me.

I lowered my head. "Sorry, Ma."

"What were you thinking? That boy could have hurt you. Then what?"

"They fine, Janet," Mrs. Charles said, waving her off. "Girls fight. No big deal."

"Hmph. Not my daughter," Ma snapped, the words slicing through the air.

Mrs. Charles raised an eyebrow and shifted back to take a hard look at Ma. "Oh really, now?"

Ma's eyes widened. "And not her best friend, either," she added, trying to clean it up. But it was too late. Clearly, she expected that sort of behavior from Monday, but not from me. And it took nothing for Mrs. Charles to recognize that. A thick moment passed between them.

"Let's go," Mrs. Charles hissed at Monday before storming off. "Come on!"

Monday jumped at the bite in her voice. Her lip trembled as she looked at me, then Ma, then back at me again.

"I said come on!" Mrs. Charles barked. "I ain't got all day!"

Monday flinched, her eyes closing as tears ran down her face. With slumped shoulders, she dragged her feet after her mother.

Ma and I watched them walk off in silence, my nerves prickling. The fear Monday had of her mother didn't seem normal. The fear I had *for* Monday didn't feel normal. Nothing about the moment felt normal.

"Ma, maybe—"

"Not one word, Claudia Mae," Ma snapped, glaring at me. "Let's go!"

Between the million and one chores Ma laid on me over the weekend, I snuck a few secret calls to Monday's house, but no answer.

On Monday morning, she stumbled into school, dazed, eyes glossy, lips white and chapped. Her uniform wrinkled and filthy, her flat twists in the same unraveling wreckage that they had been after Thursday's fight. No one would have noticed her condition, except for the fact that she smelled soaked in piss.

"Ew, you stank," Shayla sneered in homeroom. "They don't give you soap over at Ed Borough."

"Shit, you smell like one of them crazies on the Metro," Trevor cackled.

Monday walked through the halls like a zombie that day. Kids heckled, pinching their noses as she passed, and by third period, Ms. Valente brought her down to the nurse's office and gave her a fresh pair of school sweats to wear for the rest of the day.

THE AFTER

Dear Monday,
Ma hired Ms. Walker to tudoor me. Think she
gonna let them put me in the Learning Centr! Were
our you? How could you ghost on me like ths?

"Ma, please," I cried.

"Claudia, you making all this fuss for no reason," Ma
said, running a knife along some red ribbon tied around a
tray of frosted sugar cookies for the church Christmas auc-
tion to curl it. "Now, come on, we late."

I stood by the door, wool tights itching under my charcoal dress.

"You gonna let them put me in the stupid kids' class!"

Dressed in a rose-color skirt suit, she slipped on her

coat and headed for the door.

"For the last time, there's no such thing as 'stupid kids' class.' The Learning Center will be good for you. You just . . . need a little extra help, that's all. Ain't no shame in that, Sweet Pea."

The name *Sweet Pea* felt like a pacifier—a rattle shaking in my face. She was so busy treating me a like a baby that she wouldn't even try to understand that walking into the Learning Center was school suicide.

"I ain't doing it," I snapped.

Ma stopped short to glare at me. "Listen here, I've taken enough sass from you today. You want me to call your father? I'm sure there are heaps of other chores he'd like to give you. You will do as you're told and mind how you speak to grown folk. Put on your coat and get in this car. Now!"

Balancing the cookies, she flew out the door, leaving it open for me to follow.

I climbed in the back seat. Ma huffed, turned on Good Hope Road, and headed for church.

"Claudia," Ma finally said after about five minutes of silence. "Your father and I . . . we ain't out to get you. We just want what's best for you. I thought you wanted to go to high school."

It didn't matter where I wanted to go anymore. It was always Monday's plan, and now she wasn't around to help me. Or protect me. How could she just abandon me like this? What did I do to her?

"Now, Ms. Walker, she used to working with students just like you and knows a bunch of tricks to help you. We're lucky to be able to afford her at all. So take it seriously, you hear? I don't want to hear nothing about you carrying on like this up in her house. You hear me?"

"Yes, Ma," I mumbled.

Southeast twinkled brighter in December, with folks dressing up their houses for Christmas. Monday and I used to vote on the best-dressed house, always picking the ones with the big inflatable snowmen and icicle lights.

The houses by Ms. Walker looked straight out of a Christmas picture book with massive wreaths, red and gold bows, and roofs covered in lights. If Monday were still around, she'd vote for the house next to Ms. Walker's with an inflatable Snoopy in a Santa hat sitting in the middle of their yard.

Ms. Walker lived about three blocks from church, an easy walk from school. Ma drove me on the first day, just so I could become familiar with the route. She lived in a town house with thousands of pictures of her family hanging up on every square inch of wall space, next to portraits of Malcolm X and Martin Luther King. Her kitchen was filled with well-used pots and pans, and her living room was a spotless shrine for her cream sofas. The sharp edges of the plastic covers on her dining room table chairs ripped holes in my stocking every Monday, Wednesday, and Friday after school. I mean, she wasn't a bad lady or nothing. She always offered me orange juice and biscuit cookies before we started. It's just every time I stepped foot in her house, it reminded me of why I had to be there in the first place.

On the first day, Ms. Walker gave me a pack of these plastic gel filters, the size of loose-leaf paper, tinted in various colors: aqua, coral, celery, and apricot. They're supposed to help me read better when I lay them over pages in books and stuff. I held them close over my face and watched the whole room turn blue, like we were sitting at the bottom of the river.

We practiced reading and writing using work sheets and games. Some were easy, some were hard. Hard enough for me to shove the books clear across the table. But knowing what awaited me at home if I acted up, I tried my best.

Ma also asked Ms. Walker to help me with my essay for Banneker. Once again, the prompt haunted me. That's why I had to practically drag myself up to Ms. Walker's. But that day, when I opened the gate, I found the strangest surprise waiting on her stoop.

"What are you doing here?"

Michael frowned, looking around like he couldn't figure out who I was talking to. He stood up, carrying a large shopping bag, and met me midway, shoving a free hand in his pocket.

"I should ask you the same thing."

I'd never seen him in regular clothes before. Heck, I had trouble believing he even owned a pair of sneakers. But there he was, in jeans, a copper sweatshirt, and a baseball hat.

"My tutor lives here," I admitted, trying to hide the annoyance in my voice. I didn't want him—of all people—knowing, but I couldn't figure out a lie quick enough.

"Oh, you mean my grandma? She said she had a new student from church. I didn't know it was you!"

"Ms. Walker's your grandma?" I asked, skeptical. "I thought Ms. Evans was your grandma."

"I don't know about you, but I got two parents and they weren't hatched out of pods. Grandma, or Ms. Walker, is my dad's mom. She kept her maiden name."

Strangling my book bag straps, I huffed. "Well . . . how was I supposed to know? Ain't like I got your family tree hanging up on my wall that I stay studying every day."

His eyes narrowed. "Then what *are* you studying?"

An alarm went off—loud and shrieking. What if his grandma told him how I read stuff backward? Can't have the cute boy from high school thinking I'm stupid.

"Whatever," I spat, heading back to the gate.

"Claudia, wait," he said, chasing after me. "Where you going? I thought you had tutoring?"

"I . . . I got the days mixed up," I lied, walking faster.

He jogged next to me. "Can you slow down?"

"Nope."

"Just hold up a second!" He jumped in front of me. His arms extended as if to stop me, and my boobs ran right into his open hands.

"Ah!" I shrieked, clutching my coat.

"Oh shit! I'm sorry!" he hollered. "I'm so sorry! I . . . I didn't mean that . . . just please don't tell Grandma."

A laugh escaped me. "Alright! I get it! You're sorry."

Michael smiled. "Well, now that that's out the way . . . if you don't have tutoring, what you doing for the rest of the day?"

"Um . . . nothing."

"Well, you want to chill? I have to take something back to the mall for my grandma."

"The mall?" I glanced at Snoopy's red hat. "Um . . . I don't know."

"It'll be quick. Promise."

"Uh. I guess. Sure."

Pentagon City Mall is in Crystal City, Virginia, surrounded by a whole heap of hotels and big high-rise condos. Monday and I would beg Ma to take us to the mall on Saturdays. We didn't have money like that, but nothing beats trying on outfits in Forever 21, sampling lotions in Bath & Body Works, and eating fries in the food court. The thrill of walking around for two hours unsupervised—like real adults.

I didn't know how I was going to explain it to Ma: skipping tutoring, taking the Metro, running off to the mall with some boy. But I didn't care. I needed an escape, if only for a few hours. Plus, it's *Michael*—from church. Everyone's favorite Goody Two-shoes, Mr. Reliable. No one would worry about him.

The speakers hummed Christmas carols in every store decked out with garland and lights. Inside Macy's, we navigated through the crowded department store, returning two pairs of shoes for Ms. Walker.

"Sorry about the trouble, ma'am," Michael said to the cashier. "My grandma said these heels are too high for her."

From managers to customers, Michael befriended everyone in sight. I stood back and watched him work the room; it was like he was campaigning for teen mayor. He reminded me of Monday. They could both sweet-talk just about anybody. Except I didn't like Monday being all friendly to everyone—I wanted her to myself.

"No trouble, young man," the gray-haired lady said as she opened the drawer to collect his refund. "So nice of you to come all this way for her."

"It's the least I could do."

"That's so sweet. Okay, here's your change and your receipt."

"Thank you very much, ma'am. You have a blessed day."

The cashier beamed. "You do the same! Such a sweetheart."

"All set," he said to me, dusting his hands free of the shopping bag.

"You always like this?"

"Like what?"

"Like . . . extra friendly?"

He frowned, crossing his arms. "What do you mean?"

At that moment, two girls with long braids sauntered by, giggling. "Hey, Michael," they sang in unison.

"Oh, what's up, Kim? Jazzy Jaz from Georgia Ave!" he cheered, greeting them with a smile and a wave. The girls looked me over before whispering to each other as they walked off.

"You know, you'd be good on the mic," I laughed.

"Like a rapper?"

"Nah, like in a go-go band! I can see you shouting out folks."

"Ha! I keep forgetting you still listen to that old stuff," he said as we walk into the main mall. "You ever been to a show?"

"Naw. Ma won't let me. She's scared, says there's too many fights and shootings happening at them. They ain't like that anymore. But as soon as I'm eighteen, I'mma be in the front row with my name on my shirt so they can't mess it up!"

Michael bopped his shoulders, cuffing his hands around his mouth, making his voice deep and loud.

"Hey, I see you over there, Claudia, repping Southeast! South Southeast!"

"Are you crazy?" I cackled. "You gonna tell the whole world my—"

"Yoooo, big man! What up?"

A tall, lanky, light-skinned kid with a low cut called from behind us. Walking next to him was Megan from dance class. We caught eyes, and a small look of panic grew across her face that she quickly wiped away. A lump knotted in the back of my throat.

"Ohhh what up, Kam?" Michael said, dapping him up.

"Thought I heard your big-ass mouth from the parking lot," Kam said, wrapping an arm around Megan to snuggle her closer. She painted on a strained smile.

"Man, you can probably hear a tree fall in the rain forest with them big-ass ears of yours," Michael shot back.

Megan avoided eye contact. She seemed so much older outside of her dance gear. Touches of makeup, long hair pressed straight, a tight black sweater and jeans with high boots. Maybe she didn't want anyone knowing she knew me. I played it cool, like her, but I couldn't help wondering: was she embarrassed of me?

"Yeah, yeah, youngin'. You talk this much smack on the field?"

"Ha, when they let me," Michael said, turning to Megan. "What's up, Megan?"

"Hi, Michael," she said as if laughing at some inside joke.

"So! Y'all doing some Christmas shopping?"

"Yeah. Plus, she wanted to get out the house," Kam said, gazing down at Megan with tender eyes. I wondered how it felt to have a boy look at me that way. "Aye, yo, you think you can help me with that thing I was telling you about?"

"The TV hookup? Yeah, sure," Michael said, all businesslike. "But you still got to get them cables I was telling you about. And the mount."

Kam nodded. "Bet. That's up in Best Buy, right?"

"Yeah, they probably got the cheapest. All you got to do is . . ."

Something about Kam's light eyes and his crooked grin felt familiar. I tried to think back to where I might know him. Maybe church or school or maybe he lived around the hood, but I couldn't place him anywhere. If Monday were with us, she would have known. She was good at names, dates, places, and directions.

My eyes flicked over to Megan, her hard eyes locked on mine. Staring at *me* staring at *her* man. Her cold arching eyebrow chilled me to the bone. I shifted, bumping right into Michael.

"Oh my bad, y'all! This Claudia. She goes to my church."

Kam and Megan nodded and I managed a stiff smile. That's it? I thought. I'm just some girl from church. Why did he have to make it like I'm some kid he had to babysit?

"Wait, Claudia?" Kam questioned, his brows furrowing. "Oh right, Monday's homegirl."

An electrical shock sizzled up my arms, bouncing behind my eyes. He knew Monday! He must be from Ed Borough. He must've saw us together, that must be where I remembered him from!

Megan cleared her throat. "Babe! I want some ice cream."

"Oh, yeah, babe," Kam said, and turned to Michael. "My bad, I didn't mean to hold you up, cuz."

"All good! Not like I'm *that* busy."

I swallowed back the ugly thoughts I had roasting in my brain—fiery hot and ready to burn him. Megan cleared her throat again and tugged at Kam's hand.

"See you Monday, Michael," she said.

"Alright, later, y'all."

"I'mma text you tomorrow, big man," Kam yelled.

"Anytime. Cool!"

Kam and Megan walked off, with Kam sneaking a second look. I wanted to follow him, to ask if he'd seen Monday and where. Once you absorbed a fraction of her energy, she was impossible to forget. But I didn't want Megan to assume I was chasing after her man.

Michael grinned, oblivious. "Alright, you ready?"

We headed to the Apple store then two other stores, and his superstar status followed us everywhere, like the whole mall knew him.

"What's wrong?" he asked on the escalator heading down to the first floor.

"Nothing," I said, my voice clipped.

Maybe it was my silence, or maybe he felt the ruby-red anger sizzling off my skin, but his upbeat mood dwindled with each step.

"Uh . . . you hungry?" he asked near the food court.

"No," I snapped.

"You tired?"

"No."

"Um, you have to call your mom or someone?" he asked as we reached the end of the west side of the mall. He dug into his pocket, offering his phone. Even Michael, the Goody-Two shoes from church, had a phone and I didn't.

"No," I hissed, really wishing I could call Monday. The mall didn't feel the same without her.

He sighed. "Well, is there anything you want to do?"

"I want to go here." I stopped short in front of a Starbucks.

"Here? Ain't you too young to be drinking coffee?"

Ready to slap the grin off him I shouted, "I ain't a baby! And I don't want coffee anyways. It's bad for you."

"Okay, soooo, what you gonna get that's any better?"

I blinked hard before mumbling. "Um . . . hot chocolate."

He smiled. "Sounds good," he said, and held the door open like a true gentleman.

"Gooooood afternoon, ma'am," Michael said to the cashier as we approached. "Can I have two hot chocolates with whipped cream, please?"

"Name for your order?"

"Uh, hello? Don't you recognize me?"

The cashier glanced up from her register, her eyebrow arched.

Michael pointed to himself. "Chris Brown. The one and only."

The cashier and I shared a look and shook our heads.

"What? Don't I look like him?" he said with a wink.

I couldn't help snickering. "Such a clown."

"They make hot chocolate look so complicated, right?" he said as we waited by the counter. "All these machines and gadgets."

"I thought you liked machines, computers, and audio stuff."

"Yeah, but that's stuff people need! I make hot chocolate with plain hot water, powder, God's good grace, and mine turns out just fine."

The barista handed our cups to Michael and smirked. Michael took two packs of brown sugar and ripped them open, dumping them into his cup.

"What you doing?" I yelped, trying to stop him.

"Dang, what?"

"You crazy? It's already chocolaty!"

"So? I like mine extra sweet."

153

"That's too much sugar! Your teeth are gonna fall out your head into the sink."

He laughed, taking a quick sip. "Okay, Grandma."

No one called me that except Monday.

We sat on the bench outside the Starbucks, watching shoppers walk by with their massive bags, couples holding hands, and children running amok. People watching used to be Monday's and my favorite pastime. We'd spend hours cackling over folks' outfits, eavesdropping on conversations, and swooning over PDA. Sitting there with Michael only reminded me that I hadn't done much of anything without her.

Couldn't believe she'd just ditch me like this. She knew I needed her, knew if she wasn't around teachers would find out about me. She was carrying me worse than Jacob ever carried her. How could she do this to me? Why hasn't she called?

And why do I feel so alone?

Michael interrupted my thoughts. "So, like, what kind of stuff is my grandma making you do?"

I shook Monday out of my head. "She's . . . helping me, with stuff to get ready for high school."

"Oh. Do you . . . know what school you want to go to yet?"

"Banneker."

His face screwed up. "You want to go there? Everybodyyyyy and they momma want to go there. Isn't it, like, a real hard school to get into?"

"I guess, but that's why your grandma is helping me with my essay."

"What's the essay about?"

"Why I want to attend Banneker."

"Good question. Why do you?"

I swallowed back the real answer: because Monday wants to go.

"It's . . . a good school and it'll help me g-get into a . . . um, a good college."

"That's it? But any school can help you get into college. Well, that's what my dad says."

"Yeah, I guess."

"Okay, I ain't gonna front. I wanted to go there too," he said. "I mean, who wouldn't? But they didn't have football, and I really wanted to play. I was in training all summer with my dad before he left."

"Where'd he go?"

"Dubai. You know where that is? It's in the Middle East."

"I thought Pastor said he retired from the air force."

"He did. But he works out there now, fixing planes and stuff. They paying him crazy money. He said he's going to buy me a new car, so we've been looking online together."

"A car already? You too young. You don't even know how to drive yet."

Michael choked on a sip of hot chocolate. "I'm . . . working on it."

"Oh. When is he coming back home?"

He sighed. "Three years."

"Three years? Dang, that's a long time."

"Yeah, but the money is real good." Michael tensed, rubbing his knees. "And when he gets back, he's going to open some franchise business, and I won't have to pay a dime to go to college."

"Don't you miss him?"

He shrugged. "I mean, yeah, but I FaceTime and text him all day. He's seen me play at all my games because Mom Skypes him in. He'll be here in June for a three-week vacation, and we're going to drive across the country. My mom and him always wanted to do that." He slurped up the last of his hot chocolate. "Anyway, come on, we got to go. I told Grandma I'd have you back by the time your mom came to get you."

Fuming, I stood to face him. "I knew it! Ma put you up to this!"

"Nope," he laughed. "My grandma did. She said she had a student that just seemed really . . . sad and needed a friend. I swear I didn't know it was you. But . . . I'm kinda glad now. I'm glad it was you."

With all the weight that had dropped off his face, dimples bookended a sexy crooked smile. Sexy? I just called his smile sexy! I gulped, spinning away from him—my face flushing.

"Oh. And . . . uh . . . well, what else did she tell you?"

Is Ms. Walker going around telling everyone how I can't read?

He shrugged, taking my empty cup to the trash. "Just said you seem real sad. Like, depressed. She's had a lot of students before, but none like you."

"I'm not depressed," I corrected. "And I don't need anyone feeling sorry for me."

"Maybe you do."

The hairs on my neck stood up, and I let out a fake laugh. "Well, I guess if anyone's gonna cheer me up, it's gonna be Mr. Popular."

He laughed and pointed in the direction of the Metro. "Hey! Ain't my fault people love me. But seriously, Claudia, you can talk to me. If you got no one to . . . you know . . . talk to, I'm here. If you want . . . here." He pulled a pen and a crinkled-up Starbucks napkin out from his pockets. "This is my cell phone. You can call me whenever."

He grabbed my hand and placed the napkin in my palm, smoothing my fingers closed over it with a smirk that made my knees weak. I bit my lip, clutching my fist tightly before walking away. I did feel comfortable around Michael, but he also felt like a sharp needle that could pop my newly airtight bubble and hurt me.

Just like it hurt Monday.

THE BEFORE

Any time you saw students from the West Wing head to the East Wing, you knew where they were going—the Learning Center, known also as TLC. Walking in its direction was like stepping onstage with dozens of blinding spotlights. So you had to be smart about your route. If I went down the stairs, sped through different hallways and back up the stairs near the back entrance, I could throw people off my scent.

There were four teachers, and an ESL coach helped the non-English-speaking students in TLC. During study hall and after school, they reviewed homework, broke down our assignments in small chunks, and organized our class notes. Twice a week, one of the teachers would show up to each of my classes to observe. Luckily, with so many kids, you could never tell which student they were there for, and they might as well been ghosts the way I pretended not to see them at all.

This is a big mistake, I thought, trying to keep my bitter resentfulness to myself, but it bled out my pores, oozing onto my homework. They did everything they were supposed to do to help me. But when help isn't invited, it ain't nothing but an unwanted houseguest.

If she comes back . . .

If she did, we could work on our essay together. Fix up my papers, come up with new moves for my solo. I wouldn't need TLC. Together, we could fix it all back to the way it was. I have to find Monday.

The words skipped like a song in my head as I headed to my next class.

Find Monday. Find Monday. Find Monday. Find—dang, I'm late for class!

With my new route, it took twice as long to make my way. Running through the hall, I took the stairs by the parking lot two at a time and slammed right into Ms. Valente. She screamed, her papers flying up in the air and swinging down to the floor like snowflakes.

"Shit! Claudia? What're you doing back here?"

"Oh, uh, s-sorry," I stuttered, dropping to the floor to help gather her files.

"Keep your sorry. I said, what you doing back here?"

"I'm . . . going to . . . social studies."

She frowned, cocking her head to the side to study me.

"There's no eighth-grade social studies this way. So where are you *really* headed to?"

I thought about all the stories, about kids making out in the hallways between classes. Ms. Valente must have heard about those stories too.

"Not going to! I'm coming from . . . TLC," I admitted.

Her mouth formed a little O and she nodded.

"Ah, yes," she sighed. "I heard about that. They sent a memo last week."

My head popped up. "They sent a memo around about me?"

"Yes. They send memos to all the team leads—"

"What? But what if someone sees that memo on a desk or something? Then everybody's gonna know! They gonna think I'm stupid!"

She threw her hands up. "Whoa, calm down! It was an email. They send one monthly to the faculty on students who need additional services."

My eyes blurred as my heart raced.

"But what if they do? What if someone . . . and they . . ."

My knees gave in and I crashed down on the step, whimpering. My lungs burned as I tried wheezing up air. Ms. Valente sat next to me, pushing my head between my legs and rubbing my back.

"Breathe, Claudia. Big, deep breaths. Come on—there you go. Just breathe. It's okay."

But it wasn't okay. The air outside my bubble felt stiff, heavy, contaminated. How could anyone breathe in this? How was Monday breathing without me? After a few minutes of heaving at the floor, my tears spilled over, my cries echoing through the empty stairwell.

"Do you want to talk about it?" she asked. "It may help."

I dried my eyes with my sweater and I shook my head with a sniff, sighing at the floor.

"Claudia, you *have* to talk to someone. You can't keep stuff all bottled in. How about we start small, hm? Why are you walking this way to class?"

"'Cause I don't want people knowing." I looked up at her, feeling the tears boiling up. "Ms. Valente, I don't want to be in the stupid kids' class."

Ms. Valente pursed her lips.

"First of all, there are no stupid kids in TLC. That's just some silly rumor started by other kids who ain't brave enough to ask for help when they need it. Second, there are brilliant kids who go to TLC, because they want to be the best!"

"But . . . I'm fine. I don't need help."

Ms. Valente patted my knee with a heavy sigh. "Claudia, I feel like I failed you."

"You? Why?"

"Because . . . I thought you might have had a problem last year. That's why I was so determined to work with you. But I was so caught up with exams, grading, grad school, *and* planning a wedding." She shook her head. "The signs were there, I just didn't act on them the way I should have."

I scooted away from her. "So you think I'm dumb too, then."

"I didn't say—"

"First, they think I'm a lesbian. Now everybody gonna say I'm stupid too!"

"Hey! There's nothing wrong with being a lesbian—"

"Great, now you think I'm one too!"

Ms. Valente grabbed my shoulders hard. "I didn't say that! Stop putting words in my mouth. You're letting these rumors run you, rather than you running them. Now, I know you're not, and even if you were, that is perfectly alright. But don't let a bunch homophobic knuckleheaded—what's the word y'all use again? Oh right—bammas make you feel like it's wrong! I have a beautiful wife and a wonderful family, so who gives a fuck what they think?"

I huffed, holding back tears. I never heard a teacher curse before.

"Sorry," she chuckled. "Got a little carried away. But, Claudia, I think you're very bright. You just . . . absorb things differently than other students. But so do a lot of other people, and there ain't nothing wrong with that. I only wish I had said something sooner. Maybe I could have saved you some of the pain you're going through now.

"I tried to bring it up before, but folks just told me to

keep you moving. Everything about this school is driven by our ranking. No one has time to just take a moment and really *be* with our students. You're old enough to know this now, but sometimes, all you are to this school is a score that adds up with the overall score. And the higher the score, the better the reputation. You know what I mean?"

I nodded. "But there ain't nothing wrong with me! This just been a big mistake. I've just . . . there's been a lot on my mind, and Monday ain't around—"

Her eyes widened. "Wait, you mean, you still haven't heard from her? You haven't seen her at all?"

"Naw."

"I . . . I thought they told you? Or someone would've told you."

My stomach tensed. "Tell me what?"

"They talked to her mother. Her mother withdrew her from school for homeschooling."

My mouth dropped. "Homeschooling?"

She nodded. "I spoke to the social worker a week or so ago. I'll admit, I've only met her mother twice, found it kind of hard to believe . . . but it's not my place to tell a woman how to raise her child."

"But . . . she ain't even home! How can she be home-schooled if she's not even HOME!"

Ms. Valente bit her bottom lip. "She *is* home, Claudia."

"What?"

"The social worker said she's at home."

"No! She's not home. She's lying! If she was home, she would have called me!"

Wouldn't she?

"Yes, young lady. How can I help you?" an officer sitting behind a high desk asked as I entered the police station, not more than ten minutes from Monday's house. I picked it on purpose. They're used to going over to Ed Borough.

Find Monday. Find Monday. Find Monday.

Ma and Daddy won't listen, Mr. Hill ain't no help, and something ain't right about that social worker's story. No way Monday would be home and not call me. I can't go over there again without getting in trouble, but the police sure can.

I cleared my throat, giving him my best adult voice.

"Yes, hello. I'm here about a friend who lives in Ed Borough. I think she's in trouble. Can somebody go by her house?"

"Trouble?"

"She hasn't been to school and no one's seen her."

The officer frowned. "So . . . she's missing?"

The word *MISSING* popped like a hard hand on a conga drum.

"No, naw," I coughed. "She's not *missing* like that. She's . . . um . . . I just don't know where she is."

"What do you mean 'like that'?"

A tall, balding man dressed in gray slacks and a white business shirt approached, stepping between us, smiling at me.

"Relax, Warren, I got this," he said, balancing a stack of folders under his arm. "Step this way, young lady, let's have a chat. I'm Detective Carson. What's your name?"

"Claudia," I said, following him to his desk.

"Okay, Claudia, I overheard you mentioning your friend is missing. Want to tell me what's going on?"

I told the detective everything. About Monday not showing up for school and how her mom and sister were acting all weird. The detective nodded through my story, leaning back in his chair, hands folded on his belly. Shouldn't he be taking notes or something?

"Have you talked to your parents about this?"

"Sort of."

"Okay," he chuckled. "Tell me, how do you know for sure she's not home? Have you been *inside* her house?"

"Naw. But she ain't there, I just know it. And her mom keeps saying she ain't home."

"Maybe she's living with another relative. Maybe her father."

I shook my head. "Naw. She would have told me."

He smiled. "Well, sometimes, family business is family business."

"It ain't like that," I said. "Not with us."

"Hm, okay. Let's say she really is missing. Do you know if her mother filed a missing persons report?"

There's that word again. *Missing.* Why does it sound like a squealing brake before a car crash?

"Um. Naw. She's not that type of mom."

He frowned. "Trouble at home?"

"Just . . . regular stuff."

"Okay, is it at all possible she ran away from home?"

"What? Naw, she wouldn't leave me . . . like that."

He shrugged. "Sometimes girls run away from their problems rather than ask for help."

I wanted to scream "no," but then I thought about the bruises and my tongue latched itself to the roof of my mouth.

Carson sighed, rubbing his bald head. "Claudia, I want to show you something. Follow me."

We walked toward the front of station to a large bulletin board hanging by the door, filled with missing persons flyers, detailing names, dates, ages, and locations, along with photos. Staring at the wall of bright, smiling faces, I couldn't escape one glaring fact: there was nothing but girls on the wall. And they all looked like Monday.

"Is your friend on this board?"

I held my breath, scanning the wall again.

"No. But she's not *missing*, like these girls. Or . . . I don't think—"

"I want you to take a good look at this board," Carson said, his voice hardening. "Over the last few months we've

166

had dozens of girls around here reported missing, close to fifty in one week. Alleged kidnappings when most of them just run off away from home 'cause they can't do what they want."

"But shouldn't you still be looking for them anyways?"

He opened his mouth, then closed it, clearing his throat.

"Yes, but, Claudia, I want you to remember, when you come into a police station, claiming your friend is 'missing,' it means us officers have to take our focus away from *these* girls. Girls who could really be in trouble."

Tears prickled, and I avoided his glare.

"Now, if your friend's really missing and she's not on this board, then only a parent can file a missing persons report. And if her mother won't, the only person left would be her father or a legal guardian."

I sucked in a breath to keep from crying. Everyone was looking for these girls, while I was the only one looking for Monday.

"I swear, every year your father buys the biggest tree and expect *us* to manage it alone."

Ma stood on the stepladder next to our Christmas tree, her arms stretched, attempting to hook an elf near the top.

"Either this tree is bigger than last year's or I'm shrinking."

I sat on the floor, surrounded by strands of half-working Christmas lights and boxes of decorations, adding new hooks to the ornaments, replacing the ones that had rusted over the years. Ma's favorite soulful Christmas albums grooved out the speakers: Nat King Cole, Jackson 5, Temptations, and Vanessa Williams.

"You're not that tall to begin with," I laughed, detangling a ball of ribbons.

"That's no way to speak to your mother," she said, smirking. "Okay, hand me another one."

I jumped up with two wooden nutcrackers, the tree already filled with snowmen, ballerinas, black Santas, and glass candy canes. Ma loved Christmas, so the tree had to be perfect or Christmas would be canceled. Monday used to help us decorate, untangling lights and scattering tinsel. Just the thought of her made my heart ache.

Missing.

I held my breath until it burned in my chest, the word frightening. Is she missing? Missing from my life, yeah, but is she, like, missing for real? She couldn't be, she has to be home. Right?

"Ma?"

"Yes, Sweet Pea."

"I want to do homeschool."

Ma's neck snapped, the nutcracker held out in midair as she froze.

"Girl, what are you talking about?"

I gulped, twisting the ribbon around my hands. "I mean, can I do homeschool?"

"Homeschool? Are you crazy? I can't stay home with you. I have to go to work!"

She hung the ornament hard, the branch popping back up, almost knocking the other ones off.

"But Monday is doing homeschool."

Ma placed her hands on her hips. "If Monday jumped off a bridge would you want to do that too? Absolutely not, Claudia. I can't believe you'd ask for such a foolish thing."

I slumped back down to the floor by one of the boxes and peered inside. My stomach curled up with dread. There were only four ornaments left. The most beautiful ones with the ugliest history.

"And, well, you can't get no proper education with homeschooling. Not with you needing . . . extra help and all." She sighed, her voice softening. "Sweet Pea, you just need to stay in school. It's what's best right now."

I nodded, sliding the lid on top of the box, hoping she wouldn't notice. Hoping she wouldn't ask for any more ornaments. Maybe this is the year I'll break them. Shatter them so we don't have to look at them anymore and remember. But Ma would never forgive me.

"Hey! You know"—Ma beamed, trying to soften the mood—"you haven't said a word about what you want for Christmas this year. I was expecting your two-page list by now."

I shrugged, my face falling limp. I didn't want anything.

I just wanted my best friend back.

Ma stepped back to admire her work. The tree belonged in a catalog.

"Beautiful! Just . . . one little spot, right there. Alright, pass me the next one."

I swallowed, bracing myself. "There's only four left," I mumbled.

"That's okay. Just hand me one of the—" Her whole body jerked as it hit her, eyes widening.

"Four," she gasped out the word. "Well . . . okay, then. Hand one to me."

I sighed and opened the box, taking out the four crystal angels specially made for the four angels we lost.

Ma took an uneasy step toward me, peering into the box like it was an open grave. Holding her breath, I carefully unwrapped the tissue protecting the first angel. She held it in her hands. She studied their delicate features before her fingers began to tremble.

"I can hang them," I offered, springing up.

"No, it's okay. I've got it," she murmured, drifting back to the tree the way God hangs stars in the sky, gently placing each one on the branch. She stepped back to admire her work.

"There. Perfect."

"Yes, perfect," I breathed.

She took a deep breath and forced a smile. "Well, I don't

know about you, but I'm beat. Think I'm going to . . . head on to bed. You mind cleaning up down here?"

I nodded. "Sure, Ma. Of course."

Lights sparkled off the tears in her eyes.

"Okay. Good night, Sweet Pea."

She slogged toward the stairs.

I left the mess for Daddy to clean since he seemed to conveniently always have a gig the night we settled on decorating.

TWO YEARS BEFORE THE BEFORE

"What's wrong with your mom?" Monday whispered as we tiptoed up the stairs with slices of pizza and cups of sweet tea.

Ma was spread out on the sofa, tucked under a red throw. Her eyes soft and unfocused, she stared at the muted television without even blinking.

We scurried to my room, where my bags sat packed by the door for our first Christmas vacation in Georgia.

"She lost the baby," I mumbled.

"Dang, again?" Monday covered her mouth with a gasp. "Shit, I'm sorry! I didn't mean it like that."

I knew she didn't mean it, but the words picked a nerve and tears bubbled up. Ma had four babies up in heaven waiting for her. On earth, all Ma had was me, and some days I wondered if I was enough to quench her longing. Maybe I wasn't good enough. Maybe they wanted a better version of me—a version that could read and write with no problems. Maybe that's why they kept trying and failing. I hated seeing Ma in pain as much as I hated not being enough for her.

"It's okay, don't cry," Monday said, rubbing my back. "You don't want a bunch of other kids around. Then you got to share everything with them."

"I would share." I sniffled. "I share things with you."

Monday's face twitched and darkened. "It's . . . different. Trust me. You're better off without them."

Monday climbed out of the tent, pretending her last words didn't make the room turn colder.

"Anyways, I got something to cheer you up!"

"Really? What?"

"A Christmas present!"

"Are you for real?"

"Yeah," she laughed. "I didn't get a chance to wrap it, but since you leaving for Georgia tomorrow, I figured I'd give it to you now!"

She skipped over to her book bag and pulled out two matching journals, one pink and one purple, with a lock and a heart-shaped key. She handed me the purple one, a dizzy grin on her face. Monday had never been able to buy me anything before and I wanted to be grateful—instead I fought the urge not to throw it across the room.

"Why'd you do this?" I snapped. "You know I'm not good at writing!"

Monday's grin dropped. "Yeah . . . but maybe if you practice every day, you can get better. And we're both gonna do it! I'm going to write in one too, see?" She waved the pink journal like a tambourine. "Starting New Year's."

She didn't see the thorns sticking out of her sweet actions. Not like I did.

"Yeah, okay. Sure. Next year," I said, throwing the journal on my desk like a piece of hot garbage.

Her face fell as she stepped out of my way. Our bubble felt smaller, and not in a good way.

I woke up in the morning with an empty space next to me. Monday had left. As expected from the silent treatment I gave her the rest of the night. I flopped, tossed, and turned. I didn't want to fight. I wasn't mad at her. I was mad at myself. Now I wouldn't see her for a whole seven days. I wouldn't have a chance to apologize.

A fit of giggles floated upstairs.

I tiptoed to peer over the stair banister at Monday and Ma, hugged up under the red throw. *Rudolph the Red-Nosed Reindeer* on the TV, a smile on Ma's face, and a bowl of cereal in Monday's lap. Ma kissed Monday's temple, pushing her braids behind her ears. She glanced up at me and smiled.

"Morning, Sweet Pea. Come watch the movie."

Monday tensed, peering over as I thumped down the

stairs. I sat on the other side of Ma, snuggling under her armpit. Ma grinned and kissed the side of my temple like she did Monday's.

"It's nice to spend the morning with my two girls."

Monday beamed at her and focused back on the movie, passing her half-eaten bowl of cereal in my direction with a smirk. An offer. An apology.

I grinned and accepted. "Thanks."

JANUARY

Maybe I'm not the best person to talk about the bruises.

See, I'd seen a couple on Monday, here and there. But I never gave them much thought. They were always followed by the most practical excuses. I mean, kids bruise. We roughhouse, we jump, we run, we fall, and then we bruise. Sometimes we even scar. So if I did see a bruise or a cut, it meant nothing. Just another star in the sky.

I read a report that said there were over two dozen scars on Monday's body when they found her.

ONE YEAR BEFORE THE BEFORE

Monday stumbled into homeroom, her legs shaking with every measured step.

"Morning, Monday," Ms. Valente said from her desk, checking off her attendance sheet. "How was your break?"

Monday swiped a white tongue across her chapped, trembling lips, books squished into her chest. Ms. Valente looked up, her face softening.

"Monday? Everything okay?"

"I'm fine," she mumbled, barely audible, before shuffling to a seat next to me. Ms. Valente stared at her for a long while, studying her the way you would take in a stranger. Monday clutched her desk as if she thought it would be ripped from under her. Her braids were fuzzier than I'd ever seen them, the ends unraveling and dry.

Maybe she forgot to oil her scalp before bed.

I whispered, "Big news?" *You okay?*

Her bloodshot eyes flickered over, not responding.

Ms. Valente stared at her with a wary eye. She opened her mouth just as the bell rang, then shut it.

Monday carried on like a zombie, shuffling through the halls, blindly bumping into people, sitting motionless in classes, not even bothering to lift a pencil.

"What's wrong?" I pleaded during lunch. "What happened? Did Jacob do something again?"

Nothing. No signs of life. Tired of talking to myself, we sat in silence. Her eyes roamed around the palms of her hands, tracing the lines with her pinkie, her lunch untouched. Where is this coming from? I wondered. She seemed fine when Grandmamma let me call her on Christmas. Was she mad at me?

By the end of the day, I bolted for the library. She must be sick, I told myself over and over, soothing my anxious nerves. She'll go home, sleep it off, and will be better tomorrow. I wasn't halfway when I noticed a shadow following me on Good Hope Road and stopped short.

"What are you doing?"

Monday blinked up at me. The most response I'd seen her have all day. "Library?"

"But . . . where's August? You just gonna leave him?"

She froze as if I'd said something terrifying and stuttered through an answer.

"He's . . . sick. Mom . . . kept him home."

That would be her answer for weeks. Every time I asked about him, he had some mysterious illness that kept him bedridden.

By the end of the month, Monday morphed back into herself but still dodged any questions about him.

"What's up with August?" I asked on the way to the library, walking over piles of black snow, the icy breeze breaking through my gloves.

"He's sick," she said, stuffing her hands in her pockets.

"Dang, still? Y'all been to the doctor yet?"

"Yeah," she said, sniffing her running nose.

"And? What they say?"

Monday sucked her teeth. "Why you keep asking about August? He ain't none of your business!"

The words came out so nasty that they even smelled nasty.

"Dang, you don't got to talk to me like that! I just ask-ing—"

"And you keep on asking! I told you he was sick! Why don't you get that? It ain't like I have to read it for you."

I froze in the middle of the block.

"What the hell is wrong with you?" I cried. "It was just a question!"

She whipped around to face me. "And I already told you! So why you keep asking about him?"

"I guess 'cause . . . he's your brother and I—"

"That's right. He's *my* brother! He ain't yours. Just because you can't have one of your own don't mean you gotta be sweating mine!"

The negative-two-degree air ripped holes through my lungs as I gasped.

Monday winced almost immediately. "Shit, Claudia, I didn't mean that. I'm sorry."

"Whatever," I snapped, brushing by her.

"Fine, whatever. Do your own homework, then!" she screamed, storming off in the opposite direction.

"Fine, I will!"

Our first fight, and I had no idea what I'd done wrong.

THE BEFORE

On Martin Luther King Day, the church hosts its annual soup kitchen. Feeding close to three hundred people, it's our busiest day of the year next to Christmas and Easter.

Daddy and the men's ministry set up large tables and chairs in the community room while the teens decorated and handled cleanup. The media ministry manned the DJ equipment, playing gospel hits in between the choir's short performances.

Of course, Ma was in charge of the kitchen and I had no choice but to be one of her sous chefs. Like a big factory with everyone dressed in plastic aprons and gloves, we took our places in the assembly line, seasoning chicken, chopping vegetables, baking rolls, and napkin-wrapping utensils.

In the past, Monday would come help. She loved cooking next to Ma and had a knack for keeping the kiddies occupied.

"Ms. Pearl, how's my greens looking?" Ma shouted over the busy assembly line, pulling out a pan of chicken. Her hair frizzed from the heat of the hot stoves. We'd been at it since dawn, the dining room not scheduled to open for another hour.

"Almost done."

"Ms. Janet," someone yelled. "The rice is done."

"Great, we just about ready," Ma said, pouring gravy over the chicken. "Sweet Pea, watch how thick you cutting them carrots. We don't want them too big and run out."

We had enough carrots to feed the entire city—I should know since I cut them all.

"Yes, Ma," I mumbled, wiping the sweat off my brow with my sleeve.

"And smile! These folks got a lot more to mope about than you."

The guilt card always wins. I grinned wide enough to show all my teeth.

"Ooo, child, don't scare them!" Ma shook her head with a smile, wrapping a free arm around my shoulders. "Come here, let me show you something right quick."

Ma led me over to the window, looking out into the parking lot. A line had formed, starting from the door out the gate and down the street. Folks stood out in the freez-ing cold, in jackets as thick as plastic bags with clothes that could stand for a few washes. Others were draped in thick gray blankets. Daddy, along with some of the other church members, passed out steaming cups of hot coffee.

"See that? That could be me and you out there. Some of those families, they not homeless but haven't had a proper meal in who knows how long. Think of all the good you're doing these folks."

Recognizing some kids from Ed Borough mixed in with the adults, my heart sank, picturing Monday stand-ing out there with them.

"So remember, Sweet Pea, just 'cause someone got a roof, don't make it a home. We don't have everything, but we have a lot to be grateful for. You understand?"

Ma squeezed my shoulder, and I squeezed back and nodded.

"Alright, Ms. Allen, let's wrap up those buns. Keep them nice and warm. Doors are about to open, people!"

With the buffet tables set, the Sternos lit, and the food laid out, Ma gave Daddy the signal. The doors opened, and a stampede rushed into the community room, directly to the buffet. Ma spooned out slices of chicken and ham at the start of the line while I passed out rolls at the end. Folks were so . . . thankful and happy. Ma talked to just about everybody, striking up a warm conversation and sending blessings. She's never treated anyone different because of where they came from or what they had.

Throughout the day, the kitchen crew hustled to replace the empty pans. When I finished with the bread, I walked around, refilling cups of iced tea and coffee. The little kids ran in circles, reminding me of the way August and Tuesday used to play. Thinking of August, I ran upstairs to the nursery, grabbed a handful of broken crayons and a stack of paper from the bin. Clearing off a table, I dropped the supplies and watched as the kids' faces lit up. I drew silly shapes in pen and showed them how to color in the lines. It felt good to make kids laugh again. I know Monday hated how I checked up on August all the time, but if Monday was like a sister, then August was like a brother. I missed them both. I missed that part of my family.

Dad stopped by our coloring station, grinning. "Hey, Sweet Pea, your mom is looking for you."

"Okay. Can you stay with them? Make sure they keep the crayons *off* the walls and *on* the table? Teach them how to stay in the lines."

He chuckled. "What makes you think I can stay in the lines?"

"Yeah, you right. Just keep to the simple stuff," I giggled and ran off, slipping behind the buffet.

"Yes, Ma?"

Relieved, Ma nodded at Ms. Shonda next to her.

"Oh good, take over for Ms. Shonda. She needs to drive

her mother home. And grab that tray out the kitchen, will you?"

"Here, let me help you," Ms. Shonda said, and I followed her to the kitchen. "I was watching you out there. It was real nice what you did for those kids."

I shrugged with a grin. "Just keeping them busy."

Ms. Shonda pulled the last tray of chicken out the warmer.

"And where's your cousin? You know, the one you used to bring here every MLK Day?"

"Oh, um, that wasn't my cousin. That was . . . is my best friend."

"Well, where she at? She was real good at dealing with the babies."

"She's . . . at her dad's. I mean, her aunt's," I said, backpedaling. Because even though that's what everyone had told me, it felt like a lie. A big, fat lie.

I rushed back to the buffet next to Ma and took Ms. Shonda's place.

"Not too much now, just a nice spoonful," Ma directed me. "Don't want to weigh down people's plates."

Luckily, the line began to thin out until there were only a few people left to serve.

"Hey, Ms. Swaby." Ma beamed.

Ms. Swaby. Such a stick-thin, fragile old woman, I questioned whether I should weigh her plate down and if she'd have the strength to carry it.

"Hey, Janet, how are you?" she asked, a bright white smile on her smooth dark-skinned face.

"Doing just fine. How about yourself? Haven't seen you since Thanksgiving."

Ms. Swaby was one of the church elders who prayed the hardest and loudest during Pastor's sermons. She took a long, deep sigh. "Well, I *was* doing okay. Until them eviction notices came around."

"Oh no! Not you too," Ma gasped. "I've been hearing about them."

"Yes, ma'am. Been living in Ed Borough my whole life and never had no problems. Now they coming around serving everybody. This city has it out bad for us. They've wanted that land for as long as I can remember. Rather throw us all out and start with a clean slate than fix a broken toilet."

"Well, what are you gonna do?"

"Pastor is calling an emergency meeting with the city council, to see how he can help us."

"You'll let me know how I can help too, okay? Ain't right to put folks out they homes like this."

"Thanks, Janet, that's real sweet of you," Ms. Swaby said, making her way down the buffet line. "Pray for us in the meantime."

"Yes, ma'am, I surely will. Oh! Ms. Swaby, quick question for you. Have you seen . . . Monday Charles lately?"

The spoon nearly slipped out of my hand and onto the floor.

Ms. Swaby stood in front of the greens, thinking hard. "Monday Charles? Oh, Patti's daughter? Yeah, I think so. Got that crazy blond hair now, right?"

I coughed up air and kept my eyes down, trying not to shed tears in the rice.

Ma exhaled, plastering on a fake smile. "No, ma'am. She did that a long time ago. Ain't likely to do it again."

"Hmm. Really? I could've sworn I just saw her yesterday." The thing about church elders is they have the worst memories. What they say happened yesterday could have happened three years ago. "Then, hmmm . . . well, I guess I'm not sure. Ain't that something? And they don't live but a couple of doors down."

Ma winced a smile. "That's okay, Ms. Swaby. Don't trouble yourself."

"I'm sure she's fine. Ain't no one love her babies like Patti."

"You right about that. Thanks anyway!"

"Alright, now. Take care."

Ma continued serving, but I could see through her tight smile and worried eyes that she was also busy thinking.

"Whew, what a day!" Daddy said, collapsing on the living room sofa. We didn't finish cleaning up until close to ten at night.

Ma turned on the lights in the kitchen, unpacking her seasonings, placing them back in the pantry. A yawn escaped me as I flopped down next to Daddy.

"You did good today, Sweet Pea," Daddy said, hugging my shoulders.

"Thanks, Daddy!"

"Claudia, don't get too comfortable on that sofa," Ma hollered from the kitchen. "Go on upstairs and get ready for school."

"Yes, Ma," I sighed. "Good night, Daddy!"

"Good night, Sweet Pea," Daddy said. "I'll drop you off in the morning."

Exhausted but still on a high from the day, I rushed up to the bathroom. It felt good to be useful for a change. To take my mind off my problems, which seemed so trivial in comparison to everyone else's. Plus, it was fun being around all the little kids, coloring and making up dances.

Ma's voice carried upstairs just as I started the water for my bath. "Baby, something don't feel right."

"Right about what?"

"Monday."

"Lawd, Janet. Not this again."

I closed the bathroom door, letting the water run, and tiptoed closer to the stairs.

"I know, I know. But . . . baby, we ain't seen her in months. She didn't come by for the holidays or nothing. Seem strange, don't it?"

"Not to me," Daddy huffed. "There are thousands of people in this city that I don't see every day."

"That ain't the same thing and you know it. Don't it feel different around here . . . without her?"

"Different how?"

"Just . . . quiet," Ma struggled. "Like something's . . . missing. We been so busy with work and Sweet Pea's schooling stuff."

"And that's what we should be focusing on. Sweet Pea's schooling. This ain't nothing to mess around with. High school, college . . . that stuff is important. Not what's happening with her little friend."

"But it don't make much sense how she done fell off with Sweet Pea like this."

Daddy sighed. "Okay . . . I didn't want to say this before. But maybe it's time."

"Well? Say what's on your mind."

"People change, Janet. Even children. And maybe . . . well, maybe she didn't want to be friends with Sweet Pea no more. Maybe they had a falling-out or something we don't know about. Maybe them rumors from last year . . . got to her."

"Naw, I can't see that happening. Those two were thick as thieves."

"But it *does* happen, Janet. Especially with little girls. One day they the best of friends, the next day they enemies. Y'all know how . . . temperamental y'all women can get."

"Hmph. Oh really, sir?" Ma chuckled.

"Baby, you know what I mean. I can't even tell you how many friends my sister Peggy ran through over the years. She played that 'And if you don't do this or that then I'm not your friend' card more times than I can count."

Ma didn't say anything. I hoped she'd speak up. To tell him how Monday and I were different—we were sisters. But her silence felt like betrayal.

"I'm just saying, maybe it's time Sweet Pea made some new friends," Daddy offered. "Stop putting all her eggs in one basket. She needs to be more social, instead of staying all cooped up in the house like some old maid. And she's good with people! You should've seen her today! Hostess with the mostess. If Monday were around, I don't think she would've talked to half the people that walked in there today. They'd be in a corner, talking in that funny language they made up."

Ma sighed. "I guess you're right. I just never expected this. Not from Monday."

"Well, sometimes the people we love the most can hurt us the most. Claudia's about to be in high school, and she'll need to learn that disappointments are just part of life."

With a weight the size of Daddy's truck strapped to my back, I struggled through school, every class dragging on for miles.

By lunchtime, with Ma and Daddy's talk heavy on my mind, I slipped into the large bathroom stall to hide my tears. What if Daddy's right? What if Monday really didn't want to be my friend anymore? But what did I do to her to make her hate me so much—to make her pretend I didn't exist? Or what if that detective's right? Did Monday run away?

Did that picture really change us?

"Aye, who's that crying in the bathroom like that?" a voice barked.

I bit down hard on my tongue to stop the gasping tears, hoping if I just kept quiet, I'd become invisible.

"Who's in there?" I recognized Shayla's shrill voice.

"I don't know," Ashley responded.

I dried my face as someone moved into the next stall and climbed up to peep into mine.

"Oh, it's just Claudia," Ashley said, rolling her eyes before hoping off the toilet.

Shayla sucked her teeth. "What she in there crying about?"

"Probably missing her boo-thang. Thinking about them doing nasty shit."

Heat sizzled off my skin. I stormed out of the stall and ran straight into Shayla.

She pushed me back, shaking off her hands. "Whoa, chill! You tripping, I ain't into girls like that!"

Ashley and her other friend snickered.

"Whatever," I hissed, trying to walk around her. "Get the hell out my way."

"Or what?" she snapped. "What you gonna do?"

I stepped left and she stepped with me.

"I'm not playing with you!"

I stepped right and she stepped with me.

"Dumbass!" she chuckled. "So I heard you in TLC now."

I jerked back as if her elbow had pierced right into my stomach. Shayla was the one person in the entire school—the entire world—that I didn't want to know. How the hell did she find out?

Her top lip curled up. "Wait a minute, is that what was really going on? She did your homework and you ate her coochie! Is that why you crying? 'Cause Monday's not around to do your homework no more? 'Cause you too dumb to do it yourself?"

The girls stifled their giggles, sounding like squeaky markers on a whiteboard.

"Oh, naw, that can't be it," Shayla corrected herself, rolling her neck. "'Cause in that PICTURE, look like Monday was the one licking your box."

All the rage, all the pent-up emotions of the last few months, erupted at the mention of "the picture." I pulled back a fist and went to strike her but only hit air as she dodged my pathetic blow. Shayla shoved me so hard I went flying, hitting my head on the stall door and falling to the floor. The room spun. I tried to stand back up but she yanked me by the hair and dragged me.

"Helllppppp!" I screamed, kicking my legs.

"Girl, chill," Ashley said, pulling Shayla's arm. "Stop! She ain't even worth it!"

"Oh, you gonna try to hit me!"

Shayla propped me up like a doll, shoving my head toward the nasty toilet bowl. My arms shot out and I gripped on to the sides of the seat, shaking and slipping.

"Help! Somebody," I cried. My face inching closer to the water as she pushed harder against the back of my head. The foul stench of piss mixed with cleaner made my stomach heave.

"Shayla, stop, come on!" Ashley begged, pulling at her.

Never had I been so horrified of my own reflection staring back at me from a pool of water.

"No," I whimpered, my voice echoing inside the bowl, my arms trembling under the pressure. Using all my strength, I tried to find the power to fight back, when I heard the voice of an angel.

"Hey! What's going on in here?" Ms. Valente roared, her heels clicking into a jog. Shayla released me fast. Too fast. My teeth barely missed the edge of the bowl before I fell face-first on the tiles. Ms. Valente slammed open the stall.

"Claudia?" She glanced over at Shayla, standing in the

corner with a bone-straight expression.

"Ms. Valente, she started it. She pushed me, then tried to hit me!"

A moan escaped as I rolled over. Ms. Valente kneeled by my side, touching the lump growing above my eyebrow, and I winced.

"You girls go on to lunch," she ordered. "NOW!"

"What about her?" Shayla shrieked.

"I'm taking her to the nurse," she snapped, helping me to my feet.

"Ain't you gonna tell the principal? She tried to hit me. Everybody in here saw her!"

Ms. Valente stopped to glare at her. "Do you want to get suspended? Do you ALL want to get suspended?"

The girls shook their heads. All except Shayla.

"But ain't she gonna get in trouble? She hit me first!" Shayla screamed, her foot stomping.

"Well, that's what happens when you poke at a beehive for so long. You likely to get stung! Now, go to lunch and I don't want to hear nothing else about this."

Angry tears swelled up in Shayla's eyes before she stormed out of the bathroom, the other girls running after her.

Ms. Valente helped me to my feet and pulled me out the stall, checking me over again.

"Claudia, did you really hit Shayla?"

I swallowed. "No . . . well, I tried, but she was talking about me."

Ms. Valente huffed out some air, her face hardening.

"I don't want to ever hear about you fighting again. Ever! What if I hadn't walked in here? What if those other girls had jumped in? You could've been seriously hurt!"

"But . . . they were talking about me in that picture again," I said.

"I don't care! That's no excuse for fighting," she said, and pointed down the hall. "Go down to the nurse's office and get your head checked out. Now!"

I scurried out of the bathroom. My adrenaline still pumping, I only walked a few feet before noticing the stinging over my eye that made my entire face throb.

I entered the nurse's office and stopped short at the front desk.

"Hey there!" said an unfamiliar pretty young blond lady standing by a filing cabinet.

"Where's Ms. Orman?" I blurted out, my head pounding.

"Ha, I guess word still hasn't got around, huh? She retired during the Christmas break. I'm Ms. Moser."

"Ms. Moser?" I repeated.

Her smile dropped as she crossed the room.

"Hey. Are you okay? Come, let's have a look at you," she said, leading me over to one of the cots. "What happened?"

"I . . . uh . . . ran into the wall—at gym."

"Oh, wow! Are you dizzy?"

"A little."

"Am I blurry? How many fingers do I have up?"

"Three."

"Okay. Let me get you an ice pack while we check you out," she said, grabbing one out the cabinet in the back. She cracked the pack on her thigh to activate the ice beads before wrapping it in sheets of paper towels.

"Here you go," she whispered, gently laying it over my forehead. "Do you know if you're allergic to any medications, like aspirin?"

"I don't think so."

"Let me just double-check your file. What's your name, sweetie?"

It wasn't planned. The idea didn't really hit me until her name leaked out my mouth.

"Monday Charles."

She nodded and smiled. "Nice to meet you, Monday."

I can play this off, I thought. People confused us all the time. Ms. Moser stepped behind the desk and opened a file cabinet with the key around her neck. Maybe there's another address or number in her file. An emergency contact, maybe for her dad or her aunt.

"Ah, here you are," she said, pulling out a file.

She scanned through Monday's chart, squinting before her mouth dropped.

"Hold one second," she said, her voice low. "Let me close the door."

Ms. Moser peered out into the hall and shut the door.

"Monday, Ms. Orman left a note here . . . said you may stop by from time to time. Are you okay?"

The ice pack suddenly felt colder. "Yeah, I'm fine. I just have a little headache."

Worry painted across her face, she twitched nervously. "Um, is there anything else you want me to take a look at?"

"Like what?"

"Any other . . . injuries you may have . . . that you want me to examine? Any bruises?"

Those marks on her back, I thought, and the pack slid out my hand.

"No. I'm okay. Just hit my head."

"Monday, anything we talk about I promise will not leave this room. Just like with Ms. Orman."

"I'm okay," I said, wincing a smile. "But . . . um, do you have my dad's number?"

Ms. Moser opened Monday's file again, flipping through papers. Why is it so thick?

"Sorry, sweetie," she sighed. "No one else listed here but your mom. Do you need him?"

"No. I was just gonna call him so my mom doesn't have to . . . take off work to pick me up. But I'm okay. I think I can go back to class now."

She placed a hand on my shoulder, worry in her eyes.

"Are you sure? You said you were dizzy a few moments ago."

I sat up, blinking away stars. "Yeah. I'm good."

"Well, let me get you some aspirin anyways."

Ms. Moser took a generic bottle out the cabinet and filled up a cup at the water cooler.

"So, where did Ms. Orman go?" I asked.

"She retired in Florida with her daughter," she said as she handed me the pills and a cup of water. "You still have her number, right?"

I popped and swallowed the pills raw.

"No, I think I lost it. But do you happen to have it?"

THE AFTER

Dear Monday,

Reamember last year, how a clip of the Group 5 pirformnce make it on Good Morning America? Now I no why. Ms. Manis is work us hard! She's even ading more practices. I don't knw if I can ceep up. I know what you wold say if you where here: "So just quit." But I can't quite. Dance is all I got witout you.

"Claudia, you must fully extend your arms," Ms. Manis corrected, her voice just a touch above the music pouring out the speakers. "And watch your turnout."

Group Five performance is the crowd favorite. So we needed to be tight; even simple head turns had to be in sync. I was used to having Monday to practice with, be the mirror I needed to make myself look flawless, in school and outside it. Without her, my imperfections seemed jarring, like coloring an ocean carrot orange rather than cyan.

"Okay, ladies, let's take it from the top."

We split up into two lines at the far end of the studio. Megan stood next to me with her hands on her hips, focusing on Ms. Manis's direction, her feet sitting comfortably in first position. She hadn't said one word to me since our run-in at the mall, and I didn't expect her to.

"She don't say much, does she?" Shannon whispered behind Megan.

"I wouldn't either," Megan mumbled without glancing in my direction just as another girl bumped into their conversation with a sly grin. "But you heard what Ms. Manis said, so leave her be."

"You think she knows yet?"

Megan shoots her a look.

"Aye, why was Michael asking you about her the other day?"

Megan's head snapped back. "Drop it, Kit Kat."

"What? What'd I say?"

"I said drop it," she growled.

"Dang, what's up with you?"

When class ended, I raced to the locker room to change before the girls had time to join me. I slipped on my sneakers with my coat in hand and ran out into the lobby, where Megan stood waiting by the elevators.

"We need to talk," she said, her voice clipped.

I swallowed. "Um, okay."

I followed her into an empty classroom in the back of the school. Music danced through the walls from next door's Group Four lesson, loud enough that no one would be able to hear her whoop my ass for staring at her boyfriend.

"I got to ask you something," Megan said, locking the door and leaning against it.

I stepped back a few paces, putting space between us. "Uh . . . okay."

She crossed her arms and took a deep breath. "The other day at the mall . . . did you . . . tell anyone you saw me there?"

I blinked, unsure if I heard her right. "No."

She nodded. "Good. Don't."

Her words jabbed at my stomach and I took another step back.

"Why . . . you asking?"

She rolled her eyes and sighed. "'Cause, I told my mom I was taking an extra solo lesson so she wouldn't know I was with Kam."

I blinked again before a giggle burst from my lips, quickly becoming a full-fledged laugh.

"What's so funny?"

"Well, why would you go to the *mall* to sneak around with your boyfriend?"

She chuckled. "Yeah, I know. It was dumb. I guess 'cause the only other place to hang out is in his car or at his house, and I just wanted to go somewhere and be a regular couple for once."

"Well, don't worry. I won't tell anyone. Michael's the one you probably got to worry about. He knows everybody!"

The corner of Megan's lips crept up into a smirk. "Trust me, I found a way to shut Michael up. I ain't worried about him."

ONE YEAR BEFORE
THE BEFORE

Monday had tasted the sweetness of popularity and craved its high.

Every day she attempted to talk to someone new, to be seen, to stand out. Every day her head spun with ideas on how to win back the spotlight. With the braid business over and Jacob giving her death stares in the hallway, she had to come up with something new. Something big and exciting.

"I think I want to dye my hair," she announced as we walked into the library.

"Ha! Really? Your mom is gonna let you do that?"

"She won't even care," she said, dropping her book bag by our table.

"Dang, Ma would never let me. She'd kill me for even asking!"

Monday's face tensed, her pupils shrinking the way Ma's did after coming home from the eye doctor. She sat motionless, millions of miles away.

"Well, what color you gonna get?" I asked, calling her back to earth.

It took her a moment to land, but when she did, her lips curved into a smirk. "Blond."

"Blond? Now I know you lunchin'! You ain't got no business with white-people hair."

"Not like white-people blond. More like Beyoncé blond. And I'm gonna straighten it but with curls on the bottom." Monday licked her lips, thirsty for the unattainable. "There ain't no other girl in the whole school who'll be blond like me. I'mma be the first!"

We spent the rest of the afternoon flipping through magazines and websites in the media room, searching for examples of the perfect blond. It had to be the right shade of golden yellow with a tint of auburn. More natural, we thought. By the end of the day, I loaned her five dollars to buy a box of color and a relaxer at the dollar store.

That Sunday I called before church, after, and during dinner. Each time she was busy fighting with her hair. Over eight hours. All the website said was you weren't supposed to leave dye in for more than twenty minutes. By bedtime, I was pacing around my room, plotting how to convince Daddy to drive me over to Ed Borough. Monday had never relaxed her hair herself before. Mrs. Charles always brought her to some lady's house a few doors down who fixed her up in her kitchen for twenty dollars. I could count on one hand how many times she had been in that woman's house.

In the morning, I waited by our lockers, frantically hoping to catch the first glimpse. I bounced on the balls of my feet, my stomach dancing. She should've done it at my house. I could've helped.

Monday trickled in minutes before the bell, wearing my pink bucket hat, her eyes low and glassy, the spark in them missing. The wrinkled collar on her white shirt had a light brown ring of sweat circling the neck. Must have been too busy with her hair to worry about her clothes, I thought.

"Hey," she mumbled.

I grinned. "Well? Hurry up, let me see!"

She sighed as she opened her locker to stuff her coat inside. When she slammed it shut, I almost screamed.

"Claudia," she asked, eyes big and uncertain. "What color is it?"

Her hair was a violent burnt orange, her roots a rusted burgundy. Drenched in hair spray, overfried, stiff to the touch, her split ends screamed for a merciful cut. It hurt just looking at her.

"It's . . . diff . . . rent," I said, trying to keep it cool, but wishing she'd put that hat she'd borrowed back on.

Her shoulders slumped.

"I think I messed up," she said. "The instructions were . . . confusing."

"Well . . . you know, girls mess their hair up all the time. It's nothing."

"Really?" She looked doubtful, touching the crispy tips of her hair.

The second bell rang, and I looped our arms, heading for homeroom.

"Yeah! And Ma dyes her hair herself. Maybe she can help . . . fix it."

Monday struggled out a breath, as if using her lungs for the first time that day. "Okay."

Go home! Run out the back door, I should have said, if only to save her. But instead I walked into Ms. Valente's classroom first, Monday close on my tail.

"Morning, la . . . dies." Ms. Valente struggled to compose her shock.

A dead silence surrounded us as Monday slipped into her seat. I mean, you could hear a pin drop—every eyeball glued to the fire on her head. She cleared her throat and opened her notebook as if she didn't notice. I clenched my teeth and closed my eyes, knowing what was bound to happen, in three, two, one . . .

"Yo! What the fuck happened to your hair?" Trevor screamed.

208

The class erupted into laughter.

"Guys! Knock it off!" Ms. Valente warned.

"But look at her hair—"

"You need to stop worrying about her hair and start worry about your grades. And *your* hairline."

"Ohhhhh! Ms. Valente jonin' on you, cuz!"

Screams of laughter echoed into the halls.

"Well, it ain't my fault she come to school looking like a Muppet," Trevor heckled, pointing at Monday.

Monday's bottom lip trembled. She turned, staring at Jacob sitting in the back of the class. A stoic face, he didn't even blink.

Monday leaped up and ran out the room. I glared back at Jacob, his lips curling into a satisfied grin.

"Ms. Valente!" I pleaded, my voice cracking.

She nodded solemnly and I took off.

"Monday, wait," I called in the hallway, racing after her. She sprinted faster, her long legs carrying her away from me, and I pushed my legs harder to catch up. She made a left into the bathroom, straight into the larger stall, locking herself in.

"Monday," I wheezed and knocked softly. "Monday, come on out. It's just me."

"No! I can't," she cried. "God, I'm so stupid!"

"No you're not," I said, leaning my head against the door. "Open up. Please!"

Silence.

"Monday, open the door!" I jerked the handle. More silence.

"Fine!" I dropped down to the floor, lying on my stomach, and shimmied under the door.

"Claudia! You crazy! Crawling on this dirty-ass floor!"

Hunched over on all fours, I looked up at her. Monday stared down at me, wild eyed, then busted out laughing, wiping the tears off her face.

"Straight lunchin'," she cackled between sniffs.

"Me? You the one that got me chasing you down hallways and breaking into bathrooms like the po-po," I grumbled. "And you know my pressure is bad!"

She sighed, her smile fading, leaning against the wall, sliding down like a fallen leaf on the floor next to me. Side by side, just like in our tent, we sat in silence as she twisted a strand of hair between her fingers.

"He told me that I would look real pretty . . . if I was a blond. How sexy I would be . . . if I looked like Beyoncé. That he would want to be with me for real, if I looked like her."

"Who? Who told you that?"

Monday buried her face in her hands and breathed his name. "Jacob."

"You talking to him again? Why didn't you tell me?"

"I guess I . . . wanted it to be surprise. But I screwed it all up."

"This ain't your fault!"

Her face crumbled. "No, Claudia . . . it's all my fault. Everything is my fault! Everything! I just thought, if . . . if we were together . . . things would be better. But . . ."

"Better? What are you talking about?"

She struggled to talk, a story stuck inside her, but nothing came out. I couldn't believe it. They broke her. Plucked her out of our bubble and crushed the life out of her. Her body bent before she leaned over, head falling into my lap, sobbing softly. I stroked her hair, like petting a puppy. Jacob tricked her into messing up her hair. Everything that had happened to us over the last few months was because of Jacob. Why couldn't she see that? Love really does make you stupid.

"Forget about Jacob, okay? Forget about all them bammas! After next year, we gonna go to Banneker, we're gonna be on the dance team, and they ain't gonna be shit! Until we out of here, it'll just be me and you from now on. Okay?"

Monday opened her bloodshot eyes, looking up at me.

"Yeah. Just me and you," she sniffled, wiping her wet face on my skirt.

"Ew! Did you just blow your snot on me?"

"Yup." She chuckled, a smile breaking through her tears.

"Nasty ass," I laughed. "I can't believe you just . . ."

A bright flash bounced off her eyes, forcing her to squint them shut.

"Ah! What the hell!"

My head snapped up quick, but there was nothing. We hopped out of the stall, only to find us alone in the bathroom.

"What was that?" Monday asked, opening every stall to double-check.

"It was like a camera flash."

Monday peered out the gated window by the sinks.

"Could it have come from outside? Lightning?"

I swallowed an uneasy breath and glanced up at the ceiling. "Maybe one of the lights blew out?"

We locked eyes, sharing that same prickling suspicion in the pit of our stomachs. Something didn't feel right.

The second-period bell screamed, and I yelped. Monday shuddered, backing slowly into the stall again.

"I can't go out there," she whimpered, reaching up to touch her hair as if it would burn her. "I can't see him like this."

"But . . . we can't hide in here forever."

"Just a little while longer," she begged. "Please!"

I sighed, walking back into the stall with her. "Okay. One more period."

The teasing and cackling went on for the rest of the week. On Friday, Ma took Monday to the hairdresser, her first time in a real salon with proper sinks, blow-dryers, shampoos, and dyes, salvaging her locks without shaving them off. We spent the rest of the weekend watching

YouTube videos of old go-gos, working on our dance rou-tines, eating up Ma's beef stew and banana bread. I painted her nails a glittery silver with blush rhinestones, and she gave me two French braids. We were back to normal, in our bubble where it was safe, with no clue what was in store for us . . . on Monday morning.

THE BEFORE

"Hold up! Hold up! Hold up! Naw, man!" Dad yelled over his conga as the other instruments faded. "Let's take it from the top!"

Daddy went at it, slapping his rough hands against the tight leather. It's hard to describe how go-go feels in your belly. The way the funky kaleidoscope of a keyboard, guitar, sax, drums, and cowbell makes you beat your feet like you caught the Holy Spirit.

Daddy took me to Uncle Robby's house to watch the guys practice their new set. They had a huge gig for Valentine's Day, opening for the Backyard Band and UCB at Howard Theatre. Ma won't let me go to the go-go. Said it's too dangerous but I'd give anything to be up in the chop shop, maybe hold up a sign with my name so they'd shout me out, like I hear on all of Daddy's old mixtapes.

"Aight, fellas, let's wrap it up."

Everyone agreed and started packing. I slipped on my coat and gave Daddy a bottle of water as he wiped the sweat off his face.

"Whew! Thanks, Sweet Pea. Not the young man I used to be. These rehearsals are wiping me out!"

We headed down the driveway toward the car in silence, crunching over the hardening leftover snow that cracked like glass under our feet. The temperature dropped down to fifteen degrees.

"Well, that wasn't that bad," Daddy said, patting me on the back. "Getting out the house for a change. Hey, how you like our new tune? Think your friends will like it?"

I stuffed my hands in my pockets. "Kids . . . don't really listen to stuff like that anymore, Daddy."

Daddy flinched as if I hit him. "Yeah, I know. But . . . you still do, right? Long as I got my number-one fan, I'm winning! Besides, go-go ain't no passing trend—it's our culture! It's your roots, so I know you'll help keep it going! Kids tend to forget they roots but roots always the first to carry you back home."

"Yeah, I guess," I mumbled, my breath fogging.

"You alright, Sweet Pea? You awfully quiet these days."

"I'm okay, Daddy. Just . . . thinking."

"Oh yeah? I've been thinking too. Thinking about where you got that lump from and who I have to kill."

I touched the red orb on my forehead with my glove.

"I told you, Daddy, I ran into a wall in gym. Don't even hurt."

"Mm-hmm. Your mother don't buy that story either. We trying to leave you be and let you handle things on your own. You're a big girl, but I'm finna roll up on your school and figure out which one of those bammas messed with my baby."

I climbed into the truck in silence, hoping he would just drop it. I had no energy to pretend I didn't feel like a belly-up fish inside my bubble. Daddy hopped in and started the car, letting the engine heat up. A cold breeze flew out of the vent and I wrapped my scarf around tighter.

"Come on, Sweet Pea," he coached. "You know you can talk to me about anything, anything at all that's bothering you!"

"It's nothing, Daddy," I said. "Disappointments are a part of life, right?"

He raised a sharp eyebrow. "Ohhh . . . so you heard that, huh? Looks like I need to install some soundproofing in the house next."

"Looks like it."

"Well, that didn't mean you can't talk to *me*. You used to talk to me about everything!"

I hesitated, wondering where to even start, but gave up.

"You'll just think I'm being a baby," I huffed, staring out the frost-covered window.

Daddy sighed, put the car in drive, and let the radio do the talking. He took the long way home, driving through Northwest DC, passing the monuments, the National Mall lined by the Smithsonian museums, the Capitol, and the White House. Lived here all his life but still mesmerized by the lights bouncing off the marble goliath buildings. Once we were over the river and off the highway, we turned on Good Hope Road. Like day turning to night in a blink of an eye, our part of the city felt so dark in comparison when we're so full of light.

Daddy drummed his fingers on the steering wheel. "Hey, did I ever tell you about the day you were born?"

I sighed. "You mean about how Ma was in labor for nineteen hours and almost broke your hand and your eardrum screaming until you finally talked her into them cutting me out of her?"

He chuckled. "Guess I tell that story a lot, huh? Well, what about when your mother was pregnant? I tell you about that?"

I frowned. "With me or . . . with the other babies?"

Daddy winced, gripping the steering wheel. "With you. Just you."

I touched his arm softly. "No, Daddy. You never did."

He nodded, taking a deep breath. "Man, you wanted out her belly, bad. You kicked from sunup to sundown. I could see your tiny feet trying to push through her skin." He chuckled. "You were tired of cooking. You were ready for the world. Ready for this big adventure. I said 'Janet, you may give birth to the Redskins' first female kicker.'"

We laughed until his smile began to fade. "But it almost killed her, trying to keep you contained. The morning sickness lasted for months. Headaches, puking, gagging . . . she was on bed rest for most of the time with them fake contractions almost every day. Twice we went to the hospital with . . . bleeding. She looked just awful. That claustrophobia stuff can start early, even in the belly. You wanted out. Bad. And when you came out all those weeks early, even though it was touch and go if you'd make it . . . it was also a relief you were out of her."

A sharp aching ripped through me, imagining Ma in pain. The one thing I never wanted her to feel.

"Why you never told me this before?"

"She told me not to," he admitted.

"Was I killing her? Is that why she can't have no more babies? Because of me?"

"And see, that's exactly why she didn't want to tell you. She knew you'd blame yourself. You good for taking on others' burdens and making them your own. But no, Sweet Pea, you weren't killing her. And it ain't your fault. Her body just couldn't handle someone so larger than life. Your mother don't regret you one bit.

"But, boy, when they cut you out, you were glowing. Everywhere we took you, you lit up the place. Folks couldn't get enough of you—you sparked life into people.

It's like you came here with a purpose, a mission, to make others feel good. So even though your friend ain't around, don't seem right for you to stop living. You were made to light up this world, not to be cooped up in the house. I may not have said it right, but that's all I want for you, Sweet Pea."

I swallowed, lacing my fingers together.

"What if I fail my . . . mission? What if I'm not as special as everyone thinks I am?"

Daddy reached over and held my hand. "Well, I'm here to catch you every time you think you're about to fall. That's what daddies are supposed to do."

Tears prickled. "Thanks, Daddy."

He smiled triumphantly. "So! How about we stop by the carryout?"

"Thought Ma said she was cooking."

Daddy grinned. "Yeah, but I've got a taste for fried rice. So let's split it. Just don't tell your mother."

"You want me to lie?" I laughed.

"Nawwww, never that. Let's just let this be our little secret."

Daddy pulled into the parking lot of Mr. Chang's. The wind kicked up, almost freezing off my eyelids. I ran for the warmth inside and slammed right into her.

"April," I gasped.

April stepped back to balance herself from falling.

"Shit, Claudia! Watch where you—"

The door swooshed open as Daddy walked in behind me.

"April," Daddy said, delighted.

April arched her neck up to look at him, her face frozen.

"Hey, Mr. Coleman," April croaked. She shuffled backward, holding on to something behind her.

Or someone.

Little Tuesday poked her head out from behind her sister, her light gray sneakers twinkling hot pink lights with each step.

"Tuesday!" I beamed.

Tuesday slipped from behind April and ran into me, wrapping around my waist with the happiest grin on her little heart-shaped face. I squeezed, feeling her bones almost breaking through her thin coat—like hugging a skeleton.

"Hi, Clau-di-a!" Tuesday said.

I squatted down to her level and kissed her cheek, realizing how much I missed her. How much I missed all of them, my pretend siblings. I inhaled the moment just as a pungent smell hit my noise and I took another whiff. Tuesday smelled like a pissy diaper. I glanced up at April, fidgeting with her bag.

"Tuesday! How you doing, young lady?" Daddy said. "Give me five!"

Tuesday gushed and jumped up to smack Daddy's hand with a giggle.

"Whew! Got some muscle on you, girl!" Daddy smiled

at April. "How's it going, April? Long time!"

April tensed, struggling to smile, and pulled her sister closer.

"Good," she mumbled, eyes flicking back and forth between the door and us, as if at any moment she would grab Tuesday and run. And judging by the look in her eye, there would be no catching her.

"So, Tuesday, how's Monday doing?" Daddy asked. "We haven't seen her in a while."

"Fine," Tuesday said, squirming with a shy smile.

"So she's back home?" I asked, glancing up at April, her face expressionless.

"Mmm-hmm," Tuesday said, nodding.

"Oh yeah, what y'all been up to?"

"Just playing and stuff," Tuesday giggled.

"So you've been playing with Monday?" I blurted out, leaning closer.

Tuesday nodded. "Yeah. But she's always hiding in the closet."

April's jaw dropped. She looked up at Daddy, then at me before placing a trembling hand on Tuesday's shoulder, pulling her closer.

"Ohhhh! Hide-and-seek," Daddy laughed. "Ha! Yeah, I used to play that too when I was your age."

"Quit playing around, Tu Tu," April said, choking out a dry laugh. "Sorry, Mr. Coleman, Tuesday is just messing with you. She knows Monday's over by Daddy."

"Thought you said she was at your aunt's?" I seethed.

April squared her shoulders, eyes narrowing.

"You must have heard me wrong."

"Hey, how's your daddy doing?" Daddy asked, still not noticing April's trembling hands. "Haven't seen him in a long time either."

"He's fine," she said, the corner of her mouth twitching. "Um, sorry, but we gotta go. Mom is waiting on us."

"Alright, now. Y'all take care. Tell Monday to stop on by next time she's around."

Tuesday stared up at me with Monday's eyes—calm and indifferent, but needy. She grabbed my hand and squeezed it.

"Are you gonna come over and play with us?"

My heart pumped fast and I bent to her level. "Yeah, soon. I promise."

April avoided my glare and grabbed Tuesday's hand, yoking her out into the cold.

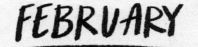

FEBRUARY

Rumors are born with legs that can run a mile in less than a minute.

Rumors eat up dreams without condiments.

Rumors do not have expiration dates.

Rumors can be deadly.

Rumors can get you killed.

There's this rumor that DC was built on top of a swamp and the Chocolate City is slowly sinking into mud. That's why the humid heat sticks to your skin like cement glue. That's why white clouds of gnats swarm like biblical locusts. That's why alligators crawl out of sewers and eat stray animals and babies left alone in their strollers.

"None of that's true," Ma told me as I hid inside.

"How do you know?" I asked.

She shrugged, shucking fresh corn for our barbecue.

"I dug into it myself. You think I'd raise my baby on some swamp?" she chuckled. "You can't always believe everything people tell you. Sometimes you got to find out stuff for yourself."

THE BEFORE

On Mondays, pieces of hope would slide down from my brain, through my throat, into my stomach, and fill me up like Ma's gumbo. Today is the day she'll show up, I'd declare, standing by my locker, watching the doors, counting the seconds. When the bell rang and she was nowhere in sight, my hope disintegrated into dread. Without Monday, there seemed to be an infinite amount of space inside our bubble. I could run in circles without bumping into myself.

Find Monday. Find Monday. Find Monday.

"Ms. Valente, can I talk to you for a minute?" I asked, lurking outside her classroom after the final bell.

Ms. Valente pushed a strand of hair behind her ear and sighed.

"Come on in, Claudia," she said. "I'm just about to pack up."

I sat on a desk in front of her as she reshuffled packs of work sheets and essays. She wore a blue—no, more like pewter, maybe even a slate—sweater over her black dress. Blue was her color; I wondered if anyone had ever told her that.

"So, what's up?" she asked, without looking up. "Trying to grade these papers before tonight's meeting. I'm a part of the admissions committee and we're starting to review applicants."

"Already?"

"Work never stops around here."

I nodded, squeezing my book bag straps.

"Are you . . . still mad at me?"

Stunned, she frowned. "Claudia, I was never mad! Just disappointed. I expected more from you than fighting. Fighting is never, ever the answer. Three against one . . . you could have been seriously hurt, or worse. You're only a few short months away from graduating. Why would you jeopardize that?"

My shoulders slumped. "I'm sorry."

"Just promise me that next time, if you're in trouble . . . you'll come find me or another teacher. Okay?"

I shook my head, thankful. "I swear. I won't do nothing like that again."

She gave me a small smile and nodded. "I believe you."

"But I need a really big favor. And you're the only one that'll listen."

She chuckled. "I'll hear you out."

I inhaled deeply. "Can you go by Monday's house?"

Ms. Valente slouched in her seat, her eyes rolling. "Claudia . . ."

"Ms. Valente, something ain't right. School saying she's home but she ain't home. Her mom saying she's at her dad's and her sister saying she's at her aunt's."

She sat up straight. "You spoke to her sister?"

"Yeah."

Ms. Valente rubbed her temple with a frown. "Hm. I've . . . met her before. Why would she lie?"

"I don't know. But I know something's wrong. And no matter how mad she is at me, I just want to make sure she's okay. I just have to know."

"Why do you think she's mad at you?"

"Why else wouldn't she call me? Why else wouldn't she want to be my friend anymore?"

Ms. Valente placed her pencil down, folded her hands together and studied my face. "Okay, not saying that I don't believe everything you're saying . . . but what if it's just that simple and she really doesn't want to be your friend anymore? You sure you can handle it?"

My hands gripped tighter before I nodded. "Anything is better than not knowing."

She shook her head and groaned.

"Okay, fine. I'll go. Not sure if it'll be anytime soon, but we'll see."

THE AFTER

First Monday was at her aunt's, then she was being home-schooled, then she was at her dad's. Nothing added up. About time I found out why.

With my door closed, I hid in our tent and dialed the number Ms. Moser wrote on a Post-it. A woman picked up on the third ring.

"Hello?"

I sit up straight.

"Hi, Ms. Orman?" I said, using my best adult voice.

"No, this is her daughter, Giselle. Who is this?"

"Um, this is . . . Claudia. I go to Warren Kent. Ms. Orman is . . . I mean, was our nurse."

The phone went silent before she coughed a gasp. "Claudia, how'd you get this number? The school give it to you? They ain't got the right."

"Um . . . Ms. Orman left it . . . for me. In case of emergencies. Can I speak to her?"

"About what?"

"I'm just . . . checking on her." I'm a terrible liar.

She sighed. "Listen, Claudia. I appreciate you calling in to check in on my mother but . . . well. I don't know if you remember, but my mother was diagnosed with Alzheimer's. You know what that is?"

Of course I knew. One of Grandmamma's friends had it. She'd pour salt in her iced tea and snapped at anyone that tried to tell her differently. Poor Ms. Orman. No wonder she retired.

"Yes, ma'am."

"Well, if you know, then you know she can have her good days and her bad. Sometimes she gets real confused."

"I'm sorry. I'm just looking for my friend Monday and—"

"Monday," she exclaimed, as if she had heard the name before. "Look, this is a real delicate time and I don't want to upset her with all that. You understand?"

"Yes. But . . . it's just a few questions that only she would know the answers to."

"That's if she could remember any of the answers at all."

"Please," I begged.

She sighed. "Okay, Claudia. If it can help you, we can try. But if this gets out of hand, I'm hanging up."

"I promise it won't! Thank you."

The phone ruffled and went silent. I jumped out of my tent and sat on the edge of my bed, staring at the falling snow softly hitting the library.

"Hello?" a familiar voice said on the other line.

"Ms. Orman? Hi, this is Claudia Coleman!"

"Yes?"

No recognition. I gulped and pressed on.

"I'm Monday's friend."

"Monday?"

"Yes, um, Monday Charles."

"What happened? Did something happen?"

Suddenly it felt as if I was standing outside in the snow in my underwear.

"Um, why you ask?"

"Well, I . . . well, what's this all about?"

"I was just wondering if you can tell me a little bit about Monday being so sick."

She chuckled. "I can't just share her personal business, dear."

"Please," I begged. "I'm looking for her."

"Looking?"

"Yeah, Monday's not at school anymore."

"She . . . Well, where is she?" she asked, her voice dropping low and serious.

"That's what I'm trying to figure out. And she was always in your office . . . I thought maybe you knew something or maybe where she could be?"

Heavy breathing sounds tracked her brief pause.

"Monday was never sick," Ms. Orman said.

I gripped the phone tighter. "Naw, Ms. Orman, remember? She had that really bad flu and was out of school for weeks. And she was always having them fevers."

"Monday was never sick. She never had the flu."

Her voice was a heavy rock thrown through a small window of doubt.

"But . . . she was . . ."

"It was all smoke and mirrors. I had to get her out."

"Wh-what do you mean?"

Another long pause, her breathing not as steady and even as before. "Hello?"

"Yes. Ms. Orman. What do you mean?" I pressed.

"What I mean about what?"

"About Monday?"

"What about it?"

It? Oh no. "No, Monday. Monday Charles! What happened to her?"

"Oh God, what if something happened to her? I got to . . . find her. I got to . . . wait. Hello? Hello? Giselle, I don't know what this is about."

"I told you this was going to upset her!" Giselle barked into the phone. Had she been listening the entire time?

"Wait, please! She was starting to remember!"

"Don't call back here! She can't help you!"

"But you don't—"

"Do your parents know what you're up to? Let me speak to your mother!"

I clicked End on the call quick, my heart hammering against my chest. What did she mean she had to get her out? Out of what?

RINGGGGGG!

I dropped the phone on the bed as if it burned my palm with a yelp. The red light blinked. Giselle was calling back to talk to Ma—to rat me out. Shit! What am I going to do?

RINNNGGGGG!

But Ms. Orman remembered something. Even if only for a split second, she remembered Monday. Which meant she wasn't lying about Monday not being sick. Ma might flip about me snooping in grown folks' business, but maybe if she hears about Monday not having the flu . . . maybe it'll burn a fire under her hot enough to help me find her!

I jumped up, yanking the door open.

RINNNNG—

I stopped short, neck snapping toward the bed. The red light held a steady green on the cordless. Ma answered from somewhere in the house. I could hear her mumbling, talking in fast whispers. My brain scrambled to come up with my side of the story. How would I save myself?

It was all smoke and mirrors . . . .

If she didn't have the flu, where did she go for a whole month? Why would she . . .

"Claudia!" Ma hollered. "Claudia!"

I flinched and inched closer to the door. "Yes, Ma," I answered.

"Michael is on the phone for you!"

I coughed out a breath, clutching my chest. *Michael? What does he want?*

"Okay," I croaked and took a few calming breaths before answering the phone. "Hello?"

"Hey! What's up?"

"Uh, nothing."

"Why you sound like that?" he chuckled.

I cleared my throat. "Like what?"

"Like you scared."

"Just . . . surprised, that's all."

"Oh, well, anyway, they having this big basketball game at my school, against our rivals next week. My mom said I can take you to it. I asked your mom if you can come and she said yes."

I gripped the phone tighter, holding in a shriek as I danced in a little circle. I'd never been to a high school basketball game. But still, I couldn't be *that* pressed.

"How come you asked my ma before you asked me?"

"Figured I'd start with the hardest part first."

"Well, how'd you know I would want to go?"

"Well, *do* you want to go?"

I paused for dramatic effect. "Maybe."

He laughed. "Well, it's next Friday. You think you'll know by then?"

"Maybe."

"Okay, so when you decided—whenever that'll be— your mom is gonna drop you off at school and my mom will drop you back home after the game."

I stifled a giggle. "Okay."

ONE YEAR BEFORE THE BEFORE

"So y'all really gay for real, huh?" Trevor said, snickering as he approached us in the hall.

"Dang, we can't even take our coats off before you come with the bullshit," Monday said, winking at me.

Trevor bit down on his fist, his face lighting up with a goofy grin as he pointed at us.

"I saw that! I was just messing with y'all, but you out in public like that, though?"

Monday rolled her eyes. "Don't pay him no mind," she whispered to me.

Any other day, I wouldn't have. I mean, the whole "we gay" rumor was plain dumb. But the way everyone in the hall stared, the hush that fell as we walked by . . . something felt off.

"What are you talking about?" I snapped.

Monday waved him off like a fly. "Whatever."

Trevor did a little dance, pulling his cell phone out of his pocket, swiping his screen open. "There you go!"

He shoved the phone in our faces and I yelped, putting a hand up to my mouth as I backed away. Monday inched closer, brows cutting a deep V down the middle of her face.

There, on Facebook, for the whole world to see, was a picture of us sitting on the floor in the school bathroom, with Monday's head in my lap. From the high angle and the way her head was positioned, as if in my crotch, wiping tears off on my skirt, and the way my head titled back with a laugh, the picture looked . . . confusing.

"What the . . . who took this?" Monday demanded, grabbing the phone out of his hand. "Who the fuck put this up?"

I read the stats below. Two hundred and ninety-three shares. One thousand likes. My mouth dried.

"Man, I don't know," Trevor said, snatching his phone back. "It just showed up on Friday."

"Oh my God," I cried, and noticed Jacob standing near his locker. His face blank, mouth closed, one eyebrow raised, staring at Monday. We locked eyes and he turned away.

"Claudia . . . ," Monday breathed.

Over the weekend, while we ate brownies and danced

236

to Junk Yard Band, everybody and their grandmamma had seen the picture. Whether from posts on Facebook or Instagram, the rumor ran up to folks' doorsteps and let itself in. Aside from her burnt hair and the way her face turned into my skirt, you couldn't tell it was Monday. But my face, my laughing smile, was clear as day. If I'd had a cell phone, I would have known about the fire we were walking into and who started it.

My parents wasted no time rolling up to the school and threatened to sue if they didn't have the picture taken down and launch an investigation. Ma filtered nosy calls, handling them with fierce grace. "So two little girls are close, and that makes them gay? What that say about you and your best friend, Sister Karen? . . . Don't your son sleep over his little buddy's house every weekend? . . . I'm not suggesting anything, just don't call my house with foolish questions!"

Monday and I hid in my room, waiting for the storm to blow over, trying not to worry about the permanent damage that would remain.

"I bet it was Shayla," Monday mumbled, pacing in a circle, thinking hard.

"Naw, Shayla can't hate us that bad," I said, soaking a cotton ball in nail polish remover. I needed to do something to ease the tension, planning to paint my nails bright canary yellow with gold tips.

"You lunchin'. That girl stays hating on us for no reason."

I felt the squeeze, the pressure building up around our bubble, threatening to break us.

"What about Jacob?" I asked.

Monday chewed on her bottom lip. "I don't think so. He wouldn't do that."

"What? He was the one who started this whole rumor in the first place! Even after you kicked his ass and he stays lying to you, you defending him?"

Monday shook her head, deep in thought. "Naw. It just don't seem like him. It doesn't seem like something he would do."

THE AFTER

"Stop, stop!" Ms. Manis yelled, cutting off the music.

I flinched mid-turn, almost falling on my face. Thank God we were alone—I couldn't handle the embarrassment in front of the other girls.

"What's wrong?" I asked, out of breath. Ten minutes of class left and I hadn't perfected the ending of my piece. We seemed to keep stopping in the middle like an unfinished thought.

With a tight-lipped smile, she gracefully walked across the room, hands on her hips.

"Claudia, is everything okay?"

I gulped. "Yes, ma'am."

"Hm." She tapped her chin twice, circling me like prey. Sweat dripped down my neck, legs tingling.

"Your parents pay good money for you to come here. So, I'll trust you'll take what I'm about to say seriously. Yes?"

"Yes, ma'am."

She nodded and spoke softly. "A dance has to have emotion—a soul. Your piece is missing *something*. A passion, a spark of life! The solos are built for you to flex your creative muscles with guidance. But I'm wondering if you're ready to do so."

I held my breath for five counts before blurting out, "I dance faster than this! This song . . . it's too slow for me."

She frowned, her eyes growing hard.

"In this life, you don't always get what you want, but you must dance through it," she said. "Listen to the piano, Claudia! It has the beat you crave. You just have to listen."

Dear Monday,

Dang, girl, did you tke ALL my cloths? Naw, I playing but ain't it crazy how you have a clozet full of clothes but never seem to have anythng to wear? I'm going to this game with Michael from church. I know wat you thinking but this ain't a date! I tore up my room something crazy looking for the perfect outfit but everything I ~~poot~~ put on, I ripe off. I can hear you now: "No, not that one . . . are you serious? You can't wear that! Girl, you lunchin', you look like you twelve!" Jus, don't be mad that I went to a game witout you. O k?

Sweat leaked out of places on my body I didn't think could sweat in the middle of winter. Guess I never saw myself going to my first high school game without Monday, and the idea of it had me shook. But like Daddy said, I had to step out and shine. Even if that meant without her.

Ma helped flat iron my hair and we compromised on some lip gloss and mascara. Dressed in black jeans, a fuzzy lavender V-neck sweater, and tall black boots, I traded my dark pomegranate puff coat for Ma's black-licorice leather jacket. The one she wore on dates with Daddy. I painted my nails eggplant, drawing dark pink bows on the tips.

We pulled up in front of the Cardozo High School steps to a sea of kids in dark purple and white. Two volunteers stood by the stairs passing out crimson flyers: *"SAVE ED BOROUGH! It's community! It's home!"*

"Okay, Sweet Pea," Ma said. "Have a good time! Enjoy the game!"

The same fear that had gripped me on the first day of school sprung up again. I couldn't just walk in there by myself. At least if I had Monday, our bubble would shield us from impending attacks.

"What's wrong?" Ma asked.

I flipped down the visor, checking my lip gloss, buying myself some time. "Nothing."

Ma raised an eyebrow. "You nervous? You want me to walk in with you?"

"Ma! I can't walk in there with you like I'm being dropped off for day care. I was just . . ."

A hard knock on the window made us both jump. Michael bent down and grinned through the frosty glass. Ma rolled down the window and his cologne hit me.

"Hey, Michael," Ma said.

He waved and looked at me, his smile growing bigger.

"Game's about to start. Let go find a seat."

A roaring crowd filled the bleachers, jumping up at every swoosh of the ball hitting net. You could smell the sweat off the brows of every player, hear sneakers squeak against the shiny floor of a packed gymnasium, and be blinded by the bright lights bouncing off the cheerleaders' curly pom-poms shaking in the air.

I unzipped my jacket as we climbed to the top of the bleachers, squeezing in the very middle of the row.

"It's high up here," I said, smoothing down my hair, hoping it wouldn't frizz in the sticky heat.

"The air's just fine," he said with a wink, scooting closer. My cheeks burned as I bit back a girly grin. *This is not a date.*

Second quarter, the Clerks with a 20–15 lead, I drank in the intoxicating electric air. A scene ripped right out of a movie that I now had a leading role in.

"Aren't you hot?" Michael said, tugging at my sleeve. "Take your coat off! Stay a while."

I pulled at Ma's jacket in the tight space, and when he helped, his fingers grazing the back of my neck, a spark flew. Our eyes locked, tension frying like water popping off hot oil. He gulped as his eyes flicked back to the game. Just static. *This is not a date.*

"So . . . uh . . . we only up by three. It's gonna be a tight game," he said, rubbing his sweaty hands over his jeans. "You know anything about basketball?"

I let out a nervous laugh. "Yeah, but I like football better."

He grinned. "That's cool. Maybe you can come to one of my games next year. Coach said I'll be starting."

I shrugged, playing it off. "Okay."

He laughed as we turned back to the game. *This is not a date.* He's just being friendly. But I wondered what Monday would have thought of it. I could picture us now in our tent, overanalyzing every word and movement of the moment. If Monday never comes back, who will I talk to about boys?

The buzzer sounded, and the announcer blared through the speakers.

"Alright, y'all! Put your hands together for the all-state Cardozo dance team!"

A storm of silver and purple sequins ran out to the middle of the floor, waving at the crowd, forming a floor pyramid, their heads down. The music started, and heads popped up with huge red smiles before the team jumped

243

into high splits and parted. I noticed Megan in the back row, her eyes sparkling as she high kicked. I leaned forward, engrossed in their routine. Michael watched me with a smirk.

The crowd cheered, harder than they did during the game. Megan looked amazing, her moves fluid, smile effortless. Grinning as she twirled, her head arching back with a laugh before she dipped, like she was having the time of her life. Maybe that's what's missing from my dancing: fun. I used to have fun.

Then I saw it. The move Monday taught me. The *boom beat beat, step step*. They did it twice before their grand finale. I stood with the rest of the crowd in awe, jumping and screaming my lungs out, like they'd won the game. That's going to be us, I thought. Monday and me, on the dance team, the crowd loving us.

That's when her sweater caught my eye. My sweater. The white-and-fuchsia one I let Monday borrow last year. A huge bull's-eye, sitting on one of the lower bleachers. My heart almost came to a full stop. But it wasn't on Monday—it hung snugly on the busty frame of her sister.

"April," I gasped, but Michael couldn't hear me over the loud roar of the crowd as the teams returned, halftime over.

With her back to me, I recognized her profile, so similar to Monday's, sitting next to a boy with a low cut, his arm roped around her waist, whispering in her ear. She faked a laugh, and he nudged her twice. He stood up, sweat-pants hanging off his ass, and nodded toward the stairs. She sighed and followed him, heading toward doors leading into the school on the far end of the gym, his hand locked right above her butt, pushing her along. She shook her head a bit, and he whispered into her ear again, more aggressive than before. Her eyes softened, seeming defeated, before disappearing through the doors. The buzzer sounded and the game began again.

I don't know what I was thinking. Maybe because she was the closest thing to Monday I had put my eyes on in months, but I leaped up and moved quickly through the crowd.

"Claudia?" Michael called behind me. I ran around the perimeter of the court, eyes focused on the door she disappeared through. Right as I passed under the hoop, a whistle blew, squeaky footsteps sounding close before two players flew in front of me, slamming into the purple mat-ted wall.

"Ahhh!" I screamed, stopping short, seconds away from being trampled. The rogue basketball hit my ankle, and the players groaned in pain, panting. The tallest one glared at me. I remembered him—Megan's boyfriend, Kam. He grabbed the ball by my feet with a grunt.

"Get the fuck off the court," he muttered and threw the ball back into play.

"Shit," I coughed out, my hand locked on my chest.

"Claudia!" Michael called again. His voice shook me out my trance, and I raced toward the doors, crashing through them.

"April!" I yelled, my voice echoing down the empty hallway. I walked aimlessly, passing the dark classrooms, stopping by the central staircase with purple-and-gold murals, staring up at the multiple flights of stairs. I kept wandering, studying the large bulletin board of photos, student trips to Italy, community garden, and spirit day . . . until I found myself in an enclosed courtyard with a glass roof—like a greenhouse—staring up at the night sky. *This* is high school, I thought, not knowing whether to be excited by the sheer size of it or scared shitless.

"Ha, stoppppp, Keith," April giggled, her voice echoing from somewhere close. I jogged, confused by its lightness. Did she *want* to be with that guy?

Suddenly, something clanged behind me, like a metal cup dropping and bouncing on the floor. A group of colored pencils scattered and rolled out the cracked door of a darkened classroom into the hallway, greeting my sneakers.

"Shhh," the boy hushed her, his voice muffled. "You making a mess."

I tiptoed toward the door, peering through the window at the boy—his pants around his ankles—squeezed between April's straddled legs as she lay on top of a teacher's desk.

I swung the door wide, letting the soft light from the hallway shine a spotlight on them.

"Shit," Keith muttered, pulling up his pants and jumping off April. She scrambled to cover herself, her mouth dropping.

"Claudia?" she mumbled in shock.

Keith did a double take. "Who the hell is this?"

April wiggled off the desk, buttoning her jeans while glaring at me. "She's . . . my little sister's friend."

"April . . . what are you doing?" I gasped, blurting out the first thought stuck on my tongue. I mean, how could she have sex with some guy in a classroom? Didn't she know what people already said about her? Didn't she know how it embarrassed Monday?

Heavy footsteps echoed in the hall and we froze. Damn, a teacher followed me. We're all going to be in trouble now, I thought. Keith held a finger up to his lips, dipping into the shadows as the footsteps grew louder. I whipped around, bracing myself, as Michael appeared.

Keith smiled, relaxing. "Oh, what's up, Mikey?"

Michael took in the scene as Keith continued to adjust his pants. His eyes narrowed.

"Are you okay?" he asked, gently touching my elbow.

"Yeah," I mumbled.

Keith chuckled and nodded in my direction. "Yo, Mikey, you robbing the cradle now?"

Michael's face hardened. "Naw, she just . . . goes to my church."

Dang, that's all I am to him? He still acting like I'm some nobody from church. I snatched my arm back, sucking my teeth. He frowned, his eyebrows pinching together.

"Um, what y'all doing?" Michael asked.

"Pssh. Nothing. Just chillin'," Keith laughed, smirking at April.

"But what *y'all* doing?" April snapped. "Why don't y'all go back to the game and mind yo' business!"

Michael sighed. "Whatever, April. You don't even go to this school. You just here to get some dick. And ain't you too old to be up in——"

A quick spark of something unsaid flashed between them before they both glanced to see if I noticed.

"You stupid motherfucker! Would you shut up with that big-ass mouth!" April shrieked, causing Michael to take the smallest step in front of me, readying himself.

They know each other. But how?

Keith watched April with an amused smirk.

"Hey, it ain't that serious. We just messing around," Keith chuckled, dapping Michael up. "And anyways, this ain't supposed to be no party." He shrugged at April. "I'll check you later."

"What you mean?" she asked, her voice pleading, eyes widening. "I thought we . . ."

"Naw, I'll check you later," he snapped, frustrated he had to repeat himself.

April shrank back, her arms crossed. Even I felt the sting of his rejection, treating her like a plate of leftovers he could reheat another day. Reminding me of Jacob . . . and Monday.

"Later, cuz," Keith said to Michael. "Catch you in the weight room."

"Yeah, later," Michael mumbled.

The three of us stood there, exchanging a few uncomfortable glances before April's foot started tapping, and then her whole body shook, teeth sucking every twenty seconds.

"What the fuck are you looking at?" she snapped, each word a claw, lashing out at us. She turned to me, throwing her hands up. "You happy now?"

I folded my hands behind my back with a wince. I'd thought I was saving her. Instead, I humiliated her.

"I need to talk to April alone for a second," I whispered to Michael.

"Are you for real?"

"Please?" I begged.

He blew out air, glaring at me like a disappointed parent, and he shook his head.

"Fine," he hissed. "I'll be in the gym."

He didn't acknowledge April as he left, storming down

the hall until we couldn't hear his sneakers squeak anymore.

April huffed, straightening her sweater. Monday's sweater. My sweater. It fit like a crop top, her flat belly out for the world to see. The way I'm sure she wanted it.

"April, I'm sorry."

Her eyes flared. "Whatever! He wasn't shit anyways."

She jumped off the table, finished readjusting her clothes, and moved about as if I wasn't standing right next to her. No use in trying to talk to her, make her see this wasn't cool. The way she operated wasn't going to change. But she was my only line to Monday.

"So, has Monday come by lately?"

She chuckled, a rough and throaty laugh just like her mom's.

"You still at this, Claudia?" She shook her head. "Okay, fine, I'll play along. Monday is at my aunt's."

"Huh? Last time you said she was with her dad."

"Yeah. That's what I meant."

"But Tuesday said she was home and she played with her."

That stopped April cold. Her eyes grew wide as she stared at the ground. Her body swayed lightly, and then she sniffed and zipped up her jacket.

"Leave Tuesday out of this," she snarled. "DON'T bring her up again."

A walking block of ice, cold and impenetrable, she tugged and straightened her tan coat, smoothing back her edges. Her hair seemed different, a shade brighter but hard to tell.

"Damn, don't you miss Monday at all?"

"Bitch, you act like you know her!"

"I know her better than you," I snapped. The words were supposed to come out like bullets. Instead they landed with a soft thud against her—light as a paper plane.

Her smirk chipped away at some of my nerve.

"Oh really? You think you knew her so well? Alright, what was her favorite color?"

"Pink," I said, sucking my teeth at the dumb question.

"ANTTTT! WRONG! Her favorite color wasn't pink. It was purple. She fucking hated pink. She just went along with it because y'all couldn't have the same favorite color."

That funny feeling in the pit of my stomach dropped lower.

"That ain't true," I whispered.

"Monday did anything you wanted 'cause you was the only one stupid enough to be her friend. She didn't have anyone BUT you. And that dude she fucked."

The word *fucked* landed hard, thumping against my bubble.

"Naw . . . Monday didn't do anything like that with Jacob."

"Ha! Who said it was Jacob?"

My tongue dropped dead in my mouth as my body went rigid.

She smirked. "See?"

She's lying, I repeated in my head over and over. April lies. That's what she does.

Her sleeve crept up as she reached to tighten her ponytail, and I noticed a spot of raw skin on her arm. A scar. As if she'd held her arm over a birthday candle and the flame had engulfed her.

"Dang, what happened to your arm?" I asked, reaching toward it instinctively.

"Nothing," she gasped, lowering her sleeve and slapping my hand away. She shoved me hard, a one-handed palm right in the middle of my chest. I yelped as I hit the floor. April stood over me, her hands balled into fists, just like her mother.

"And I ain't gonna tell you again. Quit bringing up Monday, and stay out of my fucking business!"

I stayed dead on the floor, listening to her sneakers squeak down the hall until they disappeared. Just like Monday.

THE BEFORE

"I don't know where your father is!"

Ma slapped a thick wad of dough on the counter, kneading it with her fists. When she finished beating it to submission, she'd let it rise overnight and we'd have fresh rolls for Sunday dinner.

"He know how I worry," she grumbled. "You gonna work on your homework tonight?"

"Yes, Ma," I mumbled from the table, painting my nails an ombré blue sky with tiny white stars.

The front door slammed. Ma looked up, placing powdery hands on her hips.

"Where you been? You missed dinner! Your fingers broke? You can't call nobody?"

Daddy strolled into the kitchen, tickled by Ma's snappiness.

"Sorry, baby, was with Uncle Pete. Van broke down on the BWI." He leaned down and kissed her forehead. "I didn't realize how late it was."

She huffed. "Well, wash your hands so you can eat. I'll fix your plate."

Daddy winked at me and took to the sink while Ma heated up some greens, candied yams, and baked chicken.

"Ladies, it's freezing out there," Daddy said, rubbing his hands together, grabbing a beer out the fridge. "I thought my fingers were about to break off."

He stroked my cheek with the back of his fingers and I flinched away from the cold.

"Daddy! You're gonna make me mess up my nails."

He grinned, tickling my neck. I couldn't help laughing. He's such a big kid.

"You lucky you didn't get frostbite," Ma said, loading up his plate. "It's negative two degrees out there. And with the wind chill, it feels like negative twenty."

"You should have seen us on the side of the parkway, trying to get that van to start. Almost froze to death. Van stopped in the middle of him driving—just crazy. Anyway, we swung by a service station up the road . . . and the funniest thing happened. I ran into Smokey Davenport. We played together, back in high school."

"His name's not really Smokey, is it?"

He chuckled. "No, it's Herman. Just a nickname."

Ma shook her head. "What a crazy name he gave himself."

Daddy smiled. "Hadn't seen him since I don't even know when. We chopped it up for a bit, and he told me he just saw Tip, working at the gas pumps over at the Maryland House on 95."

I flinched, hitting my nails on the table. Ma spun around.

"Tip? Tip Charles?"

Daddy sat at the table next to me, his eyes focused on his bottle. "Yup."

Ma glanced over at me quick, then back to Daddy before placing a plate in front of him. "Okay . . . and?"

He took a slow swig of his beer. "And I asked him if he had his number. And he said yeah."

I stared down at my nails to keep from looking too eager. My left ring finger and pinkie were smudged almost completely off. I tried blowing on my right hand but I couldn't cough up enough air.

"And?" Ma encouraged.

"He called him up . . . right then and there. So, I asked him about Monday."

"AND?"

Daddy sighed. "And . . . he hasn't seen her."

Ma's head snapped back. We locked eyes, both stunned.

"What do you mean he hasn't seen her?" Ma asked in disbelief.

"He hasn't seen Monday, or any of them, in over a year, maybe longer."

My mouth dropped. Ma's eyes widened. "A year!" she screamed. "How you not lay eyes on your own child for over a year?"

He chugged back his drink. "He owe Patti thousands in child support. You know that woman is impossible. Ain't no way she gonna let him see those kids without paying a toll. Tried to reason with her but it got too . . . exhausting."

"But a YEAR! That ain't right!" Ma yelled, throwing the dough in a bowl.

"I know, I know. But he hadn't been working. He couldn't pay child support, and he couldn't get a lawyer with no job to take her to court. He just got that job. But hasn't made enough to pay her back all he owes. He scared she may have him arrested. What good will that do them both?"

Ma shook her head. "That's a damn shame. Nothing should stop you from seeing your kids."

"Nothing should. But Patti sure can."

I shifted away from the table and headed up to my room in silence.

THE AFTER

"You know . . . you haven't said a word about the game!"

Bracing the early morning icy winds, I helped Ma pack her pie orders in the trunk of the car before heading to church with April's words still dancing around my head. Monday wouldn't lie about her favorite color, would she?

"Yes I did. I said it was fine."

"Yeah, but how was it being in high school? With all those kids!"

I shrugged, thinking of the massive hallways and April's shirt—my shirt—hanging off her.

"It was okay," I said, climbing into the car.

Ma hopped in and buckled her seat belt.

"But . . . did it get you excited? Could you picture yourself there?"

"At Cardozo?"

"Yeah! I heard it was a really good school. Ms. Walker mentioned how great it would be for you!"

Ma's tone felt suggestive, leading down a road I wasn't interested in.

"But I want to go to Banneker."

She shrugged. "Yeah, but it's good to have options, right?"

Options, yes. But what were Monday's options? After what April said, did that even matter anymore?

As we made our way off our block, Ma made a right on Good Hope Road rather than the left, toward church.

"Why we going this way?"

"'Cause we have to pick up Michael."

"What? Why?"

Ma took her eyes off the road for a moment to glance at me. "His mother is at a teachers' conference this weekend," she said. "Asked if we could give him a ride to service. It's too cold for him to walk all that way. I thought . . . that you wouldn't mind."

Yeah, I mind, I wanted to scream. Michael and I didn't leave on good terms. Scratch that, he didn't say one word to me. Slouched in his seat, arms crossed for the rest of the game.

Ma parked in front of Michael's house and honked twice. Michael came out in his thick gray wool coat, slacks, and dress shoes, his cold stare landing on me before he climbed into the back seat.

"Good morning, Michael," Ma said sweetly.

"Morning, Mrs. Coleman," Michael said, his voice low. "Thanks for the ride."

Ma stared pointedly at me and I held back a groan.

"Morning, Michael," I muttered to the floor.

"Morning," he mumbled.

Ma's eyes flickered between us before she chuckled. "Okay, then."

After a frosty car ride to church, we parked in the main lot and Michael jumped out, almost speeding two steps ahead of us. He greeted Pastor Duncan by the front door and ran inside. Ma grabbed my arm as we passed the stairs. "Okay, what's going on between you two?"

I shrugged, balancing the boxes of pies. "Nothing."

She raised an eyebrow. "Claudia Mae, don't you lie to me."

"If you think I'm lying, then why don't you ask golden boy?"

Ma's head almost spun off. "Girl, have you lost your mind with all that sass? You want to be on punishment for the rest of your life?"

I took a deep breath to steady myself.

"Sorry, Ma," I muttered. "Can we go inside now? It's cold."

Ma's eyes narrowed before she stomped inside.

We greeted Pastor and dropped the pies off in the

kitchen. I sat in the very back pew while Ma hung out in the nursery room. She liked caring for the babies during service. She could quiet even the fussiest one. Michael walked around like the church greeter—shaking hands and giving soft hugs. Everyone seemed at ease with him. I seemed to be the only one who noticed the strain behind his eyes, his exhaustion, as if he hadn't slept in days. He glanced at me across the room, his fake smile fading. He quickly headed to the balcony and reported to his post in the audio booth before the call to worship.

After service, we trooped back to the car. Michael followed but kept his distance, hands stuffed in his pockets, feet dragging.

Ma grinned at me as she unlocked the doors. "Michael, you have any plans for dinner?"

I cocked my head to the side, pursing my lips.

Michael glanced at me then back at Ma. "Um, no, ma'am."

"Well, why don't you come home with us? I'm making chicken-fried steak. You're more than welcome!"

His eyes brightened at the word steak. "Yeah! I mean, thank you."

"Thanks, Michael. You can put those down in the kitchen," Ma said, holding the front door open.

Michael insisted on carrying all the groceries inside by

himself. I don't think I ever rolled my eyes so much in my entire life.

"Claudia, take his coat, then help me put these away," Ma ordered. "Michael, make yourself at home."

Michael stood by the door, taking in our living room. He gently handed me his coat, staring at the TV.

"Why's your TV sitting on those big speakers?" First words he'd spoken directly to me all day.

"It's been broke for a while. Daddy just hasn't had a chance to fix it yet."

Michael slowly approached the set, kneeling like a paramedic checking for a pulse.

"Will it live?" I chuckled.

He looked up at the wall, tapping on a few spots with his knuckle, and leaned in to listen. "You know where your dad keeps his tools?"

For the next hour, Michael went to work pulling wires, drilling holes, measuring, and fastening brackets to the wall. I watched him from the kitchen, helping Ma peel sweet potatoes for mash.

After April left me for dead in the classroom, the look Michael had given me when I returned to the gym could've shredded me down to crayon flakes. Never want him to look at me like that again.

"Offer him some water," Ma said under her breath.

I glanced over my shoulder. "He's fine."

"Claudia Mae, I just about had it with you today. Offer that boy some water. Now!"

I huffed, slamming everything I could get my hands on—cupboard, cup, counter—and poured him a glass.

"Thanks," Michael said as I passed him the drink, wiping the sweat off this forehead, his sleeves rolled up and tie long gone. He took a long sip with a refreshing "ahhh," then pulled out his cell phone. "I need to look up the make and model of these speakers. What's your Wi-Fi password?"

"We don't have Wi-Fi."

Michael flinched and shook the water out his ears. "What? But . . . the box is right there!"

I shrugged. "It's doesn't work."

He sighed. "You got a flashlight?"

For the next thirty minutes, Michael rewired our modem, hooked up the Wi-Fi, and reconfigured our computer. By the time Daddy walked in the door, Michael had finished screwing closed the speakers.

"Oh, hey, Mr. Coleman," Michael said with a wave. "Glad you're here. Can you help me lift this? It's a two-man job."

Daddy dropped his bag by the door as he looked every which way, like he had walked into the wrong house.

"Who are you?" he barked. "And what you doing with my tools?"

"Hi, Mr. Coleman. I'm Michael," he laughed. "From church."

Daddy glanced over at me, sitting at the computer, then back to him. "Mikey?"

"It's Michael now, baby," Ma said, walking out to kiss him. "Dinner's almost ready. Do what the young man says."

Daddy scowled, following her into the kitchen.

"What is this boy doing in my house? Playing with my TV?" Daddy asked in a loud whisper.

"Shhh . . . that's Sweet Pea's friend."

"Woman, I said she needed more friends. Not a BOY-friend."

Michael and I locked eyes, my face a thousand degrees, praying the day would end already.

"Calm down. He's a nice young man."

"Young *man* indeed. And ain't he in high school? He too old for her."

Ma chuckled. "And you too old for me. Now go help the boy before he hurt himself lifting that thing."

Daddy sucked his teeth.

"Gerald! If nothing else, your daughter sure got your stubbornness."

Daddy marched back into the living room, grumbling. He lifted and balanced the TV on the bracket with ease.

"This TV's pretty cool, Mr. Coleman," Michael said, tightening the screws.

"Yeah, thanks. Won it at a work raffle. Just . . . haven't had a chance to fix it yet."

"My coach could use one of these for his office for when we're going over tapes. He got one of those old TVs with the fat backs."

Daddy raised an eyebrow. "You play football?"

"Offensive tackle," Michael said, smiling proud.

"Hmm. What's your forty?"

"Five-point-twenty."

"Really?"

Next thing you know, Michael and Daddy are talking nonstop about football. On and on, even through dinner. Made sense, folks just fall in love with Michael without him even trying. Ma laughed, serving Michael seconds and throwing me sympathetic looks as I sulked.

Ma and Daddy offered to clean up the kitchen while Michael and I ate dessert in the living room. I played with the flaky crust on my slice of blueberry pie before dropping my spoon, fed up with the awkwardness.

"You really just gonna stay mad at me? What you want me to say, I'm sorry?"

He sucked his teeth. "Man, I don't want your fake apology. That was just real dumb what you did. Chasing after that 'ho like that."

"How you know her? And how you know she's a 'ho?"

"You were there, weren't you? Coach always says, call it like you see it."

"Still. Don't talk about her like that. She's my best friend's sister."

He blinked in shock as if I spoke Japanese, struggling to find a recognizable word.

"But . . . that don't mean she's *your* friend, Claudia."

My tongue swelled. He was right. April wasn't my friend or even family. Without Monday, April was just a few steps away from being a stranger—a dangerous stranger.

"Anyways, I'm not mad at you. Just mad we didn't really get to chill the way I wanted to."

"You wanted to? Thought I was 'just some girl from church.'"

Michael fidgeted. "Well, I didn't want people thinking we . . . you know, unless you wanted them to. Folks talk. You of all people should know."

Was that it? He was protecting me . . . from rumors?

"Hey, what y'all talking about in here?" Daddy said, emerging with cans of root beer, Ma following.

"We were talking about your band," Michael said, winking at me. "I want to come to your next gig."

I smirked, playing along. "Daddy got a new song he's been working on."

Daddy laughed. "Just coming from the studio today."

"Really? Let's hear it!" Michael said. "We can hook it up to the speakers."

"Go on, baby," Ma cheered. "Show us what you got."

Dear Monday,

Last nite Daddy played his new song and I teach Ma some dance moves. Since today was Presidents' Day and we had off, Michael came over to chill. We watched videos on YouTube, them stupid ones you like, laughing till we cry. Then Daddy came home wit some crab legs and corn so we had a crab boil—right in our kitcen! Ma even made that sour cream pound cake you like.

I think you'd like Michael. I already know what you thinking nd NO! I don't like him like tht. Well, maybe I do. He kinda cute and real sweat.

I saw Aprul the other day and she told me some things . . . and I don't know. ~~April~~ April lies but you ain't hear to clear anything up. It's been months and you just leave witout saying nothing? What's up with that?

THE BEFORE

Somewhere in the middle of it all I started liking the Learning Center.

I sat in the back of the room with *The Secret Life of Bees* streaming through my headphones. TLC tutors gave me books on CD so I could read along, like the way Monday used to read to me. I didn't want them thinking I belonged there forever, but for the first time in months, I started to feel like my old self. My grades weren't in the trash, my admission essay was on point, and my interview at Banneker was scheduled for the next month. Aside from the constant feeling that I was forgetting to do something, I floated on a blissful cloud.

That is until Ms. Valente rushed in the room, as if being chased, bringing me back down to earth.

"Ms. E, can I borrow Claudia for a bit?" Ms. Valente said sweetly, smoothing her dress down with shaky hands, her eyes strained. "She's . . . um . . . helping me with a . . . special project I'm working on."

Ms. E shrugged, closing her workbook. "Sure, of course."

Ms. Valente gave me a tight smile, nodding at the door. I collected my books, avoiding the curious stares from my classmates.

Ms. Valente sped down the hall, her heels clicking fast. I trailed, almost jogging to keep up with her. She stopped short, glancing both ways before dipping into the teachers' lounge, slamming the door behind us and holding it as if to keep the world out. She breathed through her nose hard and stared at me, her face crumbling into a thousand different expressions, like she didn't know what to say or where to begin.

"You were right," she said, pressing the door once more before taking staggering steps toward the kitchenette. I took a long blink at the empty spot she left.

"What?" I whispered, my voice cracking.

She rinsed a mug off in the sink and let her thumb trace the rim. "I went by the house yesterday," she said, pouring herself a cup of coffee, hands still trembling.

I shifted closer, my heart racing as if I had danced for hours straight. "What happened?"

She shook her head. "That woman . . . there's something wrong with her."

We caught eyes for a second before sitting at a table by the window.

"She wouldn't let me in. Wouldn't tell me anything. I couldn't really see inside . . . but there was this little girl . . . standing in some dirty underwear. And that woman, she slammed the door in my face."

Tuesday smelled like pee, I thought with a gulp. "What did you do?"

"I called 911. I tried to get them to come by right away."

"Did they come? Did you see Monday?"

She shook her head. "Social services said an officer went by and everyone was accounted for."

"The officer saw Monday in the house?"

Her lips pursed. "That's what they say."

"You don't believe him?"

"I don't believe shit anyone says around here anymore," she mumbled. "I filed a report with CFSA. I don't care about breaking protocol. Someone has to do something."

Fear sharpened its claws on my rib cage, preparing to dig deeper into me.

"There's something else," Ms. Valente added. "Remember a time when Monday was out of school for a few weeks? Well . . . she wasn't sick."

My body suddenly felt hollow, everything inside turned to dust.

"Oh God."

"Two years ago," Ms. Valente said, talking in hushed

269

whispers, like the whole school was listening, "Monday, August, and her sisters were taken out of the house for neglect."

"Neglect? Like child abuse?"

"Neglect can mean a lot of things," she said, taking a long sip of her coffee. "But Mrs. Charles took some court-ordered parenting classes, which allowed her to regain custody. CFSA was supposed to do a follow-up visit, but I'm not sure if those visits were confirmed." She looked at me. "Did Monday ever mention . . . anything?"

I shook my head. "Naw."

"Nothing? Nothing about her mother? Was she scared of her?"

I shrugged. "I mean, who isn't scared of their mother?"

The corner of her mouth crept into the faintest grin.

"Yes, but more than normal," she pressed. "Can you think of anytime she was just *petrified*?"

My mind flashed back to the fight at school. The way Monday trembled in the principal's office. "We need to find her. Now."

"We can't barge into the woman's home and take her children. The authorities have to follow up."

I clutched my stomach, the room growing humid as more questions scratched at my throat.

"Do you think something . . . bad has happened to her?"

Ms. Valente placed her cup on the table.

"No. Oh God, no, Claudia. Nothing like that! I'm sure she's fine. She's . . . somewhere safe, but we just got to figure out where." She nodded a few times. "But you must promise me, Claudia, promise me that no matter what, you won't go near that house again. Between her, that report, and what I saw . . . I don't know . . . there's something about that woman . . . makes my skin crawl."

I nodded, knowing it was a promise I had no intention on keeping.

MARCH

March used to be my favorite month. Spring break happens in March. Good Friday and Easter sometimes happen in March. And my birthday happens in March.

April was supposed to be born in March. Instead, she popped out a whole two weeks later—on April Fool's Day no less, and she's been lying ever since. You never know what to expect with her. She falls somewhere between brownish yellow, amber, caramel, and copper with a shimmer of fairy dust.

Her color is gold, so similar to her mother, yet drastically different.

People melt, shift, and mold her into jewelry that they can wear when they want to feel regal. You're drawn to her solidness, strength, and pure beauty.

But when she is not gold, when her insides are hollowed to the point where there is nothing left, she can turn your skin green.

THE AFTER

Adele has a haunting voice. Unearthly. Triggering.

Instead of finishing Ms. Walker's work sheets in the library as promised, I stared out the window at the passing cars on Good Hope Road, holding one of my filter gels up to my face and letting the whole world turn mossy green. Michael helped download "All I Ask" on my iPod, and I listened to it on repeat, trying to find the pulse of the song.

She sings to the person she loves, knowing it's over, but begs for one last moment, questioning whether she'll love someone the same. At the end of the song, the tempo picks up, and Adele sings more desperately, pleading to hold on to one last memory of the way they were. I closed my eyes, envisioning it, trying to think of anyone I would beg for one more moment with, but only Monday came to mind.

I loved her. Well, I mean, not like that. I didn't love her in a way a girl loved a girl, like romantically. I loved her more like a soul mate loved a soul mate. Who makes up the rules for who your soul belongs to? But what if April was right? What if I didn't really know Monday? It'd explain why she'd leave me like this.

Something slammed on the table and jolted me out of the moment. Michael huffed, his book bag on the table, his face hardened. I gathered up my work sheets and stuffed them into my bag. "What are *you* doing here?"

He rolled his eyes. "You said you come here in the afternoons, right?"

"Yeah, but that wasn't an invitation," I shot back, feigning annoyance.

Michael slumped down into his seat, pinching the bridge of his nose. "Look, can we not do this today?"

I swallowed back the curse on my lip and played dumb. "Do what?"

"This," he snapped, waving between us. "This, where you pretend that everything's alright with you and that you don't want company when you *know* you do and me pretending I don't know what's wrong with you. Can we PLEASE just . . . not today!"

My mouth hung open as he ripped a history textbook out of his bag. "What's up?"

He stabbed his notebook a few times with his pen and sighed. "My dad wants to stay there. In Dubai."

"Oh," I said with a shrug until the weight of his words sank in. "Ohhhhhh!"

"Yeah. 'Oh' is right," he muttered. "He says the money is too good. And Mom could get a teaching job out there. He wants me to come visit him next month to look at schools."

"Wow," I muttered.

"And the worst part . . . they don't even have football out there!"

He slammed down his pen, leg shaking the table. No wonder, I thought. Football meant the world to him! I couldn't imagine moving to a place where I could never dance again.

"Well, what are you going to do?"

"Doesn't look like I have a choice. Mom already has her first phone interview next week."

Suddenly, it hit me. If he moved, I wouldn't have anyone left.

"You can't find anyone to stay with here?" I asked, grasping at straws.

Michael raised an eyebrow. "Stay with? You mean, like, live with?"

I nodded. "Yeah. There's a kid at my school that's staying with his aunt until he graduates. Can't you do the same? Move in with a family member until you finish school? What about your grandma?"

"My grandma?" Michael rubbed his chin. "Well, yeah. I guess I could ask her. But what about my parents?"

"You'll still see them! They'll visit you—you'll visit them. You'll all be happy."

Michael nodded for a few moments, then smiled. "Yeah, you're right. I'mma ask her. Thanks, Claudia. You got some good ideas cooking up there."

I laughed. "I've been told. And, by the way, you got the date wrong."

"Huh?"

"The date," I laughed. "You wrote down the wrong year."

Michael glanced down at his notebook and gulped.

"Oh! Yeah, yeah, you right. My bad," he said, ripping and crumbling the page out his book, then nodded at my book bag, one of my gels still poking out sloppily. "So what are you working on?"

Dread rolled up in my throat, thick and solid as cold gravy fat. "Nothing."

He gave me a knowing smile. "You know, there's this kid on my team who . . . well, goes to TLC at my school. They give him his own private tutor and everything. He does better on tests than the rest of us."

"What?"

"Those gel sheets," he admitted with a guilty shrug. "That stuff Grandma gives you. I've seen kids use that at school too."

My heart jerked and I sprung up. "Are you . . . Did you tell people?"

"What? Naw. Who am I going to tell?"

"Everybody! You know everybody!"

"Claudia, I swear. I wouldn't do that."

I shoved the rest of my stuff in my bag, tears brimming, humiliated that he now knew the one secret I worked so hard to keep from everyone.

Ms. Manis opened the studio on Saturday afternoons for freestyle, in preparation for our recital. The other girls never took advantage of the opportunity. Saturdays were meant for chilling with boys and friends. I didn't have those fun problems.

I leaned into a stretch, widening my legs to feel it deep in my hips. Happy to be alone in the one place I had real control. The one place my past couldn't touch me. The one place it didn't matter if I could read or not. A sanctuary from the outside world.

But you *can* read, a voice inside me said. I believed that voice the more I worked with Ms. Walker, read, and listened to books on tape. What scared me, though, was others . . . like Michael . . . thinking I couldn't. What he thought of me mattered.

I hooked my iPod to the speakers, setting "All I Ask" on repeat. I loved the opening. There's no warm-up—it jumps out the gate with a rumble. The harsh start helped my pacing. More familiar. But nothing about my dance screamed the elegancy it needed to. Instead of moving like water, I moved like a heavy rock.

"You have to smile." Her voice carried over the music and I spun to a stop. Megan leaned against the door frame, dressed in leggings and an oversized off-the-shoulder sweater, her gym bag slung on her arm.

"That's why you look so stiff," she chuckled. "You have to breathe and smile."

The moment someone tells me to breathe is the moment I notice the sharp pain in my chest when I'm not.

"And maybe if you relaxed your neck a little, and fell into the turn. Like this!"

She dropped the bag, slipping out of her sneakers, and galloped across the floor.

"Watch me, then you do it." She faced the mirror, elongating her neck, turning on the brightest smile, before rolling back her shoulders. She glided across the floor, spinning into a series of chaîné turns with her eyes closed, letting her neck surrender to it, the move smooth as silk.

"See? Easy. You try."

I nodded, shaking the nerves out of my arms and legs.

"Girl, you're already overthinking it," Megan laughed. "Loosen up! Ain't no one in here but us. Smile. Like a beauty queen!"

I grinned—showing all my teeth and fluttering my lashes.

"Yeah," she laughed. "Just like that."

We tried the turn ten more times, each time trying

280

to make each other laugh with silly smiles and dramatic movement. The turn became so natural I almost forgot why we were practicing it.

"Shit, what time is it?" Megan said, running over to her bag. "Ah, damn. I have to go!"

With a twinge of disappointment, I watched her slip on her sneakers, realizing I could have spent the whole afternoon laughing with her. I missed laughing.

"Hey, thanks for helping me. This was . . . fun."

"Fun? Ha! That was nothing," she said, focused on her laces until her head popped up. "Hey, what you doing tonight?"

I shrugged. "Nothing."

"I'm having a little sleepover at my house. You want to come?"

"Uh . . . sure. I got to ask my mom first."

"Cool. Here's the invite." She reached into her bag and handed me a folded-up piece of loose-leaf paper torn out of a binder with hearts and stars drawn around her address.

"See you later!" she called over her shoulder before running out the door.

"You're going to have so much fun," Ma said for the thousandth time during the car ride over to Megan's house. "Your first sleepover party!"

The moment I asked Ma about Megan's sleepover party

she flew into a frenzy. She ironed my pajamas, packed my teal overnight bag, even whipped up a fresh batch of chocolate chip cookies.

I changed my outfit three times before we left. This wasn't just some regular sleepover. This was a sleepover with high school girls—girls by default much flyer than me. But Megan invited me, so she must think I'm cool. Right?

"You know, maybe we could have a sleepover party for your birthday," Ma said, beaming at the thought. "And you can invite your new friends!"

"Really?"

"Yeah. It would be so much fun! A pajama jam!"

I'd never had a real birthday party before. That's the thing about having one friend: your experiences are limited.

"Well . . . if I have party, can Monday come?"

Ma's lips tightened, her eyes widening. "Claudia . . . we'll talk about that later."

I snuggled in my seat, unable to hide my smile. It would be the perfect test. Monday wouldn't *dare* miss my birthday. She loved birthdays more than Christmas. And if she did miss it, I would never speak to her again.

Ma pulled up to a town house in Northwest, just a few blocks from the convention center, and those first-day-of-school jitters marched their way up my spine like a parade of ants.

"Okay! Here we are! Just try to have a good time, Sweet Pea. Try to just be in the moment . . . and forget about everything else that's going on. Try to make new friends. Okay?"

What she really wanted to say: *Don't talk about Monday.* I nodded with a weak smile.

"Okay! Don't forget the cookies!"

My legs stiffened as I made my way up the porch steps. I heard the sounds of muffled music, laughter, and joy.

"Be in the moment. Smile," I whispered to myself. I took a deep breath and rang the bell. The door swung open. Bass and bright lights slapped my face.

Megan stood grinning. "Hey! You made it!"

"Hey," I said, my voice cracking. I'd forgotten how different she looked out of her dance gear—hair down, straightened, wearing tight jeans and a white tank top.

"Come on in!"

I turned and waved at Ma. Even in the dark car you could see her glowing grin as she waved back before I stepped inside.

"What's all this?" Megan chuckled, pointing at the enormous Tupperware bin in my hands, my pillow tucked under my armpit, and my overnight bag weighing down my shoulder.

"My mommy made us cookies," I said, wincing as soon at the words flew out my mouth. My mommy? What am I, five?

"Aye, cool! Well, pizza just got here. Hope you like Papa John's."

She grabbed the Tupperware out of my hand and I followed her into a living room with a huge mocha L-shaped sofa, a big flat-screen TV hanging up above the fireplace, and African oil paintings in gold frames hanging up on cobalt-blue walls.

"Hey, y'all, Claudia's mom made us some cookies!"

Some familiar faces looked up from their spots on the plush rug.

"Claudia, you know Shannon and Katherine from dance. Outside, we call Katherine Kit Kat."

"Hey, Claudia!" they said in unison, and giggled, flipping through magazines, stuffing their mouths with pepperoni slices.

"And that's Paris. She goes to school with us."

Paris sat on the sofa, playing with an iPod hooked up to a speaker. She had copper-brown hair that complimented her creamy cocoa skin and specks of freckles.

"Hi," I said, trying to match their enthusiasm. Maybe they were messing around with makeup, like Monday and I used to do, but they looked almost too polished—extra grown-up. While they were all in jeans and T-shirts, I somehow felt underdressed in my light purple sweatpants and matching hoodie.

Megan handed me two slices while Shannon switched to Chris Brown's album and joined us on the floor.

"Anyways, so like I was saying, that boy just trying to get in them drawers," Shannon said to Paris.

"And?" Paris snapped with a smirk. "So what? I'm trying to get some too!"

The girls laughed as I picked over my pizza.

"Naw, you see the way he all over her *all* the time," Kit
Kat said, stuffing her mouth. "That boy love her."

Megan rolled her eyes. "Yeah, I've seen him look at a
few chicks like that too. All I'm saying, if you gonna do it,
you wanna do it with . . . someone special. Someone who
makes you feel, I don't know, safe. Someone who's good."

Shannon bumped her with her shoulder. "Like Kam?"

Megan smiled coyly. "Yeah."

Paris shook her head. "But that's how I feel with Andre!"

Kit Kat groaned. "Fine! But you could at least play hard
to get or something. Dang!"

The girls laughed, and I giggled along with nothing to
contribute to the conversation. My experience with boys
was limited to my imagination and what Monday had told
me. Which wasn't much.

It didn't take long for the girls to devour the entire tub
of cookies, washing it down with Pepsi. I tried to keep up
with the conversations—the boys they liked, the girls they
didn't—but they talked so fast my head began to ache.

"Okay, which one of you bitches want to do my nails?"
Shannon asked, pulling a bunch of nail polishes out of her
book bag.

"Me!" I yelped.

Shannon's face tightened. "Uhhh . . . okay."

I grabbed a magazine sitting on the coffee table and scooted over to make room.

"Um . . . you sure you know what you doing? 'Cause I need my nails to look good for . . . later."

Shannon and Megan exchanged a weird glance.

I smiled. "I got you. What color you want?"

"Hmm . . . this one," she said, passing a bottle of mint green.

I started with her right hand, the others observing every stroke of paint.

Kit Kat cleared her throat with a grin. "So, Claudia . . . I heard you were running after April Charles at the game or whatever."

I swallowed, holding my hand steady. I looked up at Megan for help, but she only blinked. Of course. She must have seen me almost get trampled to death following April.

"Um . . . she's my best friend's sister."

You could hear a pin drop, the way they all froze in shock—as if they couldn't imagine me having a best friend. Kit Kat glanced at Megan, raising an eyebrow.

"So . . . y'all cool like that or whatever?" Shannon said, blowing one hand dry.

"Not . . . really." It wasn't a lie. Like Michael said, we weren't friends.

"Good. 'Cause she a 'ho."

Kit Kat snorted.

"Girl, chill," Megan said, laughing.

"What? I ain't telling her nothing she didn't know before. And if she didn't, it's better to hear it from us! Right?"

Megan shook her head and sighed. "What she's trying to say is, well, if you get seen with her . . . people gonna think you just like her. You know, like, birds of a feather flock together."

"And you don't want to be nothing like that bird," Kit Kat mumbled.

Megan shook her head. "Damn, Kat."

"What? A 'ho is a 'ho is a 'ho. I ain't gonna sugarcoat shit to make it easier for her to swallow!"

"And we all know you know how to swallow," Shannon cackled, flicking her tongue at her.

The girls laughed and my stomach clenched, thoughts crashing into one another. Is it okay to hang out with girls who talk trash about my best friend's sister? Shouldn't I be defending her? I mean, what would Monday do if she were here?

But she's not here.

She stepped out of our bubble, straight abandoned me when I needed her most. What if Daddy was right? What if she just didn't want to be my friend anymore? What would I get out of defending her bullying sister?

So I joined them, letting out a nervous laugh, pretending to be a part of their inside joke, just to belong. I missed belonging to *something*.

Shannon examined her nails. "Damn, you're pretty good."

"You want a design or something on them?" I asked.

"For real? Hell yeah!"

I took out my travel nail kit, packed in the small pocket of my overnight bag. I always did Monday's nails during sleepovers, so in my head it made sense to bring it. The room fell silent as they watched me add gold dots on every other nail with my paint pen.

"Aight. All done!"

"Wow," Shannon gasped. "Yo, this is so hot!"

"Who taught you how to do nails like this?" Paris asked, carefully admiring Shannon's hand while Kit Kat rotated the other. "This is better than the shop."

"Taught myself. It's easy once you get used to it."

"Ooo! Do me next?" Kit Kat jumped up.

"Then me!" Megan said.

For the next hour, we talked more about boys, music, and celebrity gossip. We laughed until soda spit out of our noses while I finished everyone's nails—Megan, red with black dots like a ladybug; Kit Kat, pink with silver stripes like a candy cane; Paris, French manicure with a coffee base and black tips.

Suddenly, quick steps rushed down the stairs. A woman dressed in hospital scrubs with a short jet-black bob—the spitting image of Megan—sped through the living room.

"Ladies, I'm off. I expect my kitchen to be clean in the morning," the woman said, busy digging through a junky purse.

"Yes, Ms. Forte," the girls responded in unison.

"And no playing on my—" She finally noticed me and smiled. "Oh! And who is this beautiful lady?"

"This is Claudia, from dance." Megan beamed, shooting out her hand. "Look! She did my nails!"

"Hi, Claudia from dance. Nice to meet you," she chuckled, examining Megan's fingertips. "Very nice."

"Nice to meet you too, ma'am."

"Lord, please don't call me ma'am. Makes me feel old." She winked at me as she slipped on her coat. "Okay, Meg, I'll see you in the morning."

"Ooo, Mom! Could you make us pancakes in the morning?"

"Please?" the girls begged behind me.

She laughed. "If I'm not too tired, I'll see what I can do. Later, ladies."

"Where's your mom going?" I whispered.

"She's a nurse at Howard Hospital. Night shift," Megan said, then waved at the door. "Bye, Mom!"

"Bye, Mrs. Forte!" the girls said in unison like a chorus of bells.

"Have fun, girls," she said, closing the door behind her.

The room went deathly still before everyone leaped up and scattered.

"Okay, y'all, we got fifteen minutes," Megan ordered, packing up the pizza box, careful not to smudge her nails.

"For what?" I said.

Shannon and Paris stripped off their T-shirts and jeans, standing boldly in their lacy red and turquoise push-up bras.

"I can't believe I fit in my mom's bras now," Shannon said to Paris, cupping her breast. "Crazy, right?"

I turned so I wouldn't stare. Kit Kat changed into a white crop top. Her belly button was pierced with a silver hoop and a dangling diamond-encrusted star.

"Told you they would," Paris said, slipping into a low-cut black dress. "But those regular Victoria's Secret bras are so expensive. That's why I only buy Pink. Oh dag! Meg, can I borrow your lipstick? I left mine."

"Yeah, you know where it's at," Megan said, changing into a tight burgundy striped tank dress. She hiked up her boobs so they sat right at the neckline.

"And bring down the flat iron," Kit Kat said, grinning at me. "I wanna hook up her hair."

"What's . . . going on?" I asked.

Megan smiled. "We didn't want to tell you 'cause . . . we just wanted to make sure you were cool."

"Kit Kat brought you some clothes to borrow since y'all almost the same size," Paris added.

Kit Kat dug into her book bag and passed me a skirt and a black top. "These should fit."

"I got the iron," Paris said, running back downstairs, her thick lips now rosy pink.

"Hurry up, we only got ten minutes before the cab gets here."

"Where we going?"

Megan plopped in front of me, grinning wide, and pulled out her makeup kit.

"To a party."

A breeze hit my bare stomach as I stepped out of the cab parked in front of a cream-and-brick two-story home in Hyattsville, Maryland, not far from the PG County Mall. I recognized the route as we drove. Daddy would kill me if he found me roaming out here without him.

Especially dressed like *this*.

The crop top Kit Kat let me borrow might as well have been a bra, and the skirt sat so short I'd only have to bend slightly before an ass cheek popped out. I begged to keep my jean jacket so I would have pockets to stash my money and lip gloss, but really so I wouldn't feel naked.

Following the low thud of music, I trailed behind a grinning Megan, heading around to the back. Paris, Kit Kat, and Shannon strutted like supermodels—hair, outfits, faces flawless. I stumbled down the concrete path in Megan's high-heeled boots like a clown on stilts.

The music grew louder as we approached a door under the back deck. A guy stood in front with his eyebrow raised. Megan whispered a few words in his ear as he gave us a once-over, eyes falling on me. He probably could see through my caked foundation, glued-on lashes, and ruby-red lipstick and just KNEW I didn't belong. Panicking, I grabbed my compact and checked to make sure my edges were straight, flashing him a smile. He nodded at Megan before letting us in. We clunked down the steep steps to a smoky low-ceilinged basement, full of kids just like us. Well, not like me, but older kids—high school kids. They stood in thick clusters, drinking, laughing, grinding on each other. But the room came to a standstill when we entered, as if they had all zeroed in on the one outsider in the room: me.

A boy, tall, with brown skin and a splash of freckles on his cheeks, moved through the crowd in our direction, his expressionless eyes locked on us. He's about to kick me out, I thought, taking an unsteady step toward the door.

"Hey, babe," he said to Paris, roping his arms around her waist and pulling her into a tight hug. They kissed. And I don't mean a regular kiss. I mean, they were kissing like they could drown in each other. I kept my eyes on the floor to keep from staring. Megan smirked, bumping me with her shoulder.

"Sorry I'm late," Paris cooed.

"That's okay. I missed you today."

Paris gazed up at him. "I missed you too."

Kit Kat faked a gag. "Come on, let's get a drink."

We made our way through the packed room, all eyes on us. I focused on keeping my balance as a million questions ran through my head: Who are all these kids? Whose house is this? Do their parents know they dress like this? And do any of them know my parents and will they tell on me?

On the table in the corner sat rows of half-empty bottles of brown liquor, a bag of melting ice, and a stack of red cups. Kit Kat and Megan went to work mixing drinks.

"What's this?" I asked as Megan shoved a cup in my hand.

"It's good. Just try it!"

Kit Kat sucked her teeth. "Don't be a baby."

"I ain't no baby," I snapped with a cold stare.

"Yeah? Then prove it," she spat, flicking the cup.

Be in the moment, Claudia.

I licked my lips, closed my eyes, and took a big gulp. The lukewarm liquor ran down my throat like a thousand knives, and I held back a cough.

"See, told you she was cool," Megan said, nudging Kit Kat. "She's too pretty to be all uptight."

Kit Kat laughed. "Whatever."

They giggled, the way Monday and I used to, which made me only want to drink more to erase the memories.

"What the hell are you doing here?"

I flinched, spitting out my drink. His rough voice could have brought the whole party to a stop. Michael stood behind me, so close I had to step back to look up at him. His eyes went wide as he stared down at my bare stomach. What is he doing here? This wasn't his crowd at all.

"Um . . . I—"

"We brought her," Megan said, looping her arm through mine.

Michael clenched his cup. "Megan, you crazy to bring her up in here," he seethed. "You know she ain't ready for all this!"

"And she ain't never gonna be ready if everybody keep on babying her," Megan snapped back. "How long y'all gonna keep her in the dark?"

He rolled his eyes, turning to me. "Your mom know you're here?"

Shannon raised an eyebrow, mouthing an "oh shit" to Megan and Kit Kat. Michael's only a year older than me, yet I felt caught red-handed by Daddy. How dare he try to embarrass me in front of everybody!

"Does *your* mom know you're here? Or your dad, wherever he is," I snapped. "I mean, dang! Why you sweating me?"

Michael's mouth dropped as if I punched him in the throat. He shook his head before storming off to some friends hanging by the DJ. Guilt crept in quick. Maybe I went too far.

Megan smirked as if reading my mind. "He'll be fine. Come on, let's chill over here."

We sat on a smelly gray sofa under the basement steps next to Paris, Andre, and a couple of his friends. The party was cranking, folks laughing and dancing, when it hit me: I'm at a high school party! How would I tell Monday about this? About my hair, my makeup, the nasty brown drink in my cup making my body tingle.

Michael stayed in the corner, his eyes flicking in my direction every thirty seconds. I shouldn't have been so mean to him. Talking about his dad was a low blow. But I didn't need a babysitter.

"He's all worried about you," Megan whispered. "He's feeling you."

"Naw, we just friends from church," I said with a laugh, trying to downplay it. The same way he always downplayed me. "He thinks he's my big brother or something."

She rolled her eyes. "Well, he don't act that way with other girls at school. And they all over him."

I snuck a glance of him in the corner. *Other girls?*

"What . . . what you mean?"

"I mean, girls be trying to get with him. But he don't pay them no mind. Not like you." She took another greedy sip. "When you get to high school, all the boys are gonna want you."

My heart fluttered like bee wings. "You think so?"

"Yeah, 'cause you're real pretty. That's probably why he's trying to claim you early."

The DJ turned up the music a little louder. An

"Ooooo . . ." came from the crowd, everyone feeling the vibe. Those standing around piled in the center of the room.

"Y'all, come on," Megan said, pulling us all off the couch.

At first everyone did their own thing, but then a boy jumped in the middle, doing dances that Monday and I had perfected months ago.

"I could do that," I laughed, the liquor letting all kinds of words slip out my mouth.

"Girl, what you waiting for, then?" Kit Kat shouted, pushing me into the middle.

"No! I . . ."

With her hard shove I slammed right into the boy. He smirked, popping in my face, and I laughed. He thinks he's really doing something, I thought. Let me show him how it's done!

With the alcohol, I felt lighter somehow, a weight lifted off my back. And that's when I started to move. I mean, really move, hitting every step. The boy and I battled, folks cheering us on.

"Get it, Claudia!" Megan screamed over the music. Just like that, I'm back in my living room, in my bubble with Monday, feeling alive. Next, the DJ put on a go-go track and everyone joined us in the chop shop. The song ended with cheers and high fives all around. Megan hugged me, laughing like crazy as we kept dancing. And as happy as

I felt, I couldn't help thinking that Monday had always wanted to be a part of this crowd. She wanted this life. And here I am, living it without her.

"Damn, you so sexy when you dance," a deep voice said behind us.

Megan's back straightened before she spun around. "Oh my God! You came!"

Kam grinned and she jumped into his arms.

"I thought you couldn't make it," Megan said, her face red and sweaty.

They started kissing and swaying slow. I felt silly standing there watching them, but I didn't know where else to go. The girls were back on the sofa with the boys, kissing. I mean, REALLY kissing, tongues in each other's mouths, hands up shirts, touching their mother's bras. So I stayed on the floor, next to Megan and Kam. I kept dancing, lost in the music until some boy pushed up behind me, holding my hips. I froze, looking to Megan for help. She nodded and mouthed an "it's okay."

It's cool; this is what girls do at parties, I told myself, and kept dancing—with a boy I couldn't see, the alcohol making my waist wind faster. The boy pulled me tighter to him, heat pulsing off his chest. And it felt . . . well . . . good. Like I could dance all night with him. My heart raced, wondering if it was Michael moving on me like this, touching me like this. Bet I'm not just some church girl now!

I glanced over in the corner at Michael talking to some girl with long gold braids. Smiling all in her face. Didn't he care some guy was rubbing on my booty, breathing all hard in my ear?

"Damn, I didn't know you could do it like *this*," the guy whispered over my shoulder, and my entire body hiccupped before I wiggled out of his grip.

Jacob.

"What's up?" he said with a smirk, reaching for my waist again. I shoved him, disgusted. How could I have let him feel up on me like that? How could I have betrayed Monday? My stomach heaved, and I raced to the back, cupping my mouth. I needed a bathroom.

"Claudia, wait, hold up," he called, chasing after me. "We gotta talk."

"We ain't got nothing to talk about. You did my friend dirty!"

He scanned the room, checking if anyone overheard me. But with the party popping, no one paid us any mind. He gently held my arm, pulling me toward an open room in the back.

"Come here for a sec, I gotta tell you the truth."

I snatched my arm back, fumbling, the liquor making my body extra light.

"You think I'm stupid? I ain't going anywhere with you, so you can turn around and say we did something! And I ain't never gon' do something with your bamma ass."

Jacob huffed, steadying a hand on the wall in the hallway so I couldn't pass him. "What you doing here anyways?"

"I'm chilling with my friends!"

"You mean Megan and them? Really?"

"Why you say it like that?" I snapped.

"No reason! My brother just all in love with her, so I guess she's aight."

I peeked over his shoulder at Megan, dancing with Kam, both lost in each other's eyes.

"Your brother? Kam's your brother?"

He chuckled. "Yeah. We got different dads, but we still brothers."

No wonder I thought he looked so familiar. "But . . . Kam's a good guy! And you're . . ."

Jacob's face tightened. "Man, whatever."

I swallowed. "You said something about you were gonna tell me the truth. What'd you mean by that?"

Jacob rolled his eyes. "Aight, look. Me and Monday . . . we DID do something." He took a deep breath. "She . . . sucked my dick. I didn't really want it to happen, it just kinda . . . did."

"Ew, that's nasty! You lying!"

"I swear on my moms, she did! She just kept saying she really wanna be together, was trying to come in my house and stuff all the time . . . My moms said she was too fast."

That word *fast* stuck out like a thorn threatening to pop

my bubble. No way. Monday would never do something like that. Right?

"And then you turn around and told everybody we were lesbians!"

He sighed, stuffing his hands in his pockets. "My brother said it was foul, what I said about y'all, so I went by her house to apologize. But her mom kirked out on me, chased me down the block! Guess I know why now."

"Wait, you went to her house? When?"

"You know, right after school ended. I thought I'd see her on the courts for the league games or maybe at the rec center, since she took those swim lessons, but I didn't see her all summer." His eyes went blank for a moment, as if thinking back. "Then school started, and then . . . she was gone."

My foggy brain tried to catch everything he threw at me with slippery fingers. *Rec center? Swimming?*

"She never hung out at the rec center," I mumbled.

His faced screwed up. "You kidding? She was there almost every day."

He's lying, I thought. But it was hard to ignore the way his eyes went childlike talking about her.

"Man, I be thinking about what happened . . . all the time now." He sighed, shaking his head. "You miss her, right?"

I swayed like breeze hitting a tree, my body weightless.

"Aye. Claudia, you aight?" Jacob asked, grabbing my

arm to stop me from falling.

"What's going on over here?" Michael stood behind me like a big-ass shadow, his voice booming. Jacob had to arch his neck just to look at him.

"Nothing," Jacob muttered, letting go of me. "We were just talking."

Michael gave him a once-over. He cracked his knuckles against his side, putting a hand on my shoulder. "Come on. Let's get you some water."

I nodded, ready to run away from Jacob and the thoughts that had my head spinning. As we walked off, I yelled over my shoulder, "Don't even think about telling people we danced together at this party!"

Jacob rolled his eyes. "Yeah, yeah."

Michael raised an eyebrow, leading me out of the hallway back to the makeshift bar. I didn't notice the cooler full of waters and sodas underneath the table before. He passed me a bottle of water and grabbed a Coke for himself. We leaned against the wall near the DJ, staying out of the way of folks.

"So. You chillin' with these girls now?" he asked, his voice hard.

"Why everyone so surprised? I mean, damn! You so busy worrying about me, why *you* here?"

He squirmed. "Teammates came. I couldn't just say no."

"Well, my dance-mates came, and I couldn't just say no!"

He smirked. "Dance-mates not a real word."

I smiled back at him, leaning into his arm, my balance off.

"Claudia . . . about the other day when . . ." He looked around the room. "Well, you know. I was just trying to make you feel better. I didn't want you feeling . . . different. You're just like everybody else."

I stared up into his chocolate eyes, melting in their sweetness but distracted by a strange hush that came over the room. Everyone gawked at the door as a thick group of guys entered, their eyes low and a cloud of smoke hanging above their heads. The energy in the room collapsed; even the music turned down, replaced by loud whispers. And walking right behind them was April. For the first time, we had similar wardrobes—crop top, skirt, boots, and huge gold hoops. Her hair in a high, frizzy bun, lips dark pink and glossy. Even at a party, she still seemed out of place. Megan whispered in Kam's ear and glanced at me.

The guys headed for the drinks, everyone shuffling out of their way. April followed, holding a defiant face, pretending the entire room wasn't staring at her.

Jacob scooted next to me. "Lynch mob boys. What they doing here?"

"I don't know," I grumbled, rolling my eyes. Of all the places, why he got to stand by me?

The dudes lit up blunts, heckling the other kids. No one felt like dancing anymore.

"How the fuck we gonna get rid of these bammas?"

302

someone whispered behind us.

"Cuz, we ain't going nowhere!" one of the guys barked, and the room stiffened.

"We should go," Michael whispered, hovering closer. "Before this gets ugly."

April fidgeted, bouncing on the balls of her feet, a ticking time bomb.

"Is she fucking all of them?" a girl whispered, but loud enough for April to hear.

"Girl, I don't know," another girl whispered back. "You know how them bobblehead broads from Ed Borough be."

April seemed calm, but her eyes looked wildly for an escape. Desperate, she pulled at one of the guys' jacket, mumbling something to him. He shook his head, waving her off. She tapped him again, this time more determined.

"Bitch, I said not now!" he snapped, and the room froze.

April reeled back as if shot in the face, bumping into a girl behind her. And that's when she spotted me standing against the wall—standing next to Jacob. Her eyes flicked between us. My stomach sank to the floor.

"Oh shit," I breathed.

Her eyes narrowed and she bolted for the door.

She's going to tell Monday I was at a party without her. With Jacob! She'll never speak to me again! I had to stop her.

I skipped around Michael, rushing through the sweaty bodies, up the stairs, and busting out the door.

"April!" I screamed, the cold air smacking against my moist skin. I stumbled down the path. "April, wait!"

April froze midstride, her shoulders dropping before she turned to face me. "Yeah, what?"

Alone outside, my blurry eyes could barely make her out in the darkness.

"April! Please don't tell Monday," I begged, slurring. "I didn't know . . . about all this."

April frowned, as if she had no clue who I was talking about before rolling her eyes. "Yeah, fine. I won't," she mumbled.

"Naw, for real, April. Please!"

"I said I won't, so I won't. Dang!"

I tried to rub warmth into my arms. Bad move running outside without a coat.

"Well . . . you think she can come to my birthday party?"

April frowned before snarling, "What?"

"I'm going to have a birthday party and I want her to come. Daddy can pick her up from her dad's . . . or her aunt's house, and then she can sleep over and go back or whatever."

April stepped closer to me, her glassy eyes transfixed, as if trying to look inside my head. Then she laughed. Not a funny laugh, more sinister one.

"Oh my God! Are you serious? I can't believe we still doing this." She blew foggy air and shook her head.

"Claudia, Monday's not coming."

Her tone should have marked the end of the conversation but I kept going.

"Please, it's just for . . ."

"She's not coming! Don't you get that?"

I swallowed my pleas whole and almost choked on them.

"You got some fucking nerve," she spat, her bitterness thick. "You didn't want her to go or do anything without you. Just wanted to be shut up in your house together. Now look at you! At a party, drinking and shit. Talking about throwing a party, when all you ever did was hold her back. From everything!"

Suddenly, my bubble felt like a greenhouse, the air sticky and smothering. She was right. I held Monday close like a toy I wasn't willing to share. I needed her more than she ever needed me.

"I . . . know," I admitted, my hands twisting together. "And I'm sorry. But can't I just talk to her and tell her that?"

April shook her head. "Monday's. Not. Coming. She ain't never coming back!"

"But why?" I wanted to scream. I needed to know why my best friend in the whole wide world wanted nothing to do with me. Tears hiccupped in my throat but I held them back. I refused to give up.

"My daddy talked to your daddy," I blurted out.

April swallowed, her jaw tightening. "Yeah. So?"

"So . . . he ain't seen y'all in a year."

She laughed that same evil cackle. "Three years. I ain't seen him in three years."

I bit my lip, feeling myself losing the fight. "And! I know Monday didn't have the flu."

This fact hit her in the gut somehow, her mouth dropping. The cold wrapped around us and smelled like snow.

She shook her head. "Dang, Claudia, why can't you just let. This. Go?"

"Let me talk to her and I will."

April stared through me, then shook her head.

"Fine," she groaned. "Guess they ain't leaving me no choice *but* to tell you."

My knees almost gave in. "Tell me what—"

"Claudia!"

I spun around as Michael burst through the basement door.

"Dang, I'm fine! I'm talking to . . ."

But April had disappeared, vanished like a ghost in the darkness.

"Shit," I mumbled.

Michael eyes drifted from the spot where she once stood, to my exposed stomach, then back up to my face.

"What was that all about?"

"Nothing."

He chuckled, crossing his arms. "You following her again?"

"What d'you want me to say? I've known April my whole life. She's like a big sister . . . or something. How people expect me to act like I don't know her? Ignoring her is stupid! You think I'm stupid?"

Michael blinked, then without warning he took two strides and pulled me into a hug. Not the type of hug I've seen him give other girls—with one limp arm around the neck, a Christian space apart, lasting less than two seconds. No, it was the type of hug that started with two strong hands, fingers crawling around my waist, gripping tight, pulling me up against his chest, before resting at my tail-bone. The type of hug that feels like diving into a warm bed, wrapped in down blankets, snuggling to the softest pillow in the world. The type of hug that says something, but what?

"You're right. I'm sorry," he said, his breath tickling the back of my ear before gently pulling away. "That's like, if I see someone from church at school, I always say what's up. I ain't gonna act like I don't know them." His hand cupped my cheek. "You're not stupid at all. I'm just . . . making sure you're okay."

His lips were so close it would've taken nothing for him to inch forward and kiss me. And I wanted him to. I wanted him to kiss me. But how could I ask him for something like that? You don't just go around asking boys to kiss you. Do you?

"Hey. You're shaking," he said with a small smile. "You want to go inside?"

No. I didn't want to go inside with all those people. I wanted to be alone, with him. Drinking hot chocolate, talking about music, laughing . . . my lips inched closer just as Michael brushed his against mine before he crashed into me.

No one ever tells you kissing is like an explosion of colors, bright and blinding.

Michael pushed me up against the side of the house, pressing into me, heat radiating off his chest. His tongue tasted like Coke, soft and warm.

"Dang, I've wanted to do this for a long time," he breathed as he dove in again. I wrapped my arms around him, thoughts speeding by too fast to fully process.

I'm kissing a boy, Monday! I'm kissing a boy. Just like you!

But it didn't feel right. It felt sloppy, like coloring outside the lines. Isn't this what I'm supposed to do? Monday did it. Monday did more than this. Shouldn't I do the same?

I gripped his arms and flipped him around, pushing him against the wall. His eyes widened, mouth dropping.

"Hey, what are you doing?" he chuckled nervously.

I took a deep breath before dropping down on my shaky knees, the ground cold.

"Whoa . . . Claudia."

As I reached for his belt buckle, Michael gently pushed my hands away and held my wrist.

"No, Claudia, stop!"

But I didn't want to stop. If I do this, they'll stop calling me a lesbian, a baby, stuck up. If I do this, I'll catch up to Monday. I won't be left behind.

"Claudia! Are you out here?" I heard Megan calling from the door.

The snap in her voice shook me out of daze. I fell back on my butt with a gasp, scraping my elbow on the concrete.

"Shit! Are you okay?" Michael asked, reaching for me.

The fog of blinding bright colors lifted. What the hell am I doing? Out in this cold, being no better than April in that classroom. I pushed Michael away, running back into the basement.

ONE YEAR BEFORE THE BEFORE

The picture vanished, but the memory remained. By the time the cherry blossoms started to bloom along the river, I felt a distance, a space stark blinding white, between Monday and me. Monday pretended the rumors didn't bother her while I pretended not to notice the stretch of time between phone calls and her need to go home after school rather than the library.

For weeks, she'd acted strange. Quiet, reserved. Some days, she wouldn't even show up to school, and when she did, she'd gobble down two plates in the cafeteria, sipping from every water fountain she passed, in crumpled clothes, her hair a lopsided mess.

The few times she did come over, we practiced our

dance routines, but as Ms. Manis would say, her dancing missed a passion, a soul.

And all I kept thinking was, what is happening to us?

THE AFTER

On the morning after the party, they found a body.

"Hello, I'm Christine Madden with your top headline story. Two joggers found the remains of a young girl, partially buried in the heavily wooded area of Leakin Park, in Baltimore, earlier today. The identification of the victim is yet to be determined. Investigators are currently on the scene, canvassing the area. No arrests have been made. . . ."

"Mom," Megan grumbled from under the covers on the living room floor. "Can you turn the TV down? Dang!"

Curled under a blanket next to her, listening to Ms. Forte's slippers scraping against the kitchen tiles, I replayed my first kiss a billion times over, oozing with embarrassment.

"Y'all better wake up if you want these pancakes," Ms. Forte called.

"Oooh yes! Pancakes!" Kit Kat jumped up from the couch. "I'm starving."

I sat up, my brain thumping against my skull. The cab had had to pull over twice so I could throw up. Too much of that brown stuff. Megan had done her best to clean me up, worried if I did it in the house, her mom would know. We'd brushed our teeth and gargled before heading to bed. I couldn't have been asleep more than twenty minutes before I heard the TV snap on in the kitchen.

"What they talking about, Ms. Forte?" Kit Kat asked.

"They found a girl buried in some park in Baltimore."

"Ugh . . . just another body found in *Body*more," Shannon chuckled.

"Yeah, but this is different. Police won't let this one slide, no way."

"You okay?" Megan asked, checking me over.

I nodded, still nauseous, my stomach left with nothing to purge.

"Bread will help," she said. "That's why I asked Mom to make us pancakes."

"You do that a lot?"

"Ha! No way," she whispered with a grin. "Don't want to be one of 'those' chicks. Right?"

In the kitchen, her mom set a plate of sausages on the table next to a stack of pancakes, and a pitcher of orange juice. I gulped down two glasses of ice water, my throat dry as sand.

"Well, y'all look like you had a long night," she chuckled.

"Yeah. We stayed up late watching Netflix," Megan said, sitting at the head of the table.

Ms. Forte frowned over her cup of coffee. "Claudia, what's that stuff on your face?"

I rubbed my eyes, smudging black crayon on my fingertips. I forgot to wash my face.

Megan's eyes widened before she forced a grin. "We were doing makeovers."

"Well, make sure you take that stuff off before your mom picks you up."

"Yes, ma'am," I uttered just as Megan's cell phone rang. Megan jumped up, grabbing it off the charger.

"Hello? Yeah, who this? Ohhh, hey. Hold on a second." Megan's eyes flicked over to me, biting her lips, holding back a massive grin. "Michael is on the phone for you."

The girls shared glances as I jumped up, grabbing the phone from a giggling Megan, and rushed into the living room.

"Hello?"

"Hey," Michael said, his voice unsure.

"Hey," I mumbled.

"So . . . um . . . are you okay?"

"Um, yeah."

"Oh. Well, you weren't at church this morning, and the way you left . . . I was just checking."

I vaguely remembered stumbling out of the basement with the girls and being pushed into a cab, but that's about it.

"I slept over Megan's house. Ma is picking me up later."

"Yeah. Your mom invited me over for dinner tonight."

I glanced over my shoulder at the girls sitting at the table—still giggling.

"Oh. So, are you coming?"

"You want me to?"

My heart sped up and I bit back a grin. "Yeah."

"Cool," he said, a lightness in his voice. "I'll be there around six."

At least ten seconds of awkward silence passed.

"Um, Michael . . . about last night . . . I mean, that wasn't . . ."

"Don't worry about it," he chuckled. "Too much to drink. We're friends, right?"

I swallowed the lump in the back of my throat. "Uh, yeah. Right."

"Cool. So, see you later?"

"Yeah, later," I mumbled, hanging up the phone. Had I imagined it all? The way he held me . . . I swore he *wanted* to kiss me too. Maybe I moved too fast. Fast like Monday. Was Jacob telling the truth?

I took a deep breath, heading back into the kitchen, my thoughts spinning.

"So . . . what he want?" Kit Kat said, biting into her last sausage.

"He was just checking on me," I said, keeping it vague, but my cheeks were on fire.

"So, you guys together now?" Shannon pressed.

"Naw. We just . . . friends from church."

"Girl, no boys in my choir check up on me when I don't make service," Kit Kat said.

I rolled my eyes, holding back a smirk. "Whatever."

"He likes you," Megan said, grinning.

My heart fluttered, heat trying to burst through my skin.

THE BEFORE

On the last day of March, I zipped up my coat with trembling fingers and walked over heaps of blackened snow, through the chilly winds spiraling off the highways toward Ed Borough. All day at school, I practiced what I would do and say to her. But my tongue began to stick to the top of my mouth as if painted with crazy glue, my voice hiding in my boots next to my cold feet.

During the summers, the basketball courts are a tightly packed circus for the summer league games. Folks from all over in the DC, Maryland, Virginia (DMV) area squeeze on the bleachers, spilling out into the streets. While the sun sets behind the Ed Borough houses, teams play under orange or starry skies for a cheering crowd. Ed Borough is rich and alive with lights, color, and music. But during the winters, it's like an abandoned lot, mounds of snow layering the ground, the hoops covered in icicles.

A group of boys chilled on the corner by the far entrance of rec center, and Darrell's throaty laugh echoed across the court. Maybe he's seen her, maybe he can point me in the direction of someone who has, I thought as I hiked across the snowy ground, passing a lone girl in a hooded jacket sitting on the empty bleachers, her back turned to me. I almost made it to the gate before she called my name.

"Claudia?"

April yanked off her hood, eyes almost falling out their sockets.

"What . . . what are you doing here?"

Determination sizzled. "I'm looking for Monday."

At that moment, whatever monster living inside April that would normally have popped off seemed to shrivel up and die, leaving her so drained of energy even her voice sounded lifeless.

"You know you ain't supposed to be around here. Aren't you scared your *mommy* is gonna find you out?" She gave me a once-over—from my shoes to the ribbon holding my bun. "Damn, your hair's been looking a mess without Monday doing it for you."

Insults. She always starts with them. I squared my shoulders and stuck out my chest. I couldn't let her rattle me.

"I ain't got much time. Where's Monday?"

She sighed, leaning back, in no hurry to move, then called over her shoulder.

"Hey, Darrell! Come over here for a second."

Darrell spotted me with April and jogged over, smiling.

"Hey, Claudia. What you doing around here?" he asked, his nose stuffy from standing out in the cold.

April smirked. "Darrell, didn't you fuck my sister?"

Darrell's face went blank, all the color draining. "Damn, April," he said, sucking his teeth. "Why you gotta go tell everybody?" he grumbled, kicking a plastic bottle by his shoe.

I switched my weight to my back leg to keep from falling over. Darrell met my glare, then took off running. April slapped her thigh, tickled with herself.

"She wouldn't have had sex with that bamma," I seethed. "He just wishing he did. She would have told me."

She chuckled. "No she wouldn't. She couldn't!"

"Why?" The words came out desperate.

"'Cause you too stuck up! Monday told me how all you wanted to do was stay in the house with your bougie parents, coloring and playing with dolls like some little kid. If she'd told you, all you would have done is judged her."

April liked using her teeth to rip holes in my heart. I tilted my chin up, refusing to let her scare me away.

"Look, I came here to find Monday and I ain't leaving until I do."

April stared at me, her face blank. She sighed and

climbed off the bleachers, dusting off her butt.

"Come on, then. They gonna kick us out soon anyway. You might as well see it."

"See what?"

She stuffed her hands in her pockets and headed out the gate without answering. I followed a few paces behind her as we cut through two rows of houses, up the pathway to her front door. I stepped over the crack in the sidewalk as she jingled her keys.

"Is your mom home?" I asked, holding my breath.

April unlocked and shoved the door with her shoulder. It huffed and creaked open. She took one last long look at me, her eyes hardening.

"No. She's babysitting," she said and stepped inside.

The house blew out a strange smell, like a fart, stale and pungent.

"Monday in there?"

April nodded and waved me in. I gulped, my heart racing. Monday's been home this whole time?

Stinging nerves screamed not to, but I still walked inside.

She shoved the door closed and turned on the light. Now I saw why Mrs. Charles always opened the door halfway. Right behind it, against the wall, was a large freezer chest. The kind you find at grocery stores holding frozen turkeys and precooked hams. It buzzed like a broken fluorescent light.

I stepped backward on a pile of broken naked crayons and sheets of newspaper in the middle of the tight living room. A large TV faced a black sofa, the leather ripped and cracked like paint, black trash bags taped to every window, blocking out the sun.

In the kitchen, dirty pots and pans were stacked high on the counter next to empty cans of soup. A roach crawled over a pile of eviction notices and unopened letters from the school.

"Up here," April said, her face stoic as she climbed the stairs. I tried ignoring the shivers crawling up my spine that were telling me to run and followed.

On the top on the left was a bathroom. On the right, a closed door, maybe a closet.

"In here," April said from down the hall as I glanced back down at the wreckage and the door I wanted to sprint through.

She turned on a noisy overhead fan light in a bedroom. I stepped inside, gaping before my arms went limp.

First thing I noticed was that there were no bunk beds. Just three twin beds forming a U around a room, so low they might as well have been mattresses on the floor, sheets bunched up and dangling off. Curtains hung sideways, blinds blackened by dust. Candy wrappers, bags of chips, and empty soda bottles lay scattered across the floor. The light gray walls felt like an incoming fog, with a rainbow of crayon scribble drawn at knee height. And even though we were on a whole other floor, I could still hear the freezer humming from downstairs, as if it sat right next to us.

No Monday.

"Come on, April," I said, my voice small. "Quit playing. Where is she?"

April leaned against the door frame, hands hidden behind her.

"Don't you see her?" she chuckled. "She's all over the place."

I swallowed, the smell a painful distraction. No way Monday lived here, I thought. She couldn't stand the sight of a dish in the sink at my house. She swept and vacuumed without ever being asked, made my bed whenever she slept over.

"That's her bed," April said, nodding to the one closest to the door. I couldn't help sitting on it. Just to see life from her point of view. Her sheets were rough, dusty, like they hadn't been used in forever.

April watched with an intense stare. "You want something of hers? To remember her by?"

The words cracked through my brave front.

"*Remember* her? You mean . . . she's not coming back?"

April said nothing, just stared.

My lower lip trembled as tears spilled. I leaned forward, the chest pains too much to bear. I had so much I needed to tell her. I needed one more day, one more moment.

My hand slipped, hitting something hard under her pillow. Her journal, like the one she gave me. Pink with swirls and glitter. I touched the gold padlock.

"Where's the key?" I sniffed.

April rubbed her arms with a sigh. "Still with her."

I clutched the journal to my chest, stuffing it into my book bag as I stood.

"Where is she? Just tell me," I begged. "Did CFSA take her away? Is she with her aunt? Just tell me!"

April swallowed, her eyes wild and frantic, tears pooling. I stepped closer. At any moment, she'd fall, and I was ready to catch her.

But then the front door creaked and slammed shut. Mrs. Charles's voice roared over the freezer. "April! Where your ass at?"

Our gasps stole all air in the house.

"Shit, she's home!"

ONE YEAR BEFORE THE BEFORE

On the car ride back to drop Monday home, we'd always found some go-go song to sing from the top of our lungs. "Pieces of Me," by Rare Essence stayed on repeat most Sunday afternoons. Daddy would drum along, laughing at the notes we attempted to hit of the Ashlee Simpson remix.

"Pop quiz, ladies!" Daddy said, turning down the music. "What famous go-go band started over there in Ed Borough?"

I shrugged at Monday, who only grinned. "I don't know. Who?"

"The Junk Yard Band," Monday laughed. "Girl, everyone knows that!"

"For real?"

"Yup," Daddy said. "Used to go see them play when I was a kid. Got they start with nothing but the trash cans and spoons. They wanted me to join them."

"Really? Why didn't you? We would've been rich!"

Daddy laughed. "Well, my mother wanted me to go to college, and I'd be a plum fool to turn down a football scholarship. But after I hurt my knee, I came on back home, saw them in concert, and picked up right where I left off. Music got funny a way of reminding you of what you thought you lost."

Daddy slowed down as we approached the entrance of Ed Borough, our music replaced by loud chanting. A growing crowd of protestors gathered with huge neon green signs that screamed "SAVE ED BOROUGH! It's community. It's home!"

"We need repairs, not be demolished!" a man on a bullhorn shouted.

"Daddy, what's happening?" I asked, rolling down the car window.

"Don't know, Sweet Pea," he mumbled, bringing the truck to a full stop next to man passing out flyers. "Aye, young, what's up?"

The man shook his head. "City passed the legislation."

"Damn, for real?"

"Look! There's April!" Monday whispered, pointing out the window.

April stood on the corner with Tuesday in her stroller and August, tugging at his clothes like they were burning his skin. Monday and I jumped out the back seat to join them.

"April, what's going on?" Monday asked as we ran up.

April huffed, waving off the crowd. "White people trying to buy up Ed Borough."

"What?" Monday gasped. "What does that mean? Can they . . . really do that?"

April shrugged, tucking Tuesday's Doc McStuffins blanket around her.

"Government can do whatever they want. No one owns nothing around here."

Monday pales, the happy girl in the back of the car long gone. The crowd cheered as speakers passed around the mic warning of eviction notices, bulldozers, flattening Ed Borough down to a parking lot. My stomach tightened at the sight of the camera crews.

"So . . . we got to leave?" Monday asked, a crack in her voice. "They gonna kick us out of our house?"

April blinked as if someone clapped in front of her face. She held Monday's shoulder, bending eye to eye. The most affection I'd ever witness her give her sister.

"Day Day, chill. Don't worry about it! Ain't gonna happen."

My stomach clenched tighter, icy jealously creeping up

my veins. I should be the one comforting Monday, not April.

Monday rubbed August's head as he squirmed under her. "But where we gonna go?"

"You can stay with me," I jumped to offer, attempting to hold her hand. "I can ask Ma and Daddy."

April eyes narrowed. "You don't need to ask them nothing. We straight!"

Monday's eyes flicked away as she let loose of my hand.

"Claudia, maybe you should . . . go home now," she mumbled.

The wall she put up had a purple haze. I thought we shared everything, no secrets, ever. April grabbed Monday's chin to face her. "Hey! I said don't worry about it, didn't I? I'll take care of it. Don't I always take care of it?"

"Yeah," Monday said, holding back tears.

April took a deep breath, glancing over at the crowd. She spotted a group of boys chilling near the path heading to the courts. She bit her lip as if wincing at a paper cut.

"Take Tuesday back to the house," she ordered. "It's cold out here."

Monday followed her gaze and frowned.

"April . . . don't."

"Don't what?" I asked, confused.

April and Monday shared something unsaid. But that couldn't possibly be, when Monday and I were the only ones that had a bond like that. Right?

"You know I spent a grip on y'all's uniforms this year," April said. "Now, take Tu Tu back in the house. I'll be home soon."

She sped off before Monday could stop her. Monday, mashed with disappointment, could only watch.

"Where's she going?" I blurted out.

Monday sighed, shoving the stroller ahead.

THE BEFORE

"April!" Mrs. Charles hollered. "Where this girl at?"

April closed the bedroom door. The TV clicked on. Cartoon Network on blast, yet somehow you could still hear the strange buzzing of the freezer.

"You gotta hide!" she whispered. "Under the bed, now!"

She lifted the sheet up off the floor to a black hole under Monday's bed. My mind scrambled.

"You crazy, I can't!"

"You have to!"

"April! I know you hear me calling you!" Mrs. Charles barked, her voice creeping closer. The stairs creaked.

"Hurry," April whispered, near tears, waving me on.

"But how am I gonna get out of here?"

"I don't know, but my mom will kill us both if she finds you in here."

The way she said that made it seem possible.

"Oh my God. Monday . . ."

Her eyes grew big and pleading before she grabbed my arms, pulling me close. "Look, last time I saw her alive was with *your* mom."

"My mom?" I gasped. "What? When?"

"Last summer. Now, come on, hurry up, go!"

"APRIL!" Mrs. Charles screamed, her voice hot on our necks.

No time to think or ask more questions, I ducked under the bed, crawling close to the wall, the floor covered in crumbs and black pellets of mouse shit. The mattress reeked.

April smoothed the sheet down before the door swung open. It cracked against the bed, creating a gust of wind that swept more dust underneath it. A pair of black Reebok sneakers stood on the threshold and I clasped both hands over my mouth to stop myself from screaming.

"Didn't you hear me calling you?"

"I . . . I was sleep. I just woke up," April stuttered, backing away.

"You were sleep? In your sneakers?"

April paused, crossing one foot over the other. "I—I just put them on."

"Hmm. Well, come on and help me with this child down here."

Mrs. Charles clunked back down the stairs. April stood frozen. She took a deep breath before walking out and closed the creaking door behind her.

I cowered closer to the wall, my head bumping into something hard. A book. I grabbed and angled it toward the light to see the cover.

Flowers in the Attic.

I clutched it to my chest and tightened myself to the wall.

Downstairs, Mrs. Charles flipped through channels while Tuesday let out little laughs. I counted down the minutes based on the shows she watched. Four episodes of *The Simpsons* . . . two hours, I lay hidden under the bed of my missing best friend, too afraid to move. The bedroom door too noisy, my feet too heavy, what if she heard me?

"Tuesday, where you going?" April screamed.

"Going to get my cup."

"Here! I got one right here for you," April offered, her voice cracking. "You don't have to go all the way upstairs. Come stay with me!"

"No, I want mine!" she hollered, as little footsteps thumped up the stairs. She skipped in the room, pink lights twinkling on the bottoms of her gray sneakers, dulled by dry mud. I huddled closer to the wall, my heart drumming wildly. Tuesday hopped over to her bed, rummaging around before turning back, stopping short by Monday's bed. Her feet were so close I'd only have to stick my finger out an inch to touch them. She leaped and the bed sank, her butt landing on my back. I held in a yelp, squeezing my eyes shut. She bounced three times, jumping off and skipping out of the room. Only then did I let out a gasp.

Three more episodes of *The Simpsons* and my body ached to move out of the cramped space. Ma was probably looking for me. I didn't leave breadcrumbs for her to follow. What if Mrs. Charles found me first? What would she do to me? Trembling, I let the tears fall, gripping Monday's book, trying to comfort myself with her memory.

Monday, how do I get out of here?

"I snuck out the house last night."

"Are you for real? How you do that?"

"I climbed out my bathroom window and jumped down."

"What? How you not dead?"

"'Cause I jumped onto the trash cans right below."

The bathroom. It's right by the stairs. And Tuesday left the bedroom door open.

"You can do this," I whispered, and slid from under the bed.

The sound of Mrs. Charles cackling at the start of another episode made the hairs on the back of my neck spike. Time to act fast. I stuffed the book in my bag, peeking out the door and tiptoeing into the hallway. The TV and freezer were loud enough to mask my steps as I crept through the shadows, peering downstairs, taking in the strange family portrait: Tuesday on the floor, coloring with stubs of crayons, April frozen on the sofa, opposite of Mrs. Charles, drinking a fruit punch. I crept into the narrow bathroom, gently closing the door halfway.

Just like Monday said, the window sat right above the toilet, the bathroom in the same state as the rest of the house: counter crowded with empty bottles of bodywash and used toothpaste tubes, the sink filled with hair. On the floor near the tub, I noticed an empty box of hair dye. The same one Monday had used over a year ago. My stomach sank. I closed the toilet seat, stepping on the edge of the tub to climb on top. Outside, night had fallen. Streetlights glowed down the path, toward Martin Luther King Boulevard. I unlocked the window and tried to lift. Stuck.

"Don't panic," I told myself, squeezing my eyes tight, pushing my shoulder into it, but it wouldn't budge. Monday was always so much stronger than me in every way.

"Mom, where you going?" April yelled.

I froze.

"Mind your business! And why are you screaming? What's wrong with you? Can't I take a piss in peace?"

The stairs creaked under her weight.

Hide! I could hear Monday scream.

I climbed off the toilet quick and jumped into the shower, pulling the curtain closed. The lights popped on, bouncing off mustard-yellow walls. I dropped and squeezed myself into a ball in the tub.

Mrs. Charles stomped into the bathroom, grumbling,

not noticing me through the small curtain opening. She landed hard on the toilet, and the lid hiccuped. I tightened the hold around my legs, remaining still as a rock. She would have only needed to extend her left arm to grab me by the hair.

A few silent seconds—farts, smelly, loud and wet, echoed out the toilet bowl. My stomach heaved; I covered my mouth to keep from puking.

"April!" Mrs. Charles hollered. "April! Come here."

April ran into the bathroom. "Yeah," she mumbled with a cough, lifting a T-shirt over her nose.

"Why didn't you replace the toilet roll?"

"I wasn't the last to use it."

"You were home all day and you didn't use the toilet? You a piece-of-shit liar! Go get me some!"

Through the small opening of the shower curtain, April spotted me. Her shirt and mouth dropped.

"What you standing there for?" Mrs. Charles screamed. "GO!"

April hesitated and then sprinted downstairs. She rushed back with a wad of take-out napkins.

"Here," she said, eyes toggling from me to Mrs. Charles. My foot slid an inch on the porcelain, and I gripped the side of the tub, my nails breaking against the honeycomb tiles.

"Well?" Mrs. Charles chuckled. "Are you gonna stand there and watch me? Get the hell out of here!"

April took one last glance at me and slammed the door.

My stomach flipped over twice, my head spinning, the room fading. Seconds from passing out, I heard the toilet flush, gurgling out fresh water. With a satisfied sigh, Mrs. Charles washed her hands at the sink. Just as I leaned forward to peer out, I slipped, and my sneaker squeaked against the porcelain. Frantically, I gathered myself back into a ball, holding my breath, muscles strangling around my neck. Maybe she hadn't noticed.

Mrs. Charles paused, water running over her frozen hands. The faucet shut off. She stood like a light post, listening to the silence.

For ten seconds, the world stood still.

She mumbled and shuffled back to the toilet. My heart stopped, picturing her hands inches from my neck. This is it, I thought, and I held in a whimper. But instead, she grunted and shoved at the window. It fought against her, whining, until it opened wide. Crisp air whipped in, sweet with relief.

Mrs. Charles dusted off her hands and stomped downstairs. I released my legs, slid onto my back, and stared up at the ceiling, gasping for air

Get up. She'll be back!

I scrambled up on my knees, and peered out from behind the curtain at the open door. Mrs. Charles's laugh carried upstairs.

The toilet lid bent to my weight as I climbed on top

and stuck my head out the window into the night sky, swallowing as much fresh air as my lungs could hold. Just as Monday said, two trash cans sat below. But the drop . . . how in the hell did she do this?

Balancing myself with the shower rod, I stuck my left leg out, straddling the ledge. The fall looked worse up close—a straight nosedive to heaven.

"I can't do this, Monday," I breathed. "I can't. I . . ."

That's when the dying light of her sneaker caught my eye. I gasped, nearly losing my grip and falling out sideways. Tuesday stood frozen by the closet door, her little hand held up to knock.

We stared at each other, my hands trembling until my whole body shook. Tuesday's mouth hung open, as if at any moment she could scream my name.

Either I fall to my death or that woman kills me.

"Tuesday? Tuesday! Where are you?" April called in a panic.

"Tuesday!" Mrs. Charles hollered.

Tuesday jumped, her bladder letting loose, piss running down her strawberry leggings. I didn't wait to witness the aftermath. I hopped feetfirst, dropping right into the empty trash can below, shrieking as it tipped over into the hardened snow.

APRIL

If Daddy was a color, he would be a forest green—thick, lush, calm, whispering refreshing wisdom only few could hear.

If Michael was a color, he would be bark brown—cocoa, mocha, chocolate, the color of earth. Quiet, supportive, but strong. A softness that love grows from.

Together, they are the tree I lean on when I'm weary. The tree I swing from.

The tree of life when surrounded by death.

THE BEFORE

Sometime after midnight, I stepped into the fire.

"Where the hell have you been?" Ma screamed, marching out of the kitchen. "Your father's out there looking for you now! What, you think you're grown now, that you could go off on your own and don't tell nobody? You got everybody calling everybody looking for your behind!"

Notice the difference: I'd been missing for two, maybe three, hours tops, and Ma had half the congregation out looking for me. Monday had been missing for months and no one even considered it strange.

"Ma—"

"Just WAIT until your father gets home! We ought to ground you until you're ninety!"

The house felt like there were ten ovens on broil all at

once. Ma cooks when she's nervous.

"Oh my Lord! What happened to your face?"

I blinked. "Huh? What?"

"Your face, Claudia! You're bleeding," she shirked, lifting my chin. "And why are you limping?"

I glanced at the mirror in the hall, slowly picking the clump of dust out of my disheveled hair, barely noticing the cut on my cheek, right below my eye, oozing blood. My school tights ripped, my knee scraped.

"It . . . must have happened in the fall," I said, the sluggish words tumbling out like ice cubes in a freezer door. I looked up, imagining the window right above me. "I jumped. I had to . . ."

"What fall? What happened?"

So exhausted, maybe from running in circles for months, I sighed, reaching the end of a rough rope.

"Ma, when's the last time you saw Monday?"

Her neck snapped back as if I slapped her.

"Wh-what are you talking about? That weekend before you went to Grandmamma's! When y'all had your sleepover."

"You saw her after I left."

Ma stiffened, then blew out air as she shook her head.

"Girl, I don't know what you're talking about."

"Don't lie!" I shouted, stomping my foot. Her eyes went wide. I even shocked myself.

"Ma, Monday's not with her daddy. She's not with her

aunt. She didn't move. She's not in school. No one has seen her in months. . . . And she never had the flu."

Ma blinked a few times.

I cocked my head to the side. "And something tells me you knew about her not having the flu. Didn't you?"

She swallowed and pressed a palm to her forehead, closing her eyes.

"That was . . . right after I lost the baby," she sighed. "The last one."

I remembered the way Ma curled up on the sofa, fixed to it like cement. The end of the world could have been near, and she wouldn't have moved. I remembered never leaving her side. Is that when I missed seeing what was happening right in front of me?

I breathed in deep, keeping my voice level. "I think something bad happened to Monday. Something really bad."

She wiped her hands on a dish towel and plopped down on the sofa, staring at the floor.

"You believe me, right?"

She looked up, her eyes glassy.

"Yes. Yes, I do. But . . . let's wait until your father comes home. We can decide what to do when he gets here."

After Ma helped clean me up, with my knee a thick plum, I sat in my room with two bags of frozen peas wrapped around to ice it down, wondering how I was going to dance on a busted knee.

I drummed my fingers against Monday's journal, tracing the swirls with my pinkie. Like a ticking bomb in my hands—it felt as if the world would explode the moment I opened it, unearthing the evidence of a life she wanted me to know nothing about, unlocking her past.

Shit, the key!

The metal jiggled as I picked and poked, trying to pry the latch free. I could ask Daddy to saw it open. He'd ask too many questions, maybe even take it back!

"Ah," I yelped, breaking a nail before noticing the familiar wide design of keyhole. My head popped up, eyeing the heart-shaped key hanging on a purple shoelace off my vanity. If our books were the same, were our locks the same?

Did she know one day I would have to use mine on hers?

With one click, I flipped to the first page, to her name written in purple ink under *This Book Belongs to*. My thumb rubbed against the indents in the *M* and the funny loop she made with the *Y*. Seemed like forever since I'd seen her handwriting. The pages of the thick, well-used journal were crinkled almost to the very end. We talked about everything. What did she bottle up that would force her to write an entire novel by hand?

I had so many questions, the hardest one being where to

begin. But just like a book, felt only right to start from the beginning. Slowly, I turned to the next page.

UGHHHHHH! Claudia can't read or spell for nothing! I don't know how I'm supposed to keep covering for her. I don't want her to go to the stupid kids' class, but maybe she'd be better in there.

I closed the book and chucked it under my bed.

THE AFTER

School, dance, homework, chores, church. Repeat.

Between school, church, dance, tutoring, high school applications, Ma's extra catering orders, and Daddy's band gigs, the weeks slipped through my fingers before I could catch them, inspect them. What's wrong with this picture? What's missing? But then a song would come on the radio or I would spy a splash of pink, and I would remember my missing limb.

I settled on that fact that my life had boiled down to a few steps and not much more. Daddy was right. Monday was plain sick and tired of me. I thought she was my friend; I thought she cared about me. But I was wrong. Another part of growing up, putting stupid fantasies out of your head. Besides, have April tell it, she thought I was too stuck up anyways. So, I gave up on Monday, the same way she'd given up on me, making my life a sad schedule of events.

School, dance, homework, chores, church. Repeat.

"You've been quiet," Michael whispered from across the table at the library, his math textbook laid out in front of him.

"Was I ever noisy?" I snapped as I carefully wrote out my essay. Again. Applications were due at the end of the week and Ms. Manis had added more rehearsals to prep for the recital. No time to waste.

"Damn! You ain't got to bite my head off."

That one line from Monday's journal ate at my insides, poisoning my mood daily. I wanted to pretend I never read it. That I never stepped foot in her house and pulled back the curtain on all the lies she'd spewed over the years. I wanted to forget. But the buzzing made it impossible. Whenever I was alone with nothing to distract me, the buzzing would bring me back to Ed Borough, her house, her room . . . reminding me.

"My bad," I mumbled and dug into my bag, in search of a new pen. Monday's *Flowers in the Attic* slid out and slapped the table.

"Ew. What you doing with this book?"

Flustered, I pushed it off to the side. "That was Monday's. I keep forgetting to give it back to Ms. Paul."

"Whoa, really?" Michael grabbed the book, flipping

it around as if he'd never seen one before. "Why was she reading something like this?"

"I don't know, but she's read it before. I recognize the cover."

"She's read it *twice*?" he asked. "Why?"

"Who cares? And what you know about it anyways? It's old as hell."

"They made a movie about it on *Lifetime*." He grinned. "I watched it with my grandma once. The story is wild, though! It's about these kids, two teens and little twins, who are locked in the attic at their grandma's house for, like, years 'cause their moms didn't want their grandpa knowing she had them. But their grandma goes all crazy on them, torturing, beating, and starving them. They so cooped up, the older brother and sister start having sex. And then the mom was trying to poison the kids to get rid of them so she could marry someone else for money. Wild stuff!"

I set down my pen to slip the book out of his hands.

"You're right, that does sound crazy," I mumbled. "I mean, why would Monday want to read a book like this? A brother and sister having sex? That's nasty. What would people think if they saw her reading—"

The thought chased all the air out of my lungs. I jumped up, my chair falling behind me.

Michael's head cocked back. "Claudia? What's up?"

I couldn't speak, couldn't spit the words out fast enough;

they were all jumbled and flipped in the wrong direction. Instead, I ran to the front of the library, relieved to see Ms. Paul.

"Ms. Paul!" I yelped, slamming into her desk.

"Hey, sweetie," she said, her voice a soothing hush as she scanned a pile of returned books.

"Ms. Paul, I brought back Monday's book," I said, sliding it across the desk, my heart pounding.

Ms. Paul's eyes widened. "Oh. Oh my . . . well . . . thank you, Claudia."

"No problem!"

She stared at the book as if I had placed a dead rat at her feet, unsure of what to do with it.

"So, um, Ms. Paul, I got a question for you," I started. "Is there a way . . . to see all the books a person ever borrowed from the library?"

Ms. Paul swallowed and scanned the book with a nervous smile. "No, sweetie. That's just an urban legend."

"Oh. Okay," I muttered.

"That's funny, Monday once asked me the very same thing." She sighed, placing the book in the bin. "Only place you can keep a record is when you take books out online or if you lost any."

I took a deep calming breath. "Anyway I can see . . . if I can see if Monday took any books out . . . online?"

"What . . . for?"

I gave her a shy smile with a shrug. "I just . . . want to

read the same books she has. She read so much during the summer when I wasn't around. I want to catch up! You know, we always got to do the same things."

She lets out an uneasy laugh. "Uh . . . well, that's private information, Claudia."

"Please, Ms. Paul," Michael said behind me. "She just wants to take a quick look. I think it would *really* help, since she's been missing her. We won't tell anybody."

Ms. Paul pursed her lips. She clicked her keyboard with a huff.

"I'm sorry. It's against policy." She stood up, patting her hair down. "Now, I'm going to get a cup of coffee. Michael, I think there's something wrong with my computer. Do you mind taking a look? I'll be back in five minutes."

With a curt nod, she headed for the staff lounge.

I spun around to Michael, my mouth hanging open.

He smirked. "Dang, I thought stuff like that only happened in the movies!"

"Hurry up!" I laughed.

Michael hopped behind the desk, sitting in Ms. Paul's chair, and I peered over his shoulder at the screen.

"Damn, she took out that *Flowers* book five times," he mumbled, scrolling down a long list of books. Books I've never read. Books I knew nothing about. Books that would take me forever to read.

"Any of these books you recognize?"

"Some of them, yeah," he said, concentrating as he scanned. "A lot of them are the same kinda books. Books that deal with like . . . child abuse stuff."

My stomach looped and tied itself tight. I stared down at the list, using my index finger to read the titles slowly.

Flowers in the Attic, Perks of Being a Wallflower, Sharp Objects, Push . . .

"This gonna sound crazy," he said slowly, seeming unsure. "But I think she was saying what was happening to her without actually saying it. Like she was trying to send a hint, leave clues."

"Breadcrumbs!" I exclaimed, stabbing the screen. "These are breadcrumbs! She thinks the government is watching her through her books!"

Michael rubbed his chin. "No way. No fucking way," he mumbled. "If these are breadcrumbs . . . then they would lead back to her." Michael turned to me, in shock. "Claudia . . ."

The buzzing appeared out of nowhere, like the freezer had grown legs, walked out and sat right behind me.

"There's no attic in Monday's house," I croaked out.

"Yes . . . but it doesn't mean she wasn't kept *somewhere* else. Claudia, don't you remember . . . anything?"

Her sister Tuesday. She mentioned Monday was hiding in a closet. And there was a closet right by the bathroom! She had been there, all along.

I sprinted around the desk, grabbing my coat from the

table and heading for the door.

"Where are you going?" Michael barked, grabbing me by the elbow.

"I have to go back!" I yelled, pulling away from him.

"Back? Naw, you can't go over there! Let's just call the police and tell them you've been holding on to this book—"

"Police ain't gonna do nothing. And how am I going to explain the breadcrumbs she left without getting Ms. Paul in trouble?"

"You got to talk to your parents. . . ."

"I can't! Ma and Daddy don't want to hear nothing else about Monday!"

Michael rubbed his hands against the front of his jeans. "Well, maybe we should talk to Pastor Duncan. Tell him what you found."

What's Pastor gonna do? He doesn't even know Monday. Other than April, I don't know anyone else who had stepped foot in her house and would know where to look. But there had to be someone who'd be willing to take on Mrs. Charles. Someone big and strong who could . . .

"Her dad! I have to tell her dad!"

"Her dad? Claudia—"

"Police said the only other person that could put in a missing persons report is her dad. If he does that, then they can look for her! He works at someplace called the Maryland House. You know where that's at?"

Michael crossed his arms nervously. "It's up on 95, right past Baltimore. But Claudia . . ."

"I need to find him. Tell him about the breadcrumbs and stuff."

"Naw. I—I don't think that's a good idea."

"He's the only person that's gonna take this seriously!"

Michael shook his head. "Man, I don't know."

He didn't know, but I had already made up my mind.

"Listen, I'mma find my way to him, with or without you."

He sighed, rubbing his head. "Yeah, I know. But I ain't gonna let you just go alone. Hold up."

He dug into his pocket for his phone and began texting furiously. About ten minutes later, he smiled.

"Bet. My cousin said he can drive us there on Thursday, after school. He's visiting his girl in Delaware. But then we got to get back on our own."

"How we gonna do that?"

He shrugged nonchalantly. "We'll just ask Mr. Charles to take us home."

Heavy sheets of rain blanketed Michael's cousin's truck as we unloaded in front of the Maryland House—a busy pit stop surrounded by north- and southbound highways and thick woods. The temperature had fooled me into believing spring was creeping around the corner.

"Aight, y'all be safe," his cousin said, before rolling up

his window and taking off. For the hour-and-twenty-minute ride, he didn't ask what we were up to and didn't seem to care how we planned on making it back home.

"Okay. We here," Michael said, holding the umbrella. "Now what?"

"Daddy said something about him working the pumps," I said, pointing to the Exxon station at the far end of the lot.

"Let's check it out."

With the Easter holiday approaching that weekend, lines of cars crawled toward the gas pumps. We weaved through the cars, splashing through puddles, my sneakers already soaked from the short walk. We stopped to stand on the curb next to the attendant booth.

"Okay, which one is he?"

I blinked. "Ummm . . . I'm not sure."

Michael frowned. "You mean you don't remember what he looks like?"

Just as I started to defend myself, one of the attendants, an older white man with curly white-blond hair waved us on.

"Hey, kids," he shouted over the loud rain. "Y'all can't stand here."

Quickly, I stepped up to use my best grown-up voice, taking a page out of Michael's "How to Talk to Strangers" playbook.

"Good afternoon, sir. Is Tip here?"

He frowned. "Tip? Who's Tip?"

Dang, did we come all this way for nothing?

"Think they talking about Tommy," another man said, opening the gas valve on the car next to us. "That's his nickname."

The older man laughed. "Oh right, Tommy. Yeah, who wants to know?"

I licked my lips. "I'm his daughter Monday."

He stopped laughing and stared, like he'd seen a ghost. "Oh, I'm . . . sorry. Um, he doesn't get in until six."

I checked my watch. It was only four. Behind me, Michael rubbed his hands together as if trying to start a fire and shrugged. "We'll wait inside, then."

"Y'all can cut through the store over there to get inside."

"Thanks," Michael said, a hand on my lower back as he pushed me toward the gas station mini-mart, attached to the main building. Reminded me of the first floor of Pentagon City Mall, frantic and busy; people zigzagged in front of us, rushing into bathrooms. Michael grabbed my arm, saving me from a speeding stroller, and pointed ahead at the Phillips Seafood counter.

"Let's eat. I'm starving!"

We stood on a line as long as the ones at Six Flags in the massive food court for almost thirty minutes, ordering two crab cake sandwiches and fries with two medium cherry

353

Cokes. Michael paid, refusing to take my money.

"So what you tell your mom you were doing so you can come?" Michael asked as he carried our tray, scanning the room for an empty seat.

"Told her I signed up for an extra rehearsal for my solo with Megan. That should give me a couple of hours."

He chuckled. "Man, she'll kill you AND me if she ever finds out the truth."

Definitely crossing several dangerous lines: approaching an adult like I'm grown, involving myself in family business with folks that ain't my real family, driving out of DC . . . with a boy! If Ma had a clue, she'd whup my ass! But finding Monday . . . outweighed all the risk. How could I ever even consider giving up on her? She'd never give up on me.

We sat at a booth in the back near the windows, watching the rain pour down.

"So, what are you gonna say when we see him?" he asked, taking a bite of his sandwich.

There were so many things to say I barely knew where to begin. "I don't know."

"Well, I see you thought all of this through."

"I'm winging it."

"Good thing you brought some muscle with you," he said, cracking his knuckles and fake flexing. "You know, as some insurance."

"Oh yeah, you sure figured me out," I snickered,

flinging a fry at him. He caught it in his mouth, shooting his arms up like I made a field goal.

"You know, I've always wanted to do this."

"Do what?" I laughed.

He smirked, playing with a waffle fry before popping it into his mouth. "Take a girl to Phillips."

It felt as if the rain had stopped and nothing but sunshine beamed down on us. Only us. The place cleared out and we were the only ones left in the entire world.

"Really?"

"Yeah. Well, not *this* Phillips. Ever been? It's wayyyy nice inside. My dad used to take my mom. Now all he talks about is how there's no good seafood in Dubai."

He sighed, taking a sip of his soda, gazing off.

"Did you ask if you could stay with your grandma yet?"

"Yeah," he huffed. "And they seem cool with it. But it's just gonna suck without them. I'll miss my mom, but I'm really going to miss my dad."

"I'm sorry."

He nodded with a shrug. "Anyways, so what's up with this recital I hear all you girls talking about?"

I laughed. "What about it?"

"Don't you got a solo or something?"

My back tensed thinking of Ms. Manis's last comments. "Yeah."

"Dang, don't sound so excited about it," he chuckled. "The way Megan be talking at school, it's a big deal. I've seen you dance at church and at that party. What you got to worry about? You can move!"

I took a sip of my cherry Coke. "Well, I *was* excited. But my teacher picked this slow song."

He shrugged. "So what's the problem?"

"Problem is I wanted to show out with some of the dances I made up with Monday. Slow songs ain't my thing!"

"Ohhh. So . . . that's why you want to find her?"

"No! Not just that," I said, my stomach clenching. "She's in trouble. I don't know how to explain it, but I can just feel it."

He stared at me for a moment before nodding, wiping his mouth with a balled-up napkin. For the first time, it didn't feel like a lie. I wasn't looking for her because I needed her—I was looking for her because she needed me. She needed my help.

"You watch football?" Michael asked, stealing a pickle off my plate.

"With Daddy, yeah."

"Ever see them do those instant replays?"

I frowned. "Of course. Why?"

"Well, I think sometimes, when something is going real fast, it can look real beautiful in slow motion. So, maybe you can do that. Do your same moves but slow motion."

I shook my head. "It don't work like that."

He motioned to the empty space next to our table with a smirk. "Try it."

"What? Right now? In front of all these people? You lunchin'."

"So you can perform onstage in front of hundreds of people and in front of our whole congregation, yet you can't perform in front of a bunch of tourists," he cackled. "Come on, girl! I dare you."

Monday would do it, a voice inside me whispered. She never backed down from a dare. I tilted my chin up.

"Fine," I sighed, wiping my hands clean. "This is crazy."

He leaned back in his chair with his soda and a satisfied grin. "Won't be calling it crazy when it works."

I stood up, deciding to try the first few steps of our "heartbeat" routine. Two quick pumps, dip, and a turn. I glanced back at Michael, nodding.

"Okay. So what happens when you slow it down? Like realllllll slow."

Rolling my neck, I closed my eyes to picture the steps. What would they look like slow? What if my arms weren't so sharp, but more . . . graceful? Instead of a dip and turn, what if I pirouetted?

Relaxing my muscles, I began breathing through the motions, letting my arms delicately unfold the air around me rather than slicing through it. At the last second, I thought of Megan, then of dance ministry at church, the way we ended our performance, with a low bow, arms raised to the sky. Without a mirror, I had no idea what I looked like, but the motions felt good.

Michael clapped and cheered, and so did everybody around us.

"Oh my God," I squealed, covering my face with my hands. "I can't believe I did that!"

Michael pulled me into a hug. "Told you it would work."

For the next hour, we talked through a bunch of my dances before taking our time walking back to the minimart. We stood in the snack aisle, staring out the huge windows and watching the rain pummel the ground.

"Aight, it's five to six," Michael said, rubbing his hands together. "He should be here any minute now."

"Should we wait outside?"

"And get soaked? Naw. We could see everything from in here straight." He glanced over his shoulder before walking off. "Be right back."

Night began to fall, the sky blackening. The wind kicked up, as lightning struck through the trees while puddles turned into oceans. What if he doesn't come?

Michael returned with two steaming Styrofoam cups of hot chocolate.

"Good work today, champ," he said, passing me a cup. "I asked cuz up front if he made these with milk, and he gonna say 'What you think this is, Starbucks?'"

"Thank you," I giggled, blowing off the rising steam. "How much sugar you put in this?"

"None. Coach says if I don't cut it out, I'mma end up with diabetes. I'm cutting sugar out of everything!"

I laughed. "You talk about your coach a lot."

"Yeah, he's cool." He slurped at his cup.

"So, like, I know you gonna be sad without your dad being here and stuff, but it sounds like you have a bunch of dads here."

His smile dimmed. "What you mean?"

"I mean, you got your coach, Pastor Duncan . . . hell, even my daddy, are all here for you. Some kids don't even have that."

His eyes shifted to his sneakers. "It just ain't the same. My dad . . . he's, like, my best friend."

I knew all about missing your best friend and how substitutions didn't fill the gaps left by their absence. I had fun working with Michael on my dance moves and painting nails at Megan's house, but it didn't feel the same.

"Thanks, though," he muttered, his eyes lifting to mine with a deep breath. "Listen . . . about that party . . ."

I quickly waved him off. "Naw, forget about it. Like you said, we were both drunk and things got out of hand, that's all."

He sighed. "I wasn't drunk."

The hot chocolate turned cold in my hand. "What?"

He turned, reaching to slip his fingers between mine, pulling me closer.

"I said . . . I wasn't drunk."

The rain stopped again. Lost in each other's gaze, he inched closer, stepping into my bubble, where it was warm and safe, the sun hot on my neck. He's going to kiss me, I thought. Right here, right now. And this time, I'm not drunk. This time, I won't rush.

But as I tilted my head up, I glanced through the window at a rusty tan Grand Marquis pulling up to a garage just right of the station. A man jumped out, wearing a navy workman's jumpsuit and brown boots. I recognized his eyes, his high cheekbones, his deep scowl. Monday stole so much of her looks from him.

"Look," I whispered, nodding over Michael's shoulder. "There he is."

Michael flipped around, watching Tip Charles lock up his car. I sensed Michael sizing him up, his shoulders tensing. Tip had about an inch over him in height, but in weight they could be equal.

Tip Charles ran through the rain up to the blond man, giving him a head nod as he slipped on some thick workman's gloves. Blond Man said a few words to him, then pointed over to the mini-mart. Tip Charles's face went blank before he pivoted, his back now facing us. They exchanged some tense words, and Blond Man threw his hands up.

Michael and I shared a look. This wasn't going well.

Without even glancing in our direction, Tip Charles ran back toward the garage, pulling a hood over his face as if to cloak himself. He jumped in his car and slammed the door.

"Wait . . . what's he doing?" Michael mumbled, slowly setting his hot chocolate on the window ledge. The tickling in my stomach turned sharp.

Tip Charles fumbled with his keys like someone running away from the killer in a horror movie—his face pale, eyes terrified.

"Is he . . . is he leaving?" Michael barked, and took off running toward the door.

"Michael!" I screamed, chasing him. Tip Charles threw the car in reverse and slammed on the gas by the time he made it outside.

"FUCKING PUSSY!" Michael screamed as the car sped out of sight.

"Michael!" I yelled, standing in the rain, my heart racing. "What?"

I sighed, my breath puffing in front of me. "How are we going to get home?"

"Shouldn't we call our parents?" I asked as we climbed out of a cab at the Baltimore Amtrak station, well past eight o'clock. According to my lie, I should have been home by now.

"And get yelled at for an hour and change on the drive back home? Naw. I rather get to DC first and let them kill us there."

If it weren't for the emergency credit card Michael's dad had given him, we would've been stranded in the middle of the highway, so I didn't argue. Bad enough he was about to be in as much trouble as I was. Our soggy sneakers squeaked against the marble floor inside the busy station. I kept close to Michael, wanting desperately to hold his hand, just to erase the nervousness eating at my stomach in an unfamiliar city.

"I can't believe he just dipped like that," Michael said, for what might have been the thousandth time since we left the Maryland House. "Who *does* that? After everything that's happened, he ran like we were the police!"

I didn't know what to say anymore. The shock of it hadn't worn off yet. The moment set on a loop, burning through all other thoughts.

The loudspeaker blared announcements as we passed a couple of circular wooden benches, newsstands, and gold ticket counters, TVs set on the local news hooked on every other column. We stood gazing up at the huge train information board hanging from the ceiling, clicking with departure times and gate numbers.

"Next train to DC leaves in ten minutes," I said, reading the board, as a few people rushed past, sprinting to their gates.

"Leaves from gate three. Wait over there by the track, and I'll get us tickets."

I nodded as he ran off, taking in the hectic surroundings.

"Baltimore," I mumbled to myself. The search for Monday had taken me to a whole other city, and I still had nothing to show for it. Where do I go from here? Who else could I tell? I couldn't even think of a next step since I couldn't shake the look on Tip Charles's face, just at the mention of his daughter. Why would he run?

"Authorities need your help identifying the body of a young teenage girl found in Leakin Park. . . ."

The words *body* and *girl* grabbed hold of me. I looked up at the TV on the column, focusing on the newscaster's cherry-red lipstick. Footage of the crime scene, police taping off a section of a park, and the snow-covered ground from the month before zipped across the screen.

"No missing persons report matches the young victim's description. . . . Medical reports are trying to determine how long the body has been . . . The victim appears to be between fourteen and sixteen years in age. . . ."

Before, it was all blank. Just a plain sheet of paper with empty, meaningless shapes. Only after the shapes are colored in does a picture really appear.

"Monday," I gasped, my stomach dropping, the world darkening.

Michael jogged back with two tickets. "Okay. We got five minutes. Let's go! Hey? What's wrong?"

The picture began to sharpen and cut through me. Everything clicked. I thought her being missing was the worst thing that could have happened to us. How could I have been so blind?

"She's dead," I said, staring at the TV.

Michael flinched. "What?"

"Monday. She's dead."

Michael followed my gaze, reading the lower headline on the screen. He glanced down at me then back at the TV, his face alarmed but controlled.

"Naw. That ain't her," he said, shaking his head.

My ears rang, a shrilling sound that drowned out everything around me—a BUZZ.

Michael bent to my eyesight, blocked the TV, and calmly pressed a hand on my thigh.

"Claudia, it ain't her," he said softly. "I promise you it ain't."

"Her dad lives in Baltimore," I mumbled.

"They find lots of folks in that park. But I swear to you, that ain't her."

I shook my head. "Did you see the look on his face? You said it yourself—he ran like we were the police." Hysteria began to set in, tears threatening to fall. "What if her mom wasn't lying? What if she really did take her to her dad's house? What if he lied to my dad about seeing her?"

Michael took a deep breath, his face crumbling. "Claudia, you . . . really don't remember anything? Anything at all?"

"Huh? What do you mean?"

Michael jumped like a spider bit his ass and snatched his phone out his back pocket.

"Damn," he mumbled, scrolling through new texts. "It's the church phone tree. Your mom is looking for you."

"Shit," I muttered. "But we can't leave now! We have to go to the police. They found her in the woods and they can't identify her 'cause nobody knows she's missing!"

Michael sighed with a sadness in his eyes I'd never seen before.

"Claudia, I'm sorry. I thought . . . I don't know. But I think it's time we called your mom."

THE BEFORE

The next morning, I woke up sluggish and weak. By the time I dressed for school, the chills and dry mouth swept in, followed by an aching head. I fumbled downstairs, my knee still a thick plum, to find Ma in the kitchen, sipping coffee and staring off at nothing.

"Ma?"

Waking up, she glanced at me, almost confused. "Oh. Morning, Sweet Pea," she said, her voice raspy.

I noticed her jeans and sweater. "You're not going to work today?"

She frowned. "Took today off. Your interview at Banneker, remember?"

The interview. Scheduled for April 1. I forgot all about it.

"And it's Good Friday. Got to get ready for the fish fry

this evening." She took another sip, setting her mug down softly. "Your father is on his way home. We're gonna go over to Patti's to check on Monday. I want you . . . to stay here."

She didn't say it, but the lingering thought pressed through. "Just in case?"

She nodded. "Just in case."

Shivers crept up my arms. I didn't want Ma near Mrs. Charles, or that house. What if she ended up missing too?

"Everything is going to be fine," she insisted. "We'll straighten this all out. Okay?"

I nodded, my body swaying. She stood, wrapping her arms around me for one of her tight hugs, but she quickly pulled back, studying my face. She pressed the back of her hand to my cheek, snatching it back as if she'd touched a hot pan.

"Claudia! You're burning up!"

The thermometer read 101.

"Probably 'cause you were running around at all hours of the damn night," she fussed, tucking me back in bed. "Probably caught pneumonia or something. I have to go to the store. Your father done used up all the dang Tylenol. You gonna be alright for a little while?"

I nodded.

"Okay, good. I'll make some soup for lunch."

Not long after Ma left, in the distance, I could hear the swarm of sirens, like an out-of-sync band, growing louder.

Sirens were normal in Southeast, but their urgency, and so many of them . . . my eyes popped open. I rolled myself out of bed, limping to gaze out the window, staring up at a bright blue sky with choppers hovering low. I glanced back at the library, home of all the books Monday had read. For English reading assignments, I'd skipped some chapters to keep up with her. Monday would laugh and say it's the same as fast-forwarding a movie to the ending.

The. Ending.

I raced over to my bed and dove under, grabbing Monday's journal, skipping to the last page. I don't know why I didn't think of this before. Start from the end and work my way back. I guess 'cause you always start a book from the beginning. Just like this story, you got to know a person's past to understand their present. But to find Monday fast, I needed to know her last move.

On the last page, she wrote two sloppy lines:

Tomorrow Claudia leaves for the summer. When she's gone, I'm telling her mom what happened. Maybe I can live with her, until she gets back.

Somewhere in the quiet of that moment, dread crawled in before the phone rang.

"Claudia, you alright?" Ma asked, Daddy's album playing in the background.

"Yes."

"Okay. I'm on my way back now. There's . . . just a bunch of traffic. I think something's happening over at Ed Borough. They blocking off all the cross streets."

A stray cop car came hurtling down our block, swerving past a trash can that blew into the middle of the street, sirens blaring. I only caught a quick glimpse of the driver, his face hardened. If I had any color left from my sickness, it vanished once he made a left around the library, then up Good Hope Road, following the others turning left on Martin Luther King, heading toward Ed Borough.

I don't remember the last words I said to Ma. I don't remember slipping into my furry boots or pulling my coat over my pajamas. I don't even remember running out of the house, leaving the door wide open. All I remember is pedaling down the road, panting like a dying animal.

I had to see for myself.

The weather had broken overnight, leaving it warmer than it had been in weeks. Just like DC, Ma would say. Winter one day, summer the next. Sweat dripped down into my eyes and my socks were soaked, but panic kept me moving.

Police cars blocked the main entrance of Ed Borough. Struggling with every breath, I cut through the grass path around the back of the basketball courts to Monday's side of the complex, hoping the traffic would clear. But the barriers thickened, as well as a crowd that created a semicircle, right outside her house.

I dropped my bike by the curb, wobbling up the path to join the onlookers. Yellow police tape roped around the old trees, casting shadows over the parked police cars and ambulances. The rumbling crowd grew louder. Old ladies in their housedresses, sweats, and thin coats. Men with their oversized sweatshirts, jeans. Women holding their babies, trying to tame their wild toddlers.

A policeman stumbled out of the house, his white face tinted green. He hacked and heaved, covering that same crack I tripped over with pink vomit. A hush came over the crowd. The police and medics moved at a snail's place. No urgency—meaning whatever was done was done, there was no one left to save.

A photographer appeared, taking pictures of the crowd. CLICK, CLICK, CLICK. News crews elbowed through as the neighbors started whispering. . . .

"What happened in there?"

"They saying they found some children dead inside."

"Dead?"

"Get out!"

The police tape that held us back flapped in the breeze with a smack. My heart cracked, my throat clenching so tight I could barely breathe.

CLICK, CLICK, CLICK.

"Hey, ain't that Patti's house?"

"Oh my lord! She got four babies!"

"I saw them take away April."

"Well, which one they find dead?"

"Don't know yet."

"They saying they found two kids in the freezer."

"THE FREEZER? What you say?"

"Lawd! Who they find in the freezer?"

My legs, my arms, my hands . . . everything went numb. The voices drowned out, mouths still moving but silent. I could hear nothing but my heart racing . . . and the buzz of the freezer.

BUZZZZZ.

The world spun, slow at first but then real fast. Like the way Monday and I would spin each other . . . 'round and 'round . . . fits of giggles . . . until we'd fall into the grass and look up at the sky.

BUZZZZZ.

I coughed up a breath, looking at the clouds. Only one hovered nearby, a small puff of gray, as if forgotten by a passing storm—left for dead. My eyes rolled back. Knees shaking, I staggered, bumping into something hard and solid.

Daddy.

He lifted me up, cupping a hand around my head. I clutched his neck, gripping his leafy green jacket, my whole body shaking.

"Shhh . . . it's okay, Sweet Pea. Daddy's got ya. Just close your eyes. It's alright."

He backed out of the crowd and carried me all the way home.

THE AFTER

"Oh, thank GOD!"

As soon as we walked in, Ma gathered me into a tight hug, burying her nose in my hair. "Y'all had me so worried."

I wiggled free of her grasp as Michael closed the door behind us.

"Ma, we don't have time for this! We have to go to the police!"

Ma frowned, rubbing my arms. "The police? Why?"

"It's my fault, Mrs. Coleman," Michael mumbled, his head low. "I thought if she . . . saw him, it would help her remember."

Ma sighed. "It's alright, Michael. I know you were just trying to help. Tip called here not too long ago."

"See!" I said to Michael. "I told you! Running like we were the police 'cause he knew he was up to no good. He called trying to stop us!"

Michael sighed, stuffing his hands in his pockets. Ma's eyes toggled between us. "Sweet Pea . . ."

"Ma, you have to listen to me. Monday . . . she's not at her aunt's house. She's not at her mom's or her dad's. They found a girl's body in the woods in Baltimore, near where her dad lives and . . . and I think it's Monday. I know it sounds crazy but I talked to Nurse Orman. Monday never had the flu. CFSA took her . . ."

Ma's eyes filled with tears, her lip trembling. "Oh, Sweet Pea. I . . . I thought you were getting better."

"What? No, I am better! I've been going to Ms. Walker's and TLC! That ain't got nothing to do with this!"

I looked to Michael for backup but he just stood there, staring at the floor.

"The breadcrumbs!" I continued. "Monday took out books from the library about kids being abused. She was trying to tell the government what was going on, but the government doesn't look at the books you take out after all! Her mom lied about that!"

Ma nodded with a sniff. "Okay . . . how about you sit down and—"

"Ma! You're not listening! I'm trying to tell you Monday's missing! Why won't anyone listen? Why won't anyone believe me?"

Ma froze, glancing at Michael, tears now falling. "You're right, Claudia," Ma whispered. "You were right all along. We should have believed you the *first* time you brought it up."

First time, I thought. What is she talking about?

"Honey, listen to me. Monday . . . Monday is gone. She's been gone almost two years now."

"What do you mean?" I turned to Michael. "What's she talking about?"

Michael shook his head. "I'm sorry, Claudia."

"Sorry? For what!"

"Claudia, Monday died *two* years ago," Ma said gently, grabbing my wrist to keep me steady. "Her and August were . . . were . . ."

The bursting of our bubble could be heard around the world.

"No," I gasped, trying to back away from her.

"Yes, Sweet Pea!" she said, gripping me tighter. "And I'm so sorry! You keep having these . . . episodes, where you forget what happened."

Two years! Two years? But that would mean . . .

"Wait, how . . . old am I?"

Ma took a deep breath. "You're sixteen."

"That's impossible . . . I just turned fourteen," I muttered. "You said I can have a party! I'm applying for schools!"

"Yes. Yes, you're applying for high school. Again. We

took you out of school. Do you remember your last day? Do you remember what happened?"

I tried to think back. Back to the before, but everything felt jumbled, just like how my words jumbled when I wrote. I looked to Michael for help, but he avoided my stare. *Two* years?

Ma. Her hair wasn't as golden. Had more grays than I'd ever seen. It was as if someone had swiped a gel filter in front of my face and the whole room rearranged.

BUZZZZZ.

"This isn't happening," I mumbled.

Ma caressed my cheek. "Ms. Walker has been homeschooling you for the last year. We put you in dance class to try to ease you back into things. And Michael . . . he's been by your side since the very beginning. But maybe we pushed you a little too hard. We'll try again. 'Cause everyone, and I mean everyone, wants to see you get better."

I stared at Michael. He *did* seem older than I remembered. Taller, thinner, more mature. Have I really been so blind?

"Ms. Valente," I hiccupped. "She knows about Monday . . . she—"

"She moved back to New York, not long after it happened."

The room spun both ways. "It? What . . . what happened to Monday?"

Ma shook her head, wiping her face dry.

"No!" I screamed, the rug pulled from under me. I

fell to the floor, hugging my legs. They're wrong! I know Monday better than I know myself: she loves crab chips and sweet tea, can do backflips, won the fifth-grade spelling bee . . . and she can't be dead. She just can't!

Right?

"Come on, baby. Let's get you to bed. And in the morning, we'll talk some more."

I nodded, too weak and confused to fight as one last thought hit me.

"Does April know about . . . me?"

"Yes, Sweet Pea. She knows."

MAY

Can I tell you a secret? I knew she was dead. I just hoped she'd be in the trunk of a car, chopped up, and buried somewhere. Not in a freezer, hiding in plain sight. That aggravated the pain felt by anyone who ever laid eyes on her. Once red, she became a starless sky, an endless midnight, a hole in the universe swallowing up the world, leaving everyone blind. Onyx, ebony, jet black.

A part of me was glad Monday wasn't named Friday. It would've been too tragic.

THE BEFORE

I wish my mom could be like Claudia's mom.

Last night, Mom beat August until he couldn't get up. Said he deserved it. I thought he just passed out, but when April tried to move him, he wouldn't wake up. April tried to save him, but Mom stopped her. She made April put him in the freezer. I'm so scared. I want to tell someone. But what if they split us up like before? I may never see Claudia again.

August is still in the freezer. I keep telling April we got to tell somebody. But she scared. She trying to find Auntie Doris first so we won't get split up. Everybody talking about getting kicked out of Ed Borough at the rec center. So we either gonna get split up again if they find out about August or we gonna be living on the streets like some bums.

I almost told Claudia what happened to August today. At school, everyone was making fun of me and my hair. I messed it up bad. It's like five colors. Claudia said her mom can fix it, though. That's when I almost told her. I'm scared what she might do. What if she tells her mom or a teacher? Then everyone is gonna know! What are they gonna think of us? I shouldn't be writing all this. If Ma ever finds this book, she'll kill me.

At his televised press conference, Tip Charles coughed out excuses drenched with tears.

"I didn't know. I just didn't know," he cried. "I'd call and she wouldn't let me talk to them. She wouldn't let me near them. Not unless I gave her money."

He broke down, and his surrounding family members comforted him. Monday's family. Where have they been all this time? Why weren't they looking for her too?

"Had to find out with the rest of the world that my children were gone, on the TV. It ain't right. How could she do this to my babies?"

Policed questioned April, little Tuesday, neighbors, and school officials. It didn't take long to put the puzzle together:

August had been in that freezer for a year and a half.

Monday . . . at least ten months.

Mrs. Charles wasn't home when they finally came to evict her. She wasn't there when the marshals peeked inside the awkwardly placed freezer sitting by the door and found two kids stuffed inside. She wasn't there when they ripped Tuesday out of April's arms as she pleaded. She wasn't there when a neighbor tipped officers off on her whereabouts.

Mrs. Charles was down the street, next to Darrell's, calmly smoking a blunt, listening to the sirens come for her.

A mountain of teddy bears grew outside Monday's door, spilling into the street. Hundreds of candles, burning throughout the day in a valley of flowers and "Rest in Peace" posters. Reporters stood in front of the basketball courts, combing through the tangled details of the story, as kids played three-on-three.

BUZZZZZ.

Boy, I wish you could have been there to see the funeral.

You would have seen the droves of people from the DMV line up outside Mt. Holy. The police department surrounded the block, walling us in, and news vans turning the side streets into parking lots.

You would have seen a standing-room-only church with TV cameras in the balconies, hundreds of white carnations and lilies flooding the pulpit—the old ladies in their high black hats, the gospel choir in their holiday robes, the mayor in the front row.

You would have seen the puddles—no, oceans—of what Ma called crocodile tears from fellow classmates. The same ones that had cackled at her blond hair, called her a 'ho, then a lesbian. Shayla and Ashley, consoling each other, faces wet with snotty tears. Jacob Miller sitting next to his brother with his head hung low.

You would have seen the ushers in white gloves and charcoal dresses walking around with boxes of tissues, handing out church fans and programs with her middle name spelled wrong.

You would have seen Daddy help carry in her coffin, along with some of her neighbors, dressed in dusty, mismatched suits and shoes that needed shining. Tip Charles was too distraught to carry nothing but himself to church, in a T-shirt with her face on the front—a picture from four years ago.

Speaking of pictures, there weren't many. Monday's mom had none to share. Her dad had a few old blurry ones on his cheap flip phone. So Ma gave them all the pictures she had. Almost seven years of photos of us dancing, decorating Christmas trees, trick-or-treating . . . and they cut me out of every one. Like "we" never existed. In the program, I'm always a mysterious arm, linked with hers.

Where was I during all this? The third row, in front of

a pearl-pink coffin with my best friend inside. August next to her, in an identical pearl-blue coffin. There were even less pictures of him. The Redskins players offered to pay for the entire funeral. Someone must have told them that pink was her favorite color. That someone wasn't me.

Ma's arm draped around my shoulder. She wore a black wrap dress, church heels, and a frown on her face. She scoped out the attendees, measuring them, searching for something to pinpoint a memory or recollection until it finally dawned on her. None of these people knew Monday. I questioned if I really knew her either.

"Thank you all for coming," Pastor Duncan said at the pulpit. "We are here to celebrate the life of Monday Cherry . . . I mean, Monday Cherie Charles and August Devante Charles. This home-going is particularly painful. Children should not lose their life so young . . . but we as a people must trust in the Lord. . . ."

I stared at the back of April's head in the front row, her hair in a high bun, Tuesday in her lap, with their aunt Doris waving a fan beside them. I wanted to see her face, her expression, to know what she was thinking, feeling. Did she even feel at all? I looked up into the packed balcony. With the church cameras and audio replaced by CNN, Michael stood on the sidelines with hands behind his back. We locked eyes and he nodded.

Pastor read the welcome scripture and the choir sang a hymn. After the eulogy, Pastor invited the congregation to speak in remembrance. Shayla and Ashley, linked arm and arm, were first to the mic.

"Monday was our friend at school," Shayla whimpered, looking straight into the camera. "We're gonna miss her so much. . . ."

Ashley broke down, crying harder than everyone combined. They boo-hooed before being escorted offstage by one of the ushers.

More people went up to talk. None I recognized.

"Monday was an avid reader. She burned through our summer reading list. Always willing to help put books away after reading time . . ."

"That little girl there was my heart, always willing to help an old lady out. . . ."

"Monday and August took our swimming classes together during the summer. Nothing but smiles—you couldn't help but smile when you were around them. . . ."

Ms. Valente trembled as she took the podium, her face red, her eye makeup ruined. She gazed at the audience until she spotted me, giving me a half smile before she began.

"Monday was smart, witty, funny, wise beyond her years, and ever curious about life. One of my very best English students and one of the most caring, protective friends you could ever have. I'd never met a girl so young who loved so fiercely. It was an honor to be her mentor."

Pastor finished his service, and the choir began another

hymn. Jacob Miller stood, slowly walking over to put a single pink rose on her casket. Photos snapped like clockwork. Later on, his perfectly rehearsed teary-face photo would be used for the cover of *Time* magazine. The choir sang in joyful praise, but all I could hear was buzzing.

BUZZZZZ.

Ma, confused by the theatrics, squeezed my shoulder. "Do you want to say something?" she whispered.

I shook my head no.

When you first wake up from a nightmare, you search for something to ground you—something to anchor you to reality. So, each morning after they found Monday, I stared out the window at the library, waiting for it to morph into a cave full of flesh-eating rodents. Only when it remained a clear box would I pull back the covers, step out of bed, and start a new day, with each step heavier than the last.

My toothbrush weighed a thousand pounds, my comb stung my scalp, and I found showers an unnecessary task. The smell of oatmeal made me want to vomit. Just the idea of school caused dread to swell up in my chest, and I'd sit on the bathroom floor until I had enough air to leave. I slept at all hours of the day. I'd wake up to watch the recurring news reports, showing the same picture of Monday that Tip Charles had on his T-shirt.

My best friend, my other half, was dead.

You were right, a voice inside me kept saying over and

over again as I slumped down the stairs. But being right did not give me the satisfaction I had hoped for.

One morning, I walked into the living room and clicked on the TV to the local news. Endless coverage on Monday's death, interviews with specialists and witnesses.

"Sweet Pea, I think you've been watching too much TV," Ma said. "It's not good for you."

I shrugged, changing the channel to CNN. They too were covering the story about the kids found inside a freezer.

"How about some lunch?" Ma offered. "Maybe we could go to the movies later? Or maybe just take a walk. What d'you say?"

I shook my head, pulling the red throw over every square inch of my body.

"The body of Monday Charles is now being reexamined for possible sexual trauma after a witness came forward with allegations of abuse outside of her home. . . ."

Daddy stormed downstairs. "That's it!"

He yanked the TV so hard it left holes in the walls, slamming it down on a pair of old speakers.

"I've had enough!"

A few weeks later, I found Ma in the kitchen, frying some pork chops, boiling collard greens, with a fresh tray of mac and cheese just out of the oven, and a pineapple upside-down cake in the travel case.

"We're visiting April today," Ma announced with a guilty smile. "Her aunt called this morning. April asked about you."

News vans surrounded Aunt Doris's house like a pack of sleeping wolves. Their interest was piqued as we pulled into the driveway. I carried the cake while Ma balanced the trays. Aunt Doris greeted us on the porch steps, and we hurried inside just as a swarm of cameras descended.

"Sorry about all that," she said, shaking her head. "Someone tipped them off. Everyone's trying to suck some words out knowing damn well they shouldn't be bothering these babies."

Inside felt like a dark cave, the blinds shut tight, except for a screen door leading to the sunny fenced-in backyard. And there was April, her back to the house, sitting in a green plastic chair in the middle of the lawn. We stared at her in silence, a breeze playing with her ponytail.

"April's been . . . having a hard time. Poor girl has been through it."

Aunt Doris had bags under her eyes bigger than my cheeks, black hair with graying roots. I could see some of Monday in the way she smiled.

Ma inhaled through her lips, holding back tears. "Does she have any friends we can bring by here for her?" she asked.

"Naw. Guess she just kept to herself. Not that I blame

her." She sighed, leading us over to the kitchen. "I went and saw Tuesday yesterday at the hospital. She's asking about her mother and what time Monday is coming over to play."

"Poor thing," Ma said. "Bless her heart."

I slid on a stool at the breakfast bar, watching April—a girl frozen in a picture.

"And what about you?" Ma asked, putting the trays on the kitchen counter and heating up the stove. It took nothing for her to get comfortable in someone else's kitchen. "How are you holding up with all this?"

Aunt Doris winced, rubbing her hands down the tops of her thighs as if to warm them.

"I'm managing. Just trying to take it one day at a time." She smoothed back her hair. "Patti called here yesterday, wanting to speak with April."

"She shouldn't be doing that! She knows she's not supposed to have contact with the kids," Ma said, her voice clipped.

"There's gonna be a custody trial. They're trying to terminate her and Tip's parental rights."

"Tip's too? Wow, I guess that makes sense. Not like he was around much."

"Yes, but he's fighting it," she said, pulling out a few clear plastic glasses from the cabinet. "I think he really wanted to be around but was scared of Patti and what she'd do. Courts never been too kind to black fathers."

Ma nodded. "You get a lawyer yet?"

"I got a few suggestions," she said. "Everybody is coming from every direction. I'm worried I don't know which way is up. But I know the Lord will provide."

Aunt Doris hid behind a small blanket of confidence. She looked warm, but then you realized her cold feet were poking out at the bottom.

"Well, the church asked us to give this to you," Ma said, passing her a thick manila envelope of cash donations. "Something to help with the transition of having a few new mouths to feed. Our thoughts and prayers are with your family."

"That's very kind of you. And thanks again for coming. I think seeing a familiar face would help," she said to me.

Ma smiled and rubbed my shoulder. "I think it would help us too."

"Claudia," Aunt Doris said, brightening. "Why don't you go ahead and bring April some lemonade so me and your mom can talk."

I nodded and carried the tray out on to the deck, down the steps, and through a thick cluster of gnats. April sat almost a yard away, unfazed by my approaching footsteps. Even as I placed the tray on the table next to her, she didn't stir, just stared off at nothing. She should have a better view, like one of the river, facing the cherry blossom trees, museums, and monuments. Back at the house, Ma gave me a look, pleading for me to talk.

I sighed. "Hey."

April acknowledged me with a small head turn, almost relived to see me, but then gazed off again.

"Hey," she muttered.

I pulled out the chair next to her and stared into the same abyss. I don't know how much time passed before I asked her the most basic question.

"You okay?"

She gave me a practiced nod but stopped herself, the corner of her mouth creeping into a smirk.

"That funeral was fucking bogus, wasn't it?"

I chuckled. "Yeah."

She grabbed a cup, glancing over her shoulder at the adults watching us like zoo animals from the screen door, waiting for us to play or fight.

"Did they tell you that I helped her?" she asked.

"Helped who?"

She rolled her eyes. "My mom. Did they tell you I helped stuff them in the freezer?"

The image popped in my head faster than I expected it to. I pulled my knees up to my chest, shaking my head.

BUZZZZZ . . .

April regarded me with a huff and shook her head. "Stupid freezer was already half full with August. Wouldn't close right since Monday was so tall."

I shook my head and covered my ears, the buzzing deafening.

"April, please . . . stop."

"They should arrest me too. For what I did."

"But . . . you didn't kill her."

"I helped her, though. What's that called, assisting murder or something?"

"I don't know. But you . . . were just doing what your mom told you. That ain't your fault."

"She didn't tell me to do anything. I did it on my own." Her knees bounced, holding her cup right above it. "Not sure if she was dead or alive but . . . I needed to buy myself more time."

The buzzing cut off, like someone tripped over the freezer plug.

"More time? More time for what?"

"To make a plan." April slumped in her seat. "Monday never told you anything about that month we were away?"

"No," I snapped. "And so what?"

She wrapped her arms around herself. "They split us up. Monday and August at one house, me in some teen home. Tuesday was still little, so they gave her to this white couple, and if they had their way . . . they would've adopted her. Had to *beg* Mom to get us out of there, beg her to take those parenting classes." She let out a breath. "I already lost August. I couldn't lose Tuesday too."

I shook my head. "You hated Monday that much?"

April, enraged, snatched up my collar, pulling me so close I could see the drops of gold mixed in her brown eyes.

"Bitch, do you even know what I've had to *do* to take care of her? I've given up everything for my family!" Her voice cracked and she swallowed. "But you ain't listening. Monday would have talked! They would've split us up, and who knows where we'd be? We would've never seen Tuesday again! And those eviction notices were coming around. . . . I needed a plan to get us out first."

I shook out of her grip. "You think Tuesday's better off now?" I barked. "She one step away from being one of them crazies on the Metro!"

April winced, her knee bouncing hard. "They probably gonna send me to jail, once they figure it out," she grumbled, wiping a tear out of her eye. "Not saying it was right. All I know is I got one more year before I turn eighteen. Then it'll just be me and Tuesday."

I noticed her mention nothing about Aunt Doris or her dad. "Did Monday ever tell you that I was the one who signed her up for the school lotto?"

Heat rose to my face. Another secret. "No."

April smirked, sipping her drink again. "She was so smart. Reading books, like real books, when she was four. It would've been stupid for her to go to some regular school and not learn anything. Got on the computer at the library and signed her up. Even filled out the paperwork."

She rubbed her hands together, glaring at me. "And then she met you. And it was like, she learned about this whole other world. What stuff was supposed to be like. Good home, good parents, dance school . . . Sometimes I don't know whether to hate you or I don't know what. But I never had a . . . *you* growing up. Know what I mean?"

For a change, I finally understood how our mutual resentment grew from the same seed of jealousy. I resented that April knew a whole other Monday. That they were real sisters, something I could never compete with. April resented the kind of sisters Monday and I were—soul sisters.

"Why didn't she tell me anything?"

"She didn't want you feeling sorry for her," she said.

"I would've tried to help her."

April shook her head. "How? And she wouldn't have wanted you to anyways."

"Didn't matter what she wanted! What was she gonna do, hate me? At least she'd be alive!"

April closed her eyes, wiping away a few betraying tears. "Are you gonna tell on me now?" she whispered.

April always looked so much older than us. Not just what she wore, but in her face—eyes sunken with dark circles, a jaw tight, wrinkles around her mouth. Knowing what I know now, what she had to deal with, it all made sense. So no use arguing about what could have been or what should have happened. Monday was gone—nothing was going to bring her back. And as insane as it sounds, I understood April. I understood trying to keep a secret to protect a small fraction of the life you once loved. I eased back in my chair.

"No," I mumbled.

A breeze cut through the humid air as she sighed. "First time I saw my dad in two years was on TV. They interviewed him on NBC, crying and carrying on. You see it?"

I nodded. "He seems real sorry now."

"Monday's dead. August's dead. Tuesday's in the crazy hospital. . . . Of course he sorry now!"

BUZZZZZ.

"April," I mumbled, glancing over my shoulder. "Do you . . . hear that?"

"Hear what?"

"That . . . buzzing."

THE AFTER

"Claudia, Sweet Pea? Wake up."

Daddy sat on the edge of my bed, nudging me awake. I glanced outside at the streetlights, searching for the library to hold on to something real.

"Heyyyy, there's my girl."

I threw my arms around him, tears coming hard and fast. Every time I wake up from this nightmare I cry.

"It's alright," he whispered, rubbing my back. "Hey! I got a little surprise for you."

"Another coloring book?"

"Nah, not this time," he chuckled. "See for yourself."

Daddy slid the box from behind him. I sighed, using my last drop of energy to unwrap it. I opened a shiny new iPhone in a glittery purple case, and I winced a smile.

"We've been holding off giving this to you for a while . . . trying to shield you from what happened. But I think it's done more harm than good. Maybe this will help you remember and keep remembering."

Three fifteen a.m.

I sat cross-legged in the middle of my bed, watching the minutes pass on the screen of my new phone. All it took was one swipe and punching in a few letters in the search box for articles to swarm my screen, all dated two years ago. I clicked on an NBC video link and lowered the volume. . . .

"The mayor announced today that at least eight District of Columbia's Child and Family Services Agency workers will be fired for failing to properly address the welfare of Monday and August Charles, who were found dead in their home two weeks ago. The grisly discovery has even the most seasoned detectives speechless."

"In my twenty-two years on the force . . . I've never seen anything like this. The home was filthy and unlivable. Aside from the deplorable conditions, any sound-minded building manager would have gone in the home and recognized that it would have failed several safety codes."

"During today's news conference, the mayor played tapes of two 911 calls made by Michelle Valente, a former teacher of Monday Charles, after her whereabouts were undetermined."

"Hello? Yes, my name is Michelle Valente. I'm a teacher at Warren Kent Charter School. One of my students, Monday Charles, has been missing, and I think there is something seriously wrong with her mother. She won't answer any of my questions or let me in the house! Please, you have to send someone now! Please!"

"Valente's call was not the first time someone had tried to intervene. A retired nurse from Warren Kent Charter School has also come forward claiming that she made a report. City officials are currently outlining several policy changes to prevent a similar tragedy from occurring again."

I spotted a few familiar neighbors in the next video. . . .

"Residents of Ed Borough are shocked by the tragedy that has hit their community after the discovery of the bodies of thirteen-year-old Monday Charles and nine-year-old August Charles."

"I used to see them, all the time on the courts or just playing outside but then I hadn't seen them in a long while."

"Patti never stopped talking about her kids! She loved those babies, bragged about them all the time. She said they were at their father's house and I ain't have no reason to question that."

"Nope, never seen her lay a hand on those kids. She loved them. That's why this just don't make no sense."

"I heard crying some days, but my kids cry too when they

397

about to get a whupping. I can't walk up in her home and cast stones."

"Residents are hoping this will bring light to the current property conditions and stop the city's recently approved redevelopment plan, which includes demolishing five hundred homes and rebuilding both sale and rental properties, along with retail spaces. It is not certain that the displaced residents will be approved or will receive government assistance to move back in their community, forcing most into homeless shelters.

"Multiple claims suggested Mrs. Charles feared eviction, driving her to a mental break."

"You got these buses of white folks driving around here with cameras around their necks like they're on a safari, hunting for their new home. Of course she went crazy!"

I looked outside at the library, imagining Monday's ghost sitting there, reading every book she could get her hands on, in the place she loved most. There were only four numbers programmed in the phone. I had always imagined the first call on my own cell phone would be to Monday.

"Hello? Claudia?" Michael said groggily. "Hello? You there?"

I cleared my throat, licking my lips as I clutched the phone to my ear.

"Hey? You okay? You still there? What's wrong?"

So much was wrong I didn't know where to begin.

"Claudia, you want to talk?"

I wanted to scream and cry but instead I felt numb. I took a deep breath, the thoughts pinching at my temples as I pushed out a few words. "Why didn't any reporters talk to me?"

"You mean . . . like the news?"

"Yes, they talked to her neighbors, why not me? You think they didn't think I knew things? That I wasn't smart enough? 'Cause I was in TLC?"

"How could you even think that? Don't you get it? You're the one that knew something was wrong all along. You saw what folks didn't see, which means you're smarter than everybody else—including all those folk working for the city who got fired. Just 'cause you got a little trouble reading don't mean you ain't smarter than everybody else."

"Oh," I muttered, glancing out the window at the library, wishing to hold a piece of it with both hands to keep me grounded.

"Man, you should've seen your face," Michael said with a small laugh. "After you put everything together, you were about to roll in that house guns blazing. I don't know anyone who's as smart and brave as you."

"But I didn't save her," I said, bursting into tears. "I couldn't save her."

"You *did* save her, Claudia! You saved her from that house for years and you didn't even know it."

THE BEFORE

Ma spent the entire morning beating the house into submission: dusting, sweeping, vacuuming, scrubbing, and ironing. Company's coming, I thought. Important company. An hour later, the doorbell rang. I headed downstairs in my teal church dress but stopped short mid-step, nearly tumbling the rest of the way. Detective Carson, the officer who'd refused to look for Monday, the one that made me feel stupid for even asking, stood in our doorway. His mouth dropped at the sight of me. Next to him, a woman dressed in a business suit smiled at Ma.

"Mrs. Coleman? Hi, I am Detective Woods. We spoke on the phone," the white woman said, offering a hand, her curly brown hair tied back in a ponytail. "Pleasure to meet you. This is my partner, Detective Carson."

Carson looked on the verge of a heart attack.

"Hi, nice to meet you," Ma said, dressed in a blush shift dress. Daddy stood behind her in his freshly pressed khakis. "This is my husband, Mr. Coleman. And that's my daughter, Claudia."

Detective Carson gulped. "It's . . . nice to *meet* you Claudia."

I dug my nails into my side. Is he really going to pretend we never met? That I never went to him looking for help?

"Please, have a seat," Daddy said, leading them to the living room.

"Claudia, come on down," Ma urged. "The detectives would like to talk to us. About Monday."

Clenching back angry tears, I stomped down the stairs, silently sitting next to Ma.

On the love seat, Detective Woods pulled out several files from her bag while Detective Carson set up a recorder, fidgeting, unable to meet my glare.

"Several witnesses told us you were the right folks to talk to when it came to Monday," Detective Woods said. "We're hoping you can answer some questions and fill in the gaps. As you know, Mrs. Charles is denying . . . well, everything."

"How could she plead not guilty like that?" Ma asked. "After what she's done!"

"Well, that's not entirely true. She has admitted to August's death, but she is claiming no involvement in

Monday's. She was under the impression Monday ran away and has no idea how she ended up in the freezer."

"Ran away? Really," I said pointedly to Carson. "Wonder why she didn't file a police report."

Carson stiffened before clearing his throat.

"The autopsy is a bit muddled given the conditions of the . . . bodies," Detective Carson said, eyes shifting to me then back. "Hard to determine the exact cause of death."

Ma rubbed my back. "Sweet Pea, are you sure you want to be here for this? These questions could be kind of hard."

"Let her stay," Daddy said. "She's old enough and has a right to hear what happened to her friend."

Carson and Woods shared a quick look.

"Claudia . . . I'm real sorry about your friend," Carson said. "Your mother said you've taken this pretty hard. That's why we wanted to come here, where you feel safe, and talk. Is that okay?"

I tried talking to you, but you wouldn't listen—I wanted to scream. Instead, I straightened my back and tilted up my chin. He knows what he did, living with that guilt is enough punishment.

"Yes, sir."

Daddy and Ma beamed proudly.

"Great. Now, we're trying to put together a concrete timeline of events," Woods said, flipping to a clean page in her legal pad. "We want this to be a rock-solid case, so we're crossing the t's and dotting the i's."

The detectives drilled down for information, asking us a whole heap of questions: When did we first meet Monday? What was she like? What was Mrs. Charles like? On and on, they kept digging deeper into the ground, turning over fresh soil, planting seeds of new theories.

"Mrs. Coleman," Carson said, taking a sip from his water bottle. "When did you last see Monday?"

Ma nibbled on her bottom lip. "A week after Claudia went to visit my mother. She came by one afternoon. Must have been a Saturday, since I was home. I offered her some iced tea and a sandwich. She seemed, I don't know, frazzled."

Woods nodded. "Do you remember what she was wearing?

"Yes. A pair of green-and-blue shorts with little white lace trim and a white tank top. The shorts had this sort of tribal pattern. I think it even had a little pink in it."

The detectives glanced at each other, eyebrows arching to the ceiling.

"That's very specific," Carson said.

"I bought those shorts for Claudia, for her to take to Georgia. She spends summers down there with my mother."

Woods scribbled some notes. "So did Monday take them?"

Ma's eyes narrowed. "Monday ain't never stole a thing in her life. Claudia probably gave them to her. She gave

Monday lots of her clothes. We knew, but it wasn't hurting nobody."

Woods slipped an 8 x 11 photo out of her files, sliding it across the coffee table. I tensed, digging my nails into the sofa. Are we about to see Monday's body?

"Was this the pattern?"

Ma swallowed, slowly leaning forward, easing the photo closer. I held my breath and looked over her shoulder at a fuzzy blown-up shot of a hectic tribal pattern, much like the ones I like to color. Lagoon blue, kelly green, and magenta divided by sharp black lines into shapes.

"Yes, that's it," Ma muttered, then gasped. "Wait, is this what you found her in? Does this mean that she was wearing these when . . . ?"

"We can't say for certain," Woods said.

"Oh God!" Ma cried, and leaned into Daddy, sobbing into his chest.

I dug my nails into my palms, hoping to feel something other than numbness, itching to touch the photo.

"Claudia," Carson said. "They found a unique key in one of her pockets. We couldn't figure out what it belonged to, but her sister April mentioned it was to a journal."

The room turned cold and my lungs pinched shut.

"We didn't inventory a journal at the scene. Do know what she may be referring to?"

"No."

"Claudia," Daddy warned.

"I mean, no, sir."

"April mentioned that you might have Monday's journal," Carson said. "That you might have taken it when you were over their house a few weeks back"

Ma sniffed and leaned over to glare at me, tears soaking her face. "What's he talking about? Didn't I tell you about going over to that house?"

I hung my head to avoid her eyes.

"What were you thinking?" she screamed. "What if something happened to you too? Don't you think we've lost enough?"

"Sorry, Ma," I squeaked, my lip trembling.

"Do you still have it?" Woods asked. "The journal April mentioned?"

"Yes, sir," I mumbled.

"Go get it," Ma snapped. "Now, Claudia Mae!"

I jumped at her sharp words, running up to my room and plucking it from its hiding spot.

Carson stood as I returned, taking a large Ziploc bag out of his pocket.

"Thank you, Claudia," he said, shaking the bag open. "Now, if you can just drop it in here for me."

The plastic bag snapping the air shook me out of a fog. I was holding the last of my best friend, the other half of me, the only piece of her I had left, the only way to know what her life without me was like. The boys she kissed, the books she read, the swim classes she took . . .

I clutched the book tight to my chest. "Will you give it back?"

Carson's lips tightened as he glanced at Woods. "Sorry, Claudia, we're going to have to keep it. It's evidence."

"But . . . ," I whimpered. "I haven't finished reading it yet. It takes me . . . a little longer."

"They need it for the investigation, Sweet Pea," Daddy said, standing up. "You've got to give it to them."

Tears spilled over as my hands began to tremble. "I can't. It's all I have of her!" I turned to Carson. "And you OWE me!"

Carson hesitated, gripping the bag as Woods frowned, eyes ping-ponging between us.

"Claudia, give them the book," Ma ordered.

"No! It's not fair!"

"I'm sure if Monday were here, she'd be saying the same thing," Daddy sighed, placing a hand on my shoulder. "It ain't fair at all."

A cry, the one saved deep in my belly, rippled out of me.

"Please," I gasped between sobs, doubling over in pain. "Please, I'm not ready. Please, Daddy!"

Daddy held me as I bawled, my body giving in as I slumped into him. Ma stood up to join us crying together. It was the type of crying that we should have done at the funeral, except the funeral never felt real. But here, in our home, where we spent so many hours playing, laughing, dancing, this was where we had to say good-bye.

"Come on, Sweet Pea." Daddy sniffed. "It's time."

He held up my arm with my hand gripping the journal, rubbing my shoulder. Ma kissed my cheek and whispered, "I love you" as I dropped the journal in the bag along with my heart.

"Thank you, Claudia," Carson said, sealing the bag. "I know how much this means to you. Did you happen to take anything else out of the house that might help us build our case?"

I think of the book, *Flowers in the Attic*, still hidden under my bed, and my back turned into a concrete wall.

"No."

Ms. Clark gasped as I entered the main office, forty minutes late to school.

"Claudia, I . . . um," she started but stopped, her eyes filling with tears. The rest of the office froze around her.

Mr. Hill ran in, the principal behind him.

"Claudia! What are you . . . I mean, we weren't expecting you today. Your father called and said you would be out for a little while. How are you?"

I squirmed in my uniform, hanging loose off my hips after going weeks without food sticking to my bones.

"I need a late pass," I mumbled.

"Yes, yes, of course," he said, giving Ms. Clark a curt nod. "How about I walk you to class?"

He led me out of the office quickly, as if the very sight

of me could trigger tears, escorting me from my locker to first-period English, filling my ears with promises. How he'll talk to all the teachers about my grades, homework, and finals. Not even in class yet and already regretting the idea of coming to school just to get out the house while Ma and Daddy went to work. I couldn't take the silence.

Throughout the day, whispers hit my back like kicked-up pebbles.

"That's Claudia. She was best friends with that girl they found in the freezer."

The lunch line snaked around the outskirts of cafeteria. My movements felt robotic and staggering, much like the way Monday dragged herself through school all those months ago. Go home, I thought over and over again. You don't belong here.

A broken light flickered above me. The sound lifted me out the room and dropped me in the house. I could almost smell the mattress, hear Mrs. Charles cackle, feel myself falling out of the window.

BUZZZZZ.

A heavy hand tapped my shoulder. Trevor grinned with Carl standing behind him, their smiles unnerving.

"Heyyyyy, Claudia! What's up?"

The hairs on the back of my neck spiked. They haven't talked to me all year—what do they want now?

Trevor's face tightened, straining to hold back a laugh. "Yo, I'm sorry your girlfriend got murked."

I swallowed, my fists balling up as I turned back around.

He tapped my shoulder again. "Hey. HEY! I'm talking to you."

"Don't touch me," I spat, slapping his hand away.

"Oh, so you just gonna come back to school like nothing," Carl yelled.

The cafeteria came to a halt. Just ignore him, I chanted to myself, but the buzzing grew louder, drowning out my own voice.

BUZZZZZ.

"Man, fuck you, then, dumb bitch," Trevor yelled, his breath on my neck. "I was just trying to be nice to you. Stupid, how you not know your best friend was dead? Why you ain't say nothing?"

"Hey! Leave her alone!"

I whipped my head around the cafeteria to see where the voice came from, locking eyes with Shayla, sitting at a table a few feet from the line. Ashley next to her, clutching a bottle of water, her eyes bouncing from me to Shayla and back.

"Y'all think this funny?" Shayla barked, shaking her head. "With y'all sorry asses."

BUZZZZZ.

Trevor waved her off. "Man, whatever."

"My daddy said it took four days to thaw her out the freezer before they knew it was really her," Carl chuckled. "They thawed that bitch out like a fucking turkey!"

I squeezed my eyes shut and stuffed my ears.

BUZZZZZ . . .

"Aye! Didn't she say leave her alone?" Jacob shoved Carl out the way, standing between Trevor and me like a brick wall. "Y'all lunchin'. How you going after a girl like that?"

"For real? You acting like you didn't smash that—"

"Y'all talking about Monday like y'all didn't know her too!" Jacob yelled, shoving Trevor before one of the lunch monitors stepped in. "We all knew her! We saw her every day, and now she's GONE! That shit ain't funny."

The words *she's gone* rang like a massive bell that every-one could hear.

"NO! They best meet still." *She isn't dead.*

The room tensed and stiffened.

"What's she saying?"

"I . . . don't know."

"Bit most well spent no!" *We have to save her from that house!*

"Dang, she talking in tongues. Claudia—"

"The left foot missed right gone! GONE! GONE!"

BUZZZZZ.

I screamed and screamed and screamed until I had no air left. Girls began to cry. Carl's face dropped as he stuffed

410

his hands in his pockets. She's gone. Gone. GONE!

Mrs. Valente pushed through the crowd, pulling me into her arms.

"It's okay," she sobbed, holding me tight. "You're going to be okay."

The ticking light winked at me before I felt the prick of the nurse's needle and the world went quiet.

That was my last day at school.

THE AFTER

"I've never skipped school before," Michael laughed as we walked inside Ms. Walker's house. "Well, I didn't skip school. Just left early, so it don't really count. Coach finds out, I'll be doing suicide drills for hours."

I took in the familiar warmth of the living room.

"Where's Ms. Walker?" I asked, following him into the kitchen.

"She left for the annual church retreat," Michael said, opening the fridge and pulling out two ginger ales.

"That's this weekend? Already?"

"Well, you've been having trouble remembering stuff lately," he said, placing the cans on the table.

"Right," I mumbled. It had been over a week and the shock hadn't worn off yet. Two years of my life, gone.

Monday, gone. I barely knew who I was anymore.

"Claudia. You okay?"

He rubbed both my arms, warming my skin, and I stared up into his bright, pleading brown eyes.

"So," I said, squirming, afraid I'd burst into a lake of tears. "When you moving in here?"

Michael grinned. "Started moving my stuff in last weekend. But hey, I got a surprise for you!"

We headed to the back of the house into a plain white narrow room with a small desk and a wooden twin bed propped against the wall. Michael stepped around a few boxes to a little bookcase on the floor made of milk crates.

"This was my dad's room when he was kid," he said. "He still has a bunch of his stuff here. I was cleaning out his closet when I found this!"

He pulled out a box of old cassette tapes, labeled by dates and venue name.

"Oh snap! Are these his old go-go mixes?" I asked, combing through the thick stack.

"Yeah, but want to hear something really cool?"

He popped one cassette into the old stereo. The conga beat smoothed out the speakers and my ears welcomed its rhythm, the band unknown. I shrugged at him.

"Just listen."

A guy spat over the beat, calling out folks' names.

"I see you, Claudia baby, over there from Southeast!"

"Ahhh!" I screamed. "That's me! Well, not really me but ME!"

Michael laughed. "I was trying to decide if I should throw this box away when I heard it. Now you can say you were there, even if you weren't."

I sat on the floor, in awe of the collection. Monday would have flipped if she had heard this. She would've blasted this from every speaker everywhere. She would have danced. She should be dancing.

BUZZZZZ.

"Claudia," Michael said softly. "Come here."

My stomach clenched as I pulled myself up to join him on the unmade bed he sat on.

"Hey," he whispered, tipping my chin up. "What's on your mind?"

I took a deep breath. "I remember my last day at school."

Michael brightened. "You remember? Finally! We gotta tell your moms!"

I had tons of questions, but only one mattered. "Why have you been . . . so nice to me?"

He shook his head, glancing at the floor with a shrug. "'Cause . . . she was sitting in your kitchen."

"What? Who?"

"Monday. Last time I saw her, she was with your mom."

My heart leaped. "When?"

"Like, a few days before the church barbecue. I helped my mom drop the ribs off for your mom to season."

The church barbecue was held a week after I left for Georgia. I never usually missed it, but that year it was pushed back two weeks due to rain. It would have cost too much money to change my flight.

"I walked in and thought it was you," he continued. "Y'all looked so alike it's freaky. I remembered she had these bright-ass shorts on. Then after the way everything went down, I couldn't stop thinking about it, how I saw her on her first last day. And then I thought, what if that was you? Couldn't get it out of my head. It scared me."

He slipped my hand into his and squeezed it tight. My heart raced as I gazed into his chocolate eyes. Why am I so nervous? I thought. It's just Michael—warm, tall, and solid. Michael is safe.

Michael is safe, no bubble needed.

I leaned over and kissed him. Not a drunken kiss, a kiss that felt more like flying, the air in my lungs loose instead of crushing in desperation. He smiled as he kissed me back.

Ma stood in the kitchen doorway, hands locked on her hips.

"We bought that cell phone for a reason, Claudia. You should have told me where you were," she said, her voice measured but laced with an edge.

"Sorry. I just . . . needed to clear my head." I took a deep breath. "Ma, I remembered my last day of school."

Ma gasped, crossing her arms as if to shield herself before

415

spinning on her heels, heading into the kitchen.

"Come on in here. It's time we had a talk."

I gulped, stomach squeezing against my spine.

"I think it's time I finally be straight with you, Claudia," she said, pulling out a chair. "Didn't think it would be good for your . . . recovery. But maybe knowing the truth will help."

"The truth about wh-what?" I stuttered, joining her at the table, bracing myself.

Ma took a deep breath as she folded her hands together.

"Before it happened, Monday came by here, not long after you left for Grandmamma's. She didn't say much, but . . . it seemed like she wanted to talk about *something*. I was heading to Bible study so I offered her a ride home. When we pulled up, not even a foot out of the car, Monday started crying. Something was just *off* about her that day. I spoke to your father about it, and we decided to make an anonymous call to social services. Now . . . I'm just wondering if I made things worse. If that call set Patti off somehow. And she took it out on that poor little girl."

My teeth chattered, as if a cold front had moved through my body. Ma's eyes began to water.

"When you hadn't heard from her, I thought maybe they—I mean, social services—took her out the house for good. And we, I mean, I . . . I didn't want you hating me because I had something to do with you losing your best friend."

416

Ma finally let the tears fall. "I was wrong not to tell you, because I knew you were old enough, smart enough, to understand. I'm sorry, Sweet Pea. But please, don't hate me."

I took a much-needed breath as she reached over to hold my hands.

"I could never hate you, Ma. Never!"

She wiped her eyes. "My God, it just felt like I lost another child all over again. I didn't want you seeing me like *that*. Not again. 'Cause I knew how much you loved that girl."

My lip quivered. "I did, Ma. I did love her."

Ma reached over and held my hand.

"So did I, Sweet Pea," she whispered. "So did Daddy. That's why I think it's time we . . . all got some real help. Together."

JUNE

If I was a color, I would be white, vast in my blankness. Pure, whole, virginal, predictable . . .

Boring.

The colors thrown at me didn't bleed into my canvas and leave a mark. The colors washed out with nothing but water. That's what made this story so hard to remember. It's hard facing a mirror and seeing all you are made of and all you couldn't absorb.

But I'm open to be changed. To be in a place where I can hold all the colors I love at once, appreciate what they are, and learn from them.

I'm open to new beginnings.

THE AFTER

"Last week, Thomas Charles, the father of Monday and
August Charles, filed a multimillion-dollar wrongful death
lawsuit against the city, after officials failed to respond
properly to school social workers' concerns.

"The lawsuit has created a rift between city council
and community leaders. Todd Harris, from the DC Urban
Development Coalition, feels the suit raises a fundamental
concern.

"Well, I think it boils down to one question: who's really
responsible for your well-being—your family, the government,
or your community?"

I waited patiently in line for my turn at Starbucks in Gallery
Place Chinatown. Waiting for her to see me. Waiting for us

to lock eyes and really see each other. I stepped up to the counter and she blinked, hands rubbing against her apron.

"Your hair is shorter," I blurted out. "And red. More like tomato mixed with cherry."

April chuckled. "So. You finally remembered. About fucking time."

I smiled. "I'll take a hot chocolate."

She nodded and called over her shoulder. "Taking a break!"

I had to find April. Because I trusted her, more than anyone, to keep it real with me. We sat on a bus bench on the corner of H and 7th Street, sipping in silence, watching cars drive under the Chinese archway.

"I only got fifteen minutes, so make it quick."

"How many times have I done *this*?"

"Twice," she admitted. "But this was the longest."

I shook my head. "Surprised you played along."

"Ain't like I wanted to. Your mom begged me. Said it was a part of your 'healing' and that I should take 'pity' on you. Heh! Why should I pity YOU? Ain't like you lost your WHOLE family like I did."

I bit my lip, trying to match the stinging guilt. "So. Why did you?"

She shook her head, tears welling up fast. "'Cause you ain't never stop looking for her. Never."

BUZZZZZ.

"And Tuesday?" I asked, talking over the noise. "How's she?"

Just the mention of Tuesday made her tense, an instinctive move I no longer blamed her for. Not after everything they'd been through.

"Better. In school now. Going to therapy. We . . . both are."

We caught eyes and I enjoyed the calm in the moment.

"I got accepted to Cardozo. Gonna start in the fall. And . . . I'm in therapy too."

She smiled, a real genuine one. "Good. Maybe you'll stay with us for a while."

The backstage of any recital is a hectic circus, a mosh pit of screaming girls, mothers, powdery makeup, and hot lights. That's why Daddy looked like an elephant tiptoeing around a glass dollhouse, weaving through tutus and sparkly-feathered headdresses.

"Daddy?"

He spotted me by the vanity mirrors in the corner and waved.

"Hey, Sweet Pea."

"What are you doing back here? Ma already went to take her seat."

"Yeah, I know. I passed her on the way. You look . . . beautiful."

I glanced down at my silky snow-white dress that stopped just at the knees. It flowed and moved like waves over my tights with just a hint of silver glitter. My nails matched my lipstick and eye shadow—frosted pink.

"Thanks."

"Nervous? You know I always get nervous before hitting the stage."

If he squeezed my hands any tighter, sweat would drip out. I glanced at the black door leading to the main stage, flinching at the roaring applause.

"Um, a little. I'm not on for another thirty minutes."

"Well, I was gonna wait until after to give this to you," he said. "But then I thought . . . why not, since you got some time to kill."

He whipped out a manila folder, presenting it like a bouquet of flowers.

"What is it?" I laughed. "Another coloring book?"

He shrugged as I opened the folder to find a stack of black-and-white photocopies from Monday's journal.

"Daddy," I gasped.

"It ain't the original, but it's better than nothing."

I flipped through the pages before diving into his arms, trying to squeeze all my love into him.

"Thank you, Daddy," I cried. "Thank you!"

Claudia painted my nails with this color called cherry bomb. She even painted little cherries on the tips. She

424

is like an artist or something. She is SO good! The pictures she colors are pretty too. She don't know it but I have some of her pictures in my drawer. And her dancing! In all them recitals, she's just . . . wow!

I wish she wasn't so scared all the time, though. She's afraid people will treat her different cause of the way she read and write. But if they got to know her, they'd see how smart and cool she is. Then everyone gonna want to be her friend. I can't believe out of all the people in the world, she chose me, ME, to be her best friend. Well, we ain't just best friends, more like sisters.

"You ready?" Megan said, standing beside me at the makeup mirror. "Or are you gonna sit with your nose in them papers all night?"

Sitting with a copy of my best friend's journal in my lap, reading it without mixing up my words too bad, felt like heaven. I would've sat there forever if I could. I took a deep breath, stuffing the folder in my bag, trying to hold back my mile-long grin.

"Yeah. I'm ready."

Megan shook her head. "I can't believe you."

"Huh? What I do?"

"I mean, I can't believe you're *here*," she said, gripping the table. "After everything that's happened! I don't know what I would've done . . . if that was Kit Kat."

She's right. I should've been a pile a shattered glass on the corner ready for the street sweepers to collect me. Only one thing kept me going—Monday.

"You would have danced," I said with a shrug. "'Cause she'd whoop your ass if you didn't."

"Damn, that's true." We stared at each other in the mirror for a moment, then giggled. "Aight! You up next."

"You gonna watch?"

"Girl, you already know! Let's do this! And don't forget to smile!"

I didn't forget. I smiled through every turn with my head held high, every leap, feeling Monday right next to me. Dancing in a lavender dress, sparkling, her smile brilliant. I poured my heart, soul, and all my love into every move. Just like old times, our steps in sync, having fun until the very end, as we bowed to a roaring crowd.

With Ma, Daddy, and Michael in the front row, cheering.

LATER ON

Dear Monday,

I haven't written to you in a while. I'm sure you know why.

But, girl! Last weekend, at the annual block party, Daddy's band did this cranking set, had everybody dancing. A bunch of folks that had moved away came. Even April and Tuesday! It was like a big family reunion. You should see Tuesday—she dances just like you.

Been going to this therapist every week and she said something about me needing closure. I think I know where to get it, but nobody's gonna like it.

P.S. Look how GOOD I'm writing now! I even help out my friends in TLC.

"You sure you want to hear this? Right here, right now?"

I stared up at the house. Monday's house. Its boarded-up windows, the door hanging off the hinges like a semicolon, secured with a thick chain and padlock. Thin gray clouds hung above while birds chirped in the tree, casting hectic designs on the sidewalk. I remembered it looking so much bigger.

I turned to Michael, his head almost hitting the roof of his car. His dad had made good on his promise and bought him a brand-new Dodge Charger, all black. Michael took care of it better than some people take care of their children.

"How many times do we have to go over this?" I sighed.

"I know, but do we have to"—he glanced over his shoulder—"do it right here? Even I had a hard time stomaching it."

"I know," I groaned. "I heard you the first four times."

He blew out some air, rubbed his head like a genie lamp, wishing this away. "Alright. I'm only going to play one part. Then that's it."

"Would you hurry up with all this stalling?" I chuckled.

He reached over and tickled my neck. I squealed with a fit of giggles before he grabbed my chin and tilted my face in his direction, planting a quick kiss on my lips, then another—a deeper one. I kissed him back, my lips hungry for more of his.

"Tell me the truth," he whispered. "You still hearing that buzzing?"

I sighed. "Yes."

His smile fell fast. "Then *why* are we doing this?"

"Because I need to know. I can't go on not knowing and imagining what happened."

"She could be lying," he said. "Coming out the wood-work with a new tune."

"She not lying. She's got nothing to lose."

Michael shook his head. "Your dad is gonna kill me."

"He hasn't the last twenty times you've said that."

Michael smirked and pulled out his iPhone, clicking on his podcast app before grabbing my hand.

"Okay. Ready?"

I held my breath, squeezing his hand back. "Yeah."

Michael nodded, pressed play, and Mrs. Charles joined us in the car.

"August kept putting his hands on females! I kept telling him to stop that. But he was beating up on his sisters. Them bruises you see on Monday and April you can't put all the blame on me. Final straw was when I caught him biting Tuesday. She was just a baby! I started punching him, biting him back. Told him, 'Didn't I tell you boys not supposed to touch no females?' He knew that I told him all the time. He was screaming and wouldn't shut up. I choked him, putting my hands around his throat. He fought until his eyes started rolling back, and then he was dead. Told April to put him in the freezer 'cause . . . well, I didn't feel like dealing with him."

Her voice was calm, level, smooth as silk, detailing the way she murdered her child much like the way you talk about a boring Sunday afternoon.

"Monday was a fast-ass little girl. Fast from the day she was born. Got boys coming up to my house looking for her and shit. I even heard her messing with girls too."

Michael and I locked eyes and he gripped my hand, kissing my knuckles.

"I came home early from babysitting and see her coming out of some car, in these tight-ass little shorts, talking fast, telling me she's about to leave me. I grabbed her by the neck and started punching her. She wanted to be all big and bad, trying to face me like a grown-ass woman, she gonna get beat like a grown woman. She started screaming, cursing at me and carrying on.

"I threw her in the closet for a couple of days. She kept on screaming, begging to be let out, begging for water. Every time she made too much noise I'd walk in and kick her. That last time . . . she wouldn't get up. I don't know how she got in that freezer. I didn't put her there. I would've let her rot in that closet.

"I ain't sorry for what I done. People been making excuses, talking about this and that. But I know what I did and I ain't sorry."

Michael pressed stop and pulled me into a hug. "We're never gonna play shit like that again. Ever!"

I rubbed my face on his shoulder, not realizing that I had been crying. He pulled back and kissed both of my cheeks.

"Are you okay?" he whispered into my lips.

I nodded. "Stay here."

"You sure?"

I glanced over at the house, picturing Monday hopping out of the back seat of the car, skipping up the pathway, slow and dreamlike. Her arms swinging as she took one big jump up the stairs to the landing, turning to wave at us with a silly grin. And I almost waved back at her. Almost.

"Yeah. I'm okay. I need to do this."

A fall breeze played with my freshly straightened hair as I wrapped my black knit scarf around my neck twice. I wore nothing but blue and black. Any other color reminded me too much of Monday. Still felt a pinch of guilt whenever I saw pink.

With all the eviction notices, over the last year Ed Borough slowly turned into a ghost town, and Monday's home was renamed "the House of Horrors." I shuffled closer to it, listening for the blaring television, and lifted the heavy padlock, hanging like a weight. It clanged against the thin wood. Pressing my ear to the door, I closed my eyes and listened. Silence. No buzzing, just wind whistling through an empty space. I backed away with a small relieved smile.

431

She's not in there, I said to myself. She's not in that freezer. She's gone.

"You're Monday's friend, right?"

I yelped, almost tripping over the same crack in the pathway as I had years ago. A woman sat on the stoop next door, so still she blended into the background.

"I remember, you came by here a few times looking." She buttoned up the top of her tan coat. "She told me about you. Said y'all looked alike. Like y'all could be twins."

My heart swelled at the thought of Monday talking about me with such pride, and I walked through the yellowing grass to her stoop. She looked much older up close, with a shock of platinum hair, creamy butterscotch skin, and a smile that could light up the night sky.

"I'm Ms. Roundtree. Was about to head inside. You want some tea?"

The crooked boarded-up windows on the abandoned home to the right of hers seemed like a rush job.

"No thank you, ma'am. Are you the only one left on this strip?"

Ms. Roundtree smirked. "Rodney and Kasey moved about a year after *it* happened. With everything else going on around here . . . no one wants to live next to that place. But this has been my home for a long time. Too late to quit it now."

My eyes flickered up to Monday's boarded-up bedroom

window. She's not in there anymore, I reminded myself. She's gone.

"She used to sit on her stoop a lot, looking up at them clouds," Ms. Roundtree said, sighing. "She'd cry sometimes. That's how I knew something must have happened. Hadn't heard her cry in a long time."

I eased my hands into my pockets. "Why didn't you say anything?"

She paused for a moment, collecting her thoughts. She probably heard this question ten thousand times, but this time, she seemed to have a different answer.

"I got two grandkids that live over in PG County. Can't be no more than twenty minutes from here, maybe forty with traffic. Krystal just turned twelve and Dean is about nine. Students of the month, piano lessons, violin, soccer, football, ballet . . . Their schedule got their mother ripping and running everywhere. And I'm proud of them. I just never see them. I haven't laid eyes on my grandbabies in maybe three months. They just busy. Too busy to even give their grandma a call. But just 'cause I don't see them or hear from them often, don't mean I rush and think they dead. And that's what I figured about Patti's babies. Shoo, Monday was over at your house more than her own."

Back at the car, Michael watched us from a half-open window, hands gripping the steering wheel. So damn overprotective. I nodded and smiled at him.

"I ain't making excuses," she continued. "But that's what it's like nowadays. You used to see your family, at least for Sunday dinner. This here used to be a pretty tight community. But now everybody so caught up in this and that, that you don't notice what's right in front you." She cleaned off the front of her coat and shook her head. "Sometimes I have nightmares about what went on in there."

"I have nightmares too," I admitted, kicking a few acorns by my feet.

"Oh yeah. About what?"

"I don't really remember. I just remember the . . . buzzing." I bit my lip, holding back tears.

Her face wiped blank as she leaned back. "The freezer sat up against the wall, so that buzzing was in my house too. Even after they found them, it took a while to get rid of the sound."

We both looked at the house as if someone was about to walk out the door. Goose bumps popped up all over my arms, growing up to my neck.

Michael honked his horn, and I nearly jumped out my boots. He peered out the window, waving me on.

"Guess I gotta go. It was nice talking to you." Heading for the car, the question hit me and I doubled back. "Wait! How'd you get rid of the buzzing?"

Ms. Roundtree smiled, folding her hands together. "It's all about the way you look at it. You got to decide what something is or isn't. It may have been buzzing, but I decided it's humming. Someone is just humming a song in my ear. A pretty song."

Glancing at the house one last time, I gave Ms. Roundtree a hug. "Thank you."

"Sure, baby, anytime."

I jumped in the car, kissed Michael, and we drove off, cranking up Daddy's newest song.

With Monday humming along.

ACKNOWLEDGMENTS

First, thank you, Jesus, for showing me signs when I absolutely needed them.

Natalie Lakosil, as always, thank you for being a ball of positive energy and optimism.

Benjamin Rosenthal, thank you for seeing the gold in this book when I thought it was a pile of steaming poop. You are so encouraging and have a knack for easing my doubts.

Duane Tyler Jackson, thank you for taking such good care of Oscar. You are so gifted, talented, and caring, I have no doubt in your success, pudding pop!

Tara, my best friend since the second grade, the ying to my yang, the Monday to my Claudia . . . that one week you went "missing" was the longest week of my entire life and inspired parts of this story. Love you, blueberry girl.

Drew "Droopy" Anderson, the first person to read this book, thank you for all your help in shaping this story, making it as true as possible to DC, and for reminding me of my love of poetry.

Justine Larbalestier, thank you for always pushing me to demand the best for myself. I appreciate you seeing my worth when I can't. (Also, thanks for sharing Scott Westerfeld with me.)

Laurie Halse Anderson, I cannot thank you enough for taking me under your wing! That two-day therapy session was everything I needed and put the battery pack in my back.

Shout-out to my safe space: Nic Stone, Angie Thomas, Dhonielle Clayton, and Ashley Woodfolk. Thank you for never letting me quit.

To my homies, Jason Reynolds, Justin A. Reynolds, and Lamar Giles . . . thank you for always checking on me and cracking jokes. I can always count on y'all.

To the 2017 Debuts, Class of 2k17, the Debutante Ball, the mothers of Jack and Jill, Kidlit Authors of Color, Madcap . . . your support throughout my debut year has been AMAZING! To the ladies of the Women of Color Retreat in Costa Rica . . . thank you for helping me regain my sense of peace.

Big ups to my girls, who constantly reminded me that I am loved when I wasn't feeling all that loveable while writing this book: Nicole J., Nicole W., Tiffany S., Tiffany T., Simone, Tonia, Adana, Shanelle, Jessica S., Jessica H.M., Lyneka, Crystal, Suzanne, T. Nicole, Starr, and Indigo.

To my boo, you're the best bae of all the baes.

Lastly, to missing children of color, we have not forgotten about you. We will continue to fight and give you a voice. You matter.

Turn the page for an exclusive look at
Tiffany D. Jackson's next thrilling novel

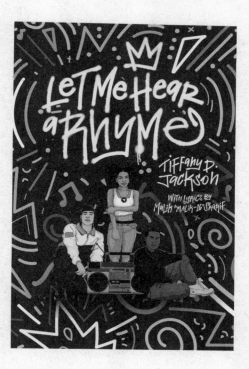

1

Quadir

You've probably seen this scene before:

Ladies in black church dresses, old men in gray suits, and hood kids in white tees with some blurry picture printed on the front and the spray-painted letters *RIP*. Pastor in the corner eating lemon cake, grandmas in their regal crowns waving church fans, while aunties swim around, refilling plates, sneaking sips of Henny stashed in their purse.

My best friend Steph smiles at me on the front of his cousin Roger's T-shirt. Roger lives in Queens, so Steph never saw him much. We Brooklyn kids don't travel to other boroughs like that. I mean, why would we?

Deadass, it's gotta be close to a hundred people stuffed in

this tiny-ass apartment, and them Sternos heating up lunch is making this place feel like we sitting inside a radiator. I don't recognize half the grown-ups walking around with long faces. They must be friends of Steph's mom. Or his pops.

I thought I'd see some reporters and cameramen at the church. For the past few days, I flipped through channels waiting to see Steph's photo cross the screen, but everyone was still busy talking about President Clinton hooking up with that intern. Like, damn, don't murders make the news no more? Don't they know who Steph was? I mean, yeah, folks die every day. But it's not every day you lose your main man.

Guess I'mma have to be the reporter and tell his story. What Ms. Greene in history class call it? Oral history, black story-telling, or something like that. Bet a real reporter would set up the scene better than I did. Probably something like:

Headline: Funeral Held for Slain Teen
On Saturday, roughly a hundred friends and family filled the victim's home in Brevoort, the notorious housing projects in the heart of Bedford-Stuyvesant, to celebrate the life of Stephon Davis, Jr.
Suspect still at large.

"Heard she almost requested a closed casket," someone whispers close by, but doing a shit job of it. "Poor thing, just been through so much."

"She" being Ms. Davis, Steph's mom, sitting across the room in the beat-up tan recliner Steph used to play in until he up all the air, standing in the buffet line snaking out of our kitchen. How could anyone eat after seeing a body lying in a casket?

And not just any old body. Steph's body.

"First her husband, now her son. Poor thing," someone says, like they don't know how to whisper.

"Poor child, they were like twins."

"Mm-hmm. Lost a brother, but gained an angel."

Mom squeezes Carl tight with one hand, clinging to the back of my cardigan with the other. But just the simple touch has my body hitting a thousand degrees.

I don't want an angel. I want my brother back.

I rush out the room, in search of air that's not mixed with perfume, pity, and fried chicken.

Sweating through the stockings Mom made me wear under the dress that I can't stand, I bust into Steph's room and throw open the window. The relief is like sticking my face in the freezer. After spending two hours fighting with Mom's hot comb last night, my hair is already frizzing. Of course. There could be a drop of rain two states away and my hair would peep it and shrink up. I wanted to wear it in my regular puffs, but Mom made a big deal about straightening it for the funeral, and I didn't have the courage to argue with her. She doesn't like me rocking my hair natural. She's old-school. She still believes in blue flames and blue grease to straighten hair when all the other girls are using flat irons.

At least she didn't say nothing about my medallion. It's round, leather, with a cut-out shape of Africa, stitched with red, green, and gold thread. It used to belong to Daddy. He wore it everywhere.

Déjà vu.

I hid in here during Daddy's funeral too. Except Steph was already in here, recording songs off the radio to make a new mixtape. He had this technique that made his tapes sound real professional. You have to listen close, one finger on the Record button, the other on the Play, half pushed down. Then when the first beat of the song he wants comes on, he'd push both buttons down real fast and it made for a smooth transition on the cassette tape. Last February, he gave Mom an R&B mixtape for Valentine's Day, and she thought he'd paid big money to have it done.

Lady of Rage stares down at me with that "Don't even try it" expression as tears rain on my dress. Would she be crying like this? I remember when I put that poster up for Steph. All he had were pictures of brothas, but ladies rap too. And no, not some models/side chicks pretending they know how to spit, rapping about all the clothes, sex, and money they get. I'm talking lyrical geniuses. Independent and strong. Everything I want to be.

"What up, Jazz?"

Quadir stands in the doorframe, squirming, looking unsure of whether it's safe to take another step.

"Uh . . . what up?" I say, sniffing back tears and quickly wipe my face dry. Dag, I don't want anyone seeing me like this. Especially Steph's friends.

"You okay? I was just . . . whoa." He gapes at the walls.

Mom used to say Steph's room looked like a magazine threw up all over the place with every artist you could ever think of: Biggie, Puff Daddy, the Lox, Mase, Method Man, Capone-N-Noreaga, Jay-Z, Big Pun. One side of the room dedicated to *The Source* magazine, *Rap Pages*, and *Vibe*. The other, movie posters: *Scarface*, *Coming to America*, *Boomerang*. You'd never know the walls were painted blue underneath his shrine to hip-hop, his first love.

Quadir gawks like he's walking into a museum. We lock eyes for a brief moment before Jarrell pushes past him.

"Yo, son. You think you a ghost or something and I can just walk through you? Move out the . . . whoa." Jarrell spins around, letting out a small chuckle. "Damn, look at all this shit!"

He grabs the basketball propped up next to Steph's bed, tossing it in the air.

On the desk is a three-disc-changer stereo with detachable speakers, covered in old fruity scratch-and-sniff stickers, so worn down the colors are faded white. Steph begged for almost a year for that thing, drove Daddy crazy over it. Daddy found one at a pawnshop, slightly damaged (one of the CD slots doesn't work) but for Steph, it was love at first sight. He almost cried when Daddy walked in with it. Stacked around the stereo were cassette tapes and cds. Dozens of them. Some named, some left blank.

"No wonder he never let us up in here." Jarrell laughs, snatching a tape off one of the piles, and reads the labels. "'The Build, Volume 1.' Yo, this fool was serious."

"You know how he is . . . was about his music," I say, feeling the need to defend Steph. He wouldn't want nobody touching his stuff, but I'm too numb to stop them.

"How you holding up?" Quadir asks. He's always been friendly, in a quiet, shy type of way.

"I'm straight," I lie, adjusting my posture. Just because Steph is gone don't mean I'm some weak girl who needs to be babied. "How you two doing?"

Quadir glances at Rell, combing through tapes. "We aight. Sorry about Steph. We know you two were close."

I swallow back the rising tears. "Not as close as you three."

"Aye, Quady, come look at this," Jarrell says.

"Yo, quit messing with the man's shit. It's why he never wanted us in here in the first place."

Jarrell blows him off with a wave of his hand.

"Check it," he says, flipping through the pages of a black-and-white composition notebook. "Look at this. All this fool ever did was write rhymes."

Quadir reads over Rell's shoulder. "He didn't even need to. He was better off the dome anyways."

"Yeah. Remember, when he called that dude 'a player who got burnt up and strung up 'cause he hit that broad up?' With his girl standing right there? Son, I was *dying* that day."

Rell cackles and Quadir can't help but snicker with him.

"Damn, that kid was good."

Quadir sighs. "Yeah. He was."

Their laughter slowly dies down and they both glance at me, like they forgot I was in the room. Yes, y'all, we're *still* at the repast for my brother.

Rell clears his throat. "Let's see what this fool was listening to."

He presses Play on the stereo, and the cassette tape hisses before Steph's voice fills the room.

"Oh shit, this must've been those tracks he was working on."

"Didn't he say he was going to a studio the night before he . . . died?"

Wait, Steph was in a studio? Like a real one?

Jarrell presses stop and ejects the tape before turning to me. "Yo, Jazz, you think I can have this?"

Quadir watches me. Is he waiting for me to crack too? Bet they expecting it, but I ain't giving them the satisfaction.

"Sure. It's not like anyone else is gonna listen to it," I say with a shrug as the little girl inside me says in a small voice, "Anyone except me."

3
JARRELL

Whenever we chill on the corner, we got to play our positions: me, posted up against the wall, Quady sitting on milk crates, and Steph leaning against the lamppost outside Habibi's bodega. Homie loves Quady 'cause he got a Muslim name even though he ain't Muslim. Can't stand me 'cause I mess up his name all the time. Not my fault I can't roll my r's and shit, but they halal food be the truth.

The spot Steph would've been standing in is looking mad empty now that he's gone.

My pops hate them type of words: should've, would've, could've. They ain't nothing but excuses. Pops don't even live with us and I'm afraid to use them words up in our spot. He's quick to make me do twenty push-ups when I try. Probably got the place wiretapped or something.

He's right, though. There ain't no excuse for Steph not being here with us. Somebody killed him for no reason.

"Damn, it's hot out here," I say, and gulp down another ninety-nine-cent Arizona Iced Tea. "Hotter than it was up in Steph's crib."

After we rapped with Jazz real quick, we took to-go plates of Mummy's jerk chicken, rice and peas, and cabbage, then bounced. I didn't want to be up in there with all them sad people and pictures of Steph staring at us. I'm sad enough as it is. Quady is too. He don't have to say it. It's all over his face, living in his voice.

"Yo, you think he knew what was about to go down?" Quady says, glancing at Steph's spot on the corner.

"Nah son. No way."

I loosen my tie, my collar wet with sweat. These church clothes be killing me. Don't get it twisted. I still look fly, and no one in the hood have these black gator dress shoes. But I had to pop a pant button open just to finish my plate. Yeah, I could've stopped eating, but when Mummy gets busy in the kitchen you never let her food go to waste. I mean, I guess I can't really call them church clothes since we only roll up in there for holidays. Now they got a new name: funeral clothes.

Never thought my first funeral would be for someone I really knew like that. I thought it would be a random kid from school or some great aunt back in Jamaica. Not my main man hundred grand. I used to wonder what Peter Parker felt when

Uncle Ben was killed in *Spider-Man*. How it felt to lose some-one you looked up to, someone you cared about. Now I know.

The shit aches, and the thoughts are giving me ruthless bubble guts. Or it could've been that Cap'n Crunch.

A gold Lexus stops at the light, its tinted windows halfway down, blasting "Can I Get A . . ." by Jay-Z with Ja Rule and this new chick Amil. The bass thumps through my chest and I'm not even in the car. They keep it up and they gonna blow out their speakers by Halloween.

Two cats stare at us, their seats leaning like they about to take a nap. We stare back. You never know what a dude is holding, so you gotta stay ready so you ain't got to get ready, feel me? And the way they did Steph . . . I don't trust nobody out here in 'Do-or-Die Bed-Stuy,' and neither should you.